Bitter Orange

DESMOND HAMILL

Bitter Orange

WILLIAM MORROW AND COMPANY, INC.
New York   1980

C. 6

Originally published in Great Britain in 1979 by Hutchinson & Co. (Publishers) Ltd.

Library of Congress Cataloging in Publication Data

Hamill, Desmond.
  Bitter orange.

  I. Title.
PZ4.H2154Bi   1980   [PR6058.A549]   823'.914   80-14024
ISBN 0-688-03711-9

Printed in the United States of America

First U.S. Edition

1   2   3   4   5   6   7   8   9   10

To Brigid –
and also Rick, Liam, Brian and many
other friends who helped so much

An episodic novel of the Northern Irish
troubles pictures the horrors visited
upon the beleagered ˆˆalone family of
Catholic Belfast, as son Vincent runs
painfully afoul of his IRA superiors,
and daughter Sheelagh becomes a triple
amputee in a terrorist bombing.

I

Grey clouds streamed high over the headland. The last tattered banners of the Atlantic storm that had been raging for three days were still in the sky, but the sting had gone. Already quick washes of blue sky could be seen. It was too early yet for any sun, but before the day was out it would bring up the steam from the gorse and heather and smooth cropped grass that lay unusually sodden for a July day.

There was a young man on the headland. He was well wrapped up, with a thick jersey, gum boots, and a woollen hat pulled well down over his ears. In the pocket of his khaki anorak he had a whistle. Round his neck were a pair of binoculars.

Lying on a groundsheet to keep out the damp, he peered constantly through the rough stems of the gorse bushes, looking inland.

Wriggling slightly to get into a more comfortable position, and putting his hand in his pocket, he wondered if he could have a quick smoke, but decided against it and settled down again.

Three hundred feet below and behind him were two men. They stood well back in a small cove, their backs to the damp rocks and their boots ankle deep in seaweed and the flotsam and jetsam tossed up by the storm. They too wore khaki anoraks and black, woollen stocking caps pulled well down. Both men were smoking, holding the butts carefully in cupped hands, the lighted ends pointing inwards. It was an automatic gesture to hide the glowing tip.

7

These two men looked out towards the sea. In the aftermath of the storm, a heavy swell was running. The seagulls, forty yards out, rose and fell steadily as the long rollers came in.

The wind blew straight onshore. It carried to them the mewing of the gulls as they wheeled and dived and came, claws outspread, to pancake landings on the water. It carried the solid smell of the sea.

The older of the two men on the beach stamped his feet impatiently. 'Sod this weather,' he said, almost whistling through his teeth in his irritation, 'sod it, sod it, sod it.'

His companion looked up at him.

'Do you think we've missed them?' he asked.

'Chrissake, we haven't missed them. We've been standing here for three bloody days now. It's them who's missed us.'

'It's been a bad storm. Do you think ...?'

'Don't bloody say it,' he said quickly, 'it's bad luck.' He kicked out at the pebbles. He bent down, picked up a couple and threw them, one after the other, as far out to sea as he could. It wasn't very far.

'They can't have gone down,' he muttered into the wind, and then shouted, 'they can't have gone down. Bloody hell, we'll be stuffed rotten if they've gone. What the hell will we do? Six months' work gone.'

'Sure it's not just the six months. It's the chance we won't get.'

They were both silent for a while, their minds running along identical lines. The work put in, the loss, and the almost certain knowledge that the chance wouldn't come again.

The two men in the cove had been waiting for a small coastal steamer to appear. Coming to the same place three days in a row was asking for trouble. But what else could they do? It was the only place that had been agreed. Changing plans now would be fatal. It might be equally fatal if they stayed much longer.

Then as if they both had the same thought, which they had, they turned again to each other. The younger was the first to speak.

'How much longer do we wait here? Three days we've been. I don't like it.'

'I don't like it neither. Some damn fool may have seen us, may have blabbed.'

'Another fag?' He gestured with his pack.

'Thanks ... here, I've got a light.'

On the clifftop above, all the interest of the nineteen-year-old was now concentrated into watching two hares playing together. They were caught in a round, sharp picture. He had his elbows firmly pressed into the soft earth, his head pressed against the eyepiece of the binoculars.

The hares lay tight to the grass, nibbling.

The helicopter came round the headland, hugging the cliffs, low over the water. The pilot had spotted them even before they heard the roar of the rotor blades, and then it only came to them in chunks, as the wind allowed.

It soared up into the air, banking round to hover some four hundred feet above them.

That was the moment the young man heard it. He froze. The feeling in his stomach now was fear.

After the first, involuntary jerk of his head to one side to see what the noise was, he had had the sense not to move again. He could just see the helicopter out of the corner of his eye. Christ! he thought, it was a big one: not just one of those wee ones with a glass bubble on the front. It was big, and solid. The door in the side was open, and a soldier sat there, his legs hanging out over the side, a gun cradled in his lap.

The young man pressed himself further into the ground, and then mentally dug himself in even more. He pressed himself harder and harder on to the groundsheet, feeling every crooked root of a gorse bush in his side, until he could hardly breathe with the effort.

Below him, the men in the cove craned their necks, watching every movement of the helicopter. It moved fifty yards further along the clifftop, but they were both still clearly visible to whoever was in it.

'Come on,' said the younger man, moving over to their pile of fishing tackle.

'What?' said the other. 'What's the matter?'

'Might as well make it look as if we are doing some fishing.'

'Don't be mad!' He looked out at the grey, heavy sea. 'With that running, anyone would know you couldn't fish. Even a thick squaddie up there,' jerking his head in the direction of the clifftop, 'would smell something wrong straight away.'

'They must have some smell in their noses, else why the hell would they be here at all?'

The clatter of the helicopter blades dropped a bit, and they both looked up again. The helicopter had disappeared over the edge of the cliff. But the clatter didn't go altogether. It was still up there, somewhere.

'We might as well make it look as if we were packing up, anyway,' said the older man.

'Aye,' sighed the other. 'If it's out there, they'll have seen it. If not, it's not coming. Either way we're buggered.

'Jesus!' he said, suddenly looking at the older man in alarm. 'The lad. What about the lad?'

'Shit!' He stared at him. 'Come on, we'd better get out of here. I don't want them questioning him without us. Christ knows what he might say.'

They threw their packs over their shoulders, and started up the path to the top.

The helicopter had gone out of his line of vision. He hadn't dared follow it, but it seemed now to be hovering right over the top of him. He was well under the bracken and gorse, but that was by chance. He hadn't thought of hiding himself to avoid a search from the air.

He wasn't very well hidden from above. He knew that. He stayed absolutely still.

By ear, he followed the progress of the helicopter. It flew off, he thought, about a hundred yards, and then came down.

He eased his head round very slowly. The muscles had started tightening up with the strain of his twisted neck.

Two hundred yards away the helicopter was on the ground,

the blades still turning. Five or six soldiers were jumping out. Some of them moved into a circle round the machine, while the others started for the clifftop path.

He saw them stop there and began to feel sick.

The two men from the cove were now almost at the top of the path. They were breathing heavily and sweating. They were frightened, wondering how the military had found them. Was this a routine patrol, or had someone blabbed?

'Steady, steady,' said the older man. 'We don't want to make it look ... hey, hang on a minute.' He drew in a few lungfuls of air. 'Don't want to seem as if ...' he puffed, 'as if we're anxious to see them.'

They both slowed down a bit and came to the top as the soldiers did. They wore red berets, and the one in the front was burly and stocky. Five yards behind him, spread out, were two more paratroopers. One kept his eyes looking steadily past the one in front, the other one turned round and looked backwards. He looked to the left and the right and back again. He kept doing this.

The man in front was a sergeant. He spoke first.

'What are you doing here?' he asked.

The older man stopped, one hand on the shoulder of his companion. He was struggling for breath.

'What is that to you?'

The sergeant didn't move.

'What are you doing here?' he repeated.

The older man held up his rods and fishing basket.

'Fishing. Fishing ... or at least trying to. No good, but. Too rough.' He wiped the sweat off his forehead with the back of his hand. The sergeant looked at him. He held a rifle, almost carelessly, but it was pointing straight at the older man's stomach.

'Who are you?' he asked.

The two men looked at each other, and sighed.

'Christ!' said the younger man, 'you can't even bloody well go out and fish these days without some bastard wanting to know who you are ... where you're going ... who your grandfather is.'

The sergeant considered them both. He hadn't room in the chopper for the two of them, unless he left someone behind. He didn't want to do that.

The wind still blew strongly, gusting over the cliff. The two men looked cold, and he wondered how long they had been there. Only two had been mentioned, but they didn't fit the description given. Were there any others?

'Are you alone?' he asked.

The younger man dropped his fishing basket on the ground and folded his arms.

'Full of the questions, aren't you?' he said, curling his lips back. The older man looked a little alarmed. 'Do you think we've some friends hiding in our pockets?'

'Right,' said the sergeant, 'put your bag down. Come on now. Down. Turn round. Both of you, turn round ... put your hands behind you heads. Move now. Right, stand still, I'm going to search you.'

'What for?' the young man asked. 'Fish?'

The sergeant nodded to the paratrooper, who slung his rifle and came forward. Quickly, expertly, he ran his hands over the men, searching inside their pockets, feeling down their legs, looking in their fishing bags. He said nothing. When he had finished, he looked at the sergeant and nodded.

'Now we'll have some form of identification from you,' said the sergeant. 'Driving licence, Post Office book. Maybe even a Social Security book.'

The men dug into their pockets, and produced driving licences. The sergeant checked them. The names were not the ones he had been given. Once again it was duff information. He would damn well moan about it when he got back, not that anyone would take any notice.

'OK! That your van over there?'

'Yes.'

'Take a look inside,' he ordered one of the paratroopers.

The man did so while they waited. After a few minutes he called out it was clear. The sergeant looked at them.

'You can go,' he said.

'Thanks very much,' said the young man, bitterly.

The older man said nothing, and they both moved off, picking up their bags. They tramped right past the hiding place. They could almost feel him there, watching them.

The sergeant watched them go. He would wait until they had driven off before he moved. He didn't think anything was wrong, but he would wait anyway. Besides, he liked the fresh air out on the headland. It cut like a knife, slicing away the gritty coating left by the city streets. He loathed those streets. Two of his friends had been killed there. One had been gunned down by a sniper. Just a single shot in the early evening. They had never found who did it. His other friend had been blown to bits.

He watched the two men get into their van and drive off, jolting and bumping down the narrow track. When it had gone from sight, he called his men and went back to the helicopter. The patrol took off.

With the wind and the clatter of the helicopter blades in his ears, the boy had heard nothing of what had gone on. He felt the two men walk past him, heard the van move off and, some time later, heard the helicopter move off as well.

The van went down the track, twisting and turning to avoid the ruts. The older man gripped the wheel tightly, staring ahead, breathing in short, shallow gasps. His face had turned a yellowish colour, and a gleam of sweat lay about the stubble on his chin. He grunted whenever he hit a pothole, the steering wheel spinning in his hands.

'Them fuckers!' he muttered to himself, again and again. 'Them fuckers!'

He had been badly frightened. He had nearly run for it when the helicopter had appeared, but he'd remembered in time that they had probably already been seen. He had only just stopped himself making that mistake.

He had been frightened before they had come out, and he was frightened now it was over. That made him more angry.

'Fuck them!' he said, out loud.

That youngster beside him, he thought, straight from the country. Didn't really know his ass from his bloody elbow. He was stuck with him, but, Christ! he thought savagely, the bugger hadn't even been frightened: didn't have the imagination to be frightened. He would be glad to get back.

The younger man twisted round in his seat and looked out through the back window.

'There's nobody there,' he announced.

'Of course there's nobody there.' The older man was very short. 'We know there's nobody there. Just come down the road, haven't we?' He pulled the wheel from side to side and changed down a gear as the road turned up a hill. 'It's there you should be watching,' he said, indicating the road in front. 'Up there. Keep your bloody eyes up there.'

The young man turned to look through the windscreen. If that was what the old fella wanted, then that was what he would do. But it wasn't likely there would be any more road blocks, not with that chopper patrol around.

He settled back in his seat, wriggling his toes to try and warm them. The van was draughty, and he felt as if he had been cold for days.

'How long will it take?' he asked.

'Round three hours. Maybe more if we get held up.'

'Are we stopping for a jar?'

'We are not indeed.' The older man was indignant. What the hell did these young fellas think they were up to? Stopping for a jar, for Chrissake, in a strange place where one might stand out like a Prod at a wake.

'It's a pity, it's a pity,' said the young man softly, almost to himself, but not quite. 'I have this terrible thirst on me after three days.' He raised his voice. 'Are you really set to drive like a bat out of hell all the way back, then?'

'I am that.'

'It's a pity,' he said again, 'it's a pity.'

The van ground its way on up the hill and towards a long tunnel of beech trees. They grew here on either side of the road, punching their way up into the unfriendly atmosphere of this high plateau. By some quirk of geology, the ground here was more fertile, and the stretch of road was a little protected from the prevailing winds by a shoulder of the hill which lay awkwardly away from the main slope. Even so, the outside shape of the trees was flattened by the prevailing wind.

Inside the tunnel it was dark and green, comfortable and cool in the heat of the summer.

As they came out, the light dazzled their eyes, and it was the older man who was the first to notice the road block. It didn't consist of much, just a few uniformed figures on the roadside, and another in the middle of the road waving them down. It was about fifty yards ahead.

'Agh, Jesus!' he sighed, looking at the camouflage jackets, 'we've just been through all this,' and he put his foot on the brake. The younger man looked up and peered through the windscreen, drawing his breath in quickly, his senses telling him something was wrong. An infinity of time seemed to drift past as the van slowed down, and he desperately tried to think what it was that worried him.

'Don't stop!' he screamed, 'they're not military. Go! Christ! Don't stop.'

The older man was about to change down into second gear to bring the van to a smooth stop, but his mind, relaxed after the climax of the last encounter, couldn't cope, and when he rammed his foot on to the accelerator the van simply stalled.

For the next twenty seconds bursts of automatic fire sliced through the thin metal, scattering glass over the road and ripping into the two men. The high velocity bullets inflicted terrible injuries, and the older man died instantly, his skull shattered. The younger man was still alive at the end of it, but though the bullets had passed cleanly through him, without touching any bones, the shock waves had damaged his spinal cord, and he lay paralysed.

It all seemed so slow to him as a uniformed figure came up the road to the van, looked into his eyes and then raised his rifle until it pointed straight at his head.

'Good-bye, you Fenian bastard,' a voice said from a long way away, and he thought how silly it was to be killed by an Orangeman like this, but it was always the way and with a very great effort he kept his eyes open as the shot was fired.

For a while the young man left behind lay where he was. He

had a feeling he was still being watched, and though his self-discipline had been very good, his back ached from the effort. He stayed still for another fifteen minutes, then he slowly rolled over and started to stretch, loosening himself before he finally got on to his feet and looked around.

There was no one in sight. The van had gone, and the soldiers and the helicopter had gone. Only the wind blew through the bracken and the gorse, carrying the gulls over the clifftop and back. Far away to his right, he could see the moorland where the turf had been cut. It lay in brown piles, heaps of soft, brown bricks drying out and just the stuff, he thought, to burn on a fire. He could almost smell it, he felt, from where he stood.

Well, he might as well start walking. He didn't think the others would be back for him, it was much too risky. The nine miles to the nearest village would take him some time, and he started down the track.

Some time later, as he came out of a long green tunnel of beech trees, he saw the van on the side of the road. Unthinkingly, he ran towards it. He looked in, and then moved quickly away and was violently sick on the road. He forced himself back again. Someone must have shot them from very close range, but he couldn't be certain as he'd never seen anything like this before. He didn't really want to be certain.

Oh Mary Mother of Jesus! he thought, I didn't know them well, but this is terrible.

Then he realized he should have been in the van himself. He stared around blindly, panic-stricken, moving quickly off the road to duck down behind the hedge. Everything seemed to revolve round in his head. Were they still there, my God! waiting for him? Then his brain started to take over again. He worked out no one would have waited that long for him – it would be too risky.

If it was risky for them, it would be risky for him, he reasoned, and, taking one last look at the van, he started walking again.

The banks on either side of him were high and solid, but

16

there were no more trees, and he hurried on, feeling very exposed.

2

He closed the door quietly behind him. But not quietly enough.

'Is that you, Vince?' his granda called out.

'It is.'

'You're late for your tea. Your ma's been waiting on you for an hour now. You'd better hurry along now and pacify the ould lady, or she'll be giving you a thick ear.'

'Right,' he replied shortly.

The last thing he wanted now was his tea. It wasn't just that he was cold and tired. He was. But he was also shocked. He'd never thought it would be quite like that. He supposed he'd never really thought about it at all. To fight and die for Ireland. Was that what it was really like? Your body blown to bits by a bomb? There was an awful obscenity to it.

He went into the kitchen where his ma was. She'd put on a kettle the moment she'd heard him come in. A small spiral of steam was already coming from the spout.

'Agh!' she said, 'you're soaked. Get them clothes off you, and I'll have your tea ready in a minute, if it's not spoiled altogether.'

She got up and moved round the table and opened the oven. Peering in she said, 'Well now, you're in luck. It's all right.' She looked up at him. He was still standing there, looking at her, saying nothing.

'What ails you?' she asked. 'Did you lose your tongue? You've been gone three days.'

He started and blinked.

'What's that?' he said. 'What's that you said?'

'I said,' she repeated more slowly, 'did you lose your tongue while you were gone? Don't you usually say hullo and give your old ma a kiss when you come in?'

'Ah, sure, sure,' he forced a grin on to his face. 'Sorry, ma,' he said cheerfully, leaning forward and kissing her cheek. Standing up he stuck out his tongue, and tapped it with a finger.

'Still there, you see. Still working just as well, though I'm not so sure you'll be pleased at that.'

'Get along with you.' She shooed him out of the kitchen. It wasn't difficult. It was barely three good paces across.

'You've got five minutes, and your tea'll be on the table.'

He went upstairs. He shared a room with Bryan, his twin brother, and his kid brother, James. It was a tight squeeze, and it didn't help that Bryan was the most untidy person he'd ever known. After three days away, it was worse than usual. He threw a coat off the bed and sat down to pull off his boots. They were soggy with water. As he pulled them off, bits of bracken fell out. He stared at them, and pulled off his socks. They, too, were soaking. He threw them across the room and rubbed his feet warm on the blanket. Then his jeans and shirt, wrapped in a bundle, followed the socks across the room. He must, he thought, be careful how he behaved. He was supposed to have been at a friend's wedding. So it wouldn't do to be acting bloody miserable and depressed. He'd have to take himself on. But what about John and Seamus? Both dead. Dead. My God! But for what? How could they be dead? Just like that. Shot to bits. They'd been doing nothing very dangerous. Well, not really dangerous. They'd not even been armed. Oh Christ! he wondered, would that have helped? Maybe not. He shuddered, he couldn't bear to go on thinking about it. What would he tell their folks? How could he possibly face them and say anything? Then he remembered he, of course, would have to do nothing like that. Because nothing would ever be said to them. There would just be the death notices in the paper. Volunteers of the IRA, killed in action. What he had to do was to keep his part in it away from his own family.

He wanted to keep that side of his life totally separate.

He looked at his hands. They were cold, and shaking, so he sat on them to get them warm. He must control himself, he thought. He mustn't relax too much just because he was home.

'Are you ever coming?' his ma shouted up the stairs.

'Yes, yes,' he called back quickly, and jumped up.

He looked into the mirror, pulled a brush through his hair, and went downstairs to the kitchen. His mother had put his tea on the table. Two rashers, two eggs, potato bread, tomatoes and a bottle of brown sauce. Two large slices of bread, a hunk of butter and a mug of tea.

'There,' she said, 'get that down you and you'll feel a sight better. You look perished. Are you sure there's nothing the matter with you?'

'Not at all,' he said, 'with this pile of food facing me, what could be the matter?'

'Well, stop dithering about and get on with it.' She bustled round the kitchen, and Vincent bent his head down so she wouldn't see it too easily, and ate his tea.

'Did you have good crack at the wedding?' she asked.

'What?' he said, looking up puzzled.

'For goodness' sake, boy,' his mother said, 'are your ears full of spuds or something? I said, did you have good crack at the wedding?'

'Oh ... the wedding ...'

'Yes, the wedding.'

'Yeah, yeah ... uh ... sure, it was great crack. Uh ... the bride,' he added, 'was very beautiful.'

His mother looked at him.

'And Bill,' she asked, 'was he in good heart?'

'Oh yes. Very good. Yes, indeed.'

'And the best man?'

'Oh yes, very good.'

He went on eating his tea.

'Better than he is at the moment?' his mother asked.

He looked up, his mouth full. What was she on about, he thought. O, my God! He gulped down his mouthful.

'Sure, course I was in good form.' He thought furiously. 'I

even,' he forced another grin, 'I even remembered the ring. Wasn't that great, but?'

'I should hope so,' his mother said drily. 'And were the bridesmaids pretty as well?'

'The bridesmaids?' he said frowning.

'For the love of God, son,' said his mother, filling up the kettle again, 'is your brain addled or something? Do I have to repeat every solitary thing I say to you? Do I have to drag every detail out of you bit by bit? Can you not put two words together and tell me what the wedding was like?' She bent down to his ear. 'I'm a woman, you know. I like to hear about these things. So stop acting like the sphinx or whatever it's called, and tell me about this wedding you've spent the last three days at.'

Christ, thought Vincent wildly, trying to remember the last wedding he'd been to. Wouldn't his mother ever stop blathering on asking questions? It was bad enough having to sit in the house with his family after what he'd been through, let alone have to try and dream up stories about a wedding he'd never been to. A wedding, in fact, that had never taken place. When he'd thought up that bright excuse, he had never thought he would be asked about it. That, he said firmly to himself, is a mistake I will not make again.

'Well now,' he said, 'you want to hear all about this wedding. Let me think. The bride was beautiful. She was dressed in white, you know. . . .'

'Aye, I thought she might be. Did she have a veil?'

'A veil?' he asked, and then quickly looking at his mother's face he went on, 'yes, a long white lacy thing. You know. Coming off the top of her head. She had a wee band of sort of pearl things round her head, and the veil fell down from that,' he went on, warming to the subject. 'She carried a small bouquet of roses. Red ones. Then she had two bridesmaids. Both in pink dresses. But both very young. Round about twelve. So that wasn't much crack for me later on. You understand,' he said, looking up as he shovelled another forkful of bacon into his mouth, 'as best man I'm supposed to be able to chat up the bridesmaids at the party afterwards. Well now, that didn't come to anything. But there was plenty to drink. They laid on a good spread, you see. Oh yes, and they had a fiddler, who played rightly until they'd poured a bottle of Powers into him. I think it was a bottle, anyway. But then he'd already had a few jars of porter. But sure nobody minded. Someone had a cassette recorder, and we put music on that, and the party went on, and his family put me up for the night in his bed. You see, he and uh, and ... Mary, Mary, that's it, had gone off for their honeymoon, so you see, the bed was empty, and uh ... and uh ... I stayed the night in it.'

He wiped up the last of the sauce from his plate with a piece of bread and took a drink of tea.

'Now, ma, I've just to go down the road to see John.' He got up pushing back his chair. 'I'll not be long now.'

He went to the door and turned.

'Is Bryan in this evening?' he asked.

'He'll be in when the pubs is shut, I've no doubt.'

'Good,' he said.

'And as you're going down the road, you can run a wee message for me,' she said.

'Ah, ma,' he complained, 'I'm in a hurry.'

'You're always in a hurry. This'll only take a wee minute. Just run into Mrs Matheson and give her this.' She held out a half pound bag of tea. 'I got a lend of it yesterday. I don't want her to be short, and I promised I'd have it back to her today.'

He took the bag and opened the front door.

'Are you out drinking again?' his granda called out from the front room.

'Indeed I am not,' he shouted back indignantly. 'I'm just down to see John. About his dog,' he added. He walked back and stuck his head round the door. His granda was sitting in his armchair, his legs covered by a blanket. His glasses were on the end of his nose and he had an open book on his lap.

'What's that you said?' he asked.

'John's dog,' said Vincent, loudly. 'John wanted me to see his new dog ... the one he's running on Saturday. He's very pleased with it, you know. I think he just wants to show it off.'

His granda looked at him over the end of his glasses and grunted. 'Along with you then,' he snorted, and Vincent went.

He walked away, desperately hoping he would find his brother, for his whole world was collapsing round him. He could hardly face his family – his younger sister Deirdre, who was seven, and James who was just a year older. If there hadn't been two deaths in the family there would have been another two after Sheelagh, just finishing school at seventeen. His ma would never understand what had happened to him. She was always telling him what a moody devil he was, never knowing what he wanted. His brother, now, Bryan, that was a different matter. Bryan was his twin, and while they looked alike they were two very different people, and Vincent was sure that Bryan, dependable and solid, would be able to help him.

The two of them had always been very close and even now worked together on a building site in the city. Bryan, he knew, had kept it going for them, because while he himself was the better carpenter of the two, Bryan was always there. Lately he'd had to do a lot of explaining while Vincent was away. Well, he thought, that would change now. He wouldn't be going away so much in future.

James Rafferty listened to his grandson's footsteps going away down the road, and he put a marker on the page of the book he was reading and slowly closed it. He ran his finger steadily up and down the spine, thinking about him.

He was worried about Vincent, who had taken to coming home very late and indeed sometimes not coming home at all, but he was, after all, nineteen now and growing up. It was time his mother cut the apron strings and let the boys go, for it wasn't doing them any good. He hoped they wouldn't get married too soon, but. It would be a long hard life for them if they did, and even more so for the girls. He thought of Sheelagh who was quickly becoming a woman, very like her grandmother though not, he thought, as pretty as she had been.

Ah! That had been a long time ago, almost a different century, or so it seemed. In the early twenties just after the war with the awfulness of the mud-filled battlefields. The way men had died there, dropping like flies as they followed their officers over the top. He could still remember the stench and horror of that time when even God was apparently against you. He had started out a cocky young Connaught Ranger, full of bounce and polish, but by the time the war was halfway through that had all drained out. He'd been left hollow and weak and he never really knew whom he hated more – the Germans he was fighting, or the British for whom he was fighting.

There had been good times after that and he had used his war experience in the flying columns of the IRA until a new Ireland had come into being, and then he'd settled down to many happy years of schoolmastering.

Now, in the North, the British seemed to be at it all again, and what to do about it, he wondered, his mind wandering on. Did anything anyone did these days make any bloody difference? If you fought them, they crushed you. If you didn't fight, you stood out as a target in your own community and then you had no friends. All this was now very different from what had gone on in the twenties. Whatever you did now was wrong in some way or another.

However, he would survive this, as he had survived the First World War – survive physically, that was. Emotionally he had been dried out long ago and left with nothing but a small, ever-burning hatred of the British.

He had tried to explain this feeling to his son-in-law, John, but John had wanted to know nothing about it. He was a hard worker and a good husband. He was even a good churchgoer and had tried to get him to take the Church more seriously. No chance of that, he thought, no chance. God hadn't helped him in the trenches and that was the end of any obligation.

All this trouble starting up again, he decided, was going to make it very difficult for the boys: rioting in the streets and such like, B Specials on the rampage and the IRA, or whatever was left of it, digging up their wee revolvers and bandoliers of lead – he thought derisively – to defend themselves. What use? he asked himself. They'll be shot for their pains. It is always the way in Ireland, North or South.

He felt the loneliness of those early war years come back. Most of his old friends were gone and his wife was also gone these many years. The youngsters of today listened politely enough – or some of them did – but they didn't really care. It didn't matter how much he told them, they only went out on the streets because they were hooligans. They would have to learn for themselves the hard practical way, and one day they might know what it was like when they were hit. It had been just the same with himself.

There was a shriek from the kitchen.

'Granda, granda, do you want a cup of tea?' It was Deirdre. She must have come through the back door, he thought, because he hadn't heard her.

'Indeed I do, Deirdre,' he called back. 'Would you bring it in here to me now?'

'Coming,' she called.

She came in pushing the door open with one hand out-stretched and stiff, while with the other she clutched a mug brimming with tea.

'Ah, you've filled it too full, child, now watch yourself or you'll have it all over the carpet.'

'No, no, granda, it's all right,' she replied, her eyes fixed firmly on the mug as she inched her way across the room to his armchair.

'Now set it down easily there,' he fussed. 'Be careful now, be careful.'

'I am being careful,' she said. 'Now you be careful too, granda, or you'll spill it and make mammy angry.' She put the mug down on the arm of his chair. 'There now, didn't I tell you it was all right?' she asked triumphantly.

'Ay,' he said gloomily, 'I suppose you did. But I have to sup it now without spilling a drop. Did you think of that now?'

'Oh, granda, stop fussing. And what's up with mammy? She seems all upset.'

'Is she now?' he wondered, watching his granddaughter set-tle herself on the carpet, clasping her knees with her arms.

'Is she mad at me for something?' she asked, looking up with big, brown eyes.

'Why would she be mad at you? Have you been a bold child?'

'Not at all. I've just been outside, playing.'

He looked down at her over the top of his mug.

'Well now, perhaps you were mistaken about it all. There's no need for her to be mad about anything.'

'Why not, granda?'

'Vincent is home.'

'Oh, Vincent is home,' she cried delightedly and clapped her hands together. 'Is he up the stairs?'

'No, no, child, he's had to go out.' Her face fell. 'But he'll not be too long.'

'Agh, once he's out,' she said, 'he stays out for hours. Sure, I'll be in bed by the time he gets back.'

'Ay, I expect you will.'

'But I want to talk to him.'

'Ay, I expect you do. You can talk to him in the morning, but.'

'You know what he'll be up to in the morning,' she said tossing her head back, 'sitting in bed yabbering away to Bryan. I think he likes Bryan more than me. Just because he's a twin. Do you think, granda ...' she paused and studied her shoes, 'do you think they really are alike? You know, that they think the same things. That they always know what the other one is doing. I mean,' she went on, 'if one of them got thumped in a riot or something, would the other one always know? I wish I was a twin. Then I'd always have someone to talk to.'

'Well, you've always got me, child, I don't move out of here very often. Chained to my armchair, that I am, so you can always come and fill my ears up.'

'Oh, granda, that's not the same. I mean,' she added quickly for fear of offending him, 'I love talking to you. You know that. But it would be nice to have someone of my own age, do you see? James, now. Well, he's only just older than me. But he's a boy. It's not the same.'

'No,' said her granda gravely, 'I suppose it's not.'

'But really, do you think they really know what each other's doing, even if they're not in the same place?'

'It seems they might. I expect they do. A bit anyhow. Indeed, I'm sure I've read it somewhere that they do.'

'Oh, granda, wouldn't it be great gas if I did have a twin

sister?' Her eyes shone at the thought of it, and he reached forward and ruffled her hair. He was very fond of Deirdre, who bounced in and out of the house, full of laughter and questions and doubts about life. She'd be just like her gran, he thought, a wild bit of an Irish girl who'd get the bit between her teeth and never stop to take anything too seriously for fear of spoiling what fun there was. Precious little fun for her at the moment, he thought. All right in school. But once out, the nastiness of the streets was all round her. Only the other day she'd been kept in for an hour because of shooting in the streets outside the school. A soldier had been shot and left lying on the pavement for twenty minutes before the army had been able to get him out. Luckily the child had seen nothing of that. But she'd heard all about it. Could hardly fail to hear.

'Deirdre,' her ma called from the kitchen, 'bring granda's mug back, and come and do your homework.'

'Coming, ma.' She got up and gave her granda a kiss on his leathery old cheek. 'Thanks for the wee chat,' she smiled. 'See you later.' She skipped out of the room.

Bryan was waiting for him in the pub down the bottom end of Leeson Street. It stood on the corner, a dingy-looking building. The windows were small and covered with wire mesh. Inside, the linoleum was scuffed and the walls were a dirty-looking brown colour, much the same as the ceiling covered with layers of smoke. There were a few marble-topped tables, covered with porter stains and the remains of the soapy water.

It was past eight o'clock by now, and the bar was full. Shafts of sunlight fell from the windows through the fug of smoke. Vincent slipped through the press up to the bar, pushing his shoulder forward and leaning an elbow on the cracked marble top. Bryan turned his head and looked at him, raising his eyebrows.

'I'll have a bottle of stout,' he said in reply to his brother's unspoken query, 'and a Powers.'

'When did you get back?'

' 'Bout an hour ago.'

'Have you been home?'

27

'Yes. I had me tea. Ma kept it for me.'

'What kept you so long?'

'We had ... ah ... we were hit by a bloody ambush,' he said softly, 'I'll tell you in a minute,' he added as the barman poured his bottle of Guinness in front of him, and then put down his whiskey and a glass of water. He paused. 'Listen,' he said when the barman had moved off, 'someone knew we were there. First a fucking military patrol came down in a chopper. I was hidden. They didn't see me, but they questioned the others.'

'What did they say?'

'I don't know, I had to stay hidden till they'd all gone. Then I started walking.' He raised his glass and, in five steady gulps, finished it off. 'Jesus, but I needed that. Listen, Bryan, it was terrible, bloody terrible. I found the van. John and Seamus ... well ... they were dead.' He stared into the bottom of his whiskey glass.

Bryan signalled the barman. 'Two,' he said, holding up two fingers, 'make them doubles.

'What happened?'

'They were hit. It was a terrible bloody mess ... There was ... oh Jesus! ... there was nothing left of the back of Seamus's head.'

'Fuck me!' said Bryan, horrified. 'How, how did you get away?'

'I told you. I was walking. I had to stay hidden when they left because of the army.'

Bryan was holding his glass with both hands, turning it round and round. He didn't quite know what to say to his brother.

'Jesus, Bryan,' Vincent said, his voice suddenly getting louder and starting to crack a bit, 'what am I going to do? They're both . . .'

'Shut your mouth, for Chrissake! Do you want everyone to know what you're up to?'

'They'll know bloody soon enough,' he said bitterly. 'How the hell can you keep something like that quiet?'

'Well, don't draw attention to yourself.' He grabbed his arm

28

and put his mouth down near Vincent's ear. 'For the love of God, get a grip on yourself.' He looked round cautiously. In the general noise and movement of the bar, no one had seemed to notice anything unusual. He then saw an empty corner table.

'Here, come and sit down over here.' He pulled his brother over. Vincent shook his arm free. Bryan grabbed it back again. 'Don't be an eejit,' he said fiercely, but softly, 'will you come here with me and stop making an exhibition of yourself?'

They both slid into the corner seat, their backs to the wall. Vincent slumped in his seat. Bryan, twisting in his seat so as to keep an eye on anyone who might come within earshot, turned his attention to Vincent.

'Listen now, Vincent, to me,' he said softly. 'What's happened? You've been out on a job, and two fellas have been killed. I know they're friends of yours. I know them too. But what the fuck do you expect, man, when you go out on something like that? What. . . .'

'I didn't expect them to get bloody well killed.'

'Well, never mind. Once you get started on this sort of thing, but, you must expect people to get hurt.'

'Oh, Bryan,' Vincent said hoarsely, his head in his hands, 'don't you understand? Don't you understand anything?'

'But I do. . . .'

'No, you bloody well don't.' He looked at his brother. 'We were unarmed. No guns. No revolvers, no rifles, no nothing,' he shouted. 'Nothing at all except a bloody walkie-talkie set.'

'Keep your voice down.' Bryan stared at him wide-eyed. 'Unarmed?' he said. 'What, what the hell was that for?'

'We thought it better, in case there was a road block. Anyway, we didn't think we'd need them. Not on that job, anyway.'

'Well, someone made a damn bad mistake there.'

'It's a bit late to work that out.'

They stopped talking, collecting their thoughts.

'Let's have another,' said Vincent and, without waiting for a reply, picked up both glasses and went, clumsily, to the bar. His mind was whirling round and round. He didn't expect much sympathy from Bryan. His brother had always tried to persuade him to give up his urge to fight for Ireland, saying granda was lot of talk but no action. He'd never told Bryan what he was going to do, that he had joined the IRA. He'd never told him that he was going up to the coast to wait for the boat. But Bryan had known. He had known full well he wasn't going within spitting distance of any wedding, best man or no. But he must make him understand. If he didn't, how could he convince himself?

He collected the glasses, and a glass of water, and holding them carefully in both hands, he walked back.

'Ah! hallo there, Vince,' he heard a high-pitched voice behind him. 'Is that yeerself now?'

He turned round. The voice came from a small, thin man with a shock of black hair falling over his forehead. Dark eyes were sunk into his face on either side of a long, thin nose. It was Jimmy Hannahan.

He nodded to him. 'Indeed it is, Jimmy,' he said. 'How's yourself?'

'A sight better than ye look, for a start,' said Jimmy, his eyes darting from Vincent, to Bryan, on round the room and back again. 'A sight better than ye,' he repeated. 'Are ye after seeing a ghost or something?' He learned forward with what passed for a smile. 'Or has someone just tried to stick a knife into ye?'

'I've got a touch of flu,' Vincent said shortly. 'I won't die of it, but.'

He moved away, leaving Jimmy by the bar, and slid in beside Bryan.

'What did that streak of piss want with you?' Bryan asked.

'Ah, fuck him,' said Vincent sharply, 'he's a wee shit, and I'll kick his bloody teeth in one day for him.'

'That wouldn't be difficult to do. But I'd pick your moment. He's got some powerful big friends, they say.'

'Ay, I know that. He creeps so far up their asses he'll lose himself one day.'

He turned his head slightly towards his brother.

'*Slainte,*' he said gloomily, raising his glass.

'*Slainte,*' Bryan replied.

They both drank.

Vincent put his glass down.

'Listen, Bryan,' he said, 'you've got to understand what I'm trying to do. I know you think I'm mad, but you've got to understand. Unless someone does something, we're going to go on as we've always gone on under the British. We don't get justice. We'll never get justice, because they are motivated by greed. They'll use violent physical force to start with. They're already doing that. Then they use extreme psychological pressure. They want to tear apart the fabric of our society, of our country. They want to stamp out all our values, traditions, customs. To get rid of our language and religion. To take away our pride and self-confidence. They've been doing it for years. They're still doing it. But we must fight back. Someone's got to fight back.'

'For God's sake, Vince,' Bryan said, disgusted, 'you sound like a bloody record. Who taught you all that – your political officer in the Provies, or what? I know all that,' he went on with a touch of anger. 'What's new about that? I've had enough Irish history bashed into my head for a lifetime. I know that.' He banged his fist on the table for emphasis. 'I know all that. But Vince,' he pulled his brother's jacket round so that he faced him, 'you don't have to kill to get it.'

'What do you know about killing? You wouldn't even take the head off a chicken. You'd pass out, you're that wet.'

'Don't be daft. Killing chickens has nothing to do with it at all. You know that. I'm talking about killing people.'

'But you don't know anything about it ... about killing. What's left, I ask you, what's left?'

Bryan said nothing. If he was honest with himself, he didn't really know what else was left. There must be another way, he thought. Killing just led to more killing. Backwards and forwards, as it had done all down the years. Anything was better than that, even if they didn't get all they wanted straight away.

'No!' said Vincent, 'it doesn't work. They've been talking for years. All those bloody politicians. Where did it get them? Nowhere. Nowhere at all.'

'Vince, are you really going to go out and kill? Are you going to take on the army? Are you going to take on the Prods? Are you going to shoot old women in the street, so help me, are you ...?'

'You're a bastard. We don't shoot old women. That's a bloody Prod lie,' he said furiously. 'What the hell do you think you're talking about? You know bloody right well that's a lie.'

'It's happened before, Vince, you know. And it will happen again. It's got to. If you start killing, there's no stopping. You get a blood lust on you. Is that,' he thought for a moment, 'is that what you felt today – a blood lust? Did you want to kill someone what you saw John and Seamus lying there covered in blood themselves – dead?'

Vincent looked away. 'No, oh, my God ... no. I just threw up.'

'You threw up?' Bryan felt a little hope for his brother. He was sure Vincent wasn't the killing type. He might be easily depressed and quick tempered, but he'd never thought of him as a killer, or, he forced himself to think it, a murderer. He groaned inwardly. It was great to work up a hatred for the British and the Prods. But it was a different matter when you were forced to do something about all that.

'Listen!' He shook his brother's arm. 'You're not cut out for this. But you mustn't let on. Not yet.'

'What do you mean, I mustn't let on?' Vincent said.

'We'll have to get you out of this. Across the water maybe.'

'Don't be daft. I can't go now.'

'But you must.'

'I can't.'

'You'll have to go, Vince. You can't stay and give it up. They'll shoot you.'

'That's why I can't give it up. That's why I can't go.'

'Vince,' he pleaded, 'do you know what you're doing? Leave this to someone else.

'Do you want another drink?' he said, after a while.

'No.'

'Will we go, then?'

'I suppose so.'

Bryan looked at his brother. His face was still pale, the eyes darkening with pain and worry. He'd never seen him look so empty. There wouldn't be much difficulty in telling them apart tonight, he thought.

'Come on, then,' he said, 'let's go.'

Jimmy Hannahan watched the two brothers go out. He didn't like Vincent Malone. There was something uncertain about the man, and he had stuck-up ideas for the class of person he was. Giving himself airs and graces just because he had a bit of learning. Not only had he done well at school, thought Jimmy, but he also had that old fool of a grandfather to fill up his head with grand ideas.

He was annoyed he hadn't managed to rile Vincent. For him not to be riled he must have something powerful on his mind. Normally, he knew, Vincent had only to look at him to fly into a temper. But not today. What was it? he thought. Ah yes! The job. He didn't know which job, but he was very certain that Vincent had been on one. Something he'd heard a week before. Some sudden flicker of interest in Vincent's eyes when someone mentioned ... agh, what the hell had it been? Guns? he wondered. No. He dismissed that thought. It wasn't no guns. Gelly? No, wasn't that neither.

He got himself another glass of Guinness and went and sat down at the table the Malone brothers had used. What was Vincent at? Then it came back to him. Something about the coast. That was it. Someone had said something about the north coast, and the storm ... ah yes ... the storm that was forecast. Nothing unusual about that. But there had been something unusual about the way Vincent Malone had suddenly lifted his head to look round at the speaker. He had thought then something was up. Well, now what was it?

He started delving around in his mind for the answer. Once again he dismissed guns as being involved. Vincent had only just joined. He wouldn't go on a job like that. He hadn't even been out, as far as he knew, and he knew quite a lot – he hadn't even been out at the training camp for a day, let alone a full

33

period of training. So it wasn't a shooting. Courier work, maybe? It was a possibility.

He had drunk half his porter by now. He looked around, but couldn't see anyone who might buy him another. So it was off, for him, and soonish. But he wanted to work out what Vincent had been up to before he left.

Courier work it had to be, he thought. And connected with the coast. Oh Jesus, of course! The lunchtime headlines had carried the story of two men shot near Ballyvoy. Unnamed as yet. But he knew who they were. Vincent must have been with them. But how had he escaped? What the hell was he doing back in Belfast with those two lying dead on the roadside, their brains and guts, no doubt, spattered all over the place? Where Vincent's guts should have been, he thought viciously.

He had downed his drink when another thought struck him. One good reason why Vincent would be back alive, and the others dead, was that he had known what was going to happen. No wonder he'd been looking pale around the gills. A bloody fucking informer he was.

He slammed his empty glass down on the table, pushed his way quickly to the door, and ran off down the street.

3

The bells woke him up. Church bells. It was Sunday morning and Bryan lay with his eyes half shut against the sun streaming through the window.

His head felt slightly fugged up, as they'd both gone on to Mulligan's place and drunk on till the early hours of the morning. Vincent had gone deeper and deeper into his black, depressed mood. Nothing was right. He didn't know what to do. Vincent got so angry at one time he had swung a punch at him, but he had too much drink taken to be effective. He had easily blocked the blow, and then calmed his brother. Ah! he thought, it had been a wild night, with talk and argument, wild singing and vomiting; with Vincent so far gone at one stage he'd had to shove his head under the tap in the yard outside. That had sobered him up betime, he remembered, but not for long.

Vincent lay beside him in the double bed, breathing heavily. The smell of drink must lie thick in the room, he thought, though he couldn't smell it himself. He wasn't surprised to see that Jamie had already upped and gone. Should he go to mass, he thought, wondering what the time was. His watch had fallen off the chair by the bed, and he groped for it, unseeing, with his hand. It was just too late, he saw, to get to eight o'clock mass. He should go, but he couldn't. He didn't feel up to it, and, anyway, he wanted to be around when Vince woke up: he didn't want him left on his own.

He dozed on, his body heavy with sleep, a slight but nagging pain in his head. The noise of the street outside drifted through the window. Cars passing, people talking, the clink of milk bottles as they were collected and delivered. That would be Ben Lucas, the rear gunner on a Belfast milk float. Very funny, he thought to himself, except it was true. At least he was almost certain it was true.

Voices floated up from the kitchen. Mammy was there, getting breakfast ready, and she would have gone to the seven o'clock mass. He could hear Deirdre singing, snatches of something or other, and the voices of Jamie and granda.

It wasn't a bad family, he thought. Better than a lot he knew. They were very close, particularly since his father had died, some four years before, and granda had come to live with them. Granda was a great one for holding the family together. They seemed to drift round and round him. He was a sort of contact point for them all; part of them, but because of the generation gap, apart from them, though he could talk about Ireland as nobody else could. Bringing it alive, making it have some meaning.

Maybe that wasn't so good, though. Perhaps that was what had really pushed Vince into joining the IRA. Granda would be delighted to hear of it. But, he was quite sure, totally horrified if he knew what it really meant. He lay on, his thoughts surfacing and then dipping again beneath the cover of sleep that lapped round him.

The hot sun on his eyes, orange sunsplash pouring over his eyeballs. The wind cool and tangy from the Atlantic, the sand between his toes. Vincent's wrist pressed against his, blood from the two small cuts mingling together. Always together, they had solemnly vowed all those years ago. They'd been only seven at the time ... or was it eight? Staying with granda down in Kerry. Oh, what a summer, he remembered. Out all day in perfect weather, swimming, fishing, and spending evenings listening to granda talk. Vince, he thought, that was along time ago, and where are we now? Ah Jesus, but it's bad, and you're in bloody great trouble.

Vince stirred, groaned and put his hands to his head. 'For Chrissake, Bryan,' he mumbled, 'do you have to shine a light in my eyes? Turn the damn thing off.'

'It's the sun, Vince. It's well gone eight.'

'Oh, my head! What happened last night? Did you get me home?'

'I did. Just. You had a fair bit of drink taken.'

'Aye, you're right on that.' He groaned again, twisting round so his face was out of the direct sunlight. 'Tell me, did I do anything mad?'

'You took a swing at me. But apart from that, we managed to keep your mouth shut. Most of the time, anyway.'

'What did I say?'

'You know damn well what you said. Or at least the guts of what you said. I'm not repeating it for you now just to ease your conscience.'

'What the hell d'you mean by that now?'

'Just what I said. You want me to repeat all that rubbish you talked last night, just to hear someone else make excuses that wouldn't stand up to damn all.'

'Is that right?'

'It is. And you know it rightly.'

Vincent sighed. He closed his eyes and rubbed his thumbs hard against his eyeballs, then pushed his fingers hard into the back of his neck, trying to ease the cramped pain. In his stomach, he felt the bitter, heavy despair again. John and Seamus, dead.

'Bryan....'

'Yes?'

Vincent lay there, rubbing the back of his neck. He hoped it would all just go away. Surely it was a nightmare.

'Yes, what is it?' Bryan asked.

'I think you're right.'

'You what?'

'I think you're right. You know,' he said slowly, looking for the right words, 'I was trying last night to justify myself. I tried very hard.'

'If taking a swing at me meant you were trying hard, then you were trying hard. I agree with you. So what?'

'Listen, you dumb bastard. I'm being very serious. I mean I was using arguments to justify what I'd been doing. Or what I was getting into. I ... I believe in what they ... we ... stand for. We've got right on our side. And if you take any struggle to the end, then you have to kill. You know.... I mean, if you're fighting for something you really believe in, and you're opposed by force, then you have to use force.'

Bryan stared at the ceiling. He said nothing.

'If you use force at all,' Vincent went on, 'then you have probably got to kill people. If you have to kill some people to achieve what you want, then you have to. And if you take that argument on to the end, then it doesn't matter who you kill. I mean,' he said, in a soft voice, 'it doesn't matter if you kill women and children.'

He looked across at Bryan, staring at the ceiling. He wanted Bryan to turn and face him. He willed him to turn. You're my twin, he said fiercely to himself. Look at me, damn you, look at me.

Bryan didn't move. Vincent covered his face with his hands.

'That's the theory,' he explained, 'the theory of how you can kill women and children. If it's the only way to get what you want,' his voice rose, 'then you have to do it.' He took a deep breath, and then in a quiet, small voice, he said: 'But I can't do that. I agree with the theory, but I can't kill people like that.'

'I'm glad,' said Bryan, without moving.

'You do understand, don't you?'

'No, I don't understand. How can I understand such a ridiculous statement? It doesn't even make sense ... but I'm glad.'

They both fell silent for a while. Then Bryan asked: 'What are you going to do?'

'I don't know.'

'What will they do to you?'

'I don't know.'

'What the hell do you mean?' he said, suddenly angry. 'What d'you mean, you don't know? You damn well should know. How the hell can you avoid trouble if you don't know what's coming? You've got to think ... think,' he shouted, the pain stabbing through his head. 'Will they have you up

38

before one of those bloody kangaroo courts, or something, and then take you out with a bag over your head and shoot you?'

'Yes.'

'What?' Bryan stared at him. 'For the love of God, you're not serious, are you?'

'Umm ... about the court, yes. Shooting me ... no. They're not that bloody daft, and anyway, I haven't done anything.'

'You haven't done anything ... yet.'

'Ay, but if I say I won't go on another job, that's not so bad as refusing to go out when I'm ordered, or backing off once I'm on it.'

'You sound very sure of yourself.'

'Well, I'm not, but I think that's what will happen.'

'Shouldn't you try and leave ... go to England ... or maybe even America?'

There was a short laugh from Vincent.

'And if I go, what'll happen to you, and mammy, and Deirdre and the rest of youse? Have you thought of that?' He spat it out at his brother. 'There's no point in my running. They'll just get you. No, no. I'll stay on. You know, Bryan,' he said reflectively, 'I went to one of those courts once. It was almost a joke. There was some wee bastard. Sixteen he was. They went through the whole rigmarole. The intelligence officer held a preliminary hearing. He made a report saying there was a case to consider. Then they convened a court ... convened, I think that was the word they used, you know, they wanted everything to be right. Well, they convened this court. Three senior IRA officers there were. The intelligence officer prosecuting. Jesus! you should have seen that poor wee bastard. Bloody terrified he was. Thought he was for a head job an' all. You know, black hood and a bullet in the head down some lonely road.'

'What had he done?'

'Robbed Mrs McTaggert of a pound of sweeties and three cartons of fags.'

'For Chrissake, is that all? They went through all that for that? What did they do to him?'

39

'Pay for what he'd taken, and clean her shop out for a month.'

'And if he hadn't –'

'They'd have kneecapped him.'

'What will they do to you?'

'I don't know. Thump me. Tar and feathering. For fuck's sake! how should I know? Maybe nothing at all.'

'I still think you should get away.'

'Well, I don't,' Vincent said firmly, 'and that's that. I don't want to talk about it. Just leave me be. I'll get sorted out all right.'

'That's what worries me,' said Bryan. 'That's just what worries me. Come on, let's get down and get some breakfast.'

Vincent felt a hand on his shoulder

'Don't turn round,' said a voice. It was not unfriendly, and it was familiar. He tried to place it. 'Vince, boyo, you're wanted down in Leeson Street. In the back room. Don't let on to nobody, and come on your own. In one hour.'

He felt the pit of his stomach heave and then contract. 'O K,' he said, 'I'll be there.'

He waited a few moments, staring at the piece of wood he had just measured. Then he picked up his saw. Steadily he made a long cut down one side, turned the plank round, made a cross cut, and put it down. He picked up a plane and smoothed off the edge. Then he drilled four holes along the back part of the plank.

The building he was working in had been burned out six months previously. The structure had been saved, but little had been left of anything inside. They'd been working on it for a couple of months now, clearing all the burned wood, re-plastering, re-flooring, and now Vincent was replacing the wooden fittings.

He enjoyed his work, the feel of wood under his hands, the smell of the shavings, the satisfaction of turning out a finished article well. He worked quickly and steadily, trying to put out of his mind the fact of his 12.30 appointment.

He set the points of the mortise gauge and divided the edge

of the work into three. He squared off the shoulder line, and gauged in the finger and cut-out lines from the face side.

He used a piece of chalk to mark the waste wood clearly, so there would be no mistakes in cutting it. He sawed down the cut-out section, skimming the gauge lines in the waste. Then he removed most of the waste by cutting across near the bottom with a coping saw. Again he squared off the shoulder line with a narrow chisel, and went on to cut the finger of the corner joint. On the through joint, he produced the finger by using the halving cut-out method on both sides – by sawing down to the gauge marks, and chiselling out the waste from both sides. He decided he would strengthen the joints even more by dowelling through from the face side, and, to get a little extra tightness, he offset the dowel holes slightly so that when he drove them home, they would force the finger against the bottom of the cut-out.

He put his work down, pleased with it, and then looked at his watch. It was almost time to go.

Don't tell anyone, the man had said. Well, he wouldn't. But he felt frightened, so he went to look for Bryan who was down in the yard, fixing some broken brickwork.

'I'll be gone an hour or so,' he said tightly, looking hard at Bryan.

'Will you now?' said Bryan, raising his eyebrows enquiringly.

'I will. Look out for me now.'

They stared hard at each other for a moment, and Vincent nodded his head a fraction. Bryan's face went pale, and set hard.

'I'll look out for you,' he said, firmly. 'Don't be late, but.'

'I'll be back.'

He turned, pushing his hands into the pockets of his jeans, and walked out of the yard. On his way, he went past the site caravan. He put his head through the doorway.

'I'm off for me lunch,' he said. He could see nobody there, but he knew Tony was behind the partition at the end. Tony was an odd sort of Englishman the construction company had brought over to keep an eye on the site. That and organizing some of the paperwork. Anyway, that's what he said he did. To Vincent he was more like a glorified watchdog than anything else.

'You're going off early,' Tony shouted. 'What's up, are you tired, or finished?'

'I've got to run a message for me ma.'

'All right, me old darling. Get mummy's message done and come back quickly. There's lots to do.'

'Ah, shut your face,' said Vincent, half to himself, turning round and striding off, 'you bloody English twit!'

He had about a mile to go, and he walked quickly, head down. It was hot, but it wasn't just the sun making him sweat. He didn't really know what to expect at the other end, for he'd been having Bryan on. It was true he had been at one IRA court before, but that hadn't been too serious. That fool of an intelligence officer had just been trying to make himself out more important than he really was, and the boy had been up for bugger all.

But he knew full well what he was up for, and he had no doubt what the summons was all about; it was far more serious. He had put a cautious word out that he wanted out of that side of the movement. He'd do other things, but he couldn't go on with the sort of operation he'd been involved with up on the north coast – or even worse than that.

He walked past Hastings Street police station, keeping to the far side of the road. It looked more like a small fortress than a police station. The door with its iron-shuttered peephole was closed, as all Northern Ireland police station doors were. But outside, along the pavement, were sheets of corrugated iron, angled up from the pavement to the wall, so that any bomb thrown at the station would roll back into the road, away from the wall. A concrete pill box stood just outside the main entrance. There were rolls of barbed wire round it, and a camouflage net over it, softening the edges and making the firing slots difficult to see; indeed at night they would be impossible to see. And crowning the station, heavy mesh wire stretched round the walls to stop anyone throwing a bomb over and into the yard. Pigs! he thought.

He crossed over Durham Street, turned another corner and walked along Cullingtree Road. He was getting into the Lower Falls area now. Narrow little streets, the houses jam-packed together; long rows of them, two up and two down. It was a depressing area. So many parts of Belfast were depressing, he thought. He remembered back to the time the Lower Falls had been under curfew. Three days. He'd been caught in a house there after the dust-up with the army. They'd been searching for arms in Balkan Street, right in the middle of the Lower Falls. They'd been searching about an hour, in the afternoon, but when the patrol tried to leave, a crowd had started to pelt them with stones. Bloody madness, to take on the army like that. But they had. The rocks had flown through the air. The troops had fired CS gas. Everyone had been choking and spluttering, tying damp handkerchiefs round their faces, some soaking them in vinegar, if they could get it, because they thought that helped.

The military had gone mad, pouring in hundreds of troops and sealing off the area. Then the petrol and nail bombs started. By ten fifteen, a full-scale curfew had been clamped on the whole neighbourhood. A helicopter hovering overhead with a loudspeaker was telling everyone to stay indoors, and by then it had been too late for him to get out. He'd had to stay in that dingy upstairs room, cramped in with a family of eight. God, he couldn't think how they'd lived there. It was awful, but he was grateful they hid him. They'd been generosity itself, and brave, as troops came crashing up the road that night, fighting their way into the area, their faces blackened, bashing down doors, searching.

Jesus! he'd lain in bed, two small girls on top of him, half smothered and sick with fear. Amongst all the other smells, the smell of fear was greatest. It was the first time he'd known it. But the night had passed, the troops had missed out the house he was in. It was two days before he got out. Bloody hungry, for they'd run out of food. They kept little in the house, relying on the wee shop down the corner – he noticed he was walking past it right at that moment – relying on it for their needs, meal by meal almost. They'd been shut up for thirty-four hours, with only a two-hour break on the Sunday. That hadn't been much help.

He turned right into Albert Street. It was a larger road that cut right through the Lower Falls. But it only seemed large because all the rest were so small. Just as it bent right towards Divis Street, he turned again, this time into Servia Street. He didn't have far to go now. What a place! he thought, and remembered this was the very way he'd come back in again, bearing the news of the curfew. The military, he remembered, had been high with excitement at all the arms they'd found as they had torn the area apart. He had had to remember all the figures, because they'd told him on no account to take a newspaper, and the batteries of the wireless had gone flat. They'd kept it on all the weekend of the curfew.

Five civilians had been killed. Sixty had been wounded, as well as fifteen soldiers. But at a special press conference in the yard of a police station, the army had produced everything they'd found that weekend! 52 pistols, 35 rifles, 6 automatic weapons, 14 shotguns, 100 home-made bombs, 250 pounds of explosives, 8 two-way radio sets and over 20,000 rounds of ammunition. Even he had been impressed with the amount. He'd never known there was so much around.

He walked across Cyprus Street, cut through into Leeson Street, and he was almost there.

Vincent stood in the small back room of the pub. In front of him, seated behind an old table, were three men he knew were senior officers in the IRA. At the end of the table, slightly apart, sat Mike Learton, the battalion's intelligence officer. In a corner, at the back of the room behind him, he noticed Jimmy Hannahan. He wondered what he was doing there, but, considering the men facing him, he decided he had more to worry about them.

The room was half dark, blinds at the two windows kept out the sun. It was also stuffy: the others had obviously been there for some time, smoking. They looked self-important, shuffling papers in front of them on the bare table.

The man seated in the middle spoke first.

44

'Is your name Vincent Malone?'

'Yes, it is.'

'Of 23 Siris Street?'

'Yes.'

'You are a volunteer in the Belfast Brigade of the IRA.'

Vincent wasn't sure whether that was a question or statement of fact.

'Yes,' he said.

'You are brought before this court, officially convened here by officers of the brigade, to face a charge of failing to obey orders in the face of the enemy.' He stopped and looked up at Vincent. Vincent stared straight ahead over the man's head. He said nothing, for he felt the cold clutch of fear in his stomach again.

'There is a secondary charge, which we will consider with the first.' He looked down at the papers in front of him. 'You are charged with giving information to the enemy or, alternatively, withholding information about the enemy which you knew would have been to the advantage of our own forces.' He cleared his throat, and looked up again at Vincent. 'You may have someone to defend you. There are four officers outside. You may pick one if you wish. They have all agreed. Or,' he said, clearing his throat again, 'you may make a statement later in the proceedings, which will be read to the court.' He stopped talking, and they all looked at Vincent.

Vincent was in a turmoil. What were they ever talking about? He hadn't refused to do anything. They hadn't asked him to do anything since the last operation. And what the hell were they on about? An informer – were they trying to make out he was an informer? Mother of God! he thought, they're mad. I'd never inform on them. It'd be more than my life is worth.

The silence grew in the close atmosphere of the small room, weighing down on everyone. He heard someone calling outside in the pub. A lorry went past. He opened his mouth to say something, but couldn't think of anything. The enormity of the charge stuck in his throat. He gagged slightly. What was he supposed to say? Guilty or not guilty, wasn't that it?

45

'Not ... not guilty,' he croaked, at last.

'I haven't asked you yet to plead. Will you please keep to the rules of the court and just answer the questions put to you?'

'Yes.'

'Well, will you answer, then?'

'Ah, what ... I'm sorry, but what was the question? I. . . .'

'The question was whether you wanted someone, an officer, to defend you. As a volunteer, that's your entitlement. Or do you want to reserve your position and make a statement later, to the court? That was the question.'

'I'll ... I'll ... make a statement later,' he whispered.

'Very well, then. Now, as presiding officer, I call on the brigade intelligence officer to open the prosecution.'

The man sitting at the end of the table rose to his feet. He picked up a sheaf of papers from in front of him and held them up.

'On the twelfth of this month,' he read, 'Volunteer Malone, the accused now before this court, returned from an operation in North Antrim. The operation had been a failure. Not least because supplies he and two others were sent to pick up failed to appear, but because the other two volunteers were killed in the course of ...'

The voice droned on. Vincent could not bring himself to listen. Dear Mother of God! he thought, how has it come to this? John and Seamus dead. He hadn't known them well, but he now felt a strong bond linking him with the two men. They had gone out together, with high hopes. He was the only one to return, and instead of some sympathy, some understanding of what he had been through, there was this awful bloody performance going on in front of him.

How had he got into this position? he thought wildly. It didn't make sense. He hadn't refused to do anything. He certainly hadn't informed on anyone, the man was talking nonsense. But he was still talking.

' ... he was then seen in a disturbed state, and overheard to say he would no longer accept orders from any IRA officer. . . .'

46

Rubbish, rubbish, he cried out, but no sound came from his mouth. He tore his eyes away from the wall; forced himself to look at the man reading out these preposterous statements. The man glanced up from his reading, caught his eye and looked back at his papers quickly.

' ... it was pointed out by another volunteer that Volunteer Malone came from a family that was not sympathetic to the cause, whatever the status of his grandfather. In particular Malone's brother was known to be very opposed to Volunteer Malone's active role within the movement. That, and the other causes I have mentioned, would make it clear that there was a leak of information. Not only did the army intercept them, but the UVF as well, with fatal results for two volunteers. The most likely source of this leak would be the most inexperienced member of the team. An inexperienced volunteer with a brother,' and the intelligence officer leaned towards Vincent, eyes suddenly blazing and a finger stabbing in the air, 'who we know for a fact was doing everything within his power to dissuade him from the course of his rightful duty.'

He threw down his papers on the table.

There was silence for a few moments. The intelligence officer panted a bit from his efforts, while Vincent felt the blood draining from his face. He couldn't believe what he had heard, and he hadn't heard it all.

'Before we adjourn,' said the presiding officer, clearing his throat and sitting up straight in his chair, 'do you wish to make a formal statement, as you indicated you wished, or do you just wish to address the court ... ah ... in your own words?'

Vincent looked at him. 'I'll address the court now, sir,' he said hoarsely and slowly. 'First, I have not refused to carry out any order given to me. I carried out the last orders given to me. That operation failed. You ... you know about that. It was no fault of mine. I did what I could. The reason I wasn't with the others was that I was hiding when the army came, and John and Seamus left without me.'

'Is that a fact, now?' said the presiding officer.

'It is so, sir,' replied Vincent, and went on: 'For someone to say they heard me saying I'd take no more orders is a lie. I never said nothing like that at all.'

'The intelligence officer has investigated the matter, and he is of the opinion the informant is not lying.'

'Perhaps you could tell me who that man is. This ... this is a serious ... ah ... matter. I want to question him.'

The three officers at the table put their heads together and talked amongst themselves. Vincent put his hands behind his back and shrugged his shoulders up and down to relieve the stiffness. He looked round the room and saw Jimmy Hannahan. He had forgotten he was there. He looked at him with contempt. And then the realization flashed on him that the person who had informed on him could be none other than Hannahan himself.

He turned back to the presiding officer.

'If it was Hannahan . . .' he began.

'Be quiet, will you?' said the officer furiously. 'I will not tell you again you must obey the rules of the court. Be quiet.'

They conferred again, and then the presiding officer looked up.

'Well,' he said, 'you seem to know who it was. Hannahan,' he called out, 'come up here, will you? Malone wants to ask you a couple of questions.'

Hannahan shuffled his way forward and stood at the end of the table.

'Well?' he said, belligerently.

'I suppose it was in the pub the night I came back that you overheard, so to speak, me saying I'd take no more orders. Is that it?'

'Ay, it was that.'

'Well now, what was it exactly that I said?'

'Ah well, I can't remember the exact words, but it was about not taking any more orders. You were getting very angry.'

'Where were you sitting, when you heard this?'

'I was standing by the bar.'

'Standing by the bar, were you now?'

'Yes, that's what I said.'

'Wouldn't that be some ten, or maybe even fifteen, feet away from where I was sitting?'

48

'I wouldn't know.'

'Well, would you like to hazard a guess?' said Vincent, warming to his questioning, and losing a bit of the fear in him. 'I won't take what you say to the inch. Just a rough sort of idea of the distance.'

'I wouldn't know.'

'Come now, wouldn't you be an intelligent man, Jimmy Hannahan? A man of quick mind and acute ears. Would you not be able to put a figure on a little distance like that now?'

Hannahan looked at him furiously. 'Yes,' he said, 'it would be about that figure.'

'Thank you. And you say you have good hearing now? There's nothing wrong with your ears, I mean.'

'No, there's nothing wrong with them.'

'I take it you can hear well, then?'

'Yes, indeed I can.'

'And able to judge noises well ... where they are coming from and what they mean?'

'Yes.'

'Now would there have been a lot of noise in the pub that night?'

'Well, I don't know about that. It was a usual sort of night.'

'Come, come, Jimmy Hannahan, you're just after telling me how good you are at judging noises. You know, an acute ear for the little sound, and a good feel for the big one. Yes?'

'I don't rightly know what you're talking about.'

'I'll tell you what I'm talking about, Hannahan, you little shit, I'm. . . .'

'That's enough,' roared the presiding officer, 'this is a court. Do that once again, Malone, and I'll withdraw your right to question anyone, or make a statement.'

'I'm sorry, sir,' Vincent said quickly, and turned back to Hannahan, whose face now gleamed with sweat. 'What I'm saying to you, Hannahan, is that from where you were standing, you couldn't hear what I was saying, so you never could have heard me say I wouldn't take orders.'

'I did hear you,' said Hannahan, hesitantly and without much conviction. 'You were shouting.'

49

'I was not shouting. And if I had been, then sure other people would have heard me say that as well. Nobody else has, have they? Nobody except yourself.' He leaned forward. 'And was it you who said I was an informer?'

Hannahan licked his lips nervously and ran his hand through a damp lock of black hair that fell over his forehead. He looked desperately at the three officers at the table for help. They obliged.

'That's enough, Malone,' said the presiding officer. 'You have made your point.' He bent down and talked softly with the other two once again. 'Captain Reegan wants to ask you a question.'

'Malone,' said Reegan, his harsh Belfast accent battering round the room, 'you say you never said you would take no more orders. Do I have you right on that?'

'Yes, sir.'

'But would I be right in thinking that though you haven't said it, you would be thinking it?'

'Thinking it?' repeated Vincent, desperately. 'But sure I haven't been given any more orders. How could I be thinking it?'

'Don't try and evade the question,' said the presiding officer sharply. 'Answer Captain Reegan.'

'Let me put it like this,' said Captain Reegan, softly. 'If you were ordered out on an operation tonight to execute a member of the RUC, who we know, for certain, has been torturing IRA officers and volunteers in detention, would you go?'

'But I haven't been asked. . . .'

'Answer,' roared the presiding officer. 'But then perhaps you don't have to, you yellow-livered little bastard. I'm adjourning this court to consider the evidence.' He looked towards two men standing at the back. 'You keep him safe till we are back.' And the three of them got up and went out.

Hannahan slipped out with them, forgotten. Vincent sat, slumped on a chair, wondering where he had gone wrong.

With blackened faces, the patrol moved carefully up Divis Street, spread out on both sides. The windows were boarded up, it was all grey; grey corrugated iron, grey concrete blocks. Grey grass sprouted miserably in the pavement gaps, the paving stones long since gone.

The patrol commander called in on his radio and reported he was passing Tennant Street. The wind-blown debris of weeks lay in the sheltered corners, but, apart from that, the wide street was empty. A lonely burglar alarm rang endlessly and uselessly, as the dawn rinsed a dirty grey into the sky.

The patrol commander looked up the street to the far end. A corporation bus was still burning there, fitfully. It was really now just a skeleton of steel struts. A group of small boys were directing traffic round it, what small amount of traffic there was at that time of the morning. Luckily, he thought, he didn't have to go up there. He would turn off into the maze of the Ardoyne before he reached those crossroads. He hated dealing with children, they were little bastards and could be very dangerous, but thump one of the bleeding perishers, and you could get your arse kicked from here to kingdom come.

Half an hour later, deep into the normally no-go nationalist area, he heard the first urgent sound of a dustbin lid being banged rhythmically on the pavement. Fuck it! he thought, nothing but aggro from now on.

From another corner in front of him, the banging dustbin lid was answered, and soon the air was full with the steady clatter of bins from all round. First it was the children. God knows, he wondered, how they got them all up at that ungodly hour of the morning. Then the women, mostly in their hair curlers, dressed in old jumpers and dressing gowns, fags drooping out of pale faces. The clattering went on, punctuated by shrill blasts on whistles. At every corner, at every front door, someone was stooping or kneeling on the ground, a dustbin lid in one hand, banging steadily up and down. They always seemed to know which way the patrol was coming, he thought; the bastards always had their eyes fixed on him as he came round the corner.

His point man looked round at him, and he waved him on, signalling to him and the others at the same time with his arms to keep a good lookout above them. This was a dangerous area. They hadn't lost a man there yet, but the previous battalion had lost two. Both single shots from a sniper's rifle.

The first soldier in the patrol flitted heavily across the street, flattening his back on the corner of the house, his eyes flickering all round. Particularly along the top windows of the houses. Luckily there was only one row to watch. The houses were very small. He beckoned. Another soldier launched himself from the cover of the corner house, ran quickly across the road, and dived into a doorway a few yards down.

'Bastards,' a woman suddenly screamed at them, and spat. Others joined in. 'Yellow bellied shits.... You murdering, fucking bastards.... You're scared of us ... come on and hit us.... While you're here your women are being screwed by them niggers in England.... Oh you shits! ...'

The bins banged with renewed energy.

An old woman, her grey hair wrapped in a scarf, her back bent with the weight of two large baskets, came round the corner past the first soldier. Neither looked at the other, though the soldier's senses were so tuned up he knew exactly where she was and what she was doing.

She spat at his feet.

Four more soldiers made the crossing. On either side of the road they stood, pressed into doorways, half an eye on the women. When the first man became the last, he moved up, leapfrogging past the others, and the whole process started again.

There were eight more crossings before the patrol was out of the area. They spread out into an open formation to move across a large tract of waste ground. Not, for once, an area laid waste by violence, but part of the city council's plans for slum clearance.

'Hey, corp!' his point man shouted. 'There's a bloke lying over here.'

'Don't touch him,' he called back urgently. He signalled the patrol to spread out all round to cover him and ran up.

He looked at the body on the ground. It lay as it had fallen, face down, one arm flung out in front. There was a blackened hole in the jeans, just above the boy's right knee. The trouser leg was covered in blood.

'Looks like a knee job, corp.'

'Right.' He turned and signalled up his wireless operator. 'Tell them we've got what looks like a knee job here. Get an ambulance out. I think the bugger's still alive.'

He looked at the body. It moved and groaned.

'Yes, it's alive all right,' he called out cheerfully. 'Another little kneecap for some quack to practise on.'

The soldier rolled Vincent over gently, protecting his leg, and putting his other arm behind his shoulders to support him.

'Don't worry,' he said, 'there's an ambulance on its way. Who did this to you?'

Vincent shook his head.

'Come on,' said the patrol commander, 'you can tell us who did it. They can't be friends of yours. . . . Crikey! they haven't half done you in. You won't be hiking around much for a long time with a leg like this!'

Hike? thought Vincent, his mind slipping from the present, it was a long time since he'd done any hiking. . . .

It had been early spring, and still cold, when their father had suggested a hike into the Mourne mountains. A bit cold, he remembered, for city-bred boys like his brother and himself, but when father made a suggestion like that, neither ever waited to be asked a second time. So at the earliest opportunity on that Saturday long ago they had caught the train which then used to wander slowly down to Newcastle.

After a hard winter, a sudden rise in temperature had filled the little Glen river that flowed from the mountain into the town. There was a rush and a splash of dark brown water and white foam as they set off up the path beside it, Vincent following Bryan and his father. As they tramped steadily along, through the cold quietness of the pine forest, their breath condensed in small white puffs. A song thrush sang in the woods near them, and under the trees was a scattering of snow drops, and the first of the crocuses. Once, as his father led them on a short cut away from the path and across the soft forest floor, they looked across a small clearing and saw gold patches of aconites picked out against the leaf brown earth. As they came out of the trees, Vincent could see far below patches of mist caught in the hollows of the land, and high above, the long scars of snow still lying along the dark edges of the mountain.

It had been a day of sheer beauty which had touched him in a way he could not explain. They didn't talk much together – for a start they never did and anyway all their energy was going into climbing up the path. When they reached the top the boys felt proud their father had got them there and even more proud when he said 'Look!' and had pointed out to them mountains far away of Scotland and England – Snowdonia in Wales, and the Isle of Man lying in between.

They had eaten at the top, burrowing into their knapsacks for their 'iron rations.' His father had always made this a joke – 'iron rations for iron men,' but they knew, from past experience, that at the last minute he would bring apples and sweets and chocolates out of his own knapsack like a conjuror, to delight them.

They knew days like that were something very special, and when they came down again to the town nestling under the mountain by the edge of the sea, his father would have a glass or two while waiting for the train back to Belfast. He would take them both in, one under each arm, winking at the barman and putting them both safely in a corner, would order for himself, and 'these two fine strapping lads with me now.' He would come and sit with them, and, while they drank their lemonade, he would start to talk. Perhaps it was the beer which helped him, for he rarely touched a drop at home, and equally rarely did he talk at any length with them.

Here, with the darkness blotting out the coloured light of the evening across the Irish Sea, dark grey all the way to England and Europe and beyond, his father would talk, and sometimes they would miss a train. Then he would slap his knee in horror and discuss with them the advantages of having another while they waited for the next train. . . .

The corporal turned round. 'Did you get the message through?' he called out.

'Yes, corp. They're coming.'

54

He turned back to the boy. One of his men had cut his jeans up to above the knee and was putting a field dressing on to the wound. The corporal had seen kneecappings before – it was a handy form of punishment on both sides. This one, he noticed, wasn't too bad. It looked as if he'd been shot through the muscles above the knee. He remembered seeing a really bad one once, where the gun had been placed right behind the man's knee, and being told later that that sort of kneecapping ruined the joint for ever. What a bloody carry on, he thought, shaking his head.

'You'll be all right, mate,' he said, not unkindly, to Vincent. 'It would help if you told us who did it.' Vincent closed his eyes. 'Oh, well, have it your way.' He wished the ambulance would hurry. He didn't like sitting out in the open like this. He kept one hand on the young man's shoulder as he looked round, checking the ground for cover, checking the houses on the far side of the waste ground, checking his men.

4

Bryan woke up and looked at his watch. It was just before seven.

He swung himself out of bed, noticed Vincent was already up, and then remembered what had happened the day before, and decided it was more likely Vincent hadn't come home at all.

All afternoon he had worked on the site, constantly breaking off his job to see if Vincent was back, until the foreman had yelled at him to get on with his work as it was bad enough having one Malone away without the other slacking as well.

Afterwards he had gone round the various pubs which he knew Vincent often went into, but he dared not be too open about asking after him, and he found out nothing at all. Late into the night he had wandered round the streets, not really knowing what to do, until finally, at about two in the morning, he had come home, exhausted, and fallen into bed.

He went down to the kitchen with the faint hope that Vincent might be there, but of course he wasn't.

His mother was down there, making breakfast.

'You're up early,' she said. 'Can't you sleep, or is it you're that eager to get to work?'

'No, no. Nothing really.'

His mother looked at him curiously but said nothing. She was getting used to the strange ways of her children as they grew up.

'If you get yourself dressed, you can have your breakfast. I'll put some on for you now.'

He hung around, not knowing what to say, until his mother told him to get out from under her feet and dress himself. When he came down again, his breakfast was ready, and he sat down to eat it.

'Shall I do Vincent's now?' she asked. 'Is he up early, too?'

'No. Don't do anything for Vincent,' he said slowly. 'He....' He paused, searching for the right words, but he couldn't find them.

'Is he not well? Is he not coming down?' she asked.

'No. He's not coming down. He's not there. He didn't come in last night. He went ... he went off for a drink with a fella and I haven't seen him.'

'Not in?' she exclaimed. 'Sure you were in late yourself last night. Were you not with him?'

'No!' he said, desperately. 'I was not. I don't know where he went.'

'Oh! He's not hurt, is he?'

'I'm sure he's not,' he said, unconvincingly. 'Sure, he's been out all night before and come to no harm. I expect he'll just pitch up to work as usual.'

'Well, if you're sure now,' she said, hesitantly. Bryan, she knew, was a very steady character, far more so than Vincent. If he said it was nothing to worry about, then she wouldn't worry. But she still didn't like the idea of them staying out all night somewhere even though they weren't children any longer.

'Are you sure you've had enough now? Do you want some more tea?'

'No thanks, ma, I'll be off now.' It was a bit early to go, but he couldn't sit around any longer. Vincent had disappeared and something had happened to him. He knew that. You didn't have a twin brother and not know what had happened to him. He remembered the look in Vincent's eyes when he had gone off the previous afternoon. The message had been clear: I'm going off to something that's bad, I'm relying on you to see me clear of it – and he knew he hadn't done that. He'd been everywhere he could think of to find him. But he had failed. Now he had to go off to work, still not knowing, and leave behind him his mother who had no idea that anything bad had happened.

What would he do if Vincent didn't turn up for work? Whom could he ask? He certainly wouldn't go anywhere near the police. Perhaps he would try the hospitals. He could walk up to the Royal at dinner time and if something had happened to Vincent he might be there.

He turned the problem over and over in his mind, unable to decide on anything definite.

In the end he pushed back his chair, telling his ma he was off because he wanted to get an early start. He put on his coat, and turned up the collar as he stepped out of the front door on to the pavement, into the rain. He plunged his hands into his pockets and, hunching his shoulders against the wind, set off on the walk into town to the building site.

His mother watched him go with some misgivings. She hadn't pressed him about Vincent, but she was sure that there was more to his absence than Bryan had made out. As she cleaned around the house, she thought about it. It wasn't so much what he had said, but what he hadn't said. She knew he tried hard to keep things on an even level in the family, and in particular he always protected Vincent.

She said nothing to the others as they came for their breakfasts and made their way off to school and work. She was tempted for a moment to talk to Sheelagh about it, but then she thought, what would the girl know about her brother's movements?

She washed the dishes and put them away, going through the routine of her housework methodically, sweeping out the kitchen, and then getting down on her knees and scrubbing the front step. She did that quickly, because the fine rain slanted down into the doorway, and her hair was getting wet.

The old man wasn't up yet, and she let him lie on in bed, where he was less bother to her than he would be if he was up.

When her work there was done, she got her shopping bag down from the back of the door, and walked along to the shops in the Falls Road.

The rain had eased off, and now only blew in the wind, but

her old grey coat and headscarf kept most of the wet off her. She did her shopping quickly, buying potatoes, eggs, some chops for their tea, and a few other bits and pieces. She nodded and spoke briefly to friends she saw, and she saw plenty of them for this was a small village in a large city. She was half home before she remembered she had forgotten to get tea, and had to trudge back again for that.

Her mind wasn't really on what she was doing at all. It was on her sons.

The two of them, she thought, alike to look at but very different in every other way. Except, that is, they were both acting very strangely these days. Hardly a word out of them. She was sure Bryan was trying to protect his brother over something. She'd seen him to do it often before and knew the signs.

She stepped round a pile of broken paving stones, pushed to one side of the road after a riot, and decided it must be to do with a girl. After all, the both of them were growing up, and it was only natural that they should go after girls, but she felt a little sad that they hadn't spoken to her about it. It was another sign they were getting older and further away from her. She didn't want that to happen. She found she needed their company and their confidence since her husband had died four years ago.

He had died peacefully enough in his bed, she thought bitterly, but only after being beaten up months before when he tried to stop a gang of young hooligans from stoning a house just down the road. He'd seemingly recovered, but he hadn't really. It looked as if he was over the beating, but something else was broken inside him.

The boys had been a great comfort to her, and then her father had come to live with her. He had been a great diversion, an endless talker who had kept the children amused for hours, and indeed half the neighbourhood as well. Somehow it had filled the gap, little by little, until she felt she could be herself again. The boys had taken to him. Vincent in particular, with his quickness and fiery temper, had been much influenced by his republican stories, and had taken it all very seriously. She never allowed herself to think on logically, and connect him with the fighting going on against the Protestants and the British Army.

The old man was up. 'Yarra, Mary,' he shouted, 'have you them all fed and away to work now?'

'I have, I have,' she called back.

'Have you a cup of tea there ready?' he called.

'If you come down, it will be ready,' she shouted back, and put on a kettle. The time it would take for him to fight his way into his clothes would be more than enough to boil a kettle.

'What's the matter with you?' he asked when he got down. 'You're very down-looking this morning.'

'Agh, I'm worried about Vincent.'

'Why's that?'

'He wasn't in all last night.'

'Oh!' said the old man, slightly taken aback. 'Is that so?' He thought for a bit. 'Well, he'll hardly come to any harm. He's a big fella, and well able to take care of himself.' He drank his tea noisily, and looked over the top of the cup at her.

'What does Bryan say?' he asked.

'Sure he doesn't know a thing. If he does, he's not saying.'

'Well, bad news travels fast, so if you haven't heard anything on him, then he's probably all right.'

'Don't be silly,' she said, sharply.

'For pity's sake, girl. Stop worrying your head about him. He's a big boy now. He's grown up and must lead a life of his own. Don't you understand that?'

'Of course I do.' She was angry now. 'Don't you think I don't know about children growing up, and letting them be? He's still my son, but. Is that a crime then, to worry about him missing?'

'Come on, come on,' he said, soothingly. 'There's no need to get all steamed up about it.' He reached out and put his hand on her arm. 'Hush, girl. Don't fret so. He'll be all right.' He left his hand there for a few moments, calming her, in the same instinctive way he had done as a boy, gentling his ponies. He felt her grow easier and he stood up.

'I'll be getting that window pane fixed upstairs,' he said. 'Did you get me the putty I asked for?'

'It's here.' She went to the kitchen cupboard and rummaged around inside. 'It doesn't look very much. Will it do?'

'Agh, yes. A little goes a long way with this.' He took the putty and started squeezing it in his fingers, rolling it slightly to soften it. On an impulse, she leaned over and kissed him.

'Thank you,' she said. The old man looked down at her and smiled. She would be all right now, he thought, it had never failed with the ponies, nor the children. When he put his mind to it he could calm almost anything.

She was standing with some washing in her hands wondering how she was going to dry it when there was a banging on the front door and she heard an excited voice calling for her. She put the washing down, opened the door, and there was young Patrick Hoggan. She wondered momentarily why he wasn't at school.

'Mrs Malone, Mrs Malone, you're to come with my da.'

She saw Mr Hoggan's car behind the boy. His father was leaning across the passenger seat.

'It's Vincent,' he called out. 'I'm after having a call from the Royal. He's had an accident. I'll run you down. Just get your coat.'

'Vincent!' she cried.

'Aye. They won't say what it is. Come on, will you?'

She turned and called up the stairs to her father that she was off to the hospital to see Vincent.

'What's that, what's that?' he shouted.

'It's Vincent. Sure, he's had an accident. Mr Hoggan's here with his car.' She hurried through to the kitchen to get her coat, talking to herself. 'Oh, Mother of God, I knew it! I knew something bad had happened.' She threw her coat on as her father came down the stairs.

'I'll come with you.'

'You will not. Sure, I don't know how long. . . .'

'I'll come with you,' he repeated firmly. 'If the boy's bad then you'll need some help.'

He put on his old cloth cap and, taking her by the arm, moved her out and into the car. Young Patrick jumped up and down in excitement on the pavement, but his father shouted at him to be off home and tell his mammy he was away to the hospital with Mrs Malone. The boy looked disappointed he wasn't coming and waited till the car had driven off before he ran back down to the pub.

All the way up to the hospital, Mary Malone kept saying she knew something had happened. The old man told her to hush until she found out what the matter was.

Mr Hoggan said he would wait for them; she hardly heard but the old man thanked him, and they both went in.

The sister caught them just before she got to the small side ward where they'd been told he was.

'Mrs Malone?' she asked pleasantly.

'Yes, yes. I'm Mrs Malone. Is this where my son is?'

'Just a moment before you go in, Mrs Malone.' She looked enquiringly at the old man and he said: 'James Rafferty. I'm the boy's granda,' and the sister nodded.

'Mrs Malone, your son has had a bad shock, but he will be all right. We had to operate, but he's come round now. He'll be in a lot of pain, but you can talk to him for a while.'

They went in with her.

He was lying slightly propped up on pillows with his leg, huge and white in plaster, stretched out. His eyes were closed.

She went across hesitantly and stood by the bed, looking down.

'Vincent,' she said softly, 'I'm here.'

He opened his eyes.

'Mammy!' He held out his hand, and she took it. She felt like crying and fought back the tears. He looked so young and small again.

'Are you all right?'

'Yes.' He nodded. 'It's very sore, but.'

'Aye, I'm sure it is.'

He closed his eyes again.

'Sure, we've been mad with worry when you weren't there this morning.'

She wasn't quite sure what to say to him. She just wanted to hold his hand and make him better again quickly and look after him and ease his pain.

'Bryan was up half the night looking for you.' Bryan hadn't told her that, but she knew.

He opened his eyes.

'Was he now? I'm glad.' He sighed. 'Sure, I thought I'd been forgotten altogether.'

'You're never forgotten at home, Vincent. You know that well enough.'

They lapsed into silence again, and old Mr Rafferty looked around the ward and cleared his throat, and then got hold of a chair and brought it to Mary Malone to sit on. Without letting go of Vincent's hand she sat down, and then straightened up a corner of his pillow.

His granda stood behind, twiddling his cap in his hands. 'What happened to you?' he asked.

Vincent closed his eyes again, and said nothing.

'What happened, Vincent?' This time it was his mother. 'Did you get run over?'

'Mammy, I don't want to talk about it,' he said softly. 'It was an accident. That's all. I'll be all right.'

'You can tell me what happened, but?'

'Mammy, leave it. It's no matter.'

Mary looked at her father and shook her head. She didn't understand. The sister came in and said that perhaps he ought to have a rest for a wee while, but they could come back later that evening if they wanted to.

'Is there anything you need?' she asked Vincent, as she got up.

'No, thanks,' He shook his head and tried to smile but the pain stopped most of it. 'Will you be back?' he asked.

'Aye, we'll come back later.' She patted his hand, and the two of them left.

In the corridor, she turned to the sister and asked her what had happened to Vincent. The sister looked her calmly in the eye, and then taking her by the arm walked along with her.

'He was shot. In the knee. They call it kneecapping, Mrs Malone.'

63

She stopped and stared at the sister.

'Kneecapping?'

'Yes. It is very unpleasant but there's a lot of it happening. His is not too bad, though he'll probably always have a stiff knee.'

Mary Malone walked on. She couldn't believe what she had heard. Kneecapping was something the IRA did to people they wanted to punish for something. But what had Vincent done? He wasn't tied up with the IRA. He couldn't be, or she would have known about it. What a terrible thing. Did Bryan know? She looked at her father as they came down the hospital steps.

'Is he in the IRA?'

'I don't know,' he said, 'I don't know.' He was very shaken by what he had heard. He was an old man now, and to him the IRA had always been something very special, even after the movement had been split in Belfast. But the thought that his grandson had been punished by them, punished by being shot in the leg, was something he couldn't take in. It was the forces occupying the country which the IRA should be shooting, not its own people. He couldn't think what Vincent could have done to merit that treatment.

'Perhaps it's better if you say nothing.'

'Nothing?'

'Nothing.'

She nodded her head slowly. 'Perhaps it's best, perhaps it's best,' she said, almost to herself, and walked across to Mr Hoggan's car.

Further up the Falls Road from where the Malones lived was St Matthew's Presbytery. It was at the top end of the road, which ran like an artery out from the city centre: an artery used by Catholics. It gave its name to the area through which it ran, so that if you came from the Falls, you were automatically a Catholic. Such was the way it worked in the North: each to his own area, his own school, his own collection of names, religion, loyalities and culture.

It consisted, this Catholic area, of a huge maze of small

streets, of rows of small terraced houses, yards and alleyways, all red brown.

The streets reached out and merged with a similar area that grew off another artery from the city centre – the Shankill. This area was different in that it was exclusively Protestant.

The streets interlocked the areas, the areas interlocked with others. You could travel from one to another, and a stranger would notice little difference.

Each had its separate identity and each had its boundaries rigorously defined. Perhaps a few outward signs might give some indication. The red, white and blue kerb stones, the slogans on the walls, the graffiti.

The city was a collection of villages, each in itself relying traditionally on the support of the extended family for its continuing existence.

Employment was local, and it was kept for the locals. It never occurred to those living in this city that they had no overall name to describe themselves – as Londoners, Dubliners or Parisians would.

St Matthew's Presbytery was part of this structure, one of the locking devices that held it together, along with Protestant Orange Halls, Free Presbyterian Churches, Republican Clubs – and people fearful of change.

The building itself lay some way back from the main road. Tall iron railings surrounded it, backed by dank growths of rhododendron bushes, and a gravel drive, mossy at the edges, led from the iron gates to the front door. It was large and grey, with ivy growing up beyond the first-floor sash windows. Three well-scrubbed steps led up to the door and a gleaming brass knocker, and a bell-pull hung to the right under a small brass plate.

To one side was a lawn, often damp, and covered with worm casts. A small path wandered round the back to a high wall, topped with broken glass, and a locked door. Beyond lay a tarred school playground, and the shrill noise of children.

From the other side, there was a view over the city. On bright days it extended clear over to the Holywood Hills on the other side of the Belfast Lough. More usually, however, the shipyards that lay between were just a smudge of grey under the city haze. It was a grey city, under a grey haze. Spirals of grey smoke from the rows of houses in the maze below joined the two.

The door to the playground opened, and a young priest came through. The weather had improved since the morning, and the warmth was making him perspire. He was rather stout, with a shock of black hair, and he pulled out a large red hand-kerchief to mop his forehead. Father Farrell had been in the parish for just over a year. He was still getting used to it.

He had been brought up in a small country village in South Armagh. With his quick, enquiring mind he had done well at school and later at Maynooth, the elite Roman Catholic train-ing college for priests.

He had spent four years at the Vatican, something he had never considered, in his wildest dreams, but then, feeling he had to get back to the grass roots of his faith, away from the rarified, intellectual atmosphere of the Vatican, he had come back to Northern Ireland. He left behind a city that he had grown to love – the burnt sienna of the beautiful squares, the bustle of Roman life, the pavement cafés and the hills where he felt so much at ease.

It had been a rude shock. But it was what he had wanted, asked for, and got. He did not complain, even inwardly to himself; instead, he rejoiced in the problems that faced him, and wept for the people as their homes, lives and families were ripped apart by ever increasing violence.

The violence he had experienced had been largely that of a great storm; the battering, ravaging effect of nightly rioting, the burning of homes and factories, the wholesale movement of people terrified for their lives. He had not seen much actual killing, although he had seen plenty of the after-effects, felt the pang of time slipping by, of life ebbing away as he tried to administer the sacrament of the sick.

More often he found himself repeating the formal confes-sion, 'Oh my God, I am sorry for all my sins, I love you and I will try not to sin again,' repeating it again and again in the hope that the dying person might in some way respond. He

66

never got used to it, but he had come to cope with it. Cope with keeping the fright out of his face and actions and despair out of his voice.

He had been sent for by Father Mulligan, a priest who had spent years in the parish. Father Mulligan, he knew, did not like to be kept waiting, and so he hurried along to see him.

'There's one of your young lads down in the hospital,' Father Mulligan told him. 'You'd best get down there right away.'

'Who is it?'

'Vincent Malone.'

'Sure, he's hardly one of mine,' exclaimed Father Farrell. 'I'd be lucky if I saw him at mass twice a year.'

'Well, now, I think you might find him in a more agreeable frame of mind to see you,' said Father Mulligan. 'He's after having his knee shot away.'

'Oh, my God! What was that?'

'An IRA thing. You know,' Father Mulligan said testily, 'one of these IRA punishments. They have what they care to call a court – and pass their own judgements and sentences. I'm sure I don't know what the place is coming to ... all this nonsense, and the security forces just look the other way.'

'Ah, come on, now, Father Mulligan. It is hardly the fault of the military if they miss a thing like that now.'

Father Mulligan looked at the young priest over the top of his spectacles. He was an old man, and the years lay heavily on him. He'd been through too many riot-torn years and military occupations to view what happened with anything other than a strong degree of cynicism.

'If it wasn't for the military, there would be no trouble. The IRA would have no one to fight. If the British had any sense, they would have realized that long ago.'

Father Farrell said nothing. Instead, he turned slightly towards the sideboard, to look for his cycle clips. His years in Rome had taught him how to make use of an innate sense of diplomacy. He leant across and picked up the clips. He threw them lightly up and down in his hand.

67

'Have you just heard about Malone?' he asked. 'Has he been there long?'

'He was picked up by a military patrol early this morning. I'm only just after putting the phone down on his mother. I suppose,' he sighed, 'you'd better be seeing her too. She's not taken it too well.'

Father Farrell looked out the window, across the lawn and over the rooftops of the city. There was something wrong about the Malone boy being kneecapped. It wasn't that the boy was particularly religious, or devout – he wasn't. He knew that well enough. In fact, like his grandfather, he had very little to do with the church at all.

But on the few occasions he had met him, usually when visiting his mother, he had never got the impression that the boy would be the sort to get involved in anything like an IRA court and a kneecapping.

'It's very unusual,' he said, half to himself. But old Father Mulligan heard him.

'What's that?' he said sharply. 'What's unusual?'

'Malone being involved with the IRA.'

'Nothing unusual at all,' he snorted, and glared at the young priest. 'There's no discipline left any longer. Parents allow their children out all over the place. No control.'

'That's the point I'm making,' said Father Farrell, gently. 'It's not an undisciplined family. It's a very close family. And,' he went on, nodding his head up and down slowly, 'despite the fact the men rarely go to mass, if ever, indeed ... despite that, I just don't get the feeling in that house that they would be tied up with the Provos.'

Father Mulligan looked at him with some exasperation.

'The fact of the matter,' he said coldly, 'is that young Malone had got himself tied up with the IRA. A bullet in his leg is not something from my imagination. It is a fact, Father Farrell, and I suggest you get down there without too much extra delay, and give the boy what comfort you may. Mind you,' he said turning back to his book, 'you'd probably find the mother more in need of comfort than the boy. From my observation of that young man over the years, he's not as soft as he might look.'

'Oh, dear!' said Father Farrell. 'I'm sorry, I didn't mean to suggest I didn't believe you. And you may well be right about the boy, and even the family. Perhaps I misjudged the situation.' He smiled. 'It has happened before, you know, Father Mulligan.'

Father Mulligan looked puzzled.

'What's happened before?' he asked.

'Mistakes ... you know, misjudgement.'

'What are you talking about?'

'I'm sorry, Father Mulligan. I was just saying maybe I had made a mistake about the Malones. I was, I fear, trying to make a little joke of it. I'm afraid,' he added lamely, 'that it wasn't a very good one.'

'Mmm, well, you're right about that, at least. Levity is hardly called for at this point. There's a boy you could help lying in hospital, and a mother who certainly could do with some sympathy.'

'Yes, yes indeed,' said Father Farrell, once more gazing out of the window. 'I'll go straight away.'

His visit to the hospital was brief. He found Vincent in a side ward, his leg heavily bandaged. He had a brief word with the ward sister, and went across to the bed.

'I'm sorry to see you like this, Vincent. How are you feeling?'

'How anyone would feel with a bullet through their knee. Bloody painful.'

'I'm sorry.'

'Are you now?'

'Yes, I am. Is that anything I can do for you?'

'No.'

'Has your mother been to see you yet?'

'She was in just now.'

'I see,' he paused. 'Is she away home then?'

'Maybe.'

'Well now! Are you sure there's nothing I can do for you? I'll be popping in again tomorrow.'

'Father, it's not yourself I don't like. It's your calling. I haven't time for it. You'd be doing yourself and me a favour if you didn't come. But no doubt me ma will talk about it all. You'd do her more good. You'll get a cup of tea from her, too,' he added.

'I see,' said Father Farrell slowly. 'I see. Well then, I'll be away. Perhaps I'll have a word with your mother. Good-bye then. Get yourself well soon, and God bless you.'

'Good-bye,' said Vincent.

He left the hospital on his bike, and cycled slowly back up towards the Lower Falls. He waved to some people, and stopped to have a talk to one whose child was shortly to take his first communion.

It took him some time to reach the Malones' house, for he lost his way in the side streets. They all looked alike to him, and he hadn't been in the area for long.

As he rode down the street, some small children skipped along beside him calling out to him, and telling him it was a pet day for the rain had stopped, and the sun was out again. He said it was, but a bit hot for cycling, and they laughed.

'Are you for Mrs Malone's?' one called.

'I am,' he puffed, and the children ran ahead to tell her the priest was coming.

She was at the door when he arrived, looking flustered and pale. She had been crying.

'It's good of you to come, Father.' She grabbed his hand with both hers, and he felt them shaking. 'It's a bad day we've had.' Tears started in her eyes again, and she rubbed them with the back of her hand. 'Come in, come in.' She turned and raised her voice. 'Sheelagh! Are you getting a cup of tea for Father Farrell? Sure you must be raging with thirst. . . .' She stopped, embarrassed that she had gone on shouting with him only inches away.

'Cycling is thirsty work for a man of my size,' he muttered as she led him into the front room and sat him down in an arm-chair. He was relieved to find the old man out. He felt he couldn't cope with his acid remarks about the Church, and Mrs Malone, at the same time.

Sheelagh came in with a plate of cakes. Her eyes, too, were red, and she was clumsy with the plate. He felt very sorry for them.

'Well, now,' he said, balancing a cup and saucer on his knee, 'that's a terrible business about young Vincent. You must be very shocked.'

'Oh, Father!' sobbed Sheelagh, 'will he be all right? He's hurt very bad.'

'Of course he will,' he said, comfortingly. He reached out to pat her hand, but she was just too far away, and he felt his teacup sliding. 'They'll look after him very well. They're very experienced, you know.' He started talking quickly, bringing them the soothing comfort of the Church. He hoped in particular that Mrs Malone would be strong enough to take the shock. He wasn't sure she would. There were some things he ought to find out, however, and when they both seemed quieter, he brought the talk back to Vincent.

'How did it happen?' His voice was gentle.

Mrs Malone hesitated a moment, looking away from him.

'I don't know, Father. I don't know at all.'

'He's never been mixed up in that sort of thing,' Sheelagh said quickly. 'He's not the type.'

'Not at all,' her mother agreed. 'He's a very good boy. A bit wild at times, and moody. You know, he gets very depressed sometimes. I've never heard no talk, but ... no talk that he was mixing in with men like that.'

'Was it the Provos who did it?'

'I suppose it was. He won't say anything, but.'

'I know,' said Father Farrell. 'I've just been up to see him.'

'You have?' She was surprised at that. She knew Vincent thought nothing of the Church.

'It wasn't a very happy visit. He doesn't like us, as you know. But I thought I might help. I was wrong.'

'Oh! I'm sorry about that, Father. He's a very wilful boy when he's a mind to it. Just like his grandfather in that. It's all right,' she smiled, and he noticed it gratefully. 'You'll be gone by the time he gets back'

Father Farrell smiled back. She offered him another biscuit, and Sheelagh, who had been out of the room, came back with a plate of ham sandwiches, and put it in front of him. He groaned inwardly at the sight of them. He was always getting caught by the hospitality of these people.

'He seems to be in a lot of pain,' he said.

'Oh, he is. He's a strong lad, but. He'll get over it.'

'How badly damaged is the knee?'

'Well, now, the doctor was saying that the bullet went through from the back, and lodged up against the kneecap itself. So he still has that not broken.'

'But, Mother,' said Sheelagh, 'the doctor said he'd have a very stiff leg. He told Vincent he'd not be playing games again.'

'Sure and when does he get time for that anyway? That doctor doesn't know the half of what goes on. They give me a fright every time I go near them,' she said, turning back to Father Farrell. 'What with the white coats and those things hanging round their necks and all their chat. Sure I'd be dead before I went to one of them.'

'Oh, Mother,' Sheelagh laughed. 'You're talking a terrible load of old rubbish. What happens if you're ill now? You're not saying you'd rather die than go to the doctor, are you?'

'Well, no, I suppose not. You know what I mean, but.'

'How will you look after him,' Father Farrell asked, 'when he's home again?'

'Sure as soon as he's able now I'll pack him off to my sister in the South.'

'That's nice,' said Father Farrell.

'Yes, indeed. He went down once before, with Bryan. They camped out – some old hut up in the hills there. They always said it was the best holiday they'd ever had.'

'And you wouldn't let me go, Mother,'

'Indeed not. You were much too young. Anyway, it's not the sort of thing for a young girl.'

'Oh, Mother! I'd have been all right with Bryan and Vincent.'

'Hush now, Sheelagh, Father Farrell doesn't want to hear about that.'

72

'Have you ever been camping, Father?' asked Sheelagh.

'Yes, I have. In Italy. We took some boys down one summer to the coast. It was very hot, and we swam and walked a lot. It was grand.'

'Now Sheelagh,' said Mrs Malone, anxious to make an end to this particular conversation, 'would you run along and fetch Deirdre home from school? They had some trouble up there last week,' she explained to Father Farrell, 'and I don't like her to come back on her own.'

'Ah,' said Father Farrell, rising out of his armchair. 'As it happens, I'm going that way myself. I'll walk with you. Mrs Malone,' he said, shaking her hand, 'thank you for the tea. I'll be thinking of you now, and I'll be praying for you, and for Vincent's recovery. God sends these tribulations to try us and our faith. But if we keep it, we'll pull through. If there's anything I can do now to help, you'll just let me know?'

'Oh yes, Father. That's very kind of you. Just pray for Vincent. He doesn't think it does any good, but I know it does.'

The classroom was very quiet. The endless afternoon stretched on, and the heat of the summer day lay heavily on the children. The sun had already gone behind the main school building, and only half the room was filled with the yellow shafts of light, through which the chalk dust slowly stirred.

Forty-three children had their heads down over their exercise books. Their pens scratched slowly, some painfully, as they did their copying.

Each child sat at an individual desk, their chairs attached to them by cast-iron bars. They were old and scruffy, pushed together in pairs to form lines reaching to the back of the room. At the front, two big pipes ran along under the blackboard which covered nearly the whole wall. In winter, the pipes were hot, and the children would wait for their teacher and warm their hands.

It was basically a drab room, the paint old and dark. Years ago the dark paint had come from the idea that it would hide the mess the children would make. But the drabness had been taken out of the room by bright posters. They were pinned up

73

all round the wall, together with the children's drawings, essays, projects and other bits and pieces that made up their work.

Deirdre sat in the third row from the front. She knew school was nearly over for the day, and she couldn't wait to get out. She knew her ma or Sheelagh would fetch her, and probably she could persuade them to buy her an ice-cream on the way home.

Then the bell rang, the teacher told them all to put away their books, and the scramble to get outside started.

She came through the gates at a run, and stopped suddenly as she saw not only Sheelagh, but Father Farrell there as well. He had his bike with him, and she thought he looked very hot. He waved to her, and she walked over. She always felt a bit shy with him, and so she stood in front of him, one foot behind the other, and kept her eyes down as he patted her on the head.

'Well, now, Deirdre, you're looking in the pink of health, though a bit hot, I'm sure, like the rest of us. Have you learnt a lot at school today?'

'Yes, Father,' she said. 'We've done writing and drawing. And we've done sums. I don't like those, but.'

He laughed. 'You'll have to work hard at that, even if you don't like them. Isn't that so?'

'Yes, Father.'

'Agh, I'm sure you will. Now here's Sheelagh to take you safely home. But listen,' he went on, 'you've got to be a brave girl. There's some bad news at home.' She looked up at him quickly. 'It's not too bad. It's your brother, Vincent. He's had an accident and hurt his leg.'

'Vince!' she cried. 'Oh no. Not Vince. Is he hurt bad?'

'He was hit by a bullet. Last night. He's in hospital, and he'll be all right.'

'Oh, poor Vince.' She moved across to her sister. 'Was it the army that shot him?'

'No,' said Sheelagh, 'he won't say much. But we don't think it was the army. Isn't that so, Father?'

'That's right. He was found by a military patrol this morning. They picked him up.'

74

She stared at them both, reaching out for her sister's hand. She didn't really understand what was going on, except that Vincent was hurt. But she felt a rising fear inside her, and she swallowed hard.

Bryan came in much later. It turned out he had heard the news at work, and had been to see Vincent. He had been drinking since then, and his face was flushed and sweaty. Sheelagh had never seen him so angry, but he was so tight-lipped that no one felt like saying much to him. He nodded curtly to his mother when she put his tea in front of him, and snapped at Sheelagh when she asked where he had been. The two young children stayed out of the kitchen.

He pushed his plate away when he had finished and looked at the two women.

'People murder, and are murdered in their turn, and do foul things. What are they fighting for?' he asked, a sneer in his voice. 'Freedom! Freedom to go on murdering and maiming those who don't agree with them. It'll be a fine country to live in then ... with the smell of burning in the air, and the screams of children in our ears and everything destroyed. Bastards!'

5

The summer heat gusted the air warmly into her face, so the long black tresses of her hair blew about it.

It raised a shimmer of haze across the wide valley, and softened the higher slopes of the mountain beyond.

Drenched in sweat after her climb, she sat still on the short-cropped grass, her legs straight in front, her skirt pulled high. Her blouse was unbuttoned almost to her waist, and stuck in damp patches to her body. She was still breathing heavily, but evenly.

Round her neck she wore a thin gold chain and cross. It was her only personal ornament, and a touch of red on her lips was her only concession to make-up. She had none of the gentle prettiness of a town-bred girl, none of the softness of figure nor the hardness of eyes. Her face was large and open with big brown eyes and a wide mouth. Indeed, she was a big girl all round – a country girl, or so one would have thought.

After a while, as the sweat dried on her, she looked up and around. Putting her fingers in her mouth, she gave a piercing whistle, and waited.

Almost instantly, a brown and white terrier appeared from behind some gorse bushes. Bounding over, tail wagging furiously, he looked up at the girl, head cocked to one side.

'Hungry, I suppose,' she said to the dog. 'Are there no rabbits, or are they too fast for you?'

She delved into a small canvas bag she had carried over her shoulder, and brought out a biscuit which she broke in two. Tossing one half to the dog, so that he leapt into the air and caught it with a snap of his teeth, she put the other in her own mouth.

The heat drained the landscape of colour. It was burnt out and lay heavily under the sun. There were no trees in this place, so there was no shade, and no coolness. Even the sea, far away to her right and well below her, seemed hot, though she knew it wasn't.

She wasn't used to this heat. Normally, the country was cool and green, with soft rain constantly seeping into the hillsides and valleys, keeping everything fresh. She thought people must like the heat because they only found it on holidays, lying on beaches far away, with nothing to do but apply sun-tanning lotions, swim, eat and sleep.

She leant forward, her elbows on her knees, and shaded her face from the sun with her hands. Across the valley she thought she saw something move. She slipped on her dark glasses to cut the glare a bit more, and looked across again.

The movement she thought she had seen was near a small white cottage. She had seen the cottage as she had come over the pass at the top of the valley, and it had looked deserted at that distance, a tumbledown shack that had once, long ago, housed a family in this bleak and unfriendly place.

Then she saw the movement again. Someone was walking out from the back of the cottage, across a piece of open ground. Then the movement was lost behind an outcrop of rocks. She sat still and watched, waiting to see what happened next. She couldn't tell, from this distance, whether it was a man or woman. Perhaps, even, it was a child. The tiny movement she had seen through the heat haze could almost have been anything. Not an animal, however, the movement had been too full of purpose for that.

From her canvas bag she took out an Ordnance Survey map and unfolded it, holding it high with outstretched arms to get the folds in the right place. Smoothing it, she examined the detail to see where she was, and also to see if she could find the cottage on it. She looked up once or twice to try and get her bearings, which wasn't easy in such a featureless place, and with the heat haze obscuring some of the higher peaks. But she

77

found it. A dotted path was where she was, and following the contour lines down the valley and up the other side, she came to the cottage. Just beyond it, the contour lines formed a series of tiny V's, and running down the middle of them was a thin blue line.

She looked up again at the cottage, pleased that she had been able to locate herself on the map so quickly. She loved maps, particularly Ordnance Survey maps. She liked the feel of them, and the detail they gave. And she really liked being able to use them to know exactly where she was. It gave her a sense of power. Not much, but just a little over all the other people who didn't know as much. What a silly thing to think, she thought to herself, but so what, that was how she felt.

Now she knew what she was looking for, she spotted the man as he walked back to the cottage, carrying something. A bucket. Ah, yes, that was it, a bucket. He had been to the stream behind to get some water.

She lay on the grass, chewing a piece of grass and wondering what she should do. The unnatural heat was so heavy, it dulled the normal sounds of the valley. She could hear nothing. It dulled her senses, too. Perhaps the man over there – she wondered why she presumed it was a man, but she did – perhaps the man over there was some fabulous IRA leader, chased by the British forces across the border, and now hotly pursued by the Gardai. He had come up this lonely valley to make a last stand in that little cottage. Maybe years ago he had singled it out as the place where, if necessary, he would die.

For goodness sake, she said to herself suddenly, what a load of old rubbish. She cast her mind back over the events of the past few weeks in the North, and no outrageous feat of arms by the IRA against the British sprang naturally to mind. Ah well, then! Disappointed, she thought it might be a hippy. Well, that would be a change at least. Dropouts, weren't they called, with long hair, sandals and jeans. Dirty, too, probably. So perhaps, after all, it was just a youngster, using the cottage as a booley house for the summer, while he tended his father's sheep.

Mind you, she said, musing, that would be interesting now. It was a practice that was dying out, and she'd never seen anyone at it herself. Her father had told her about it. How the farmers' young sons used to spend all summer up in the mountains, minding the sheep, living in a booley house. These were, traditionally, a sort of beehive affair, made by stacking up corbelled stones. No mortar was used, and the roof was covered with sods. The boys would always bring up provisions, and sometimes get re-supplied. But often they had to make do with what they caught, rabbits or hares, fish from the stream. Of course there would always be a stream near a cottage like that, for both water and food. Three or four different varieties of heath berries were also worth eating, especially if there was a bit of cream to go with them.

That must all be fun, she thought. No school all summer, but a fishing rod, maybe a gun, and all your time your own, except for a few sheep to look after, and, of course, the fact she'd never be allowed to do it because she was a girl.

Girls in Ireland, she thought, damn it! Always expected to stay at home and look after the men. Do their washing and cooking and every damn thing for them. She even used to watch her mother peel apples for her father, and he never raised an eyebrow or thought it unusual. Well, she wasn't going to get caught like that! Oh no, not little Mairead. She was going to carve out her own track. And what, she thought, was she going to do about that fella over there?

He was back inside the cottage now, and the stillness of the valley was complete. The only movement now was a thin stream of ants, seemingly busy going from nowhere to nowhere, just a couple of feet away from her face. Funny she hadn't noticed them before.

She watched them for a while, one line going one way, another coming back parallel to it. Sometimes the ants bumped together, and swerved round each other, and went on purposefully. They knew exactly where they were going, and what they had to do. What a lovely, simple life, she thought, the life of an ant. Wouldn't that be lovely for me – and then realized quickly that, of course, it was just the sort of life she might well lead. So she would not be an ant, she decided. She would not follow along in a line, with someone always in front, and another at the back. No, she would go her own way, it was the only way she could go.

Having made this momentous decision again, for naturally it wasn't the first time it had been made, she dragged herself to her feet, and whistled for her dog. He appeared from behind a bush to see her already striding off down the hill, heading straight for the cottage on the far side.

It took her half an hour or more to get there. At the bottom of the valley, there was a tangle of boulders and gorse in a deep crevice which hid another small stream. There was little water in it, but she was almost smothered by the sudden smell of damp earth, after the dryness of the uplands.

She was panting again as she came up to the cottage for she wouldn't let up on her striding out, and it had been a sharp pull up. She scrambled over a broken-down stone wall some twenty yards from the cottage, and then stopped, suddenly frightened. What was she doing in such a lonely place, approaching a stranger who might be anyone at all? Well now, what to do? she asked herself, and without thinking further, called out:

'Hullo there, is that yourself, Tom?'

She swung her bag round, and whistled to her dog. She wanted it to look as if there was nothing at all unusual for a girl like herself to be out on the moors on her own. In fact, she wouldn't mind if whoever it was inside thought she maybe owned the cottage, or at least had something to do with it.

'Hullo, Tom,' she called out as confidently as she could, 'come out of that place and stop skulking or I'll. . . .'

She broke off as a head appeared around the corner. It was young man with a shock of black hair. She suddenly seemed surprised she'd never seen him before.

'Afternoon,' he said quietly, looking at her, 'but the name isn't Tom.'

Mairead stood there, her mouth open. She stared at him.

'Oh!' she said. 'Oh! Well, I'm sorry.' She caught hold of herself. 'I expected to meet a friend of mine here. I thought, when I saw the movement in the cottage, that it was himself. I hope I didn't startle you,' she added brightly, smiling.

'Not at all. Though I wasn't expecting to see the likes of you up here.'

They both waited expectantly. Neither said anything. The terrier sniffed around the man's trousers, and he bent down and patted him on the head. They both felt awkward, not quite knowing what to do next, for, unknown to each other, they were both out of place.

'Well,' she said at last, 'is it the politeness that is suffocating you?'

'No!' he said. 'But I had better get along. I've quite a lot to do.'

'Ah yes, yes. Of course. Indeed, and so have I. I have to . . .' She looked up and around, avoiding his eyes. 'I have to inspect the cottage. Just to see ... ah ... you know ... if everything is all right. I usually do for Tom.'

His eyebrows went up. 'It's your cottage then,' he said, surprise in his voice, 'I didn't know that.'

'Well, why should you know?' She walked firmly forward. What was she getting herself into? She'd passed him before he realized what she was doing, and he turned after her.

'Hang on a minute, would you?' he called.

She looked round and saw him limping towards her. He was limping quite badly. It was something she hadn't noticed at first.

'I've a few things in the cottage,' he said. 'I'd best take them out. I didn't know it belonged to anyone. To tell you the truth, it doesn't look as if anyone's been inside for years.'

She saw his face wince with pain each time his right leg hit the ground.

'Are you all right with that there?' She nodded towards his leg. 'If you didn't expect me up here, I certainly never expected the likes of that. What in heaven's name are you doing out here on the hill with a game leg like that?'

'I had an accident,' he said shortly. 'Let me get my things out, and I'll be away.'

He was annoyed with the girl, and it showed. He hated anyone to notice his leg, though he knew it was hard, it not quite impossible, to miss his limp, especially when he was tired. But every time someone looked at it he felt, my God! they know what happened. They can tell by the limp I have the sort of man I am. He felt sure everyone knew it hadn't been an accident, however much he insisted it was. He was sure they all knew he'd had a bullet smash into the back of his knee. And that meant, in turn, that they would know he had been convicted and sentenced in an IRA court, and he just could not bear anyone knowing that.

He fought to keep down the cold surge of sick anger he felt. Steady, steady, he told himself furiously, get a hold of yourself, man. The girl means no harm, means no harm. Indeed, you fool, she is so open about the leg, she really accepts it for what it is, a broken limb. He forced the calmness back on to himself, using the force of his stomach muscles to bear down and settle himself, physically as well as mentally. So often, for him, it was all one and the same thing.

He heard her talking as she led the way into the cottage. It was dark inside, or at least semi-dark after the brightness outside. And it was hot, and very stuffy, for he'd only unboarded one of the windows. What was that she was after saying?

'... no trouble at all. Sure I only came to see if the place was still standing. It's a very solid structure, mind you, but being miles from nowhere then ye've no idea the young hooligans and layabouts who might get after the place.' She looked up at him. 'Oh Jesus, I didn't mean yourself now. You don't look like, well, look like....' she paused, and laughed. I'm always putting my great foot in it now. But you know what I mean. You know, you do look, well, you do look perfectly all right.' She ended rather lamely.

'That's civil of you. I'm glad I'm not in your category of your hooligan or layabout.'

His rucksack was lying by the wall, and he walked over to it. Next to it, laid out neatly, was a sleeping bag, a small saucepan and kettle, and some smallish cardboard boxes which he had taken out of his rucksack. He started to gather his bits together.

'Oh!' she said. 'You're sleeping here, are you?'

'Yes, I'm sorry. As I said, I hadn't realized this place

belonged to anyone, or I'd never have stayed here.'

'But for pity's sake, it doesn't matter. Anyway, I've no right to stop anyone sleeping here.'

'I thought it belonged to you, or was it Tom?'

'Tom?' she said, surprised. 'Oh, I see. You have got a nasty suspicious mind, haven't you? Well now, no, it does not belong to the both of us, but we have an interest in it, Tom and meself. But please now, don't you go rushing off. There is no need.'

He put his things back on the floor, and fished around his pockets for a cigarette. He offered one to her, silently, but she shook her head. Leaning back against the open window, he drew in, and then blew the smoke out in a long, thin stream across the room. He turned, hunching his shoulders, and looked out through the window, itself in deep shadow from the overhead sun. He saw far down the valley.

In the shallow V shape some two miles away, where the valley ended and the ground dropped steeply down to the next plateau, he could just see a line of darker blue. The sea, merging, almost, into the washed-out sky. It seemed a long way away, like so many things in his life at the moment. Far away from the North, and much further away than the drab violence of Belfast. What it would be, he thought, to live in this country, free, free from the constant threat of gunman and bomber. But he was free of them, certainly, at the moment. His aching leg reminded him that he was probably free from it all for ever. They would hardly bother him again after what they had done.

In the distant haze, higher up on the slopes to the right of the cottage, he could now see a few sheep. There weren't many, and they were totally alone on the hillside, with just a hawk lazily high above them, using the thermals to swing in a long arc with barely a movement of its wings. A black speck hanging in the sky, looking for some sign of small life below.

But there was no life below, nothing moving in the heat. Everything was hiding in what little shade it could find, and the hawk had no luck.

He felt a tiredness in his shoulder, and the depression coming on him again, and he wondered if it was the girl who had made him feel like that. He didn't want to see anyone. Least of all a girl he didn't know, and one who bounced around in such a way. What was this Tom she was supposed to be meeting here, or was she just stringing him along! If she wasn't, he thought, wearily, then he'd have to move on, and he didn't want to do that either.

Jesus! he thought angrily again. All I want to do is to keep out of everyone's way, and even in this bloody spot miles from bugger all I can't do it. Some damn woman has to come along. Just my luck! He wished to hell she would go away. But she was still standing just inside the door.

He refused to turn and look at her. He thought if he didn't his irritation might go, and he could then handle the situation.

'I thought you wanted to check the place over,' he said tightly, 'just in case I'd made a mess anywhere.'

He heard her take a few steps round the small room, and then open and shut the door that led to the second room in the cottage. Then there was silence, and he could hear no movement at all. But he still wouldn't turn round to see what she was up to. He held his breath for a minute, straining his ears to try and hear the faintest sound that might tell him what was happening. There was nothing, and he began to feel the emptiness of the cottage.

When he couldn't bear it any longer he turned abruptly, but there was no one behind him. Four strides took him to the door, which he flung open. But there was no one in that room either. Where the hell had the girl gone, he wondered, and what was she up to?

He went back to the window, and then he saw her. She was sitting on the grass just outside, her arms round her knees, her head flung back, and she was looking at him grinning.

'Is this a game?' he asked sourly.

'Oh! catch yourself on,' she laughed, 'you look so hatchet-faced I thought you were after my head . . . or worse. Come on out here and tell me what's the matter with you. It's much less stuffy.' She waited, and he looked at her, holding her eyes. She stared back.

His hair was so black, it stood out against even the darkness of the room behind. But his face was pale. She had noticed a slight touch of pink where he had recently caught the sun. But it was obvious he wasn't used to it. Without doubt a city fella, and from the sounds of him, from the North. And that leg of his. She wondered what he had done to that. By the look of him when he walked on it, it wasn't an old wound. Something quite recent, she thought. He was a gloomy fella, quite ready to take her head off, so being one who was always ready to move in directly, she moved.

'Are you on the run?' she asked him, without batting an eyelid.

He looked somewhat startled, and flushed.

'I am not,' he said firmly.

'But you have all the makings of a man on the run. Now don't be mad at me,' she said quickly, 'I'm not the sort to go round opening my mouth. But if you are on the run, you won't be running very far with that leg of yours. You. . . .'

'You leave my leg out of this,' he shouted.

'Ye've no need to shout at me. All I'm saying is that with that leg you can't get very far, nor fast neither. You may even need some help.'

'I don't.'

'Is it a gunshot wound?' she ploughed steadily on, seemingly oblivious to the state he was getting into. 'That sort of thing needs attention. You could get a sort of gangrenous infection. Have ye had it seen to?'

'I have that.'

'So it is a gunshot wound. Was it bad?'

'For Chrissake, woman, would you shut up and let me be?' He glared at her. She smiled back. 'I do not want any treatment. I do not want any advice. I do not want to be disturbed, which is why I came to this place. I thought it would be well out of everyone's tracks.'

'There's a lot of things you don't want.' She got up and brushed the dead leaves off her skirt. 'Is there anything ye do want? A cup of tea, perhaps? Sure I could do with one meself. It's a great thing, you know . . .' she disappeared from sight round the corner, but her voice came remorselessly on, ' . . . a great thirst-quencher in this terrible heat.'

85

She came into the cottage, and ignoring his back, picked up the kettle.

'Aha!' she said, feeling its weight, "'tis already filled, mister,' she called out, staring at this back, 'you were about to make yerself a cup of tea, weren't you? Own up. And not even offer me one. Goodness sake! What hospitality in such a lonely place. Now, it has to be heated up. I'm sure you must have thought of that, and got something ready. Something very clever and easy, I'll be bound. A Primus stove it must be. Oh ho! A Primus stove. Where have you put it, mister?' She looked around, but couldn't see it. Then she threw up a hand in mock triumph. 'Of course, now, what an eejit I am. There's nowhere you'd put it, of course, being a self-made man, but in the kitchen.' She advanced on the door and threw it open with a flourish, peering in.

'There you are,' she called out, 'right where I thought 'twould be. Now, do you have a light on you or perhaps ye'd like to light it yerself?'

Vincent had listened to all this with growing concern. He didn't think of himself as having any great experience with women, and he had never in his life come across anyone like this. He felt he was suffocating under the flow of words, and the presence of this girl. He began to wonder if she was, perhaps, a wee bit light in the head. He felt obliged to do something, in case she did something daft and set the place on fire.

'Don't touch it,' he called out. 'I'll light it myself.' Perhaps if he gave her a cup of tea she would go.

She gazed at him in open, half-mocking admiration.

'Well, now. I never thought I'd see the day of a man making himself a cup of tea.'

'Did you not? It does happen sometimes.'

'Not in my part of the world.'

'And which is your part of the world?' he asked, automatically, forgetting he didn't want to strike up another conversation.

'Kilmulpeter.'

He didn't say anything, but busied himself with the methy-

86

lated spirits and pricking pin, and getting the stove alight. She handed him the kettle she was still holding.

'You're not too talkative now, are you?' she said, in more of a statement than a question. 'Do you know where that is?'

'Yes,' he said, wearily, 'I do. I caught the bus there. You know that is the only way to get to this place, unless you are prepared to spend a week or more walking across the hills from the other side. So why ask me such damn fool questions?' He pumped away at the primus until it was roaring, and sat back on his heels. 'The tea is over there.' He indicated a tin by his rucksack. 'There isn't any milk. No sugar, either.' He chuckled to himself at the thought of scoring a point over her. He suddenly thought it quite funny, and laughed.

'You're a good-looking one when you smile.' It was the first time she had seen him smile, and he looked very different. Anyway, she knew it would probably annoy him if she said that, and she wanted to spark him.

She was right. His face went grim-looking again. He scowled at her, and turned his attention back to the kettle.

'A watched pot never boils,' she said.

'Jesus, woman! Would you ever give over with that jabbering of yours?'

'If you'd talk a bit, I would. Maybe.'

'Talk!' he exclaimed. 'What would I talk about?'

'Yourself, for a start. What about that leg, now? How did that get hurt?'

'Oh! Me leg? Well, now it was a bus that ran me over. Late one night. I was coming home with a few jars on me.'

'A bus?'

'A bus. But it was no ordinary bus, mind you. It was burning.' His eyes widened, and he made a bit circle with his hands. 'A runaway bus. I was tearing down the hill, and it followed me. I slipped, and the side of it hit me knee as I fell. So that ...' he said, looking at his knee, 'is why I have a bad knee.'

'Is that so?' she said, astonished by·this tale.

'Oh! It is.'

''Tis hard to believe.'

'Is it?'

"Tis.'

'Why so?'

'Well, where would you get a bus burning, and then career-
ing down the streets out of control?'

He lifted the kettle off the primus and poured the boiling
water into a mug. The tea bag floated to the top, and he stirred
it round, slowly. He picked out the bag, looked round, and
then put it down beside him on the floor. He handed her the
mug.

'Are you not having one yourself?' she asked, taking the
mug.

'I am. When you've finished. I have only the one mug.'

'Thanks.'

He watched her sip the hot tea.

'Have you never seen a burning bus?' She shook her head
slightly, and he went on. 'Not even on television?'

Her eyes widened. 'You mean . . . ?' she said, hesitantly,
and looking round as if to look north across the border. 'You
come from the North?'

'Yes.'

'Where from?'

'Belfast.'

'Oh, Mother! But that's terrible. All that fighting and carry
on. Is it really as bad as they say?'

'It is.'

For some reason this worried her, but she couldn't work it
out. It wasn't just that this was a good-looking fella she had
found in the most unlikely place. Nor was it the small air of
mystery which surrounded him, staying in this empty, lonely
cottage, miles from anywhere, with his bad knee. She put the
mug down carefully on the floor, and then sat down beside
him, cross-legged, and smoothed out her skirt. She thought for
a few moments, then picked up her mug in both hands. Sipping
it slowly, she looked at him across the rim.

'I've never met anyone from the North before,' she said.
'Anyway, not anyone from the Troubles. Why do they do it?'

He gave a short laugh. 'You may well ask. All sorts of
reasons. Getting the British out, for one. Getting the Prods off

our backs, which is probably the most important, though one goes with the other. I don't know. Better jobs, despair ... the feelings have been there a long time.'

'Are the British very bad to live under?'

'It's not so much that. They're an arrogant lot, surely. It's not so much what they do, but. It's what they don't do. They just let the Prods do what they like. They won't interfere, and so we come off second best.'

She shook her head. 'And so you're on the run from all that. Sure 'tis no wonder.'

'I never said I was on the run. I am not on the run. I'm here to get my knee mended.'

'Don't start on again,' she said, quickly. 'Sure it doesn't matter if I believe you or not. Burning runaway buses, indeed!' She paused for a moment, and then went on: 'All that rioting. Is that what you do? Throw stones at the soldiers?'

'It is not. The only stones I ever threw were at the Tartan gangs that come up our street. They don't do that often, mind you. Usually at night. But we sort them out.'

'Is it very rough?'

'Yes. Sometimes. I have seen a whole street on fire.'

'Oh, my God! As bad as that?'

'Yes.'

'Did you ... did ye ever see anyone killed?'

'Yes.'

'What ... what ...?'

'It's enough to see someone killed, without having to talk about it.'

'I'm sorry.'

'It's no matter. If you haven't seen it happening, you can't really believe it.'

They sat together, talking quietly. He told her what it was like, living up in the North, in a city divided into blocks of Catholics and Protestants. He talked about his twin brother, and the time they had both been off to Port Stewart and spent a whole weekend by the sea. The huge long beaches, and the swell and crash of the Atlantic rollers. The fish and chip shop where they had eaten most of their meals, and how they had knocked off a whole carton of beer cans, and got drunk in the sand dunes, and roared down the beach as it was getting dark, stark naked into the sea, to the astonishment of some evening fishermen working the incoming tide. He talked about his sister Sheelagh, 'about your age, I'd say, young and pretty,' and Mairead had laughed: about his small brother Jamie and, of course, his baby sister Deirdre. He admitted he spoiled her. 'That's what small girls are for,' he said, adding she was the spit image of her mother, who had been a noted beauty in her day.

'Is that your whole family?' she had asked, and he had said, 'Oh, no!' He then talked about his granda, who had been a schoolteacher, and was a raging Republican. He knew every bit of Irish history from the Kings of Tara and more besides. He could account every English atrocity and always heaped venom on Cromwell.

Mairead had protested that in sacking Drogheda and Wexford, Cromwell was only abiding by the rules of war at that time, which said a city could be sacked if the garrison did not surrender at one, and instead made a siege of it.

'That argument wouldn't impress my granda,' Vincent said. 'In fact, he wouldn't even listen to it.'

'Would he not?' She sounded surprised. 'But it is a matter of historical fact.'

'That would make no difference,' said Vincent, with a rare flash of understanding. 'It's the feeling that matters, not the fact.'

The afternoon wore on, and they suddenly hit an awkward patch of silence. Both came back to realizing where they were. Vincent felt he had spoken too much, let too much of himself go to a girl he hardly knew. Mairead sensed the change.

'Are you sure you're not on the run?'

'Listen. . . .' He paused for a moment. 'What's your name?'

'Mairead . . . Mairead O'Donnell.'

'Well, Mairead, let me give you a wee bit of advice. Never ask a man if he is on the run. If he isn't, it would annoy him to be thought of so. If he is, he wouldn't tell you, and he might get nasty besides. If he wanted you to know, he'd let on, somehow.

The less you know about such things, the better. As it so happens, I am not on the run. And stop exercising your mind about my leg. What's happened to that is as I told you. It's sore. I'm half crippled with it, and so I like to keep to myself. That's why I'm here. And before you ask me, my name is Vincent. That'll do. Just Vincent.'

She nodded her head slowly, as if she understood everything he had said, her hands clasped in front of her, her fingers twisting together. She thought about his family, and wondered about his father.

'Are you like your father?' she asked. 'You haven't mentioned him.'

'No,' he said shortly. 'I am not. He had a lot of guts. He died after he was beaten up by a gang in our street. Not straight away, of course, so they couldn't call it murder. But after a suitable interval of three months or so, he died.'

His mood had changed again, and she wondered what sort of man she had chanced upon. A moody fella, with a lot of charm, but up and down like a yo-yo, and very edgy about his leg. She didn't for a moment believe that business about a bus, though it was so improbable it could be true.

Perhaps he had been very drunk when he did it, whatever it was, and he was ashamed of that. It might even be a bullet wound, though he'd hardly be wandering around so far from medical care if it was. On the other hand, that might be the reason. Oh dear! she thought, what a muddle.

Aloud she said, still looking at the ground and then her hands: 'I'm sorry. I'm not meaning to pry. But if your leg is bad, it should have attention. Proper attention. Our doctor is very good. He's had a lot of ...' she searched for the right phrase, not wanting it to be too direct, but then not wanting him to miss the point, 'a lot of experience with all sorts of severe wounds ... injuries ... the sort you get on a farm. You know, accidents with machinery and the like.' She looked up and caught his eye. 'He has,' she said firmly, 'been in this area for a very long time. He knows it and all the people very well.'

The ache in Vincent's leg came again, and he felt himself

sweating. To take his mind off it, he relit the primus and put the kettle back on. They had talked so much he had forgotten his tea.

If he understood the girl right, she was saying the doctor had Republican sympathies. If he went to him now, it would be the same as admitting he was an IRA man on the run. Well, he wasn't. He had finished with them, and he was damned if he would give anyone the idea that he was still tied up with them. So he gritted his teeth and held out his hand for the mug.

'If you've finished, I'll have some now.'

He took the mug, poured in hot water, added a tea bag and stirred. While he did so he kept his face away from her. Then he hauled himself to his feet and limped towards the door.

'I'll take this outside. It's a bit cooler there now. I need some fresh air. And thank you. I don't mean to be rude, but I don't need any attention, medical or otherwise.' He leaned against an outcrop of rock, and lit a cigarette. 'You have a long way to go,' he said, pointedly, 'and it wouldn't do to be caught out here in the dark.'

She looked at him with exasperation but said nothing. Instead, she gave a piercing whistle, which made his head spin, and the terrier appeared.

'Come along, Spot,' she said, 'we're not wanted. 'Tis sudden, but 'tis true. Thanks for the tea,' she called over her shoulder, and then she was away, swinging down the valley with long strides, the dog running about her.

He stood for a long time, without moving, watching. Her figure got smaller and smaller until he could see it no more. Then he went inside.

6

Vincent woke up in a foul mood. He couldn't think why. He hadn't been drinking. In fact, he hadn't had a drink for the two weeks he had been up in the hills.

His knee ached. Perhaps that was it. The wound was still red and sore to touch. It was stiff, but he exercised it hard, and by the end of the day he was always very glad to get into his bed. However, this was the start of the day, and the whole empty time stretched before him.

The morning sky was clear, and he could hear a lark singing. He wondered if it was too clear to stay fine all day. He was really a townsman, and he knew very little of the signs and ways of the country. But he was learning quickly.

It was a black depression that had hit him, he could recognize that much. He felt very alone, and he wondered at the uselessness of everything, and the foul luck that had brought him in front of that IRA court. He spat as he thought of them, mean-minded wee bastards, who reckoned they could do anything to anybody.

He had blacked out of his mind the actual moment of the shooting, with the terror before it, and the total helpless fright and the pain that followed.

He relived that moment only in nightmares, and he had just woken from one. His body was still in a sweat. Dear God! Would he ever get it all out of his mind? He felt like lying on his bed all day, doing nothing, but he knew he could not really do that. It would go against everything he had set himself to do. Some people might call it a holiday. Well, perhaps it was, but it was also unpaid and unwanted. He'd had to borrow money from Bryan to come, and even Sheelagh had forced some on him, telling him he should take it with good grace. He had, in the end, and hugged her warmly and just stopped himself crying.

So he forced himself out of bed, wincing as his leg touched the ground. It was always very painful first thing in the morning, but if he worked on it, the pain would wear off quite a bit during the day.

He made himself some coffee, drinking it black because he had long since run out of milk. He spread Marmite on some hard crackers and swallowed them down. He was never very hungry at the start of the day.

He decided he would walk up into the hills that morning and try his hand at fishing. He remembered a stream where he and Bryan had fished the time they had camped here. It was a long time ago.

He had a rod lent to him by his uncle who had greeted him warmly and said little about his leg other than to offer some sympathy. He had also lent him some flies, and given him a stream of instructions on which ones to use and when. But then he had seen Vincent's blank face and, taking pity on him, had selected one brownish fly, whose name Vincent still couldn't remember, and said that was the one to use if everything else failed. It was a regular killer, his uncle said.

So after he had eaten, he put the rod over his shoulder and set off up the hill. He followed a small, winding path made by the sheep, and then broke from it and went right, over a rise and down a steep slope to the valley. He skirted round a small stand of trees, and came to the pool. It lay calm in the early morning sun, the stream on either side rattling and roaring away.

He put his bag down, and tied on the brown fly. The rod swished through the air behind him, and he cast out the line three or four times until he felt it was out enough, and then let the fly settle gently on the water. It wasn't as gentle as he had hoped, but then he was well out of practice.

It was hard to see the brown fly in the boggy water, but he

concentrated hard and was able to follow it being taken down by the current.

He tried a few more casts, but had no luck, so he walked up the stream a bit, and tried again. He enjoyed the peacefulness of it all, but he was also quite anxious to catch something, for he hadn't much food left in the booley. Moreover, the thought of fresh trout sizzling over his fire was making him feel hungry already.

After about an hour of casting with no result at all, he sat down on the bank and lit a cigarette. The sun was breaking through the morning haze now, and he threw off his jersey and wondered if he would have to jump into the stream and catch a fish with his bare hands. He blew smoke out through his mouth and watched it drift away, and then remembered with a start the girl he had met the previous day.

Mairead ... that was her name. A good-looking girl, he thought, though she had irritated him beyond measure. He'd been furious that she had been so open about his leg: that she couldn't see he didn't like anyone making any reference to it. He remembered he'd done a lot of talking, and that was unusual as well. He didn't talk to girls very much. Most times all he would need to do would be to smile and nod, and the girl would be his. He did his talking with the boys. This Mairead, however, had chatted in a way he wasn't used to at all, and had even got him talking back.

He flipped the cigarette away from him and wondered if he would see her again. He thought it unlikely, but if he did, he would work on it. A bird like that, willing and able, up in his little hut on the hills, would add enormously to his holiday.

He started fishing again and was so lacking concentration by this time that he almost missed a gentle pull on the line. His first thought was that the line had snagged on something, and then he suddenly realized that he had a bite. He waited for the second tug, and then struck hard, and the line screamed away.

He wasn't very experienced at this, but he knew roughly what to do. He let the fish run a bit, and when it slowed, he drew up the slack on the line, and this time held it steady so the fish had to pull against it and tire himself.

95

The fish tried another run to the far bank, and Vincent let him go again, and again pulled up and held him. On the next run he walked along the bank, the delicate tip of the rod bending under the strain.

Once the fish rose, and he saw the gleam of silver as it came out of the brown water. It was a big fish, and his stomach contracted with the excitement of having to try and land it. He was terrified he would do something wrong, and the line would break, and he would lose it.

Up and down the bank he hobbled, his knee forgotten until he half twisted his leg on a clump of grass, and came down heavily on his bad leg and gasped at the pain. But he didn't let up. He had never caught anything like this before in his life.

The minutes passed by, and he hardly felt the fish tiring, for he was tiring too. He began to wonder how the hell he was ever going to get this fish on to the bank when he heard a voice behind him.

'I suppose you have a licence for that?'

He daren't look round. He was concentrating everything he'd got on his fish, and as it was a woman's voice, he was damned if he would take much notice anyway.

He hobbled along the bank again, his leg aching and his arms beginning to tire now as well. He was getting desperate to land his fish and be done with it all, and now this wretched woman was standing watching him, and he had no doubt who it was.

He heard her laugh behind him again.

'You're a big fella to have so much trouble with a wee fish.'

That did make him glance round, and he saw her sitting on a boulder, her arms round her knees and her hair hanging loose. That was all he had time to take in, for there was another yank on the rod and he was away again.

He was sweating now with the effort and at his wits' end as to what to do next. If the girl hadn't been there, he would have been tempted to let it go.

'Walk a wee way down,' she called. 'Then just ease him across towards you. The current will bring him if you do it gently.' He heard her run past behind him, then saw her out of the corner of his eye down by the bank ahead. 'Come on!' she shouted. 'Ease him over here towards me.'

She was kneeling where the bank flattened out and shelved very gently into the pool. So he did as she suggested, and moments later the fish flopped on to the bank. Mairead picked up a bit of wood and, holding the fish by the tail, hit it with a downward movement on the back of its head.

Quickly she opened the mouth and tugged at the hook until she got it out, and then washed her hands in the water. She was so quick it was all done by the time he got to her. He was panting.

'Well, now,' he gasped, 'that must be the biggest trout I ever caught.'

'Trout!' she yelled, looking up at him. 'Sure 'tis no trout. 'Tis a salmon, and a very fine one at that.' She picked it up, hefting it in her hands. 'About five pounds, I'd say. 'Tis as well I'm not the bailiff asking after your licence.' She laughed at the thought. 'Sure you have one, no?'

'I do not, and you know it. Thanks anyway. I'll just get my bag.'

He walked across the grass to where he had left his bag and brought it back. Wrapping the salmon in some paper, he put it in and closed the flap. He washed his hands, and then lit a cigarette. He offered her one, but she shook her head and he said: 'Oh yes! I remember, you don't smoke.'

He sank back onto the grass, feeling exhausted. He made himself comfortable and looked at the girl through half-closed eyes. She was a fine-looking girl, there was no doubt about that. She was wearing jeans, and a boyish shirt with a wee scarf. He noticed again how well tanned she was.

'Don't you work?' he asked.

She looked puzzled. 'Yes, I do. Why?'

'You seem to have plenty of time off, then. This is the second day you've been up here.'

''Tis the weekend, you ninny. I don't work at the weekend. 'Twas Saturday yesterday, and 'tis Sunday today.'

'Oh!' He felt slightly abashed. With him one day was merging with another, and he had forgotten what day it was.

'What do you do, then?'

'I teach. Small children. I teach them everything and anything. Except at weekends. I have those to myself.'

'Do you come from these parts?'

'No. I come from County Galway. My father has a farm there. But I had the chance of a job here, and so here I am.'

'So what are you doing out here again? Exercising your dog? Where is he, but?'

'Oh! Spot's around here somewhere. Rabbiting, I expect, though I haven't seen many around. 'Tis a lovely day again.' She lay back with her face up to the sun, and closed her eyes. 'Tis a long walk you had up here this morning.'

He sensed she was going to say something about his leg, so he spoke quickly. 'Sure it's not so far now. My brother and I used to come here. Sometimes we used to run and arrive so hot we'd throw everything off and swim.'

'Do you swim a lot?'

'No. We don't get out of Belfast that much.'

'Do you not!' She sounded surprised. 'With all that bother and fighting and whatever up there, I'd have thought you'd get out as often as you could.'

He shrugged. 'We just don't seem to get round to it.'

She lay on in the sun, and after a while she asked him if he was hungry. He said he was. She jumped up and ran across to fetch her basket. She pulled out a couple of cans of beer, a loaf of bread, margarine, cheese and a tin of meat.

'Is that your lunch?' he asked.

''Tis ours.'

'Oh! Were you so sure of finding me here?'

'I was.'

He watched in silence. She was a very pretty girl, and she looked very much at ease, sitting cross-legged on the ground, the loaf in her lap, competently cutting and spreading. Her dark hair kept falling forward, and she constantly brushed it away with the back of her hand, or tossed her head to one side.

With a little sound of exasperation, she suddenly undid the scarf round her neck, and, throwing her head well back, she caught her hair and tied it.

'Meat or cheese?' she asked him, glancing up and catching him looking at her. He was slightly embarrassed, and muttered something about not minding what he had.

'Well, if you can't make up your mind, I'll give you some meat, and you can have some cheese later, if you've a mind to it. Here,' she said, throwing him a can of beer, 'try some of that. 'Tis still quite cold.'

He caught the can, and when he opened it the beer frothed a little at the top. He raised the can to her, and smiled.

'*Slainte!*'

'Wait a wee minute,' she said quickly, 'while I open mine.' She did so and raised her can in the air too. 'Here's to your leg getting better soon.'

His face reddened, and for a moment it looked as if he would throw his beer away. But he couldn't. He knew she was attracted to him, and he didn't want to do anything that might spoil that. He felt an urge to take her there and then, but he fought it down. He wasn't absolutely sure of her. She was something new. The usual signs and signals he would exchange with a girl – almost subconsciously – wouldn't necessarily work in this instance. He felt they might, but he didn't have the confidence to let himself go.

His fingers tightened round the beer can, and he forced a smile. 'I hope it will,' he said, and feeling suddenly perverse, added, 'I suppose you want to nurse it. That might help.'

She held his gaze, saying nothing. In the end he broke, muttering, and drank some beer.

She passed him a sandwich and he took it, eating quickly, looking at her between mouthfuls. The tensions between them heightened his hunger. She broke off a hunk of cheese and put it slowly into her mouth. She was still looking at him as she ate. 'You're a hard bastard,' she said, and he was surprised. He hadn't expected anything like that. He was about to say something, but she passed him another sandwich, and he took that instead.

'That knee of yours needs a wee rub,' she told him. 'Ye shouldn't just keep hammering it the way you do.'

His mouth stayed open in mid-bite. He couldn't believe what he had heard.

'A wee rub!' he said, hoarsely. 'A wee rub!'

'Yes.' She was quite calm. 'What's so surprising about that? There's no benefit it staying hurt, just of the sake of it. Is there?'

'You mean you want to rub it?' His voice was still high.

She put the rest of the cheese into her mouth and moved across to him. He stayed absolutely still, watching her.

'Pull up your trouser leg, man. Come on.'

When he didn't move, she reached down and did it herself, exposing the knee and the red scar. She felt quite bold, for she had really expected much more of a fuss from him. But he lay on the ground quite still. Not wanting to look at his leg, nor Mairead, he looked instead up at the sky. Out of the corner of his eye, however, he saw her take a small jar from her bag and open it. Then for the first time he felt her hands, firm fingers spreading a cool cream around his knee. First along the line of the scar, and then gently probing the strained muscles.

After a few minutes he felt himself relaxing, and she noticed the almost imperceptible movement. Through his closed eyelids the orange burst of sun colour shifted and moved, darkening quickly whenever she touched a particularly sore point, and he flinched. He smelt the warm grass and the dryness of the earth and heard the small noises the river made behind them. Her hands travelled down his leg. She worked slowly and rhythmically.

'You should learn to relax more often,' she said quietly. 'You're terribly stiff and tense. Did they really let you out of hospital like this, and no treatment?'

He grunted a reply, not wanting to tell her he had refused to go back for treatment. He wondered now what was happening to him. He could feel the girl close over his body, hear the soft movement of her clothes and catch her body scent.

She paused to rest, and he thought of opening his eyes to look at her, but the drowsiness made them too heavy. He took a deep breath, and sighed as he let it out.

'That's a big sigh,' she murmured, 'for a fella who's supposed to be all relaxed.'

He felt her hands come down on his leg again, pushing up from the knee, first with the thumbs and fingers, and then the heel of the thumb until finally both her hands were flat on his thigh, and then they lifted and started all over again. She had moved her position and was kneeling over his leg now, straddling it. He knew this because her hair had brushed his face and he had half opened his eyes and seen her head bent down and her shirt beyond, unbuttoned.

There was a softness about her that he wanted to touch, and as her hands moved round his thigh muscles, he felt himself hardening and he thought how awful that this should happen and he not knowing whether she would take him and it was now too late to make any further moves to discover what she might do, other than to move directly.

So he brought up his arms, and it seemed the most natural thing to do, slipping his hands inside her shirt and cupping her breasts, feeling their heavy roundness and the quickening nipples.

She drew her breath sharply, sliding her hands further up his leg. 'You are a bastard,' she said firmly and grinned at him. She went on rubbing his thigh, and then moved to lie down beside him. But he kept his hands where they were, holding her above him.

'You're hurting me.' Her face puckered. 'Please be gentle.'

He held her there for a while, and then let her down beside him. He ran his fingers down from her throat, over her breast and down to her stomach. His hands were hard from manual work.

'Get your clothes off,' he said abruptly, sitting up and unbuckling his belt. He pulled off his jeans. 'Come on, come on. Don't sit around.'

She did as she was told, and they came together quickly. She babbled away in his ear, but he said nothing. He took no notice even when, rolling on to some old, sharp bracken, she cried out.

When it was finished, Vincent pulled on his jeans quickly and, lighting a cigarette, lay back. Excitement and depression hit him at the same time. When Mairead came close to him again, kissing him, he made an impatient movement, and she moved away and got dressed.

Mairead felt very close to him. It hadn't quite gone the way she had expected, but then she realized she hadn't known quite what she was expecting anyway. He had been rough. There had been no gentleness in him. At one time she would have been appalled at the thought of what had just happened. Now, she felt excited, and she wanted to continue the closeness she felt to the man lying beside her on the grass, smoking, gazing at the sky but saying nothing.

A lark sang above them, and she narrowed her eyes to search for it. She saw it, hanging against the blue sky, a small grey body pouring out its song. She felt contented, secure now in the knowledge that she had Vincent. This strange, brooding man from across the border was hers, and she wouldn't let anything take him away from her.

Later, they fished again, or rather Vincent fished, and she lay on the bank watching. For a man from the city, she thought, he was quite good with a rod. He worked up the bank steadily, and round the deep pool at the bend in the stream. She watched the cast fly out behind him, and then snake forward to settle lightly on the water. He fished for an hour, or maybe it was more, she couldn't tell and she didn't really care. He caught nothing, and in the end came back to her and said they would go on. He wanted to walk, he said, indicating she could come with him if she wanted to, but that he wasn't too concerned if she didn't.

He led the way, striding out ahead. She wanted to walk beside him and hold his hand, but she knew he would not like that. She was aware enough to know that the hold she had on him was slight, if indeed any hold at all. She would have to work on whatever was there to make that hold stronger.

She noticed he walked quickly, despite his limp, and from the set of his shoulders knew that his knee hurt him. There was no other way the pain would show, he was too proud for that, and also, for some reason she didn't know, he was ashamed of his disability. He couldn't help his limp, but everything else he could control, and he did.

They walked on through the early afternoon, high up, the slopes falling away from them, shimmering in a blurred, purple haze, and there was hardly enough wind to blow out a match. The sweat stained his shirt, and only occasionally did he stop, as if to look at the view, but really, she thought, because he needed to rest.

He seemed to know where he was going, and brought them in a wide circle so gradually that she was surprised, when they came to the top of what had seemed an endless series of ridges, to see the hut below them again in the valley.

When they got back, Vincent cleaned the fish, washing it out in the small stream that flowed by a few yards away. When he came back, the gutted salmon swinging from a finger through the gills, he found Mairead making up a fire.

'I'll do that.' He was brusque and took no notice of the surprised look she gave him. 'You can get some potatoes out, if you want to do something. We'll cook them as they are in the fire.'

'Why don't you sit down?' she said, almost adding, 'and rest your leg,' but stopping herself just in time.

He stiffened slightly even at that, wishing the girl would stop sounding so concerned about him. The last thing he wanted was some woman fussing around him. He had seen it happen to his friends, and they all took it very easily, but he himself wanted none of it. All he wanted was Mairead, and he had had her once and would have her again. She was very attractive, and she was very open. He saw she couldn't hide her feelings, and he was drawn to that. She had a sort of open innocence about her. He couldn't find the right phrase in his mind, but she seemed to be able to meet him on equal terms. She didn't cling.

'Are you here long?' she asked later, as they both lay on his outstretched sleeping bag.

'A week more.'

'And then ...?'

'I go back.'

'I suppose you do,' she said, softly, 'back to Belfast and all the terrible goings on there.'

'I don't want to talk about that.'

She rolled on her side, reached out and ran a finger down his cheek. He didn't move.

'What do you want to talk about, then?' she asked. 'There are so many things you want to cut out of your life. You'll have nothing left if you go on like that.'

He looked up at her. She was very pretty. 'Rubbish,' he said. 'Why should I want to talk about things like that when I've got you here?'

'Oh really!' she cried, delighted. 'That's a lovely thing to say.'

'Is it now?' he replied drily. 'It might well be lovely, but it's true.'

She smiled down at him, and he reached up, catching her round the neck, and pulling her down. For a moment she stayed there, and then tugged her head away.

'For pity's sake,' she laughed, 'what are you going to do all next week when I'm away? There aren't any other girls around.'

'Where are you going?' he asked.

'Back to work, of course. For another three days, anyway. Then it's the start of the summer holidays.'

He fell silent for a while, thinking about that. He was going in a week, so he might as well make the most of it while he could.

'Will you be up again?' he asked at length.

'I will,' she said simply.

'When?'

'Tomorrow. After school. I'll be up around half four.'

'How do you get here? Is it far?'

''Tisn't too far. A couple of miles or so on me bike, and then I walk. 'Tis no bother.' She got up and started to dress. 'I have to be back early tonight,' she told him. 'I have lessons to prepare for tomorrow.'

'I can't imagine you as a teacher. I didn't have one like you when I was at school.'

'Just as well,' she laughed, and he laughed with her. The sound bubbled up in her throat. He was relieved. He had hoped she would be a girl with no complications, and that was exactly what she seemed to be.

He lay on his back and watched her. The late afternoon light filled the small room with a slight reddish glow, touching his few possessions, his rucksack and a pile of tins in a corner – and catching her face.

'Your nose is red,' he said.

''Tis not!' she cried in alarm, her hand flashing up to touch it, the other holding her jeans half round her knees.

'It's burnt something terrible.'

She felt her nose carefully, then looked at him and saw he was laughing again.

'You're a bastard,' she shouted, 'I always knew it.'

'And if you don't hurry, it'll be dark by the time you get down the valley, and some hairy monster will get you.'

'It will not indeed. I'll tell it you're up here and will come and fix him if he so much as lays a hand on me. Now listen, will you, for a minute. I'll bring some stores up tomorrow. No ...' she held up a hand as he started to open his mouth, 'don't start your arguing again. 'Twill not be much. Just what I can get into me basket. And I'll choose what I get, so just keep that tongue still in your head.'

'OK.' He smiled at her.

'See you tomorrow. Don't be exhausting yourself before I get here.'

'I won't,' he shouted after her as she went through the door. 'Get along with yourself and don't be late.'

He heard her whistling for her dog, and then the silence of the hill country fell about him again. For a long time he lay still, until he felt a breath of cold across his bare body, and he got dressed and lit a cigarette.

She came the next day as she said she would, and on the following day as well. Each time she brought up some provisions for him. She didn't bring very much, just enough for herself and a little extra for him. She was very careful not to appear possessive, nor to challenge his independence in any way.

In turn, he made it clear he enjoyed her company, and her body. He clung to her sometimes, and she felt he didn't really know what he was doing. It never entered his head to wonder what Mairead really thought about it all. He was engrossed only in the immediate physical need they both felt.

On Wednesday night she came up later then usual, and he found he had been waiting for her, looking anxiously down the valley to see if she was on her way. When he did see her coming slowly up the path, a small figure in the distance, he set off down to meet her.

'What's all this, then?' he asked, indicating a rucksack on her back.

'A change of clothes, and a sleeping bag,' she replied.

'You're staying the night?' he asked, and she smiled at him, and he realized he had asked a stupid question.

'I'll take it, then.' He stood in front of her, and turned her round, taking the rucksack off her back, and swinging it on to his own.

''Tis the end of term today,' she reminded him. ''Tis Wednesday. I told you so. I don't have to be in with those wee dears in the morning, and I'd rather be with you instead.'

So she stayed, and the next day it was Vincent who volunteered to walk down the valley and ride her bike into the village for provisions. She didn't argue with him, but she tidied up the place while he was out, and he said nothing about that when he got back again.

They walked on the hills and fished in the river, and at the end of the week he decided he would spend a few more days away. He said it would help to get his leg better. She noticed he was now able to talk about his leg, if only briefly.

They decided to spend a few days by the sea, and so they packed up and walked down the valley together, pushing her bike into the village to lock it up in the school.

They spent another week together, pretending they were a honeymoon couple so they could get into a little boarding house which was all they could afford. They walked along the cliffs, sat on the beaches, swam, talked and drank in the local pub. He found himself talking about feelings he never knew existed. Mairead seemed to be able to draw him out of himself, or maybe it was that he was far from home and able to look at himself from the outside.

He again talked a lot about the North, and about his family. He told her endless stories about his grandfather, old Mr Rafferty, and how he was forever beating Irish history into them all.

Vincent didn't laugh very much, but when he did, she did too, and her deep-throated laugh would send him wild. They would roll around on the springy cliff turf, over pink clumps of sea thyme, and fight and struggle their way to exhaustion.

But Vincent could also go into a deep depression. A black mood would take over, creeping with icy fingers round his stomach, clamping his head. He would stare for ages out to sea, saying little except: 'You don't understand ... you've no idea what it's like up there ... no idea at all.'

'Is it really that bad?' she would ask softly.

'Oh, yes!' he would say, 'bad as that, and worse now.'

He would relapse into silence, and they would walk for miles along the cliffs, wrapped together in the blue sky and sea, warm in a south wind, the song of a skylark quivering above them out of sight.

Sometimes the swirling nightmare of that awful evening in Belfast would come back to him. It was worse at night, senseless and frightening. Figures looming and lunging at him out of the darkness; the red blaze of burning homes; Bryan hauling him away to be shot; his mother screaming at him for informing on his companions; the riot police roaring up the street in a haze of tear gas. The dream changed from night to night, but one thing remained constant: the awful sensation of the pain he was about to feel but never did because he always woke up before the shot was fired.

He would take her hand and squeeze it till it hurt. She never cried out. She knew he was trying to squeeze the black badness out of himself.

She was also beginning to think that he couldn't.

'I don't know what to do,' he once told her. They were sitting in the small pub, tucked away in the corner. It was a concession by the owner, for he didn't approve of women in pubs. But he had a soft spot for Mairead and said she could come in with her young man, but to take him into the small cubicle at the end of the bar. The bar itself continued on into it, but it was screened off from the rest of the drinkers. It was private, too, which helped. So they sat there, under a large old mirror advertising Jameson's Redbreast ten-year-old whiskey.

Vincent had been cheerful all day. They had laughed and joked, lying on the beach, wriggling their toes in the warm sand and rushing with shrieks into the cold blue sea.

Now, in the friendly warmth of the pub, the blackness came down on him again.

'I don't know what to do,' he said despairingly. 'Everywhere up there there is hatred. Hatred that spits at you, with a gun most ways. The Orangemen are arming more and more. . . .'

'Well, wouldn't you arm yourself, if you were them?' she broke in. 'Of course they're going to. They're frightened everything they have will be taken from them.' She pulled a face. 'Mind you, they're not far wrong in thinking that, from what I've heard.'

'I hate them,' he said, his voice tense. 'I feel I could kill them when these things happen. Is that bad?' he asked her. But she just looked quietly back at him, saying nothing, knowing she could make no decisions like that for him.

'It's not just history, you know,' he went on. 'I used to think it was, with my granda going on and on about it. But it is happening now, Mairead, now. Sure, I've seen a whole street burnt out by Protestants. . . .'

'And I suppose you have never seen the results of the IRA in action? You know, those fellas who are defending the Catholic population? It takes two to quarrel,' she went on, 'have you ever thought of that now?'

'Aye, I have that,' he said, bitterly, 'and have you ever

thought what it's like always to be beaten, and beaten by Orangemen?'

He looked down into his glass. The Guinness lay heavy in the bottom.

'I feel I could kill them, but I know I won't. I know I can't. I can't, Mairead. Don't you see?' he said fiercely. 'I just can't kill like that.'

She said nothing. The noise of the pub went on round them, but they sat on in their own small cocoon of isolation.

The next day the depression had lifted. Vincent was up early, full of energy, and after breakfast they persuaded a fisherman to come out with them for a couple of hours, and they fished for mackerel. They took turns at rowing, much to the fisherman's amusement, until their arms ached and they had to give up. They baited hooks and threw the lines over, and pulled in the fish, gleaming silver out of the sea. That evening their landlady cooked them for supper.

It was their last evening. Nothing happened to spoil it. But despite this, Vincent felt a blackness in the background, nudging the edges of his consciousness. He knew the brightness of the moment could never last, just as well as he knew Mairead thought that it would.

When she suggested she come back with him to Belfast for part of her summer holiday, he found to his surprise that he agreed straight away.

And so, for the first time in her life, Mairead went north of the border.

7

Vincent's mother greeted Mairead warmly, though with some surprise. She wasn't used to putting up girlfriends of her sons in the house, and indeed, it was all a bit of a squash, for there wasn't much room. They borrowed a mattress and put it on the floor for her in Sheelagh's room. The two girls hit it off almost immediately.

Old Mr Rafferty himself hadn't even blinked an eye and had hardly stopped talking since she had arrived. He was delighted he had someone from the South to talk to and to show off as a real Irish girl.

As she busied herself around the house, helping where she could, he had kept up a non-stop barrage of Irish history, only pausing now and then to ask her if she really did know what he was talking about

'Yes, indeed, Mr Rafferty,' she would often say, 'we did learn about that in school.' Once she added, 'Mind you, I never knew it all in such fine detail before. You've a fine head for facts and figures, now, Mr Rafferty.'

The old man beamed his pleasure at that. 'Aha, yes,' he would shout, 'and wouldn't you know it better than those two numbskull grandsons of mine. I'm always telling them the history of their country, but they don't take it in. Too busy dashing about the place, they are. Never listen. Never, never.'

'Oh, Mr Rafferty, you're a wee bit too hard on them now. Sure, and aren't they really two fine boys. From what they tell me they know a lot of what's going on. I think they must listen to you more than they let on.'

Mr Rafferty would then humph and grumph and clear his throat. It was about the only thing that would ever halt him in his stride. He would never admit it, but secretly he was very pleased that Mairead thought the boys had taken in his endless Irish lectures.

He was an old man now, his eyes sunk into his face and his neck rising, scrawny, from a collarless shirt. It was old and much patched. A gold collar stud held the top together, and he was forever putting up his hand to feel it, his fingers rubbing the top and turning it round and round.

He was delighted to discover that Mairead was a teacher, for he, too, had once been a teacher, out in the country, away from the narrow grimy streets of the city. In his small village school he had taught generations of children, trying to keep them away from too much of the Church's influence. He didn't really hold with the teachings of the Church, though he had brought up his children as Catholics.

When the war came, though, the population of the village had dropped so much that the Church had, reluctantly, closed the school, and he found himself out of a job. He had moved to Belfast, where all he could find was unskilled work. He had tried for a job in the shipyard, but they weren't keen on taking Catholics, especially unskilled ones. In the end he had been taken on as a clerk, and he had the sense to keep his mouth shut and his Republican ideas to himself while he was working. He knew news of his reputation had come ahead of him, but work was too difficult to get to run any risk of losing it.

In the evenings, though, when he came back tired and hungry after a day's work, he had never failed to talk about Ireland's past. He would get particularly incensed about the years of the Great Famine over a hundred years ago, and how the laws against the Catholics had made so many of them incapable of standing up and defending themselves.

His children had always known when he was about to launch into all this. He would sit back and carefully light his pipe. Then he would pour a small tot of Powers into a glass, or even better, poteen, if he'd been able to come by any. Then he would call to his wife for a glass of water. This he would set by his glass of whiskey, lean back and begin.

'This struggle of ours,' he would say, 'goes back a long way. It is not religious now, whatever you hear of Protestants and Catholics. But it is tied up with religion, totally ... totally. And I'll tell you why. It's because this whole fight of ours to be free, to be Irish, has always been a fight to be a Catholic, without any restrictions, without any penalties.

'Listen here now,' he would go on, leaning forward and jabbing the air with his pipe stem, which would always go out at this point and never be relit until the end of the lecture. 'Listen here and I'll tell you. The Battle of the Boyne, won by William of Orange on his white charger there, it wasn't just a victory for them, by God! It was total annihilation for us.

'You know what happened?' he'd ask.

'Yes, da,' the children would dutifully chorus, 'the penal laws were brought in.'

He'd take a gulp of whiskey at this stage, and wipe the back of his hand across his mouth. One day he was talking along these lines to Mairead. He was well into his stride, more than he had been for some time because his grandchildren, especially Bryan and Vincent, just wouldn't sit and listen to him any more.

'Do you know, girl,' he roared, 'what that does to a people? Do you know, do you know? Well, I'll ...'

'Yes, Mr Rafferty, I do know. Sure am I not a teacher like yourself, and what's more I come from the South anyway. And besides, I've been here a few weeks now.'

'Well? Well?' he demanded. 'What's the answer, then?'

'It means every God-fearing Catholic had a duty, yes, a duty, moral and binding, to evade the law and practise his own religion: to be free to make his own choice. He had to attend illegal meetings. He had to be secret and cunning, always concealing the truth.'

His mouth dropped open in amazement, and for a moment he could say nothing. Then he clapped his hand three or four times on his knee.

'Oh, you're a darling girl,' he shrieked at her. 'Oh, my brightness, you have it right, and that's a deal more than any of those grandsons of mine would. I couldn't have said it better myself.'

'Indeed, Mr. Rafferty,' she said drily. 'I think not, too. 'Tis just as you've said it yourself on three occasions in the past two weeks now. I'm glad I have it right.'

He took no notice of her gentle sarcasm but slapped his hand on his knee again, swallowed his whiskey and banged the empty glass on the table beside him.

'My God! But you're right, you're right. And what would all that do to a man? Those stupid bloody British, they didn't know what it would do. They didn't know how dangerous it was to let that sort of life become a habit.'

She poured him another glass of whiskey, and he took it in his hand, warming it. He looked at Mairead, and she gazed back at him calmly. He liked the girl. She had a spark to her that he appreciated, and, what was more, she was prepared to talk to him, and listen as well. She was going to a dance later that evening, and Vincent was going too. He wondered what sort of hold she had over him, for it wasn't the sort of thing he normally did, especially since his accident. They were young to get married, he thought, it was a mistake. But then he'd heard neither mention it, and wondered at what youngsters got up to these days. It wouldn't have been like that when he was young.

He slumped back in his chair and stared at her. A silence grew between them.

'Mr Rafferty,' she said after a while, 'that was all a long time ago.'

He gave a short, dry laugh and took some whiskey.

'No, you're right. We've improved on that situation a wee bit.' He paused and looked at her closely. 'But in here now,' he tapped his chest with a finger, 'in here, in our hearts, we're empty because the Orangemen have taken all our rights now.'

Mairead didn't answer. She wasn't sure of herself any more in this strange city. People's emotions, and the general tension, were beginning to have an effect on her. There was a bitterness here that she knew of from the history books, and the tales her father had told her down on their farm in County Galway. The theory, however, of the fight against England and Protestant

113

domination, which she knew by rote as she had just demonstrated, had not prepared her for the reality of it. She had been horrified by what she had seen in Belfast, the scenes of devastation and violence which everyone else seemed to take for granted. After one or two attempts at asking why everyone allowed it to go on, she had stopped, and kept her thoughts to herself. 'I don't understand,' she had once said to some friend of Vincent's, and had quickly been silenced by the retort – 'You don't have to live here, so of course you don't understand.'

She came from a large family and was one of seven girls. She had one brother, younger than herself, and it was a happy family, with a lot of laughter and singing and general nonsense going on most of the time. There seemed little of the same atmosphere here in Belfast, in the Malone house, although the old man made a brave attempt at it. They were nice enough people, and she got on well with them, especially Sheelagh, who was younger than she was, and who adored her brothers.

She longed now for the openness of the country life she knew. It wasn't grand, nor sophisticated, but she felt happy there, teaching her small children and walking in the hills. Back in his own environment, Vincent no longer seemed so exciting.

She wondered what her parents would say if they knew where she was, but she had deliberately not let them know. Her grandparents would be even more horrified. She had last seen them that spring, and they and the cottage they lived in seemed little changed from all the other times she had been there as a young girl. The kitchen, where most things went on, was bare and whitewashed, and stairs without bannisters led up to the loft, which was their bedroom.

Her grandmother would wear a coloured shawl tightly wound round her head, for all the world like a gypsy woman, but still sprightly, despite her age. Her husband was frail. They spoke in Irish and chickens picked around on the floor and the back door was invariably open even in the evening, to let in the warm coloured night of the west. The coast there was barren and rocky, and the cottage stood in a tumble of small fields, enclosed by unmortared stone walls.

In some way, the old man sensed her feelings. 'Are you thinking of home?' he asked.

She smiled at him. 'I am that,' she said, and then pulled herself together. She would be going back, and she could sort out her feelings there.

She got up.

'I'm away to get myself ready for this dance tonight,' she said. 'The boys will be back soon, and I don't want to keep them waiting.'

'No, indeed,' said Mr Rafferty, 'that would not do at all.'

She sat on her chair at the edge of the room, her knees tight together, her hands clasped in her lap. Cigarette smoke drifted up to the few streamers in the rafters above, and the music of the fiddles and the accordions swirled across the figures dancing and jumping around on the floor.

Mairead and Sheelagh had spent a lot of time getting ready for this dance, and even more time persuading Vincent to come. He didn't like dancing, and had said so, while Bryan kept quiet in the background.

In front of her, four girls had put their handbags on the floor and were dancing together round them, their movements small and timid. She was staring at them when Bryan came out of the crush round the bar, body hunched protectively over the drinks he was carrying. He pushed his way across to Mairead. His face was damp in the heat; his hair slicked down and his tie made him look more awkward than he really was, and Mairead smiled at him. Bryan grinned back.

'Where's Sheelagh?' he asked, putting his drinks on the floor beside her chair, and then giving her a glass.

'She's away dancing with some fella.'

'Oh!' Bryan peered round. He couldn't see his sister, but he picked up his own drink and went on looking round the room.

'Who's she with?' he said at last.

'I don't know. It was just someone who came and pulled her on to the floor. She seemed to know him,' she added.

'What?' he said after a pause. He leant across slightly his head on one side to pick up her voice above the noise.

'I think she knew him.'

'Oh.'

'Nice-looking fella,' Mairead said to Bryan's ear. He still wasn't looking at her. 'Where's Vince?'

'He's up at the bar. He'll be here shortly.'

'Will he?'

'What?'

'Will he, I said.' He turned to look at her now, wondering if she'd taken too much drink. 'It would be a wonder,' she said softly to herself. 'Sure and he hasn't been near me all evening.'

'What?'

'Nothing.' She raised her voice a bit. "Tis nothing.'

Bryan wished his brother would come back from the bar. He felt very embarrassed sitting here with Mairead, and he'd run out of things to say to her in this noisy dance hall. His inclination was to take her out where they wouldn't have to shout at each other to be heard. He wasn't much good at conversation, and this didn't help. Her foot tapped time to the music, and he wondered if he should ask her to dance. Vince should do that first, he thought, but he wouldn't. He knew Vincent would never drag himself away from the bar. It just wouldn't occur to him to come and look after Mairead, and he certainly wouldn't bother about Sheelagh unless she got into trouble. Bryan was also rather frightened about getting close to Mairead.

'Are you two sitting there all night?' Sheelagh whirled out of the press of dancers and back in again, and Bryan looked blankly at Mairead so that she wouldn't be able to tell that he really wanted to dance with her in case she didn't want to dance with him, and then she smiled at him again. He got to his feet and held out his hand.

'Thank you,' she said simply, holding tight on to his hand, following him onto the floor. 'You don't have to if you don't want to.'.

'That's all right,' he said stiffly, not quite sure what to do, but very conscious of the crowd all round him. He tried to get his feet going to the rhythm of the music, and allowed

Mairead to steer him through to a less crowded corner. They were pushed against each other, and then flew apart as the crowd thinned. He began to get the feel of the music, and she felt very light at the end of his arms.

'That's better,' she smiled at him.

'I'm not very good,' he apologized.

'No, I mean your face.' He looked puzzled. 'You were so stern when you came on to dance.' She laughed suddenly, and threw back her hair. ''Tis great music. Come on,' and she yanked at his arm, twirling her whole body in time to the scraping melody of the fiddles. He caught her mood, and as he relaxed and started to dance with her, he lost track of everything else; the dancers around him, Vincent at the bar, the three fiddlers and the accordionist on the platform, their arms pumping up and down, their feet beating out the time on the floor. He caught her hand and spun her round by her waist, and when the music stopped she clung on to his arm, laughing and panting with strands of long black hair stuck to her face.

'Great, great,' she gasped, 'wasn't that great? Come on, you've earned your drink now, and I need one too.'

They sat and drank and danced again and Sheelagh nudged him in the ribs and said she'd be calling him Vincent next. Bryan looked embarrassed but Mairead just laughed again. She'd had quite a bit of drink taken and what with the excitement and the dancing she was flying high and fast, or so Bryan told her when he felt her getting out of any sort of control at all.

'Rubbish,' she shouted, giggling and slapping him none too gently on both cheeks at once. 'This is how you should enjoy yourself.' She gulped from her glass. 'Are we dancing again, then? Ah no! Sure I've a better idea. Where's Vincent?'

'No,' Bryan cried out, trying to grab her arm, but she'd already gone, pushing her way through to the bar. Bryan followed. He had forgotten about Vincent, and he wished Mairead had too, when he saw his brother push her hand away from his arm.

He stopped and watched. Vincent obviously had more than a few drinks taken, he could see that clearly enough. Mairead's shoulders sagged. He saw the brightness in her switch off. Oh, you bastard, he thought savagely, why do you do it? When she saw him waiting she threw her head up and smiled but it wasn't the same and her eyes were very bright.

'Can I leave you home now?' he asked gently.

Picking up her shawl and handbag she nodded, and followed him out into the night.

The sun came up along the northern shores of the Belfast Lough, touching the massive crag of Cave Hill. It washed over MacArt's Fort on the edge of the cliff and moved quickly down over the wooded slopes to the ornate pile of Belfast Castle.

The grass was soaking from the heavy night dew, and across the lawn were the tracks of a hare about its business in the early light. Here, the summer stillness was broken only by the dawn chorus and the colour of the summer flowers.

But across the slowly waking city, the noise of the shipyards carried far in the clear morning air. The clang of metal on metal, and the deeper thuds as something really heavy was moved.

Almost in the city centre, seagulls wheeled and cried above the mail packets, fussily mooring alongside Donegal Quay after the crossings from Liverpool and Heysham. They were at the head of the line, just below Queen's Bridge, and behind them other ships lay along either side of the narrow Victoria Channel, which led out past the harbour airport, built on reclaimed land, to the open lough itself.

In the forward part of the ship, the first-class passengers still lay asleep in their bunks. So did those in the steerage area who had managed to get cabins, but the bulk of the steerage passengers were only too willing to move off and get back on to firm land.

Wrapped in warm clothes – for some had been on deck all night, sleeping in sheltered places – and clutching parcels and heavy cases, they lurched and shuffled across the deck to the gangway. The crew were already taking the tarpaulins and planks off the holds, and the deck cranes were swinging over to start the business of unloading.

Leaning over the rail, Danny Loughran watched the passengers move away from the ferry and disappear into the huge, soaring sheds that lined the side of the quay. He, too, was well wrapped up, with a scarf round his neck.

He hardly moved, except to stamp his feet from time to time to try and get some warmth into them. He stood where he was instead getting off, as he wanted to, because it gave him a good vantage point to see on to the quayside. He wanted to get off, because he hated sailing. Above all, he hated sailing on the Liverpool – Belfast ferry. He was a terrible sailor and usually very sick. The previous night hadn't been too bad. It was a summer crossing and had been fairly steady. But he still had a stale taste in his mouth, and his guts felt empty. He felt like drinking pints and pints of hot, sweet tea, and eating an enormous breakfast. He wouldn't feel human until he did so.

Over his shoulder was slung an old army pack. It was the only luggage he had. He believed in travelling light, and on this trip, above all, he had had to do just that. He had spent just one day in Liverpool, going across on the night ferry. He had paid a visit to a man he had never met before, and whose name he still did not know. All he knew was that he lived on a council estate on the edge of the city, in the end of a row of terraced houses. The man designed bombs. He was one of the best.

Danny had gone to see him in desperation because of a series of disasters in his own bomb squads. Own goals, he thought viciously, that's what the bastard press called them. Four of them, in four months.

He couldn't afford any more. But he thought he had the problem beaten. The answer lay in the basic design of the bomb. It had been too complicated – one bit of wiring he knew had been a shot in the dark, and so particularly dangerous, especially if the bomb was handled the wrong way.

He had been told that he'd been forcing the pace too much. He had protested that the army were keeping on top, despite the greater difficulties they faced in defusing bombs. So he had had to change the design. He was told firmly not to believe everything that was put out, and it suddenly dawned on him that the army had been leading him on, forcing him to extend himself so far he would make mistakes. That, of course, was just what he had done.

The last of the early departing passengers were straggling off the boat when he saw his man. He was standing by the opening to the shed, his hands in his pockets. He stared at him until the man looked up and caught his eye. He gave no hint of recognition. But then, instead of shaking his head, which Danny knew meant all was clear and he could come ashore openly, he just turned deliberately round and walked off.

Bugger it, thought Danny. It meant he had to get off and slip through the shed and into the town on his own. It hadn't been a signal to go completely to ground – just a warning there was some security activity going on nearby.

There was no point in waiting. Apart from anything else, he was clean. There was nothing on him which would give anyone the slightest idea he did anything out of the ordinary.

His story was that he had been across for the day to discuss a greyhound with a breeder in Liverpool. He had, in fact, done just that, as any check would show.

So he picked up his bag, and walked firmly down the gangplank and across the quay.

The summer morning was fresh and bright. The few people around at this early hour moved briskly along the pavements. No one took any notice of him. He felt more at ease back on his home ground, despite the stricter security and the warning he had just been given.

As he walked round the Albert Memorial and into Victoria Street, he saw the road block. There seemed nothing unusual about it. It looked the same as any others. An olive-green troop carrier was parked half on and half off the pavement. It was squat and ugly – and commonly called a pig. Two policemen and two soldiers were stopping random cars. The rest of the patrol covered them from various positions.

He took all this in at a glance, not slackening his pace at all. He was relieved to see they were only stopping cars, and he walked on firmly past, inches away from the muzzle of a soldier's rifle – a soldier who was crouched down on one knee by the wall, and carried his rifle easily. He didn't look tense, like so many of them did, but watchful, a professional – he'd done it all before.

He looked directly at him, as he had always taught himself and forced himself to do. It was the only way to do it – stare them down. Show no hint of weakness, ever. They went for blood if you showed weakness. The soldier caught his eye for a brief moment and looked away. He could still see Danny out of the corner of his eye. You wee shit, thought Danny, you're good. Won't even let me distract you for a moment. Wouldn't I love to blow you up? See you spattered all over the street. Perhaps I will one day.

He caught a bus from the city centre, out to his home in Ballymurphy. When he got there, his wife was waiting for him. As he walked through the front door, she tossed bacon and sausages into the pan, and followed that up with potato bread and then some tomatoes. She knew when he came home from this sort of trip he was always hungry.

He was, very often, also bad tempered and very irritable.

'There's a cup of tea for you,' she called out, 'and your breakfast will be ready in a minute.' He came into the tiny kitchen, and she turned to him, pushing a strand of hair away from her face. 'Joe Murphy's in the back room. I'll bring it in there.'

'Pour a cup now.'

He took it with him into the back room, closed the door and sat down.

'What was all that about?' he asked. Joe was a big man, slow moving and ungainly. His fat face always looked greasy, and he wore jeans, held up with a big leather belt, with his stomach spilling over the top. He was Danny's intelligence officer.

'Dunno. Usual road block. Put up as the boat docked.'

'Looking for anything in particular?'

'How should I know?'

'Well, did anything happen last night?'

'No, not much. . . . Oh, I see . . . no. No, I don't think it was nothing to do with that.'

'Do with what?'

'What do you mean?'

'Jesus!' Danny exploded. 'You're only after saying the road block was nothing to do with what happened last night. So what did happen last night? I'm not a bloody mind reader.'

'Uh ... nothing ... I'm getting muddled.'

'So am I. What happened last night?'

'Sorry. Nothing happened. It was very quiet. The road block must ... must have been chance. That's all. Nothing to get mad at. Drink your tea.'

His wife came in. 'Here, I've done you a fry.' She slapped a huge plate of food in front of him and followed it with a plate of bread and butter.

The room they were in was small. A heavily patterned and brightly coloured carpet ran from wall to wall. Lace curtains hung across the window, looped up on either side. On one wall was a crucifix, and, above the fireplace, surrounded by yellow-glazed bricks, was a religious picture. There was a settee and an armchair, covered in brown. Danny sat on the settee, his food in front of him on a low table. He crouched forward and ate quickly, washing his mouthfuls down with gulps of tea.

Joe waited until Danny had finished eating, wiped his mouth on his handkerchief, and sat back. Then he asked:

'What's up now?'

Danny scratched his ear. 'I reckon I know what's been going wrong. Partly, anyhow. I'm going to kip for an hour. Then I want to see the lads. Usual place, behind Stracey's. Better make it an hour and a half from now. And I want all four of them. Right?'

'Right.'

'Do you want a cup?'

'No, thanks, I've had one, waiting on you.'

Joe got up, and went to the door. He turned. 'Hour and a half, then?'

'Hour and a half,' said Danny.

The four men were waiting for him at Stracey's. They sat in the stuffy back room, with the windows shut and covered with blackout material.

It was a well-guarded pub. There was only one apparent entrance, and that was round the back, for the normal front doors had been blocked off. Customers had to come down a side street, through a door in the wall, and up a narrow alleyway before they got in. By the first door, as they entered the alleyway, there was always a man, sometimes two, lolling around on the stack of beer barrels.

Once along and inside the pub door there was another man, officially there this time, with a little desk and a notice which said, 'Security – all bags checked here.' This man would examine any parcels or bags brought in and give the men a frisking. Those who went to the pub sometimes noticed that the frisking was a good deal more efficient and thorough than many they were used to getting in other parts of the city.

Everyone who passed this search, and no one had yet failed it, then went right into the bar itself. But at times, one would nod casually to the security man and walk straight on and up the stairs which lay ahead. As these people turned the corner on the stairs, they would be confronted by yet another man. This was never a surprise to anyone who came up these stairs. Only those who were meant to ever came up at all. If, by chance, some stranger did get through, then he would be very surprised at the guard on the stairs, because the guard was always armed, very obviously, with a sawn-off shotgun.

Danny passed through this security screen with hardly a nod in anyone's direction. They all knew him well and were waiting for him.

Danny was one of the new breed of IRA leaders. He was young, about twenty-four, and he was tough and militant. He had been one of the first to press for a breakaway section, after the appalling loss of face they'd suffered in the early days, when the Protestant gangs had rampaged unhindered through the Catholics' streets, rioting and burning them down. He remembered standing, almost helpless with rage, with nothing but a brick in his hand, watching armed men slip past the flames, and toss petrol bombs into yet more houses. One man, one old guard of the IRA, had managed to find his revolver somewhere. He had probably dug it up from his back garden.

But he had had a go. About the only person to do so or, more to the point, able to do so. That had helped a bit. But never again, he had sworn at the time. Never, never, never would they be caught like that again.

As he'd helped to reorganize the housing of the homeless and the growing tide of refugees who were fleeing South across the border, he had started to ask questions. Why had this happened? The only answers he could get said that the IRA had decided to 'go political,' and stop using guns and force to achieve what they wanted. He had argued that this was madness, especially now. Others had argued, too. They had pleaded with Dublin Command for guns, ammunition.

They desperately needed help, they said, up in Belfast. Anyone could see that. And they would need it in Derry, and other places, too, before long. They had to have some way of protecting themselves.

The exchange was long, and furious, and desperate. It failed. And so the split came. Those left behind to carry out their wet, pussy-footing policy came to be known as the Officials. The men who were looking for guns, ammunition, explosives and anything else to fight with, became the Provisionals.

He had been one of the first to go to a training camp in the wild Antrim hills round Glenarrif. It had lasted two weeks, and he supposed he had learned something, if only that it was a very uncomfortable way of living. They had three old Lee Enfields, and a small amount of ammunition, one Thompson machine gun and four .45 Colt revolvers – the traditional IRA weapon. They had drilled and practised with these, running up and down over the hills, hiding in ditches and behind walls. They had, in the end, been allowed to fire half a dozen shots each from the weapons. That was about the size of it.

But what had interested him most of all was the visit of the bomb officer. He had shown them two Mills grenades. He had explained how they worked, but that had been all, because the man only had two of them. But he had also shown them how to make their own bombs. Nothing very sophisticated, sugar and sodium chlorate, ordinary weedkiller they could get anywhere. There were a few spare fuses and detonators, and they were able to practise a bit with those. Danny had produced a bomb which had quite spectacular results. Instead of using a cardboard box as the container, he had got hold of an old bit of piping. He had rammed a plug in solid one end, poured in his mixture, fixed the detonator and fuse, and sealed up the other end.

He had waited until last to demonstrate his bomb, and he told no one what he was going to do. He waited while the others, one by one, set up their bombs, lit the fuses and then retired to a safe distance to watch them blow up.

When his turn came, he merely said, 'Watch this. I'm going to throw mine.' And with that he had lit his fuse and hurled the cast-iron pipe into the hedge some twenty yards in front of them all. Everyone had remained rooted to the spot, first staring at the place in the hedge where the bomb had landed, then at Danny.

It went off with a fair old crack, a cloud of smoke and the whistle of flying metal. The visiting instructor had his hat whipped off his head by one piece and went very white when he realized what had happened. Danny was firmly instructed 'for Chrissake be careful, those things are dangerous,' but his kudos rose enormously. From that moment on he decided to stick with making bombs.

He looked around at the men in the room who were waiting for him to begin – waiting to know what he'd been able to achieve during his trip across the water.

He began, quietly, giving them a run-down of all he had done, only he didn't tell them exactly where he had been. Only one man knew that – one of his best men, although he didn't like him much himself. Jimmy Hannahan had worked for him since he'd come out of prison some time before. He had been put inside for murder but had escaped. He kept very much to himself now, keeping out of sight most of the time, but he was a hard, acid wee man, and very useful, and Danny trusted him.

He turned to him. 'Jimmy, I want those alterations sorted out quickly. I want them done fast.'

'OK.'

'I want to start hitting back. We want them angry. We want

the Prods out and fighting. Then we can really hit them. They're all talk now ... they don't care how much the military is hit. So get at them,' he emphasised. 'Shops, stores, you know the sort of thing. Don't worry that they are soft targets – they still matter.'

'I don't worry.' Jimmy's hand fluttered up to scratch his ear. 'I think you should be hitting people, but. That would bring them out.'

'Just you get on with hitting their property. You know where their loyalties lie – more to the half crown in their pocket than the crown across the water. Get their prestige buildings – hotels, if you can make it. But get it done.'

Jimmy nodded briefly, and the meeting broke up. One by one they left, until only Danny remained. He sat for a while, thinking. Then he, too, left, and the small dark room was empty again.

8

The breeze, gusting up the Belfast Lough, heeled the yachts over so that their small, triangular, white sails angled close to the choppy water. The sky was blue, and the sun brought life to the flowers massed around the city hall, which, with its green tarnished copper dome, looked like a huge Victorian wedding cake.

If a city could have been scrubbed clean of the blood and guts, and the dusty, lung-choking harshness of an endless civil war, then it was on a day like this. The dark night had passed with its heavy potential for death unfulfilled. No small child lay waiting to be measured for its white coffin. No young man had another death or injury lying easily on his conscience.

The dust carts had gathered up the debris, at least in those areas where they could operate. Rain had washed the streets, and even the puddles sparkled.

Mairead and Sheelagh also sparkled that morning. It was a crisp day, one to get the blood tingling and the brain racing. A day to feel alive and active. The two girls giggled and chatted together as only two young girls can do.

They were going shopping after breakfast. It would be window shopping at first, and maybe later they would do some buying. Sheelagh was looking for a long red dress.

They had a five-minute walk to get to the Falls Road where they would find a black cab. The first time she had done this Sheelagh had felt terribly grand, catching a cab into the city. But that had been long ago, and the novelty had worn off, and anyway it wasn't really a cab, but a sort of mini bus. All the real buses had been taken off these routes because so many had been hijacked and burned, or made into barricades. Some said the cabs were run by the Provos, to make money. A stupid story, she thought. With the place stiff with British soldiers that was very unlikely.

The driver, she saw with some satisfaction, was someone whom she had been to school with. He nodded cheerfully as she and Mairead pushed their way on to the back seat.

Fifty yards from where Sheelagh and Mairead sat in their black cab waiting to be taken into the city, two other young people were preparing to do exactly the same.

One was a young boy of nineteen. His long greasy hair fell dankly on to his shoulders, framing a thin face. He wore thick-soled shoes and jeans, and his denim jacket fitted too tightly, the sleeves barely reaching his wrists. The young girl with him looked about the same age and was dressed in the same way. In fact, she was a year older, and the boy's sister.

They, too, were excited, but in a different way. The palms of their hands were sweating, and their stomachs felt empty and small. They didn't realize it, but the adrenalin was pumping round their bodies, boosting them up for what they had to do.

The boy looked again at his watch.

'Five minutes.' The girl nodded, saying nothing. She knew that in five minutes it would be half past ten. Then they would move. Not before, not after. They had been very firm about that. Keep it all very simple, they had said. Then there is less to go wrong. The whole thing should only take half an hour.

Again the boy looked at his watch. . . . This time he said nothing. Hardly a minute had gone by. . .

The girl sat beside him, her hands clenched tight and gripped between her knees. She wore a brown coat with a faded check pattern over her jeans. At her feet, just to one side, sat her shopping basket. It had an old jersey stuck in the top.

They both sat well back from the window, they'd been told to do that as well. It was an empty house, and above all they didn't want to attract any attention. They would go out the back way, turn left, walk down the street, turn left again at the end, and walk straight on until they came to the black cab stand. They would wait their turn with everyone else, and get into a taxi in the usual way. Time and time again they'd been told to do nothing unusual. This was most important. Too many things had been going wrong recently, and they wanted this operation to work properly.

'No fuck ups,' they'd been told tersely by a man they'd never seen before. He had put a cardboard box carefully into her shopping bag and said, without expression, 'Do exactly as you're told, and it'll all go like clockwork.'

With the taxi full at last, the driver moved off, weaving his way down the Falls Road towards the city centre. On either side the pavements were full of people hurrying along, or moving in and out of the small shops and past the gaps and empty spaces left by fire and bombs.

At street corners and outside pubs were the inevitable clusters of old men and young boys. They leant against the walls, hands in pockets, staring out across the street, waiting and watching for nothing.

"Tis a grand day,' said Mairead to no one in particular.

An older woman sitting across from her, their knees almost touching in the cramped space, looked at her closely.

'It is grand,' she agreed, and then said, 'You're from the South, then?'

'I am that,' said Mairead.

'Agh,' the woman sighed. 'I went there once. 'Twas lovely. You don't get them young hooligans there.' And she chatted on about her visit.

'Time to go!' the boy said suddenly. He had been staring hard at his watch for the past thirty seconds, willing it to move on round at the same time. He felt cold inside.

'Come on,' he said roughly to the girl.

'Do I have to carry that?' she said, still sitting on her chair, and looking at her shopping bag.

'Yes, you do. I'd look a right fool carting that old shopping bag around town with you. You carry it. You're the girl doing the shopping.'

She took a deep breath, stood up and carefully took hold of her bag.

'Will you carry it like a shopping bag?' he said, biting off his words. 'Don't make it look as if it was full of eggs.'

She remembered the man saying that. So her brother was remembering things, too. She supposed that was good. She wasn't too sure of her brother. He was always full of his own bravado, but she wasn't sure he thought about anything too hard. Still, if he remembered what they'd been told, and stuck to it, they'd be all right.

They walked quickly out of the back door, turning abruptly left into the street without looking round. She reached out and took hold of his hand, and for a moment he looked shocked.

'You're my boyfriend,' she said simply, looking straight ahead. Acutely embarrassed, he held her hand, and they walked on. The eyes of the street corner watchers followed them.

As casually as they could, they walked into the city centre and made for the coffee shop that had been chosen for them. It was packed with people, but the girl managed to find two seats while the boy bought two cups of coffee. Again, that was exactly what they'd been told to do.

When they finished they got up, paid and walked out.

Under the table, where they had been sitting, they had left their shopping bag.

Dr Jennifer Platton was tired. She had been up late the night before attending to an emergency case, a perforated appendix which had become complicated and taken much more time to deal with than normal. Then this morning she had had her usual list of surgery, removing a bit of gut from one patient, sorting out an ulcer in another.

She nodded her thanks to the operating nurse and walked out. In the lounge, she sank into a large armchair with a cup of black coffee and relaxed.

She'd worked in the Royal for nearly two years now, and it

was something she would never have missed. She had always wanted to do surgery, and she had tried hard, and very successfully, to get as wide an experience as possible. For wide experience, she thought, nothing could beat the Royal.

She had been through just about everything. The hospital was only five minutes from the city centre. Whenever there was trouble the ambulances would arrive, singly for shootings, in waves for bomb explosions. Within minutes of an incident injured bodies would arrive. At first she had been shocked, shocked by the, to her, senseless killings and appalling injuries. She could still be shocked, but by now she was able to keep a protective cover around her. She didn't think she was hardened to it, probably just immunized.

After taking a shower she felt rather better, and went along to the TV room in the east wing. Here, the windows looked out on to the Grosvenor Road that led down to the city centre. It was almost a straight run all the way down.

It was very peaceful. She should have been off duty by now, but she had offered to stand in for another doctor for a couple of hours, and would be tied to the hospital for most of the time. But she would be able to get away later in the afternoon for a short while, and she remembered there were some things she had to pick up from a store in town.

She checked her bleeper that was switched on and closed her eyes.

Mairead and Sheelagh pushed their way through the crowd of shoppers in the city centre, moving from shop to shop looking for the dress. They had seen one beautiful dress but decided it really was too expensive. Mairead had tried to persuade Sheelagh to buy it, but Sheelagh had firmly said no. She was very careful with her money, and she was determined not to be extravagant.

Mairead offered to buy them lunch at a little restaurant off Royal Avenue, but Sheelagh again said it would be a waste of money, they could have something when they got home. Mairead then persuaded her that they should at least go and have a coffee.

The coffee shop was crowded when they got there, and they waited for a few minutes for a couple of seats to become free.

'Here, over here, Sheelagh.' Mairead clutched Sheelagh's arm and pulled her across through the tightly packed tables to a seat by the window.

They sat down, smiling briefly at two other girls who were also sitting there. Sheelagh reached down into her shopping bag and pulled out a piece of blue cloth. She held it up to the light by the window.

'Well, now!' said Mairead, looking around. 'Do we sit here all morning waiting for someone to bring us a cup of coffee, or do we get it ourselves? Get it ourselves, I think. Wait here,' she said to Sheelagh. 'I'll nip over and get them.'

She got up and moved away to the counter, while Sheelagh sat and looked out of the window. She felt a bit unhappy that she hadn't found what she wanted. Everything was so expensive. There were some shops further down the avenue she hadn't tried yet. They'd do that after their coffee.

Mairead pushed her way back, carefully holding two cups of coffee. She had spilled a little in the saucers. She put them on the table, sat down and swept her hair back out of her eyes.

'Thanks,' said Sheelagh, pulling a cup towards her, and spooning in some sugar. She looked up at Mairead. 'Has Vincent said anything?'

'You must be joking. He wouldn't say anything. He'd sooner swim across the lough in winter than ask me that.' She stirred her coffee. 'No, if I'm to marry Vincent, then I shall have to drag him to the church.' She looked at Sheelagh and smiled. 'That's one thing I will never do. He's got to ask me, and it's going to be a fair old time before he gets round to that.'

'Oh, he's terrible!' said Sheelagh crossly. 'What's the matter with him? He's no brains in his head at all.'

'Well, now, I wouldn't say that quite, but he's a lot to think about at the moment.'

'All he's got to think about is where he's going to get his next drink.'

'That's not very fair. He's not really like that.'

'You don't think so? Well, he's been my brother for a long

time now, and I know him well. He's always been a bit funny that way.'

'What do you mean?'

'Well, he's sort of … I don't really know. He goes very quiet sometimes, talks to no one. Gets very moody and cross with everyone. There's time he hasn't a civil word for anyone.'

'I know, I know,' Mairead said quietly, 'but I think I can deal with that. If I have the time.'

Halfway up the Falls Road was Mrs Mullen's sweetie shop. It was a small shop, full of bits and pieces. Everything she sold was in small amounts. She was used to handing over just an egg and maybe a bit of bacon for someone's breakfast. Or a couple of cigarettes. She kept a plate of them loose on the counter. She had learned long ago that people never thought ahead. It had been an unconscious process, the knowledge just seeping in. It wasn't that they didn't have any money. Dear, no, she told herself. It was just that they lived for each moment, and so they were always forgetting to lay in provisions.

Her doorbell clinked. It hadn't rung properly for almost two years now, but her ear was tuned to the sound. She shuffled out of her back room in her slippers.

A young couple stood there. She couldn't see much detail in their faces, for her eyes weren't what they used to be, and they were standing silhouetted against a sun-filled window. Two dark figures, she thought.

The boy asked for two ice-creams. His voice cracked slightly as he did so, and the girl giggled. Mrs Mullen peered at the two dark shapes over her glasses. Up to no good, she thought crossly.

Mrs Mullen often thought young people were up to no good, and as time went on, nothing happened to change that attitude. Indeed, she put down the troubles of the past few years to the fact that young people were now so ill disciplined, and had so little to keep themselves occupied.

She watched these two suspiciously as they went out through the door licking their ice-creams.

In the large red-brick hospital, not a mile from the shop, Dr Jennifer Platton lit a cigarette.

She knew she was smoking too much, but she couldn't stop. Not only was she feeling tired, she was feeling very tense. She told herself it was the troubles outside that made her feel like this, and that once they were sorted out, she'd be able to cut down again.

She looked at her watch. The doctor she was standing in for would be back in about half an hour. As long as there weren't any emergencies, any more perforated ulcers or whatever, then she felt she could just about get through the rest of the day without too much trouble.

In the coffee shop, Sheelagh and Mairead sat squashed together on small chairs at a small table. Sheelagh wondered if the discomfort was worth it.

'Do you fancy another cup?' she asked.

'Not at all!' Mairead replied, raising her eyes. 'I think we should be off – if we can ever get out of here – and get round the rest of the shops before dinner time.'

'OK then. Let's go.'

'Hang on a wee minute. I'll go and pay for this.'

Mairead got up to walk across to the cash register. Sheelagh bent down to pick up her shopping bag.

Three-quarters of the way up the Falls Road, a young couple were looking for a telephone kiosk. They couldn't find one that was working. The two they had found had had the phones ripped out. However, had they managed to find one that worked, it would have been of little use.

'Do you have that two pence I gave you?' the girl asked.

The boy searched his pockets.

'I have not,' he said. 'What happened to it?'

'Look again!' the girl demanded.

Again he searched his pockets. He looked up at her.

'Jesus! I must have given it to that old woman for the ices.'

The two men who'd organized the bomb planting operation

were well pleased with the way it had gone. For once, every-thing seemed to have worked as they had planned. So often in the past, some little thing had gone wrong during the compli-cated procedure, and there had been a disaster. This time, they thought, things should be different.

The man who had designed the bomb had kept it simple. There was no anti-handling device in it, for the plan was that it should go off before any explosives' expert would get to it.

He had impressed on the bomb carpenter the vital necessity for making a strong but very light box to hold the bomb. It had to go into a cardboard container when it was finished, and be small enough to fit into a normal shopping bag. The electrician who designed the circuit was a man with a lot of experience. He was a professional electrician, who knew his job back-wards. It was the first bomb he had worked on, and he had taken a great deal of care soldering the circuits. But he, too, had been told not to put in any anti-handling devices. There were to be no extra micro-switches, and no false circuits to confuse anyone who might try to defuse it.

Further down the organizational pyramid, the bomb officer had taken over, and carefully inserted the explosives and the detonator. There had been room for only three pounds of gelignite. But it had been good stuff, smuggled away from a store in the South only half an hour after it had arrived from the closely guarded explosives factory. There was no identification on it, no means of telling its source.

There were two bomb layers, a young boy and his sister. They were to lay it on their own. There would be no armed back-up for them – no one to hold people at gun point while it was being laid. They'd been told to leave it under a table in a city centre coffee house, and phone a warning half an hour before it was due to go off.

Sheelagh found her shopping bag and stood up. Mairead had just turned from the table.

At that moment, only a few feet from them, two metal con-tacts came together, and the bomb exploded. It was the one part of the operation which didn't go according to plan. It should not have gone off for another forty-two minutes.

The shock front of the blast waves spread out, at first faster than the speed of sound. The wave consisted of a short positive phase, followed by a much longer, but less distinct, negative phase. Heavy obstacles deflected some of the waves. Other solid material was changed instantly into gas, creating an enormous increase in volume and pressure.

The effect on people was devastating. The two girls nearest the bomb died instantly. As their arms and legs were torn off, the energy wave went into their mouths and upwards taking away the tops of their heads. In the milli-seconds that followed, they lost more of their bodies, until all that was left was their spines, held together by vertebrae.

Mairead and Sheelagh, only a couple of feet further away, knew nothing. They just swam into black unconsciousness.

The shock wave, travelling at some 13,000 miles an hour, had also pulverized the floor immediately beneath the bomb. But it slowed down quickly, and the rest of the damage was done by the blast wave which followed it, at about half the speed.

It had the pressure of pent-up gases behind it, and it went through the coffee shop tearing off limbs, perforating ear drums, smashing furniture which in turn became deadly missiles.

For a few micro-seconds, a fireball went with it, singeing hair, removing eyebrows and eyelashes.

The blast wave bounced back off the side walls, reinforcing the original explosion. As more furniture was hurled around, the roof collapsed on to the people below in a cloud of dust.

The screaming started almost straight away.

In the television room, Jennifer Platton was stubbing out her cigarette when she heard the dull thud of the explosion. Moments later she heard the ambulances start to go out.

'That sounds like trouble,' she said. 'I wonder where that one was?'

One of the interns looked up and shrugged his shoulders.

'We'll know soon enough, I expect.'

Jennifer looked at her watch. The doctor she was standing in for was due at any moment. If he arrived before a casualty, he would be able to deal with it, and she'd be able to go and get some rest.

She lit another cigarette, and sat back again.

It seemed only a few minutes later that she heard the sound of ambulance bells. She looked up automatically out of the window. It was a very distant sound, and normally if there was a casualty on the way, her bleeper would have gone off.

She stared down the road. At the far end she could see not just one blue flashing light, but what seemed to her like a continuous stream of blue lights. She could see at least eight coming up the road towards her. Eight! she thought. That could only mean some surgical disaster. My God! and I'm only sitting here with two interns. They were both with her now, all at the window together. She waited no longer.

'Let's go!' she shouted.

The three of them ran down the corridors to the main emergency entrance. When they got there, the first ambulance had already emptied itself of patients.

Emergency was starting to fill up, and Jennifer stood for a moment and thought hard. I mustn't let this get out of hand, she said to herself. Now think! What is the most important thing? Control! Keep the system working.

A nurse pushed by to the phone on the wall. It was the only available phone. She picked it up and dialled. She was very brief when it was answered.

'Explosion. Lots of casualties. Come.' She was phoning the east wing. This was the residents' wing. With a pool of about thirty doctors. At this time of day there would be about twelve or thirteen there, and a lot of students.

Every few seconds, it seemed, the big plastic doors swung open, and ambulance men pushed in more people on stretchers. Nurses were already directing the flow. The most seriously injured went straight into the resuscitation area. An anaesthetist was already there, sedating the first casualties and starting to set up the tubes and IV's ready for surgery.

The routine was working smoothly. The less seriously

injured were being taken to individual cubicles. Those who were just shocked would be given some tea, and then put out again. Two medical students had arrived and were helping with the initial examinations as the stretchers came through the doors.

There was a eight or nine in by now. Some patients looked terribly injured. She saw an ambulance man she knew.

'Tommy!' she called out. 'How many?'

'A hundred. Maybe more. It was a coffee shop and store.'

'My God! A hundred.'

She fought down a momentary rise of panic at the thought of the work load they would all face.

She called over to a student.

'Keep by this phone for the time being. I don't want everyone using it. Get on to the main block first. Tell them, briefly, what's happening. I want their four theatres prepared. Then phone all the other theatres ... neuro-surgical, orthopaedic ... all of them. Get them to do the same. And anyone else you can think of.'

She moved back into the resuscitation area. It was a gory sight. A number of broken bodies were lying there, festooned with tubes and drips, very still amongst the comings and goings of the doctors and nurses. The head nurse came across to her.

'It's pretty bad, doctor,' she said. 'If the rest are like this, we're in trouble. Sixteen limbs missing from this lot alone – either totally missing or partially amputated.'

'Right. Let's get our priorities worked out. We can get the worst of this lot into the theatres pretty fast. I'll start writing them up.'

Jennifer glanced quickly at her watch. Hardly three minutes had gone by, and she knew then that the rest of the day was going to go in a swirl and haze of unconnected memories, one patient merging into another, the operations, the scrubbings, the calls, decisions, distraught relatives, deaths, severed limbs, labelled and put into sacks to wait for the forensic boys at the end of the night.

She pushed her hair back, walked into the cubicle and started.

Sheelagh lay on the cubicle stretcher. She was aware of little except constant swirling black waves, a floating sensation, as if she was on the edge of the sea, floating in and out, in and out on small waves lapping up on the beach. Someone was calling her. She thought it was her name, she couldn't be sure. But she knew someone was calling her, desperately needed her.

She just went on floating, in and out, in and out, the black waves lapping over her. Her thoughts seemed to blow away from her. Each time she thought she was about to grasp an idea, work out what was happening, it all floated away beyond the reach of her outstretched fingers. She groped after them, but it was too tiring, and she found she'd stopped groping without making any decisions about it herself. In and out, up and down, gently she floated on her black sea by a black shore, her thoughts just out of reach.

Her long black hair lay spread about her face, white, almost transparent. There was no injury there. It was a pretty face.

Jennifer looked down. The girl lying in front of her looked so small, so tiny, she was almost like a baby. She was white as a sheet. There was little or no blood left in her.

Jennifer noticed immediately that the IV was being fed into the girl's jugular vein. This was unusual. It wasn't the best place, and then she saw why.

One of her legs was gone below the knee. The other had been torn off higher up. Her right arm was hanging on by a bit of skin. She only had one whole limb left.

That was why she looked so small, and why the drip was into her jugular. She hadn't another decent vein left to put it into. She was in deep shock. She had pumped out almost all the blood she had. Jennifer checked all the obvious bleeding sites. They had all been controlled. The girl, Jennifer decided, just had to have more blood, and quickly.

She would get a second IV set up, and find a vein in the girl's left arm. She would also get a pump on to it, to squeeze the fluid in faster. This girl would have to be the first on to the operating table. She must be the worst casualty, Jennifer thought, anything worse and there would be nothing left at all.

In the background she could hear someone screaming,

above the cries and moans and general pain of the casualty and resuscitation areas. Some girl kept shouting out, in a very weak voice, the name Sheelagh. Sheelagh, she was calling, are you all right? I'll look after you.... Sheelagh ... Sheelagh.

The girl who was shouting was further down the room. Jennifer went to her and found she was also badly hurt, though not as badly as the first girl she had seen. The nurse was trying to quieten her down, but even under sedation her shouting was an automatic shock response to her injuries. Nothing would stop her.

One leg was badly broken, with a lot of damage round the knee. Her face was covered by a rash, evenly spread right across her face. Jennifer had seen that sort of rash before. It was caused by thousands of minute splinters; wood, pulverized by the explosion and sent flying across the room at supersonic speeds. They were so small, and there were so many of them that they would never come out.

Jennifer knew the girl was scarred for life.

Mairead was more conscious than Sheelagh. She knew something terrible had happened. She was in great pain, but she couldn't reach Sheelagh. She didn't know where she was or what was happening. She was aware of bright lights and some movement. There was pain in her throat. Apart from that pain, the only sensation she had was of being in a huge cavern, where everything was muffled and quiet and where there were no sharp noises.

There was only a sharp pain in her body. What had happened? Where was Sheelagh? My God! Sheelagh! I'll look after you. Sheelagh, Sheelagh, are you all right?

Around Jennifer the whole casualty area was now working at full pace, but it was only just coping with the enormity of the disaster.

The casualty clerks and other staff had come in. They had to get down the names and addresses of those who could talk. It was all very crowded, there always seemed to be ten times more people around than there should be.

She went from stretcher to stretcher, writing up the patients, assessing which should have priority in the operating rooms, keeping out of nurse's way, but trying to ensure she also kept an overall grip on what was going on.

On the sixth stretcher she came across a young man with the worst injuries yet. His head was badly damaged, and there was a huge wound across his chest. Three IV's fed into him, and a nurse stood next to him.

'I don't think he's going to do, doctor.'

Jennifer examined him quickly. 'There's a chance,' she said. 'But I think you're probably right.'

'His father is here.'

'What!'

'His father is here. I've told him the boy's about to go into surgery.'

Jennifer looked at the boy. It was touch and go whether he would make it. She hated having relatives in at a time like this. That side of the operation was always difficult to control. Her job was to save lives. She hadn't the time to console relatives.

But the boy might not make it off the operating table, she knew that.

'Tell the father he can sit here until the boy goes into surgery. But warn him . . . warn him.'

'I've already done that.'

'And keep him away from me. I haven't time to talk to anyone. Let me alone.'

'Very well, doctor.'

Twenty minutes had gone by now since the first of the casualties had come crashing noisily through the swing doors. It was time to get them on to the operating tables. She would be assisting the senior orthopaedic surgeon, Dr Golding. She decided it was time to scrub up and get ready.

She had seen eight ... no ... it must have been about fifteen patients. These had been the worst. She realized that others coming in now would be less seriously injured.

She walked up the corridor. The girl who had been screaming for Sheelagh was still screaming as she was wheeled to the operating room. From what the nurse had said, Jennifer presumed the girl they would be dealing with first was Sheelagh.

The anaesthetist had the girl just about ready. Pentothal had been injected into the small body, and she had been intubated and anaesthetized.

Because she had lost a lot of blood, the anaesthetist had taken a CVP line and slipped the long tiny tube down the girl's jugular and into her heart. It had taken about thirty seconds to slide in, and then she had connected it up to a manometer. Going right down into the heart it would measure the actual contractions of the heart muscles, and so give an accurate reading. The mercury would jump up and down. The less blood, the lower the reading. It should read eight or ten millimetres of mercury.

Jennifer scrubbed up. She slid into her green gown, mask and gloves and was ready. Dr Golding was ready too.

She glanced at the manometer. It read barely two. The girl was still in a extremely shocked condition. She was also in a terrible mess. Jennifer started to re-check there were no major vessels still bleeding. The girl couldn't afford to lose any more blood.

'Has the blood come yet?' asked Golding, looking at her over the top of his mask.

'Not yet.'

'How much is coming? Six pints?'

'Yes.' She nodded.

'OK. Let's get to work. We'll clean up first. Scrubbing brush,' he called out and took one.

'Scrubbing brush,' said Jennifer. She would take the other leg.

She held out her hand and took the scrubbing brush. Bomb blasts usually peppered people with grit; very often they would be tattooed over the exposed, and even unexposed, parts of their bodies. This was the only chance she and Golding would have of cleaning up. Straight scrubbing.

She took the left leg. Working steadily, she used the scrubbing brush straight on the raw stump, cleaning the ragged edges, working out the grit and dirt. It took her about ten

142

minutes of hard work. She finished about the same time as Dr Golding.

Normally, as the assistant, she would do the cleaning up at leisure. There wasn't time now, and they both worked flat out.

'Scalpel.'

She took the scalpel and cleaned away some of the ragged flaps. Across the table, his head almost touching hers, Golding did the same.

She wanted a clean stump, but it was important to leave enough so there would be a cushioning effect for the artificial leg that would follow.

She preferred using a scalpel all the time. It was the best way of getting rid of dead tissue. With her left hand she clamped the forceps on to the raw flesh and cut through. She never used scissors. They had a tendency to crush as they divided the flesh. Anything that was left she wanted to be as vital as possible.

There didn't seem to be any other foreign bodies in this stump. It was amazing, she thought, where some bits of metal got to. Sometimes she would find a small opening, maybe only half an inch wide. She would explore it with a finger and often find a huge lump of shrapnel behind.

As she cut she irrigated the wound with an effervescent hydrogen peroxide. She just poured it on. There was nothing very delicate about this sort of surgery. It was a race against time. A race against the effects of massive shock and dehydration.

The stump looked clean now. She couldn't be sure it was surgically clean, so she didn't close it. That could be done later.

Dr Golding looked across at what she was doing.

'Bring the ends together,' he said.

'Just put on a padded bandage,' she told the nurse. 'I hope our luck will hold. We've had very little gas gangrene so far.'

She nodded, her eyes peering over the top of her mask, quiet and calm. She bandaged up the stump.

The blood from the bank had arrived and was being steadily pumped in. A bit of colour was coming back into Sheelagh's face. The pressure was coming up. The normal pressure should

143

be 120/80. That was the pressure Sheelagh's heart should give to her whole circulatory system with one squeeze, one contraction: 120 on the squeeze, 80 when the pressure came off.

Jennifer glanced at the manometer. The pressure was still way down.

She finished the stump, turned to let a nurse wipe the sweat from her forehead, for it was hot under the theatre lights and the strain was beginning to tell. Moreover, she suddenly realized that she had been on duty for a very long time.

She looked down at the arm. It was hanging by only a few bits of fibre and skin. She saw it was completely devulsed. It wasn't cleanly cut at all, it was absolutely mangled from the wrist down.

Dr Golding ordered some more blood. It was essential to have enough in the body to keep the girl's heart operating. If there wasn't, she could be in serious trouble.

'What about this?' asked Jennifer, indicating the arm.

Golding came round and had another look at it.

'Do you think we can save it?' she asked.

Golding glanced up at the monitors on the walls. Then he picked up the arm, and his gloved hands felt over it, gently probing. He shook his head.

'The bones are all gone,' he said. 'They're traumatized. Look ...' he picked up the arm again, 'all the muscle tissue here is gone.'

'So it's a non-starter?'

'It's a non-starter,' he repeated simply.

Jennifer didn't hesitate. She took the scalpel, and together they finished off what had really been an amputation in the first place.

'Pressure's going up,' said the anaesthetist, sounding happier for the first time that night.

Jennifer felt happier too. They had been at it now for over two hours. It had been very exhausting, physically and mentally. She felt great the girl was still alive. A wave of relief washed over her.

'At least we've managed to do something for this wreck of a human body,' she said.

There seemed to be no other injuries. She examined her chest as well as she could. Nothing apparently there, she decided, but there was always the risk of the lung being damaged by the blast.

That probably wouldn't show for a day or two. But if the lining of the lung had been damaged, fluid and blood would pour into the lungs. If this happened, there would be a serious problem of respiration. It was something she could do nothing about now, she would just have to worry about it later, if it happened.

'Just wheel her to the ward as she is,' Golding said. 'It'll save doing it all over again. She's to be on anaesthetics all night. Keep that ventilator going, too. She'll probably have to have it for two or three days.'

'Well,' said Jennifer, 'I hope she'll pull through all that. It's been a terrible shock to her system.'

'I think it should do. She should be OK now. Jennifer ...' he put an arm on her shoulder, 'come on. Let's get a coffee. Thanks for your help on that one. But I don't think we're over yet.'

Sheelagh was wheeled out, and in the corridor an elderly man was waiting to come in. His white hair was matted with blood.

Jennifer walked past. She took off her gown and threw it into the tub. Her mask and gloves followed.

Behind her, the nurses and orderlies started to clean up the mess and debris in the operating room, working fast now as the old man waited his turn.

She knew it was going to be a long hard night.

Every theatre in the hospital was now working flat out. Four main general surgery theatres, an orthopaedic theatre, both casualty threatres and one used for neurosurgery. In another wing, three further theatres had been brought into use.

Doctors and nurses had arrived as the news of the explosion came out on radio and television news bulletins. They didn't bother to phone in to see if they were needed. They knew they would be. Chest surgeons, plastic surgeons, neurosurgeons, anaesthetists, radiologists – they all came in and worked on whatever came up first.

It was a long, long night. More and more relatives and friends came crowding into emergency to find out what had happened. The ambulances began bringing in bodies. They were quickly labelled D O A – dead on arrival. The ambulances were also starting now to go direct to the mortuary as the rescuers dug deeper into the rubble of the coffee house.

It was dawn by the time they had all finished, and Jennifer felt a great weariness come over her as she watched her last patient being wheeled away. She came out of the theatre, and for the first time that night she became aware of the smell. She was used to most hospital smells. She would never get used to this one. The smell of burnt hair and flesh. It was right inside her nose. It clung to her hair and clothes. All she wanted was a bath, a great hot bath to scrub away that smell, and a spray to spray over her and inside her and up her nose and anywhere at all to get rid of the smell.

But she knew, from before, that it would be days before it went.

9

The wounds caused by that summer day explosion in the city cut deep into Vincent. The numbness they produced at the beginning hid the full extent of the damage until it was too late ever for him to recover.

He had heard about the explosion on the radio. The flow of pop music had been interrupted by a news flash announcing the explosion, and the fact that there had been a number of dead and many injured. There had also been extensive damage.

It was the sort of news he had often heard before. It was a commonplace occurrence in his part of the world. This one did sound rather more serious than usual. But he and Bryan had only wondered idly between themselves where in the city it might have been, when they heard the dull boom of an explosion.

But neither the sound nor the news flash prepared him in any way for the news which greeted him when he got home. It was his half day and his mother normally got him his dinner on those days.

His granda was sitting slumped in his chair in the front room. His mother was out, which he found a little surprising.

There was a stillness about the place which he did not appreciate, but which he should have recognized as a sign that people were missing who normally should be there.

.He'd gone into his granda and asked him what was up.

His granda had answered slowly, speaking quietly and staring straight ahead, not looking at Vincent.

They've gone, he had been told. Gone to the hospital. Why, what was the matter, he'd asked urgently, wondering what could have taken them to the hospital, indeed wondering for a moment if his mother had finally had the heart attack she was always threatening to have.

But no. It had been almost worse than that. Indeed, it had been far worse. All he had got out of the old man was that the two girls had been injured in the bomb explosion in the city. Mairead and Sheelagh. Sweet Jesus Christ, let it be nothing bad, he thought desperately, lapsing unconsciously into a call for help. He tore to the front and raced off, his stiff knee giving him a lopsided gait, down the street. Shit and fuck the bastards, he screamed to himself ... and ran and ran.

To Vincent, the hospital was one vast muddle. A place of chaos, seething with people. He had pushed his way into the crowded foyer of the emergency room, looking for someone he could get some information from. He despaired of ever finding anyone as he looked around.

Every chair had someone on it. Others stood about. They looked worn and haggard, lost in their own individual pools of worry. He found an information desk and gave his name. The woman had looked up quickly and said, yes, was he a relation of Sheelagh Malone, and he said yes, her brother. She'd told him to take a seat and someone would take him along to where his mother was and she would tell him what was happening.

His mother had been able to tell him little. She was in a state of shock and could hardly speak. Deirdre and James sat on either side of her looking small and frightened and tired.

He remembered that evening as a blur. The doctor telling him the awful news about Sheelagh, and his urgently asking after Mairead. Mairead O'Donnell. Yes, the doctor said, she had just come out of the operating room. His mother had already asked after her. Her injuries were bad, but not as bad as his sister's. No, he couldn't see her now, she still hadn't come round from the operation. Yes, he could wait. Then the doctor had gone, and he had sat on. His mother said little, but cried from time to time. James started to chatter, but Deirdre said nothing at all. She just sat, scuffing the toes of her shoes on the floor under her chair.

In the end, Vincent had packed his mother off back home with the children. They couldn't sit there all night, and they needed their dinner. So she had gone, and he sat on, his mind a mixture of whirling thoughts and blank, very empty moments, out of which he would come with a sudden jerk to remember what had happened that day.

He stopped noticing the other people who sat around him, talking, crying, asking questions. He retreated into a space of his own, blocking out sounds of the hospital, the sight of the rows of stretchers along the corridors and the peculiar smell of the hospital, with the added awfulness now of burnt clothes, hair and flesh.

He had never been as close to violence as this. Even the ambush in North Antrim, terrible though that had been, had been nothing like this. And, so far, it was all in his mind. He had not seen Mairead, nor Sheelagh. He had not seen the explosion. He had not seen the ambulance men moving into the rubble, searching.

Unlike the young policeman now being treated for shock, he had not seen or heard any terrible sights. He hadn't come across a young girl, every stitch of clothing ripped from her, along with her arms and legs, nor heard from the shapeless red mass on her shoulders – as the policeman had heard – continuous screaming.

Someone brought him a cup of tea. He drank it down quickly and gratefully, the hot liquid scalding his throat. He lit another cigarette and sat, hunched forward on his chair, looking at the floor. Bryan arrived, bringing with him some sandwiches. They both ate, saying little to each other after Vincent had told him all he knew. They sat side by side, looking exactly alike, even the small differences between them rubbed away by their shared despair. Both had the same shock of black hair, swarthy looks, blue eyes and slightly hunched shoulders. They were dressed differently, but that was the only difference. And Bryan did not smoke.

Later the doctor had come and told them there would be no

149

way of seeing Sheelagh that night. They would have to come back the following day. She was in the intensive care unit and would be for some time. She was also still totally unconscious. The doctor looked at them both. Which one is Vincent? she had asked. Vincent had nodded.

The doctor, who was short and attractive in a plump sort of way, had looked at him quietly and said Mairead O'Donnell was calling for someone named Vincent, she supposed it was him, and told him he could have a few minutes with her.

Bryan had waited for him, and he'd come out pale and shaking. It had been terrible. Mairead had just gripped his hand and gone on whispering his name, and then Sheelagh's name, and then his, again and again. He had tried to say something to her, but found no words would come. Her face seemed covered by a red rash. He knew, because the doctor had told him, that the apparent rash was, in fact, thousands of tiny splinters. She would always look like that.

Father Farrell was with Bryan when he came out. Vincent came up close in front of him, his eyes glaring out of a white face.

'Go away,' he said tightly. 'Go away from here. You're all like bloody vultures. Good for nothing but the death throes of people. Don't you go near that girl upstairs. She's not for the likes of you.'

Bryan had put a restraining hand on his arm, but he had shaken it off angrily and walked away. He wanted no more part of this nonsense. All this rubbish about God and how he would help you overcome sorrow and despair. They would be telling you next that God was actually on your side. Balls. He didn't need any help like that.

Over the next few weeks Vincent lived his own life, keeping very much to himself but spending lengthy periods down at the hospital. Sheelagh remained unconscious for a long time, and Vincent would sit with her, holding her left hand lightly. It was the only limb she had left, he thought bitterly. Bryan would come down with him, and he would sit with Mairead and talk to her, for she'd come round far more quickly than her friend.

Somehow it seemed natural that way, for Vincent, when he tried sitting with Mairead, could think of little to say. He couldn't bring himself to talk directly to her anyway, for he couldn't bear to look at her face.

Bryan could talk to her, and Vincent left him to it, grateful he was spared that ordeal and content to sit with Sheelagh with whom he needn't talk. It was all a slow and painful process for them. Sheelagh, in her intensive care room, hardly knew what was happening. She slipped in and out of a grey twilight world, sometimes exchanging odd sentences with her visitors, but not often.

She had one long rambling conversation with Vincent, convinced that she was on holiday in Portstewart, and complaining that her mother didn't allow her out swimming, nor to the local disco. Feeling sick, he'd played along with this and was astonished to find how easy it was.

He was with her when she discovered, almost by accident, that she had lost her legs. She had complained about pain in her feet and without thinking he had blurted out, surprised, that she didn't have any feet, so how could she feel them? She had tried to push her head up, struggling and weak on one arm, and looked down the bed. Then she had screamed, a nurse had rushed up and given her an injection, and she had lapsed back into sleep.

The incident did nothing to help Vincent. If anything, it churned him up even more. The doctor, whom they had got to know quite well, tried to explain it. Byran seemed to understand, but Vincent couldn't grasp what she meant by phantom limbs, that it was quite normal for people who had lost limbs to go on feeling them, even feeling pain in them or imagining they could use them. 'I'll talk to her,' the doctor had said. 'Lost limbs need a lot of explaining. Sheelagh's lost three of hers, and we'll have to do a lot of talking to her. It won't be easy.' The next morning she had come in and pulled the screens round the bed and talked to Sheelagh quietly for a long time.

Vincent started to find excuses for not going to the hospital. The sight of the wards, the smell, the constant feeling of pain and strain had got through to him. He would go down sometimes with Bryan, but leave him there, saying he had work to do. Bryan never complained, never questioned him and that helped a bit, but not much. Nothing seemed to make sense to him any more. He couldn't understand why Sheelagh complained all the time that her feet were cold, despite the hot water bottles and extra blankets the nurse put into that flat, empty space at the end of the bed. When Sheelagh said she was wriggling her toes to keep them warm he began to think she was going mad.

He talked about it, just once, to Bryan. They were in the pub, sitting in their usual corner away from everyone else. Vincent's temper over the past weeks had done nothing to encourage anyone to come close. Moreover, he was still largely avoided after his brush with the local IRA, though there was some sympathy for him at the severity of the punishment he'd had.

He sat back on the bench, his hands in his pockets, his legs stretched out in front of him, his working boots crossed one over the other, muddy and covered with cement.

Bryan sat forward, leaning over the table, his glass of porter held in both hands. He gazed moodily into his beer. It was mid-afternoon, and they had both been laid off work for the second time that month. The construction work had stopped because the compensation money hadn't come through. They spent most of their time these days rebuilding.

It had become a joke in the building trade that businesses were blown up deliberately, just to get the compensation. Mind you, they had to rebuild to the original purpose of the building, but it was still worth it. There were even stories that some people approached the Provos and offered their buildings as bomb targets. The Provos put it out that they'd have nothing to do with that, they were revolutionaries, not anarchists or criminals. But who knew what went on? All Vincent was concerned about was that he and Bryan was both out of work and Sheelagh and Mairead were badly ill in hospital.

He had begun to feel like killing someone.

'You're joking!' said Bryan.

'Maybe I am,' Vincent replied. 'Then maybe I'm not.'

'Then you're mad."

'No, I'm not.'

'You're not serious,' Bryan said, making a statement, rather than posing a question. 'Just because you've had a gutful, and Mairead is in hospital ... and Sheelagh.... Of course you feel fucking mad. But killing someone. Not you. You can't do it.'

'Look, we've....'

'You can't do it. We've had this out before. Remember?'

'I remember that. Of course I fucking remember that.'

'Well, then?'

'Well, what?'

'Oh, shit, Vince! What about all those fancy arguments you had about killing people? All that stuff you hand me about it doesn't matter what they do, you can't just kill someone. You were the person who said all that, not me. You had good cause to feel like killing someone. You couldn't do it. You're angry and sick now. That's not enough to make you kill someone.'

'Oh, yeah? You just want to feel how I feel now. Last time was something else. Listen, boy.' He leant forward, nearly slipping off the seat, and so he sat up straight, pushing himself back into the corner of the bench. He picked up his whiskey, holding it tightly in his hand. 'Listen. I don't know quite what I think any more. I don't know if I even fancy Mairead any more. Yeah, don't look so fucking surprised. You've seen her. Listen, she was great. Just great. But I could never marry her, you see. She was too bright for me. She didn't really fit in here. Too much education. You know her father owns a bloody great farm down in County Galway? Bloody big for that part of the world, anyway. She was great to have around, but she didn't fit. She knew she didn't fit. She knew that, didn't she? Bryan!' he said fiercely, shaking his brother's shoulder. 'She knew that, didn't she?'

Bryan looked at his brother sadly.

'Catch yourself on, Vince. I don't know what's got into you. If you didn't fancy Mairead, why bring her up here? What are you trying to do to the girl?'

153

'I don't have to do anything now,' he said bitterly. 'It's all done. She'll never be the same again.'

'Don't blame yourself for what happened. She wanted to come. She doesn't blame you.' Bryan paused and looked at his brother. 'She says she's sorry for you.'

'Sorry!'

'Yeah. Sorry. She thinks you're blaming yourself for it all. But she says it could happen to anyone. She says bad things do happen, that you can't always help it. And when they do, the best thing to do is to try and make something of them, use them somehow to make things better. You know what I mean?'

'No,' said Vincent shortly. 'No, I bloody don't. I just can't stand it any longer. You talk to her. I can't. She's not the girl I knew, Bryan. She just lies there and says nothing. There's no bounce....'

'No bounce!' Bryan, scandalized out of his mind, almost shouted at his brother. 'What d'you mean, no bounce? The girl's lying there with a leg badly broken and a face full of bloody splinters and you say she's no bounce.' His voice rose. 'No bounce, what the hell are you talking about?'

He pushed himself angrily back in his seat and stared in the opposite direction. His raised voice had turned a couple of heads. He felt embarrassed. He felt worse about his brother. What was Mairead going to do with Vincent gone stark raving mad?

'Bryan, you don't understand....'

'Too bloody right I don't understand.'

'Oh, for fuck's sake,' he said wearily, 'will you listen for once? I'm after telling you I don't *know* what I think any more. I'm trying to sort this out. I need your help. There's no one else I can talk to. I don't know what's happening to me.'

Bryan said nothing, but he relaxed a bit and settled down again on the bench. He drank some beer and wiped his hand across his mouth. Vincent swallowed his whiskey and signalled to the barman for more. He waited till he had come and gone again.

'There are some things I have to sort out. I can only talk to

154

you. Maybe you can help, maybe not. But there is no one else. Mairead is ... well ... she's a woman, and they have their place. I'm not one for ever to keep them in the kitchen or anything like that. They need to be allowed to do their bit, you know. Mairead, well, I fancied that girl real bad. She was great. But don't you see that was all before this happened? She's not ... she's not the same girl. Don't you see that? How can she be the same? So how can I feel the same?

'But I'm mad that I don't. I'm mad that it's all gone. I feel empty and sick inside. It's all gone, and there is just pain and aggro and sickness and ... nothing, just nothing. I can't go on with her. And if I find another girl it won't be the same because it can't and I will remember her, and I know she needs me or something and I know I'm doing the wrong thing, but, Bryan, I can't help it. And that's why I feel I can kill someone. For what they have done. Bryan, don't you see they have fucked us all up, and I want to kill the bastards?'

Bryan's head reeled. He knew his brother was a moody character, but he had never seen him quite like this before. He had no idea he felt so bad about it all. Well, they all felt bad, and sick inside at the whole mess. But to talk as he did about killing people was something else altogether.

'Who are you going to kill?' he asked simply, thinking it might be an idea to bring the conversation round on to a practical basis and so get rid of some of the emotion.

'I'll get who did it.'

'But do you know who they are?'

'Bloody Prods. UVF probably. I'll get them.'

'How do you know they're Prods?'

'They blew up Sheelagh and Mairead, didn't they?'

'For Chrissake. That doesn't mean they were Prods. There's a lot of talk it was the Provos.'

'Balls! You listen to me. I'll tell you. Remember the night before it happened? A bomb went off in Boyne Square. You know where that is, right in the middle of Sandy Row. The Prods were mad at it. Burnt out two houses and some old woman died in the smoke. Then the night before that – across the river, up Woodstock Road, another bomb ... and shooting across at the Prods from the Short Strand. D'you not think the Prods were mad about that as well? D'you not think they'd do something about it? Of course the café bomb was theirs. Stands to reason, they were hitting back. So would you. Don't give me that Provie rubbish. It's balls, and you know it.'

'It's not balls, Vince. Everyone thinks the Provos did it.'

'They haven't claimed it.'

'No, they haven't, but. . . .'

'They always claim it. So if they haven't claimed it, they haven't done it.'

'Vince, you know that's nonsense. For God's sake, it wouldn't do them any good. The whole thing must have been a mistake.'

'Why must? Why *must* it have been a mistake? It's just the sort of bastard thing the Prods would get up to. You know what they're like.'

'Listen, Vince, and listen carefully. No one has claimed that bomb explosion. Too many people were killed and injured. It wouldn't do them any good. It could be Prods or Provies. It's likely to be Provies, but any one would be mad to claim it. However, be that as it may, if you think it was Prods, how the hell do you think you'll go about dealing with them – or killing them, as you say?'

'I'll find them, and then I'll kill them. Just them. Then I'll blow up their houses, and their shops and their schools and their pubs and their factories. I shan't kill anyone else. I'll just make their lives a bloody misery, and I'll frighten the shit out of them ... women and children and the whole bloody lot. They've fucked up my life ... our lives. They've been sitting on us for centuries. They've done it too long. . . .'

'Look, Vince,' Bryan broke in, desperately trying to get through to his brother, to break him out of his almost hysteri-cal pattern. 'You're talking rubbish. I can't help you. You know you are talking rubbish. Why don't you talk to someone else? Father Farrell might help you. . . .'

'And if he gets in my way,' he was furious now, 'I'll kill that pansy-footed fucker as well, God help me!' He stopped, and half closed his eyes. He started taking in short, shallow breaths of air, and then spoke, very slowly. 'I don't want him around, Bryan. Understand? And don't you talk, neither. Informers have a way of being dealt with. Look what happened to me,' he patted his knee, 'and I was no informer. See what I mean?'

Bryan stared at him, shocked beyond belief.

There was a spell of warm weather, which blanketed the narrow streets with a sweaty heaviness. Each back yard was like an individual oven. The front and back doors were open hopefully to catch a breeze that never seemed to come.

The men on the street corners were in their shirt sleeves again. They lounged and smoked, watching life go by and waiting for the same pattern to begin the next day. Only an enormous effort would get them to break free from the constricting boundaries of their village existence in the city. But this effort was past them. To be truthful, it probably never entered their heads to do anything about it. This was where they had been born and brought up. Their schooling had been here, and so had their work, when they could get it. There wasn't much around.

Life in the rest of the city went on as normal, dedicated to business and making money. It ebbed and flowed round the Protestant and Catholic enclaves, shrugging off the effects of the bombs and bullets that came out of those areas, and mourning its dead when necessary. Massive injections of financial aid from the parent country across the water insulated it from the worst effects. They also served to insulate minds.

The nightly horror of the television news bulletins had a numbing effect. On a national scale it served to isolate those on the mainland from the people in the Province. After all, it was a different country, and indeed, people were now starting to ask why they should bother with it at all. Locally, a nightly diet of Provincial politicians, on the whole mind-numbing in their repetitiveness, turned the warring factions, more and more, in on themselves.

It was a reliable sign, if anyone cared to see it, of the massive revolt which was taking place.

The Catholics, the minority group, unable to expand out-
wards, had turned back in on itself. It was feeding on itself:
trying desperately to create a group identity.

In the Protestant enclaves, there was a growing awareness
that there was a just cause for grievances abroad in the Province. But this awareness did not extend very far, and it did not
mean a recognition that the privileged position should be
shared. Rather the thought of what might be lost produced
outbursts of anger, and these were directed against the cause
of that feeling – the minority group.

The rights of both sides became lost behind the smoke of
battle.

Vincent wasn't around when Mairead came out of hospital,
and it was Bryan who went to fetch her. He had persuaded her
to spend a couple of weeks with them while she regained her
strength, and her parents, who had come up to see her, had
agreed.

Mairead had been to see Sheelagh before she left hospital.
Indeed, she'd spent quite a bit of time with her one way and
another pushing herself about in a wheelchair. Sheelagh was
still in great pain, and Mairead would talk to her for long
periods, quietly, gently, giving her encouragement to carry
one. It wasn't easy. At times Bryan would come in as well, and
then the three of them would even find things to laugh about.
Once Vincent had joined them, but despite Bryan's efforts, the
talking had dried up. Vincent had little to say. He took little
notice of Mairead, and his presence, brooding and remote, cast
a shadow on the group. He had brought some grapes which he
absent-mindedly picked at until they'd all gone. No one else
had any, and Vincent didn't even notice.

He wasn't someone Mairead talked about anymore. She
carefully avoided any mention of him if it was at all possible.
But after that visit, Sheelagh asked her what had happened
between them.

'It's all changed,' Mairead told her in a small voice. 'It was
difficult before, but since the bomb I can't get through to him.
Sometimes you'd think 'twas himself that had been blown up,

not us. I can't get through to him.'

'He doesn't see you much now, does he?'

'No. He didn't even meet my parents when they came up North. They wanted to see him, see what had lured their daughter away to all this. They saw Bryan instead.' Mairead smiled a little. 'I told them not to worry, 'twas like looking at the same person.'

'Yes,' said Sheelagh. 'But he's not the same, is he?'

'No.' Mairead looked away, and Sheelagh reached out her hand and caught the sleeve of her dress.

'Mairead,' she said softly, 'isn't it Bryan who comes to see you now?'

'Yes,' she whispered.

'He's soft on you, I can tell.'

'Yes.' Mairead's eyes started to fill. 'It's very difficult, Sheelagh. I feel so awful about it. But Vincent has changed. He doesn't come near me. And Bryan ... well, Bryan's been a great comfort.'

'Has he said anything to you, you know. . . .'

'No, nothing, but I know he wants to. . . . He's asked me to spend a couple of weeks here before I go home.'

'Oh, yes, yes.' Sheelagh's eyes lit up. 'I don't want you to go. You must stay as long as you can. Oh, but ...' her face fell. 'What about your parents, won't they want you back quickly?'

'They do. But they say it would be a good idea to build up my strength a bit before I travel South.'

'Did they like Bryan?' she asked.

'Oh, yes, yes, they did. They didn't say anything, but I know they liked him.'

'Good.' Sheelagh sighed and seemed to slip back into her pillows. 'Hold my hand, Mairead, hold it tight. . . . I'm glad they liked Bryan. You like him too. We need you, Mairead ... don't go away for too long.' Tears started to pour down her face, losing themselves in the pillows. She cried quietly, desperately. 'I'm hurt so bad. . . . No one can help me. . . .'

'Hush, hush. Don't fret so.' Mairead stroked Sheelagh's hand, but she went on crying helplessly.

The nurse had come along in the end and, seeing the state

Sheelagh was in, had given her some pills. The scene stuck in Mairead's mind almost more than anything else. The small, unnaturally small figure in the bed, shaken with silent sobbing. She had looked out of the tall windows, out across the city she had known for such a short time. Neither she nor Sheelagh had been back out since the day of the bomb, and even now, as she listened to the girl beside her crying quietly, and held her hand, she could see a pall of smoke over the city centre. Another bomb and more deaths, she thought. More injuries like her own, or even worse, like Sheelagh's. She knew she herself had been lucky, despite the damage to her face. She still had her arms and she could see and talk and hear, and she was sure her leg would mend.

As the drugs started to work, Sheelagh quietened down. until she was asleep. What a way to live, Mairead thought, what a waste. And when Bryan had come to fetch her some days later she felt suddenly drained and weak and very alone. His concern for her made her weep, which he couldn't understand, and when he gave her a huge pair of sunglasses to put on, she kissed him. It was the first time. They wheeled her out, her large, plastered white leg stuck out in front of her, and her new crutches across her lap.

Old Mr Rafferty had been delighted to see her back. His tall figure was still erect, and he talked as much as he ever had before, but some of his spirit had ebbed away. There were other changes she noticed, too. The atmosphere in the house was tense, and Bryan's mother was always on edge. Two or three times Deirdre woke up in the middle of the night screaming, and each time it was she and Bryan who had to sit with the little girl until she had calmed down, her fears smoothed away, and she was asleep again.

The second time it happened they sat on together on the side of the bed after Deidre had gone back to sleep, talking in whispers.

'I'll be sorry to see you gone,' Bryan told her.

'I know,' she whispered back.

'It's all finished with you and Vincent now, isn't it?'

'Yes.' Her voice was so small he could hardly hear it. The

light from the landing was just enough to let him see the features on her face. The rash that spread across it was lost in the shadows and he thought how beautiful she looked. He knew then quite clearly that he didn't want her to go.

'You've been a great help. I don't know what we'd have done without you ... Sheelagh especially. She really needed you. Me too,' he added.

She didn't say anything, and Deirdre moved restlessly in the bed. Mairead stroked her head. Bryan sat still wondering what to say and how to say it for by now he was terrified that anything he said could destroy the feelings he knew were building up between them. There had never been any awkwardness between them, and he didn't want any now.

'I'll come with you when you go home,' he said, making up his mind. 'You can't go on your own.' He spoke naturally, not even thinking about making an excuse for Vincent.

'I'd like that,' she said, and he felt very pleased. The threat of awkwardness vanished.

'Your parents won't mind, will they?'

'No. They like you. Anyway, they know you're coming.'

'What?' he said out loud.

'Shh, you'll wake the child.'

'What do you mean?' he whispered. 'How do your parents know?'

'Because I told them. Or I told them you'd probably bring me down.'

'Didn't they ask about Vincent?'

'Yes.'

'And ... what did you tell them?'

'I told them ... it was my mum I really told ... that I'd made a mistake. I knew it wasn't going to work. It wasn't just the bomb, it was before that.'

'I see.' Bryan's voice was now very small as well.

'People change, Bryan, when they're away from their own. Vincent changed. Maybe it wasn't him changing so much as the different setting making him look different. Maybe I wasn't quite what he thought I was, either. Perhaps I didn't fit into his world.'

'Of course you fit in here. Everyone thinks you're great,' Bryan said hotly.

'I don't think Vincent did. It was all so different here. And he's not very good at being hurt. He takes things badly.'

'I know. He's always been like that.'

'Yes. . . .' She paused, looking across at him and then reaching out her hand to touch his. 'There's another thing, Bryan. I know how you feel ... or a bit how you feel, anyway. I don't want to hurt you, but I don't want to make a mistake again.'

'No,' said Bryan. 'No ... I suppose you're right.'

'So it would help if you came and stayed in my home for a wee while.'

'It would?' he queried blankly.

'Yes. Don't you see, Bryan? We know each other up here, but it's very different. It would help ... you're not upset, are you?' She squeezed his hand. 'You mustn't be upset. It's very important for me to see how you fit into my life or maybe I should say into my sort of surroundings.'

'Is that why you told your parents I'd be coming?'

'Yes.'

'You were very sure of yourself.'

'Please, Bryan ... it's not like that. If only you knew. I'm not sure of anything anymore ... I just hoped that ... maybe. . . .' Her voice faltered a bit, and then she went on. 'Maybe you would understand ... and that you would come down ... because ... because I want you to very much.'

'I'm sorry,' Bryan said. 'I didn't mean to sound like that. I find it all very difficult, and I don't really know what to think. I didn't think this would ever happen to me like this. What with Vincent and all, you know. We might look alike, but we're not really.'

'I know you're not. That's probably why we're like this now. But, Bryan, I'm a bit muddled up, too. I don't really know why everything has changed so much since I came here, but it has.'

'Let's wait and see what a change back to home will do then, shall we?' Bryan stood up. 'I think we should go back to bed now, or we'll be up all night here. Come on now.' She stood up next to him, and he put his arms round her. He gave her a hug

162

and kissed her on the forehead. 'Don't worry,' he told her gently, 'we'll sort something out together. Things will get better.'

Father Farrell, despite the effect of the heat on his corpulent frame, walked up and down the presbytery garden, trying to come to terms with himself. He knew he had to do it on his own. There would be little help from outside. The minds of too many people were already well camouflaged behind their individual barricades.

God above could be a source of inspiration. But before he could appeal for help from that quarter, he had to know exactly what arguments he would employ. This was the difficulty.

The sweat ran down the back of his neck, trickling steadily on down to soak his black jacket. He felt increasingly uncomfortable but decided this was probably good for his soul – and his concentration.

As a young boy in a large family, he had been well protected and loved. It hadn't altogether been an easy childhood. Money had been tight, and there had been little for luxuries. But by and large it had been happy. His first real taste of the Protestant ascendancy had been during the IRA border campaign in the fifties, when suddenly it was brought home to him what it meant to be a Catholic living in the North: especially one with nationalistic ideals, romantic though most of them were at the time.

He had been so shocked the first time a gang of youngsters had screamed abuse and mocking taunts at him that he had run all the way home without stopping, arriving in a state of utter, terrified exhaustion. The shock came not so much from the abuse, but from the fact it came from boys he had known and played with for years.

He had seen more of it when his elder brothers had tried to get work. Three of them had been lucky and got jobs locally. There wasn't much around, however, and his fourth brother had tried in Belfast. He was a good mechanic, but every time he had a job within his grasp, he had been told that it had gone.

He had wondered at the time if it had anything to do with the fact his brother was always asked where he lived, and where he had been to school. He had never been asked what his religion was, so he didn't think it had anything to do with that. He knew better now, and he also knew that in predominantly Catholic areas, the system worked the other way around.

He had seen the civil rights movement get under way, or rather he had read about it. He knew what it had achieved before it fell to bits and into the lap of the IRA. He felt, and understood, the fear the Protestant had of the Catholic community. In conversation with them, though, he had never been able to persuade them their fears were based on a false premise. He found that the fear of being ruled by 'Cardinal Redsocks' in Rome was all too real for many of them.

The sun beat down, and he surrendered, moving across the lawn to a bench in the shade. He took off his jacket as another concession to the heat, feeling that as he had made one, he might as well make two. He mopped his brow with a large handkerchief and stared at the city below.

He didn't condone violence. He thought what a ridiculous statement that was, even though he'd made it to himself. But violence was such a part of Republican life now that to condemn violence was almost to condemn the goal for which it was being used. He believed in a United Ireland, so he didn't think he could do that. However, he didn't believe in unity brought about by force. He could see clearly the arguments on that, and accept the Protestants' viewpoint. They were, after all, the majority, but not, of course, in the whole of Ireland, he thought on. What a tortuous situation!

The heat made him dozy, and, unable to come to any clear conclusions, he started to nod off. He slept fitfully for a while and was only woken up by the noise of children coming out of school. He felt heavy with the sun, and groaned as he thought of what the incredibly wizened Mrs MacBride, the housekeeper, would have produced for his midday meal. Stew again.

He shuddered, and, getting to his feet, he lumbered off into the cool labyrinth of the presbytery.

The phone was ringing. He let it ring. It persisted. He hit his chest for so unchristian an act and went to pick it up.

'Father Farrell here.'

'Is that Father Mulligan there?' a voice asked.

'No. It is not Father Mulligan. It is Father Farrell.'

'Oh! Well, now ... ah ... it was really Father Mulligan I was after. Who ... who did you say you were, Father?'

'I am Father Farrell.'

'Oh yes! The new one. Well now, it was Father Mulligan. ...'

'Father Mulligan is out, and I'm not all that new. I have been here for a year, or thereabouts. Now that wouldn't be Mrs O'Keefe I'd be talking to, would it?'

'Ah well, Father, never mind. I'll ... I'll. ...'

The phone went dead, and Father Farrell sighed. Mrs O'Keefe would never learn. She tried it on at least twice a week, phoning up poor old Father Mulligan and pestering him with cries for help. He might have guessed it was her straight away. Goodness, he thought, looking round the dark, wood-paneled hall, I wish I could throw some white paint around this place. Even on the brightest of days it was gloomy. After the airy brightness of Rome, he would never get used to these gloomy northern houses, with their heavy furniture and thick velvet curtains.

The phone rang again. Surely that couldn't be the dreaded Mrs O'Keefe again so soon. He picked it up.

'Father Farrell here.'

'Oh! Father Farrell. I'm glad it's you. It's Mrs Malone here. I don't know how to say this. ...'

'Why don't you just try, Mrs Malone? I'm listening.'

'Well, Father, I'm in a bit of difficulty here, you see. It's a bit awkward asking you to help, you see. It's not as if ... as if he ... ah ... takes much notice of you. But he only seems not to ... I think he really does respect your views; ...'

'Mrs Malone,' Father Farrell interrupted gently, 'I presume you are talking about your son, Vincent?'

165

'Oh yes!' she cried. 'It's Vincent. Father, I don't know what to do with him, and with Sheelagh still here very poorly, and Mairead and Bryan away home to County Galway. Vincent just isn't himself anymore. He's sort of going to bits now. Do you think you could possibly see your way to popping in for a wee cup of tea this afternoon? Just sort of casual. You know what I mean?'

'All right, Mrs Malone, I'll do just that. I was coming down that way this afternoon anyway. To go to the recreation centre.'

'Oh, thank you, Father. Thank you very much. Good-bye.'

Father Farrell rode a bike because he thought it would help reduce his waistline, but it seemed to have little effect. It did, however, create some amusement, particularly among the children, and that was probably worth something, he thought, in these times.

So after his dinner, and feeling over-full with Mrs Mac-Bride's stew, he set off down the hill. The sun was high, and there was a column of smoke over the city. He could just hear a jangling of bells. Ambulances, he supposed. He could also hear what he took for gunshots. He stopped the bike and listened. The gunshots went on, crackling away faintly from the other side of Belfast. It must be some fierce old gun battle, he thought. Very unusual for the time of day, he considered. Gun battles were normally, though not always, fought out during the hours of darkness.

He sat on his bike, his left foot just balancing him on the edge of the pavement, and listened on. The children were all quiet now in school. There was little or no traffic passing on the road by the laurel hedge. The crackling went on, with some deeper noises, and he realized in the end that what he was listening to was the noise of the shipyards, floating towards him from near on two or three miles away. Gun battles! he said to himself. Whatever next? You're getting too jumpy by far in this place. Just catch yourself on, and get along with your work.

He pushed himself off the pavement, and freewheeled down the hill.

Father Farrell had seen Mrs Malone at fairly regular intervals since the appalling accident to Sheelagh and Mairead, but it had always been in church. He hadn't been down to their house for months. While he was happy to see Mrs Malone, and indeed got on very well with her, he always felt uneasy when the two boys were around, particularly Vincent, who made no secret of his dislike for the priest. He frankly doubted Mrs Malone when she said her son secretly respected him. That remark was more likely to be one made in desperation to get him to come down. It was a sign of how bad things had become in the Malone household.

He had heard one or two stories, always unsubstantiated and often, he thought, tinged with malice, of how Vincent was slipping into bad habits with bad companions. Bryan, he knew, was still much the same: pleasant, but distant. The lessons of the grandfather had sunk in well.

But despite these forebodings, he was unprepared for what he found when he got to the Malones' house.

As the door opened, he could smell the sickness and decay. Sheelagh had only been home a short while and was still confined to bed for most of the time, so there was bound to be some of the air of a hospital ward around. But not, thought Father Farrell as he stepped across the front door step, like this. It was really very bad.

Mrs Malone met him. She looked drawn and haggard, as she had done for months. He could hear voices arguing upstairs. It was a very small house, and he in particular felt its smallness. There was no soundproofing to speak of, and as he didn't want to hear the details of any quarrel, he went into the kitchen.

When he had come here before, this part of the house had always been spotless. The kitchen table against the wall was always scrubbed clean, and a tea tray laid on it with plates of bread and butter, and often some barmbrack as well. Now, the place was a mess. It looked as if no one had been near it to clean for weeks. Empty dishes lay piled up in the sink and across the table. Old clothes lay on the floor, the window was streaked with dust, and again there was that smell of decay. Mrs Malone was harassed. Too harassed, he thought gratefully, to see his acute embarrassment. She pulled out a chair.

'Sit you down there, Father, and I'll get you a cup of tea.'

He squeezed in between the chair and the table. She busied herself putting on a kettle, and he winced inwardly as she casually rinsed out a dirty cup under the cold water tap, and put it on the table in front of him. When she started to cut bread, he rapidly interceded on his own behalf.

'It's very kind of you, Mrs Malone, but I couldn't eat a thing. I'm just after having my dinner, and you know how much dear Mrs MacBride makes one eat.'

'Agh, come on now, Father,' she protested, 'a cup of tea is nothing without a bite to go with it.' She went on buttering the bread.

'No, no, really, I'm quite full, thanks all the same. Just a cup of tea will do rightly.'

Mrs Malone looked disappointed. Her shoulders sagged a little. Years of habit were ingrained into her, and she found it difficult not to push food into everybody at the slightest opportunity. Indeed, she felt a bit ashamed she only had bread to offer the priest. At one time, when things were better, there would have been jam to go on it, and cake, and soda and wheaten bread, and maybe some sponge cake as well. She didn't have the money for that now. She knew that. She didn't have the inclination to bother, either, but that was something she didn't recognize.

Father Farrell, however, recognized it. Even in his short time in the city, he had begun to recognize and distinguish the various signs brought on by the wear and tear of continuous troubles. Mrs Malone had almost got over the death of her husband, but the shock of the accident to Sheelagh and Mairead had been traumatic. He knew that the sight of her daughter, some three feet shorter than when she had last seen her, and white as a ghost, was etched on her mind forever, clear and sharp and terribly lasting. He felt that must be almost worse than any bereavement.

He knew also that she felt a certain responsibility for

Mairead, Vincent's girl from Galway. Her injuries, he remembered, hadn't been quite so bad, but her face had been covered with tiny splinters so it looked like a red rash. A permanent rash, he thought, the poor wee soul! He wondered how she was getting on at home. But Mrs Malone was the immediate worry right now, and he dragged his thoughts back to her.

'Mrs Malone,' he said, kindly, 'sit you down right there in that chair. Never mind the bread and butter, but I would love that cup of tea.'

He wanted to get up and pull a chair out for her, but in that small kitchen it was easier to stay where he was, wedged in his own chair, and try and reach out for one. He knew, anyway, that Mrs Malone would hardly notice what he did. All she would be sensitive to would be any atmosphere he created. So he set about creating one which would calm her down and allay some of her fears, whatever they might be.

Mary Malone sat down and looked across at the young priest. She saw he had a shock of black hair, and dark eyes. The same colouring as her two boys, the twins, but that was where the resemblance ended. For this priest was a mountain of a young man, with a round, red face. Moreover, his eyes were kindly, which was more than could be said for her two eldest. Vincent's eyes had been hard for a long time now but, since the bomb, even Bryan had gone cold and withdrawn. He said little but she knew he and Vincent quarrelled furiously before he left.

She felt tired and depressed. Rheumatism was getting into her knees, and they ached continually. Deirdre, too, had taken her elder sister's accident badly. She had also adored Mairead, and missed her when she went home after leaving hospital. Mrs Malone didn't think she was much use to Deirdre in her present state and Sheelagh was bed-bound. Dear Mother of Jesus! she thought, I'm done trying to keep up with all this.

'Would you like me to see her?' She suddenly heard Father Farrell talking.

'She's asleep now. I'll let her be. Maybe you would say a prayer for her? Dear knows she needs it.'

'Of course I will.'

There was silence for a while. Her mind wandered, and then she thought she heard Father Farrell asking about Sheelagh again.

'She's still very poorly,' she answered in a thin voice. 'Very quiet. She says very little, you know. She's very weak still.'

'Can you manage with her at home?'

'It's very difficult. There's so little room.' She wiped a greasy hand across her forehead. 'It was a mistake to bring her back. She should have stayed in hospital.'

'But she wanted to come back, didn't she?'

'Oh, yes! Of course she wanted to come back. And the doctor said it would be better for her. Help her mind, you know. But. . . .' She broke off and stared at the wall above his head.

He waited.

'Vincent is very difficult. I don't know why. You know, Father,' she leant across the table to look closely at him, 'if he wasn't my son, I'd think ... I'd think...' she stopped again.

Again he waited. He knew her pauses were noticed only by himself. She had no idea she was not talking continuously, or, indeed, behaving in any unusual fashion at all.

They both sat like that for two or three minutes. A fly buzzed up and down the window pane, searching for a way out. But despite the warm weather, the window was tightly shut.

'Do you think he's in trouble?' she asked, suddenly.

'What sort of trouble?'

'You don't think he could be in trouble with the Provos, do you, Father?'

He shook his head. 'Mrs Malone, I wouldn't be knowing if he was, nor if he wasn't. Vincent might be . . .' he searched for the right phrase, '. . . might be rather inclined to that sort of thing, I suppose. Am I right?'

'He's acting very peculiar.'

'He's living through difficult times. It's not really surprising that he's affected.'

'I think they tried to get him into the Provos before.' She was looking out of the window, though there was nothing really to see. 'I don't know what happened. But Bryan said it would be all right, not to worry. And then Bryan had this job, you know. On the building site. And he got Vince there with him, fixed him up. Fixed it with the foreman. Vince is a good carpenter,' she said earnestly. 'He's very good and works very hard. It's just that he couldn't get a job for so long, you know. Oh! My goodness!' She laughed, and Father Farrell started back a little, it was so unexpected. 'You know, Father,' she went on, 'it must have been queer old fun on that site, with Bryan and Vincent the exact spit image of each other, and no one to tell the difference. When they were small, they would do terrible things together. And they would always blame it on the other so they'd never get caught. Oh my! You can't tell the difference between them yourself, can you, Father? Nobody can except me. There's no difference between those two that anyone can see. It's just that they are different inside,' she added sadly, 'very different.' And one has a bad leg, thought Father Farrell to himself, but didn't say anything.

Mrs Malone prattled on, talking about this and that, and telling stories of what her two boys had got up to when they were young. She laughed occasionally, and Father Farrell listened patiently, presuming – rightly as it happened – that she was far from the point that was really bothering her.

He drank a cup of cold tea and was grateful the question of bread and butter hadn't been raised again. The room was stuffy, and he was sweating. He wondered how on earth he could afford to go on having his jackets cleaned if the weather stayed as it was.

He became aware that she had stopped talking about the twins, and was talking about Deirdre. Deirdre, she was saying, had been very odd lately. She had even taken to wetting her bed. At this Father Farrell sat up straight. What was the woman talking about now? he thought wildly. If she was really talking about her child wetting her bed at night, then it was surely a question for the doctor, not him. He said as much, interrupting her flow of words.

'Ah no! Father, I've been to the doctor. He can't find anything wrong. But it's not that, you know. . . .' She looked at him, her eyes wide and her mouth trembling. Dear help me! Father Farrell thought. What is coming next?

'You see,' she went on, 'she gets these sort of fits, like. If she hears anything outside, like a riot, or the army passing by, or the fellows rushing back after a football match, she has a sort of fit. Her fists, Father,' she raised her own off the table, and clenched them tight. 'Her fists go like this, and she clamps her teeth together, and she shakes. White, white. She goes white in the face, and then she starts sweating. It's terrible. She can't stop. She goes on. And on and on. I can't stop her. She's like a bit of iron. Absolutely stiff. It's terrible. . . .' Her voice rose and cracked, and Father Farrell reached quickly across the table and took her hand. It was rigid.

'Mrs Malone, Mrs Malone,' he said urgently. 'Look at me. Listen to me. You must stop. Mrs Malone!' he shouted now, loudly and suddenly. 'Take hold of yourself.'

He pushed back his chair and, still holding her hand, shuffled his way round the table. The back door opened, and Vincent came in.

'Here!' he said. 'Take hold of your mother. Gently now, she's in a bad way. Mrs Malone,' he said, soothingly, 'you're all right now. Come on, now, just relax. That's it . . . that's it. . . .'

He turned to the boy. 'You'd better get your mother lying down, and perhaps give her a cup of tea . . . and maybe a wee drop of something. Have you something in the house?'

'Aye, we have. Some whiskey.'

'Well, now, get that into her, there's a good fellow. Get your mother sorted out now and I'll drop in on Dr James and get him to come round as soon as possible.'

'You'll find that difficult, Father,' said Vincent, shortly.

'For why?'

'There's trouble up the road. The army's blocked it off. There's a couple of barricades burning there. You won't get through.'

'Oh, my goodness! That's bad. Very bad. Well, I'll just have to see what I can do.'

He tried, but he was soon back. There was no way through, and it looked as if the rioting would go on for some time. It was impossible to tell. So they made some more tea, and Vincent went up to sit with Sheelagh, while he sat on with Mrs Malone.

As she sat alone with the priest in her kitchen, Mary Malone started to feel a bit better. She couldn't understand what had happened. It was the first time she had felt like that. She wasn't totally aware of the connection, but she sensed that what she had been describing as Deirdre's problems were also her own.

She had just managed to maintain a hold on herself after the bombing, and the awful shock of seeing her eldest daughter cut down. It had shaken her very badly. But the crying she had done, she had done alone, undetected even by her closest family. She had been pleased with the way she had held out. It had happened to other people, and they had had to learn to live with it. Now it had happened to her, and she would have to learn as well. She thought she was learning.

But for Mary Malone, and Deirdre, there were to be more blows that would penetrate into their subconscious, causing psychological damage that would become apparent in the months ahead. While not appreciating the full extent of this damage, Mary Malone had enough natural common sense to realize that her problems stemmed from the violence of the street fighting that took place round their area.

The first night, it had been an awful shock.

They thought they were safe in their street, with the huge, strongly constructed barricades at either end. Iron stakes had been driven into the road. Corrugated iron sheeting had been put up, supported by lumps of concrete, hi-jacked cars, a bus and other bits and pieces. There was a narrow passage through for those who lived in the street. It was always guarded, usually by young boys during the day, always by men at night, armed with pick helves. Although it wasn't obvious, there were also guns around.

Mrs Malone had been out late that night, doing her stint on patrol. It consisted mainly of making sure the men were well supplied with hot tea and something to eat. She was to finish at two in the morning, and she was waiting for the last half hour to slip by, when she saw the first petrol bomb she had ever seen.

She was gazing down the street, away from the top barricade, thinking of nothing in particular. It seemed to move very slowly, in a high, twinkling arc. Tumbling over and over in the night air, it landed against the wall of a house on the far side of the street, and a splash of flame ran up the wall. Then it went out. It seemed so small and ineffective. Was it really a petrol bomb she had seen? she asked herself. She thought they were much more dangerous. Hadn't the army threatened to shoot anyone caught throwing them?

Then three came over together. Again the slow arc of tumbling light. She opened her mouth and screamed.

'They're petrol bombing. Petrol bombs ... quick!'

As they hit the house this time, the noise was different. She heard a window breaking. She saw the splash of flame run up the wall again. But as the men came running from the barricade, she also saw a flame in a downstairs room.

There was a shout from behind, and she turned to see more petrol bombs landing. There were more shouts. Doors and windows were thrown open, and soon the entire street was in an uproar, with men, women and children fighting the blaze.

'So you see, Father,' she said, 'it was a terrible shock. We thought we were safe there. You know, with the barricades up, and the men on patrol. And where was the army that night? Sitting on their asses,' she answered herself with uncharacteristic coarseness.

The night had got worse. Two houses had been completely gutted. Her two boys were nowhere to be seen, and she had no idea where they were. She was terrified that something would happen to her and she would not be able to look after Sheelagh, who would soon be coming out of hospital. Agitated, she had moved in and out of her house, and then discovered that young Jamie was no longer around. She had screamed for him from the front door, staring into the shadows and past the bright light of the burning houses. But the noise had drowned her words, and they had been lost, and she had run up and down the streets looking for him, and then her heart had missed a beat as she realized she had left Deirdre alone in the house. She had gone back totally distraught and unable to think what to do next, to find Deirdre out of bed crouched by the window staring wide-eyed into the night.

Jamie was curled up in Deirdre's bed, fast asleep.

The following day it had been the turn of the army to attack. The men from the street, enraged at the ease by which the gangs had petrol bombed them the night before, and convinced that the army had stood by and let them in, hi-jacked two buses and burned them in a barricade on the main road.

The army had produced their token force, a platoon of men. They stood down the road, waiting, helmeted and visored, with long, transparent shields to ward off stones and bottles. In their heavy flak jackets, they looked like some form of medieval soldiery. They were more mobile than that, but not as mobile as the mob of jeering, stone-throwing youths who had confronted them.

The army decided it was one thing to have barricades around people's homes, quite another to have them blocking main roads. They would have to go.

Two bulldozers moved in, supported by the troops off the ground. A loudspeaker call for the people to move off the streets was greeted by derisive shouts and more stones. An army snatch squad raced into the crowd, pick helves flailing, and tore back out again bringing a young man with them. His feet were hardly touching the ground, and he was screaming, you fucking bastards, fuck pigs, let me go bastards, until a soldier casually swiped him across the mouth with his fist and he stopped.

There was a momentary, very brief lull after this, and then for ten minutes the soldiers stood and took a barrage of rocks and stones, broken metal gratings, and ball bearings and darts fired from catapults.

In the background, army reinforcements rumbled up. Soldiers crouched in darkened doorways on either side of the street. The bulldozers sat quietly. In front of them in a line across the road, the riot squad waited. The officer in charge watched curiously as the crowd in front of him melted away. He opened his mouth to give the order for his men to get to the sides of the road under cover.

The first shot rang out, and he screamed 'Cover.'

There was a scramble to the side of the road, and a jeer went up from the darkened alleyways around. The soldiers started moving up the street, leap-frogging from one dark doorway to another. It was a slow process, and there was another quick burst of fire from up the road. The soldiers froze. They didn't return the fire. They had no real idea from where it was coming.

Mary Malone had watched all this from the dark shelter of a street corner, clustered together with half a dozen other women and children. It hadn't occurred to her to get out of the immediate area. Riots seemed to have a hypnotic effect on those who weren't directly involved.

She craned her neck round the corner, pushing past the shoulder of a man who stood there, also watching. She saw a flicker of light from the second floor of a building about two hundred yards away, just where the road bent round and went out of sight. Then she heard the shots.

'That'll sort them bastards out,' muttered the man in front.

Looking up the other way, she saw about one hundred and fifty yards of empty road. The street lights still shone down. At the crossroads, the traffic lights went from red to green, and nothing moved. The army were up there somewhere. Beyond the lights she could see the remains of the barricade. The flames were dying down, but the wreckage was still across the road, blocking it.

She heard three separate shots. They were very distinct. Very close. She smelt a whiff of cordite. With a shock she realized the gunman was only feet from her, crouched down behind a post box. She saw him raise both hands again, and this time she saw the flash from the revolver. He turned, crouching still, and ran towards them on the corner, pushing his way through, his path cleared by the man who had been standing in front of her.

176

Someone tugged at her sleeve.

'Come on back, Mary,' said one of her neighbours. 'The boys say the army's to come in and clear them barricades.'

The women hurried together, their arms folded across themselves and their heads down from habit. They reached their own barricade and slipped through.

The noise behind them was growing as the army moved in with their bulldozers to clear the main street. The grinding and crushing softened as she moved further away down her own street towards her home.

She found Deirdre up again, with her face pressed to the window, wide-eyed.

'Get yourself off to bed this minute,' she called out angrily. 'You've no cause to be up at this hour. Goodness knows what might happen to you.'

She pulled the child from the window and put her into bed, pushing James across. He was fast asleep. 'Now get yourself to sleep or you'll be no good for school in the morning.'

She closed the window completely, as if to guard against any further trouble, and went carefully down the tiny narrow staircase that led straight to the living room. It was cramped and untidily crowded.

The front door burst open. Vincent stepped in. In the flickering half light, she saw him looking wildly round. His hair stuck out, he was panting hard, and in his right hand he had a revolver.

'Vincent, what. . . .'

'Get yourself out of here. Quick. I'll get Deirdre and James. Move. Move.'

She stood still, unable to grasp what he was saying, and totally unable to contemplate just moving out of her house.

'What for?' she asked.

'The bloody army's about to come down the street, that's what,' he said savagely. 'I heard them giving orders for all these barricades to come down. Get the children. Quick. Where's granda?'

'Sure, he's in bed, where else?'

'Well, get him out. Those bastards won't stop at anything if they get in here.' He went quickly to the back door and looked out. He called over his shoulder, 'Bryan's just coming. He'll see you out. Go across to Rooney's and wait there. I've got to go. But hurry!'

He hurried out, and Mary Malone went back up the stairs. She was starting to pant. Too many things were happening. What was Vincent doing with a gun, with the army about to come down and search the whole place?

She went in and woke the old man. He was very sleepy and she had to shake him a few times to get him to listen to her.

'Will you get up?' she screamed at him. 'The army's after pushing down the barricades, they'll be here any moment.'

After repeating this two or three times, she left him to struggle into his clothes and went to the front room to get the two children. Deirdre was out of bed again, staring out of the window.

'Mammy, mammy,' she whispered, 'they're coming now. Look!'

Mary Malone looked out the window to see the barricade at the street end start to move. It heaved and shuddered up and down, and bits started falling from the top. There was a tearing, grinding noise as the giant bulldozer broke through. Clouds of dust rose up, and through this were fired gas canisters. They burst open, and the choking, eye-smarting gas swirled round and down the street, quickly getting through even the closed windows till she and the children were forced, coughing and hacking, down the stairs.

She remembered being told that vinegar on a handkerchief was good to help stop the effects. She grabbed a bottle from the kitchen and splashed some on to a handkerchief, quickly finding another and doing the same for the other child. She bent down to share one, her eyes streaming.

The old man came down the stairs in a hurry.

'What the hell's going on here?' he roared, and stopped abruptly as he took in a mouthful of gas. He was a tall man, this old schoolteacher, and afraid of no one. He had a shock of white hair which he normally was careful to comb down. Now it stood up, almost straight on end.

'Get back to the kitchen,' he shouted at them, and went for the front door. Mary Malone watched him step outside. Through the dust and the noise of the collapsing barricade, she watched the helmeted figures of soldiers come looming through. She went cold. 'Come back,' she screamed, but the old man either did not hear, or took no notice.

Two soldiers raced up to him. 'Get back. Get back inside your house,' they ordered, and Mary shivered as she heard the English voices.

'Piss off,' the old man roared back. 'This is my house and I'll do what I like in it.'

'Get inside,' the soldier shouted again, and raised his baton.

'Go fuck yourself, you English pigs. Go on, hit me, hit me. I'm only seventy-one. But I'm Irish. . . .'

The soldier dropped the baton from his hand and let it swing from his wrist. He grabbed the old man by the front of his shoulder, and pushed him rapidly back towards the front door. At the last moment, the old man turned, broke loose, and was through the front door and had it slammed for protection before the soldier knew what had happened. He hammered on the door.

'Open up. Open up before we break the bloody thing down.'

'I will not,' yelled the old man from inside, and upstairs Deirdre screamed, again and again.

There was a crash of glass. The second soldier was getting through the front window. Most of the window frame went with him as he forced his way through. He grabbed the old man and threw him back. He opened the door and, half through, yelled to his mate to come on in.

The old man seized his chance and threw all his weight against the door, trapping the soldier's head. The soldier kicked out behind him and bellowed in fury. But the old man, still leaning on the door, jumped to one side, and the boots missed him.

'Fire a baton round at the bastard,' he shouted hoarsely to his mate.

'Hang on, Fritzy, I'll get him.'

The second soldier started through the broken window. By

this time, Mary Malone had come back to her senses, and she was outraged at what was being done, not only to her house, but also to her old father.

As the soldier came through the window, his helmet caught on a broken strut and came half off. She leapt forward and grabbed a handful of his hair and pulled. She swung her arms from side to side.

'That'll teach you, you great pig.'

The soldier dropped his rifle into the room, and she jumped on it with her feet. His head was still down, but he could see what had happened to his rifle.

'Fritzy!' he yelled, choking. 'The bitch has got my rifle.'

Fritzy struggled free from the front door, and threw the old man back against the stairs. He reached round Mary Malone from the back, grabbed both her wrists, and with a jerk upwards, pulled her away. His mate gave out a great shout of pain, for Mary had kept her fists tightly clenched. He pushed her back into a chair and pulled his mate on through the window. He turned on the woman, his bulk filling the room.

'You're lucky we didn't leave your face like we left that woman in Andersonstown,' he told her. 'Now who else is there in this house apart from that old fool on the stairs, and that child screaming its guts out upstairs?'

Mary Malone stared at him, suddenly finding a hate for these soldiers she had never thought existed. She hated the way they lorded it out in the streets, sweeping through them like gods, crashing into her house, tearing down windows, frightening her children, and where had they all been the night before when the MacManuses had been burned out?

'Where were you last night, you bastards?' she spat at him. 'Whoring it up with some Prod tart I've no doubt, while her man burned down this place. Get out of my house,' she screeched at him. 'Get out. Get out. Get out!'

The squaddie gazed at her impassively. He'd seen and heard it all before. Grotty, dirty people in grotty, dirty houses. Christ, how could they live like this, he wondered. I'd cheerfully crack all their heads in and put the whole place to the torch. This was just the sort of house where some bastard Provo would be hiding out.

'If you don't tell me, I'll look myself. Keep an eye on this woman, Al. I'm going upstairs.'

She looked at Father Farrell.

'I don't know what happened up there. Maybe nothing. Maybe the child was frightened out of her life anyway. I would have been if some damn great soldier came charging into my room like he did. He just shouted down after a few minutes that I'd better come up and do something about her. Then they left.'

Father Farrell sat still, his tea cold in front of him. He was smoking, and Mary Malone was also puffing nervously on a cigarette.

He leaned forward and placed his hand over hers.

'Now don't you worry too much, Mrs Malone. I'll have a word with the doctor.'

He didn't think it would do Mrs Malone much good. Nor the child. But he felt he had to try something – anything.

10

The summer lingered on that year, stretching itself into early autumn, almost fearful to end the dry warm days because of what the long dark winter months might bring.

On the Sperrin mountains, which spread across the heart of the province from Donegal towards Lough Neagh, the heather was mostly withered and brown. The mountains were gently contoured, spreading for some forty miles from east to west, and cut through with lovely valleys like the Moyola, the Owenkillew, the Ballinderry and others.

Here and there were a few sprays of late purple flowers to catch the evening sun. There was a smell of autumn in the air, with a dampness rising from the valleys at dusk. But during the day, dwarf gorse shone yellow in the sunshine, and the spikes of molinia grass were a splash of orange against the bright green clumps from which they rose. Jays called harshly to each other in the thickets, and the martins still flitted to and fro, not yet started on their long journey south to the sun.

As the air thickened with the slowly approaching night, the ghosts of the past seemed to move across the immense moorland at Beaghmore. The dark figures which appeared were the Stone Age people's standing stones, about a thousand of them. And at Beaghmore Castle, their ancient clock still had its six stone hands pointing towards the midsummer sunrise, as they had pointed for the past six thousand years.

Deep in the mountain range, and deeper still in one of the huge forests, was a small camp. It didn't look much like a camp, but rather more the sort of place forestry workers would use. There was a clearing, and a wooden hut on one side, its structure weatherbeaten and sagging. A wisp of smoke rose from a corroded chimney pipe, but no light showed through the two windows that faced the clearing.

Danny Loughran had spent two weeks in this hut. He wasn't a country-bred man, and he didn't like it. Neither did three of the four other men who were with him. However, they were all going back to the city the next day, and so they were more relaxed than usual.

They sat around smoking and drinking tea. They also had out the bottle of whiskey which had been carefully kept for this last night. Danny had ruled from the start that there would be no drinking on the course.

By and large he thought it had all been a success. He had hand-picked the four men. Three from Belfast, and one from Strabane. He had wanted all the men from the same area so that they would fit into the local scene more easily, but that hadn't been possible. Still, he now had a team that was thinking his way, that would operate together and stick to instructions. There had been too many half-cock operations, he emphasized to them, which cost time, effort and sometimes lives as well.

He had constructed his bomb team pyramid. With his knowledge of explosives – and he had spent a long time poring over military text books from America – he had put himself at the top. He was the designer, who would conceive the bomb with its circuitry and its anti-handling devices. He was the man who would try and think of something different each time, some clever device to fool an army expert, and kill him.

From Belfast he had brought a carpenter, although he wasn't very good, and an electrician. The man from Strabane was also an electrician of sorts, but he had a lot to learn. However, he had to be included because the Belfast electrician worked full time for the post office, and wasn't always available. These three would make the circuits and the micro switches and build them into the bomb casing in a way to confuse anyone who might try and defuse it.

He saw the carpenter on the same level as the electricians: a man who had to use his skills to make the containers, using wood or metal, or whatever was necessary. The man he had for this wasn't very skilled, but he was the best he could get, and he hoped he would improve.

The fourth man was older, and Danny called him the bomb officer. He was a retired quarry foreman, well used to handling explosives, and his job now was to do just that. He had to collect, store and make up the various explosives for each bomb, and put the whole thing together with a detonator. His name was Michael. Danny had used him before, and he remembered with a shudder the dreadfully unsophisticated bombs they had made then. The Co-op mixture it had been called – sugar and sodium chlorate. Now they were on to a better thing – gelignite. This was the proper stuff, Polar Ammon Gelignite, expensive, but worth it. Normally it would cost £10 for a 50 lb case, but he had to pay the black market rate of £1 for 1 lb. However, it was untraceable because it wasn't coded in any way. Thank God! he thought, otherwise the ton a month that came over the border would stop coming.

There was a fug in the hut. It smelled of unwashed bodies. The water was kept mainly for cooking and drinking. Though Danny didn't wash much anyway, even he was beginning to feel the need. He looked across at Pat, the post office engineer, and wondered if he felt the same. Pat was a slight cut above the rest of them, and he was certainly looking uncomfortable. Perhaps Pat was the sort who had a bath every day? He laughed to himself at the thought.

'What's so funny?' Pat called over.

'You. You look so bloody miserable.'

'It's not miserable I feel. It's just dirty. I haven't had a decent wash since I came here.'

'You normally bathe every day?'

'Yes.'

'I thought so.'

'Why's that?'

'You look so bloody miserable. Like I said.

'Pat,' said Danny, after a pause, 'I'm going to need more

184

help on these circuits ... and this micro-switch system you've got.' He kept his voice low. 'I must be able to get hold of you more often. Peter here doesn't know enough about them. There must be some way of reaching you at work.'

'Well, I don't like the idea. You know that. The more I am contacted, the greater risk of being lifted.'

'Yes, I know all that.' Danny felt irritated. However well the two weeks had gone, he knew his pyramid was not totally sound. This was one weak point – not having immediate and easy access to Pat. The other was himself. He had bullshitted a bit about his knowledge of explosives. Of course he knew about them, but not nearly as much as he had made out to the others. He had a feeling Pat knew this as well, or at least had guessed at it.

'We could use some code,' he said, at last.

'We've been through this before. What happens if I don't answer the phone? And if you start asking for me ... it's too dangerous.'

'Shit!'

'Listen! If you're really in trouble, try it. Phone. If I'm not there, or whoever answers the phone even if it is me, ask for the Samaritans. If it's me, I'll know why. I'll then meet you half an hour after work, in the pub.'

'If it's not you ... ?'

'Then insist that the number you have is the right one – that it must be the Samaritans. Say you are desperate. The guy on the other end will be astonished – or he may even think it is very funny. Either way, he's bound to tell someone about it, and as I share an office, it is almost certain to be me. It's worth a try, anyway. And I'll meet you on the same basis.'

'What if you aren't there ... or if he doesn't tell you ... or tells....'

'Then I shan't meet you.'

'But what....'

'Danny,' said Pat patiently, 'it's the best I can do. I can't risk anything else. You know that. I know that. I don't want to end up in the Kesh, interned for a year. I'm sure,' he added, 'you don't want me to either.'

185

'No, no.' Hastily Danny waved his hand. 'Now, if it's in the morning. . . .'

'Then I'll meet you round the corner in Murphy's instead. Quarter to one. Is that OK?'

'Yeah, I suppose it will do. I don't like it, but.'

'I don't either. Different reasons, probably. But I still don't like it.' He pushed his chair back. 'I'm going for a slash.'

'Good idea. I'll come with you.'

The two men went out of the hut, getting one of the others to put a bucket over the lamp before they opened the door. They stepped outside into the dark and picked their way across the clearing. There was a slight evening breeze now which moved through the trees, masking the smaller sounds of the night, and carrying the faint scent of woodsmoke from their fire.

They stood side by side, a few feet apart.

'What are you doing about Hannahan?' Pat asked.

'Told him to keep well out of the way. I don't want anyone even to start looking for him. He should be OK, for he's not much around anyway.'

'What did go wrong?'

'I don't know. He says a warning was phoned. Why he picked a place like that, but, God knows. He was supposed to put it right in a Prod area.'

'He says a warning was phoned.'

'So he did. You think they would have cleared the place if they'd had one?' He looked over at Pat, who shrugged his shoulders. 'Jimmy says they didn't take no notice of the warning. You know what I think? I think there was no warning.'

'I think you're on. Jimmy just doesn't want to admit making a mistake. . . . How long will you keep him out of sight?'

'Ha!' Danny snorted. 'Not long. We need him. I just want him to be a bloody sight more careful next time.'

'Well, for what it's worth,' Pat said carefully, 'I think he is careful. I think he means to do just everything he does.'

'You do?' Danny looked at him sharply.

'Yes, I do.'

In the silence that followed they both heard a fox barking down in the valley.

'What's that?' asked Pat, lowering his voice, for the night suddenly seemed very still about them.

'Dunno. Fox maybe. It's a long way off, but.' He offered Pat a cigarette. 'You know, Pat, I've bullshitted a bit about those explosives. Not much, mind, I do know quite a bit. But I don't want any more fuck-ups. That's why I need you.'

Barricaded behind the high steel mesh fence round the police station, the Royal Ulster Constabulary were getting their nightly bombardment of rocks, bottles and petrol bombs. The steel shutters were down on the windows. The peephole in the front door was covered by its steel shutter.

The policemen were cramped because their station also held an army detachment. In the yard, brown Land Rovers stood next to grey police vehicles, and along the back wall was squeezed a line of squat, ugly-looking 'pigs,' ready to take the troops out when they were called.

Outside the front, in a heavily sandbagged and concreted pill box hung over with camouflage nets, two sentries peered through the narrow firing slits. Their field telephone lay beside them, unused. Everyone inside the station knew what was going on. The sentries would only use the phone if they wanted permission to open fire, or saw something very unusual happening.

Earlier that afternoon a young boy had been killed in a nearby street, crushed to death when a heavy Saracen armoured vehicle had been reversing round a narrow corner. The driver had been moving slowly, but children and adults kept swarming round him, shouting and throwing bricks and stones. Usually they were quick enough to keep clear, though they often left it tauntingly late. The young boy had done just that. He hadn't moved at all, and he had been caught between the Saracen and the wall, and crushed. He had been in one of the driver's blind spots, and was dead by the time he had been got to hospital barely a quarter of a mile away.

A deputation of women had marched on the police station,

and three had been allowed inside. They wanted the army taken out of the area. They had been told this was not possible. To the police inspector's horror, an army captain had commented that it had been the height of stupidity to allow children out on the streets in such a situation. The captain had made his comment quite gently, and was shaken by the fury of the response. The women had shrieked at him that he was nothing but a filthy, murdering bastard, and that from now on he would be a marked man. 'You'll be the next to go,' they shouted at him as they were led out, 'there'll be a bullet with your name on it next.'

So they were now all sitting inside, taking the results that the evening inevitably brought. On one side, buses were burning in the Falls Road. Further up on the other side, in Ballymurphy, crowds were gathering, and stones and milk bottles were already flying through the air. The Henry Taggart Memorial Hall was again under attack. It housed an army detachment, and the hall itself had long gone from view behind sheets of corrugated iron, steel mesh fences and camouflage nets.

Across the city, in the Short Strand area by the docks, a soldier on foot patrol had been hit and wounded by sniper fire. The army said the shot had come from a church tower, but that was off the record. In Londonderry, two explosions had rocked the city centre. In Newry, near the border, crowds of Catholics and Protestants were facing each other, with a line of troops in between.

In the darkened Springfield Road, where all the street lamps had long since been smashed, the crowd grew thicker and noisier. The company commander decided it was time he put on a show of force. He wanted to move in a company on foot to block the road to the city centre, and then clear the crowd. It was his first tour in the province, and he was a bit edgy.

His request went up to the commanding officer, and on up the line, through different levels of command, to the army commander himself. Back down again came permission to block the road, but not to move in and clear the crowd. Not yet, anyway.

Standing in the deep shadow of a side street corner, Vincent watched the build up with some satisfaction. It was just what he wanted. A diversion which would let him slip unnoticed down through the back streets with his explosives. This would be the third time he had used a riot as a cover for planting bombs, and he found it far better than going in cold, when nothing was happening.

This time he would have to be very careful. For the first time he was taking his personal battle right to the heart of the enemy camp. His previous bombs had all been planted round the city centre, except one. That had been in a garage on the outskirts of the city.

Tonight he was going into the Shankill Road. He had decided to burn down the post office there. It would be a symbolic gesture, if nothing else. But it meant he had to walk across from his own safe area into the Protestant area which wrapped round the Shankill.

He had decided he would do it openly, carrying his bombs in two carrier bags, which he would leave outside the post office. With a bit of luck he would merge into the general background, and it still wasn't too late in the evening for someone to be walking around with a couple of bags.

He pulled his coat around him and, feeling a slight dryness in his mouth, picked up his two bags. He walked down the street, away from the noise of the crowd, moving steadily into the dark mass of back streets that lead to the Shankill. He knew this area well, and had already walked it during the day. Left into Canmore Street, past the rows of little front doors, all the same except for the coats of paint. He couldn't see them now, but every now and then he spotted a dim, blurry figure in front of a door, or standing by the small front gate, silently watching and listening.

He crossed into Southend Street. It was only a few yards long and he was soon through it. He jigged slightly right through Nixon Street, the palms of his hands moist now, the handles of the carrier bags digging in. He was unarmed. He had decided all along he wouldn't carry a revolver. He didn't fancy shooting it out with anyone, least of all the army with their powerful, automatic rifles. If he was caught by one side or the other, he had just the faintest chance of talking his way out. If he was found to be armed, there would be no chance at all.

The tension in him mounted. It always did at this stage. He had to stop in the next street to arm his bombs. He would then be inside the Protestant area, and if he had to dump his bags in a hurry, at least the damage would be on the right side. The bombs were timed to go off within an hour. He had used the clothes peg technique. The pressure of the opened peg would slowly expand the soft wire which held it open. A drawing pin in the end would finally make contact, the circuit would be complete, and the bomb would explode. Six weeks in a quarry outside Belfast had taught him a lot about explosives. The foreman there had thought he had a natural flair for the work. That had pleased him enormously. He now carried the bags even more carefully than before. It needed a lot of concentration and effort, as he had to look as if he were walking normally.

While he felt the tension rise inside him, he also felt his brain was quite clear. He felt as if he were two people, one with the physical excitement of what he was doing, the other cold-minded, knowing exactly what to do.

He turned the corner out of Seventh Street into a wider road which led directly up towards the Shankill. When he got to the end, he would only have a few yards to go. He had worked out his route so that it would bring him out almost immediately opposite his target.

Vincent gripped the bags tightly and walked on, his shoulders back, looking firmly ahead.

This would be the seventh bomb he had planted, and so far it had been an amazingly successful run. Four had gone off, causing a lot of damage. One had been defused by the army, and one had been blown up by them, and that had caused some damage, too. No one had been killed. Each time he had telephoned a warning. From the start, his words had always been the same. 'This is Shamrock calling' he would say, 'with a bomb warning.' He would give the approximate location of the bomb, and the time it would go off. He usually allowed three-quarters of an hour.

No one had done very much after his first warning, apart from clearing the area. The fire that one had caused had gone on most of the night.

The next time he phoned he heard a quickening interest in the voice at the other end. But he had over-ridden the voice, given the warning, and rung off. From then on he never listened at all but put down the phone immediately after he had spoken. Working on his own he had never attempted, nor had he ever thought of, claiming responsibility on behalf of any-one.

This had caused a flutter of interest in the press, when it became apparent something unusual was happening. But as all the explosions were in the so-called neutral areas, or in Protestant areas, the papers had blamed the Provos. It was, he thought, what they always did, anyway.

He moved confidently but carefully deeper into Protestant territory, along pavements whose scruffy kerb stones were still painted a loyal red, white and blue. He knew it was the beginning and the end of an operation like this which were the most dangerous times, and where sudden failure was most likely. Well, he had come a long way from his carefully set up bomb-making factory, and he was determined that nothing would go wrong at the last minute.

He drew closer to the Shankill, which was lit, and where he would be more exposed than ever. He would walk across the road to the post office, and bend down as if to read some information on a poster by the letter box. He knew there was one there to read because he had already checked. He also knew that as he did so, immediately to his right would be a darkened corner where he could rest his bags quite naturally. He would then straighten up slowly, read something off another poster just to the left of the first one, turn round and amble away.

He came to the end of the road, automatically looking left for traffic, and then to the right. To his horror, he saw three men slouched against the post office wall.

He glanced left again, to gain himself some time, while his brain went cold and started to race.

He couldn't hesitate for more than a fraction of a second. Obviously the post office target was out, completely. He couldn't just turn back, the men had seen him. It would look unnatural. So that was out. He didn't want to walk up and down the road with his carrier bags, but he had to do something, fast. Turn left or right? He turned right.

That would bring him, momentarily, closer to the men lounging against the wall on the far side. They weren't taking any interest in him.

He walked down the street towards the city centre. He forced himself to the outside of the pavement as a young couple came past him in the opposite direction. He kept telling himself to do nothing that might make it look as if he had something to hide. Walk naturally! He was finding it increasingly difficult.

He was past the men now, and he could feel the hairs on the back of his neck prickling. He dare not look round. He felt terribly vulnerable. The carrier bags felt heavier and far, far bigger than they actually were. Every eye in the street must be on him, wondering who he was. His nervous system told him that. His brain told him it was rubbish, and to keep walking along and find a suitable side street to get into.

Left, right. Left, right. He forced his feet along, his eyes peering through the shadows of the street, searching out the pools of light under the street lamps. Two things he must watch out for: people, who were a hazard, and a suitable escape route. His brain analysed each message brought to it, and told him the route ahead was still clear.

Twenty yards away, a group came out of a door and moved directly across the road. Those people were no danger, and they had just come out of what must be a pub. The signals his brain took in told him the pub door was not on the edge of the street, but down some small passage. He walked on.

Further down the road, his eyes then took in a much larger group of people walking up towards him. They were waving things around. Scarves. They were also making a lot of noise, which grew as they came closer.

His brain flashed danger signals to him. He knew he could not allow himself to walk through that crowd. They might jostle him. They might ask who he was. They might offer him a drink.

At their combined closing speeds, they would meet in about twenty seconds.

Could he cross the road, even though that was away from the direction he wanted to go? He looked across. The answer was no. The crowd extended to that side as well.

His brain told him there was only one course of action. It would put him into greater danger than he had planned, but there was no alternative. He would have to turn right into the alleyway leading to the pub.

If it was long enough, and no one came in or out of the pub while he was there, he might just be able to walk to the end and back again while the crowds surged past the entrance.

As he turned right, he could see the detail. They were all youngsters, jumping and singing, holding their long tartan scarves above their heads with both hands, and waving them from side to side. Their jeans, boys' and girls' alike, were cut off shortly below the knee. Tartan socks led down, in most cases, to huge wedged boots and shoes. Their legs looked like coloured matchsticks stuck in a plasticine base.

No other sight could signal so clearly that he was in enemy territory.

A black alley faced him. It was fifteen yards to the door at the end. His brain told him it was long enough for what he wanted, and he walked slowly down it as the wave of noise and colour passed across behind him.

There was a dustbin by the door. He turned as he got to it, passing the bag from his left hand to his right, where he just managed to hold them both together. He lifted the lid and carefully, swiftly, put the two bags into the dustbin, and put the lid back on again. He walked back up the alley towards the road, unbuttoning his coat and slipping it off. He turned it inside out, and threw it over his shoulder.

The main body of the crowd had passed. Only the stragglers

remained. He joined them, unnoticed, and left them some twenty yards later, to slip down a darkened side street.

He moved more freely now. The main danger was behind him. If he were challenged now, he might just be able to make a run for it. His knee was aching from his efforts to disguise his limp. He had to think about it constantly, or it would become very noticeable. Here, in the dark again, he could afford to relax a little, but not much. A follow-up search would be narrowed down considerably if the target was a man with a limp.

In every street he would slip into a darker shadow and glance back to see if he were being followed. Nothing moved. All the curtains were tightly drawn, scarcely a chink of light showed anywhere.

He now had to find a phone. This was another difficulty. There were few around, and most had been broken. It was one way of stopping people informing and passing on anonymous information to the police.

Telephone, he thought. I must get to a telephone. I have always got to one before. I shall do it this time. I must do it this time. I can't kill people. Only those who injured Mairead and Sheelagh. These people I can kill, if only I can find them. Jesus! I wish I could find them and tear them apart. How much of my life have they fucked up? All of it. It's all changed. Nothing's the same anymore. It's all coming and going, this way and that. What the hell does it matter what happens next?

Does it really matter what happens to me? he asked himself, kicking viciously at the kerb stones. I could be picked up by the army. If they do it here in this street, they will thump hell out of me. I am not in my own area. If they get me in the next street, over the Peace Line, they will probably just thump me. What the hell!

I must find a telephone. That bomb will go off. It will tear that place apart. I don't want people getting killed. I just want those bastards to know that I hate them. I hate what they've done. I hate everything about them. Oh shit! Does it really matter anymore? The bomb will go off. The pub will burn down. It should have been the post office. That would have been better. But it had to be just a bloody pub. Just a pub!

He stumbled on, a stab of pain shooting up his thigh. His knee ached appallingly now. Would he ever get used to that, he wondered, and where the hell was the phone?

He came out on to the main road and looked round him. He was safe now, back on his own territory. The phone was fifty yards away. When he got there, it was being used, and two girls and an older woman were waiting outside.

He looked at them. They weren't talking to each other, so they were all on their own, he thought, and waiting, each one of them, to use the phone. The way women chatted they would be all night.

He went straight up to them.

'Excuse me, excuse me,' he said quickly, 'it's an emergency.' He opened the door of the kiosk. 'Excuse me, but it's an emergency. My wife's having a baby. I must phone the hospital.'

'Piss off,' shrieked the girl inside. 'I've heard that one before.' She pulled the door shut and turned her back on it.

He pulled it open again.

'It's a matter of life and death,' he shouted. 'I must use the phone. I'll only be a minute.'

'Piss off. I'm not going for that one.'

He looked round despairingly for support. The two girls regarded him blankly. The older woman looked at him, and he shrugged his shoulders. She was from his own street, and he knew that she knew he wasn't even married.

'Oh, you bastard bitches!' he said under his breath, and walked away.

What now? he thought. No chance of getting that phone without a great fuss. Find another. Where?

He limped off down the street.

The barricades were still burning. Further up the road he could hear the noise of the crowd still round the police station. So the army hadn't gone in yet.

The next kiosk he found had nothing but bare wires hanging from the wall.

He moved on.

Four army vehicles whined past him, bulky and menacing

shapes in the half dark, going at quite a pace towards the police station. He hardly noticed them. He was getting really worried now about finding a phone. Where the fucking hell was a phone he could use in this bloody city where nothing fucking worked because everyone blew it apart all the time?

By now he was well out of the Falls, and away down towards Divis Street. In fact, he was nearly in the city centre by the time he found what he wanted. He dialled the number, fishing two pence out of his pocket while he did so.

The phone at the other end was lifted. He heard the signal, and pushed in the coin.

'This is Shamrock calling,' he said quickly, 'with a bomb warning....'

'You're too late, Shamrock,' a voice cut in from the other end. 'It's just gone off. What an unpleasant little shit you must be.'

He held the receiver to his ear, stunned. He suddenly realized the call could be traced, and smashed it down on the cradle. He was furious. It was the first time he had been caught out. He didn't like it. He thought of himself as being very professional! A perfectionist who ensured that everything always worked.

He cursed steadily to himself.

High in the Sperrin mountains, Danny and Pat and the others were getting ready to go to bed. They had finished the whiskey, and the fire was low. They all felt a gentle ease of contentment. They were warm, they were fed, and they were going home in the morning.

Pat lay on his bed, stretched out, his red pyjamas well hidden by the blanket which he had pulled up to his chin. He was just a bit embarrassed by his pyjamas. The others wore nothing at all, that is, if they ever got out of their underpants. He lay flat on his back and stared at the ceiling.

Everyone was in or getting into bed, except Danny. He sat on the edge of his, hunched, his hands gripping the sides. He felt a tiredness about him that came from days spent in the open air. He wanted to go to sleep, but he also wanted to hear the late-night news. There had been earlier reports of trouble in Belfast and other places, and he wanted to know what was going on.

He reached over and switched on the radio. There was a blare of music, and he turned it down for a few minutes, until he heard the time pips. He automatically checked his watch. Then the news started.

Two people were killed and twelve injured – some of them seriously, when a bomb exploded outside the Orange Bar pub in the Shankill Road this evening. Reports are still coming in, but there appears to be extensive damage to the pub, which caught fire, and to buildings on either side.

It's understood the bomb was placed just outside the entrance. Eye witnesses say the young couple who were killed were walking out the door when the bomb exploded. No one has yet claimed responsibility for. . . .

The news reader went on with more details of the explosion, and talked about the crowds round the Springfield Road police station, and other incidents across the province. The words flowed over Danny. He wasn't listening anymore. The news about the bomb explosion had excited him. Every time he heard of a Protestant building being blown up or burned down, he felt a surge of elation. He got even more elated when he heard of Protestants being killed or injured. It was the same when a policeman or soldier was hit. He got the same tight feeling in his stomach. The only damper this time was that he had not been involved in it himself.

He was restless now. His fingers gripped the edge of the bed more tightly and his eyes blazed. But he said nothing, forcing control back into his body, and his mood wasn't noticed by any of the others.

He just sat, feeling a glow of satisfaction all over him. It was great.

But who had done it? he asked himself. He had heard the stories of some man who went round planting bombs as part of a personal war against the Protestants. He felt there was something odd about this particular explosion. He knew his people hadn't planned to plant anything like that, although that could have been changed while he had been away. But as it was his own job to organize these things, he thought that unlikely.

The warning had come too late. Personally, he wouldn't give any warnings at all, but he had been firmly overruled on that by the Central Committee. All the other unclaimed bombings had had warnings. This one, he decided, had probably had one as well, but the army had just fucked it up. Hadn't got the people out in time. So they had just blamed it straight on to the IRA. They hadn't actually done so yet, but Danny knew they would get round to it sooner or later.

The thought irritated him. He always claimed his bomb explosions and his executions. Why did they blame him when he didn't claim them?

However, if the warning had been too late, something must have gone wrong. If it was just one man involved, then that, he thought, wasn't surprising. A lot of things could go wrong with an operation like that. If it was just one man, though, he must be bloody good. Danny did a quick calculation and reckoned it must have been the fifth or sixth bomb this man had planted. He didn't know how many had been planted and failed to go off. But six in as many weeks wasn't bad for someone on his own.

He switched the radio off and climbed into bed. He cursed, and climbed out again to go across the room, collect the lamp, and turn it out. Everyone else was asleep.

He pulled his blankets over his head. He would have to find this man, whoever he was. He did seem very efficient. He pulled the blankets down again.

'Did you hear that news, Pat?' he asked quietly.

Pat grunted. 'What's that?' he mumbled.

'Did you hear about the Shankill bomb? On the news just now.'

Pat struggled up on to an elbow, suddenly interested. 'I did not,' he said. 'What was it?'

'A bomb in the Orange Bar. Two people dead and plenty injured. No warnings ... not in time, anyway.'

'Inside the pub?'

'Ah ... no. It said maybe just outside. By the entrance. Hit two Prods as they walked out, so it did.'

'Whose was it? One of ours?'

'No. Not ours. It didn't say. Looks like that man we were talking about the other day.'

'Oh! That one.'

'Yes. I think we should try and find him.'

'It would help.'

'I'll get Joe to start looking when I get back. First thing.'

Pat lowered himself back into his bed. 'I'm getting to sleep,' he said.

Danny sat on, gripping the side of his bed. His stockinged feet swung slowly back and forwards in the dark. He sat there for a long time, thinking hard, before he climbed back into his bed. Then he lay on his back, looking into the darkness of the small, stuffy hut. Despite his tiredness, he couldn't get to sleep.

The Shankill Road was now blocked by a crowd of very angry people. They were shocked at what had happened to them, that someone could get into the heart of their area and plant a bomb, and get away again.

The ambulance and the fire brigade had to push their way slowly through the crowd, while a self-appointed group of men tried to clear a way for them. The gap closed behind them, and there had to be a lot of shouting and pushing and yelling of orders and instructions to get the ambulance out again with the injured and the dead.

The scene was lit by flames from the buildings, now well alight, and the arc lamps of the fire brigade. In their dark blue coats and yellow helmets, the firemen hung on to the powerful hoses which snaked back through the glass and rubble, pouring jets of water into the burning pub. The hiss of steam, the roar of the fire which now and then burst out into huge red and orange flames, the crackle of the radio sets, and the shouts of the people, filled the air.

The immediate area around the pub was kept clear. But on the heap of rubble, a dozen men or more tore at the bricks with their bare hands, passing them down a line to be dumped some distance away.

The bulky size of the fire engines blocked this scene off from most of the crowd. Those near craned their necks forward to see. Those at the back kept asking what was happening.

On the fringes of the crowd, women stood in little groups, their arms folded, talking, as they always did, about the lack of security, and how the government, the police, the army and everyone else was soft on the IRA.

Small children wandered around their feet.

Surprisingly, there were no television cameras to record the scene. One crew which had arrived had been roughly handled. The others would probably appear later when feelings had cooled. Already there were complaints, which would mount the next day, that television was ignoring this because it was an IRA bomb in a Protestant area. There were also very specific threats as to what would happen to any television crew if it did turn up.

It was a familiar cry to those few journalists who mingled, unnoticed, in the crowd.

I I

Danny and the others left early in the morning. They packed up carefully, making sure they left no mess behind, nothing which might connect the site with them.

Two days before, they had spent an afternoon at a fishing camp further to the south. If anyone wanted to know what they had been doing, then they could say they had been on a fishing holiday. Virtually everything they had done was checkable, and clean. They drove in Danny's own car, and had with them their own fishing gear which they had used. They had even left a couple of trout in the back for a day, just to make sure there were some traces of fish around, if ever a search became that thorough. Danny didn't think it would, but he did not want to take any chances.

The early morning mist lay low on the ground, filling the hollows. As they dropped lower it covered the fields so that just the hedges and trees stood out, markers of a shifting and insubstantial base. The sun had yet to warm any colour into the landscape. Beyond the middle distance, the countryside was painted, grey and flat, merging into an undetermined horizon.

The men drove steadily south and east, along the small country roads, towards Cookstown. Hitting on a larger road, they increased speed, and before long they were on the M1 motorway, with a fast forty-odd miles to go to Belfast.

Danny kept his speed just under seventy, and his eyes examined the road in front and behind. He and the others, he knew, were clean. But you could never guarantee anything in this game, and so he wasn't going to do anything which might attract the attention of the police.

The low, flat countryside slipped past quickly on either side. There was very little traffic on the road, and he thought how stupid they had been to build such a motorway sticking like an unwanted finger half way across the province. It would have made more sense to have built one to Dublin, or even one up to Derry. But that would be too much for those so-called loyalists to stomach. 'Mustn't do anything to strengthen the links with the nationalists,' he mimicked to himself. That wouldn't do at all.

However, the road was useful to him at the moment, and anyway, there were more important things to think about.

We have taken a knocking, he admitted to himself. It was something he was reluctant to admit to anyone else – but he had been forced to do so. The army was doing better, and they had suffered a lot of casualties because of this. A lot of arrests, too. The police were doing better as well. Their intelligence had improved. Of course, they wouldn't know the extent of their success. But he knew, and he knew his organization had been dented pretty badly.

That was why he was back in charge. He was very pleased. He had headed the unit a year before, but automatically had lost his position when he was arrested. By the time he got out, another man had filled the post and was firmly in control. Fortunately for Danny, the man had been soft. He had got out and fled the country after some of his members had battered a young girl to death for informing.

The matter had been brutal, but informers had to be wiped out quickly. Danny thought the job was his, but it went again to someone else. Then, three months after that, there had been another chance. The man had been picked up by the police and charged with murdering his father-in-law. My God! thought Danny, what a fool that man had been. His father-in-law had caught him with his latest bird in a pub. There had been a punch up, and the old man's head had caved in. What a way to go, he thought. What a waste for someone to go to jail for that. All the same, he was delighted.

Now he had his old job back, and things, he felt, could only improve. He turned off the motorway just before Belfast to go up to Andersonstown to drop off his men. Pat himself lived in Bangor, some fifteen miles on the other side of the city. He could catch a train there, Danny had told him. His wife could meet him with his own car at the other end, and, Danny added, dredging out the small residue of what he had that passed for humour, he could keep her happy with his fisherman's stories.

Danny didn't want to take Pat home, anyway. He felt uneasy in his house. Pat had moved some years before to this area, where he now had his own semi-detached house, which even had a garden. The first and only time he had ever called, Pat had been out mowing the lawn, and his wife had been sitting in a deck chair, reading a book. He had been totally put out by the whole incident.

As they moved off the slip road, they came to the first road block.

Two Land Rovers had pulled up on either side of the huge cement blocks that lay in the road to slow cars down, and force them to zig-zag through. They could also be joined together by steel poles to block off the road altogether.

'Where are you going?' A young soldier had his head by the window.

'Andersonstown.'

'Is this car yours, sir?'

'Yes.'

'May I see your driving licence?'

He checked the licence, peering at Danny's face, and then back again to the blurry photograph.

'Would you get out, please, and open the trunk.'

Danny hid his annoyance at this whole procedure and got out. While one soldier rummaged through the trunk and all their fishing tackle, another slid a mirror, mounted on small wheels, under the car. He walked round using it to inspect the underside of the car.

The corporal wandered over and peered into the trunk as well. He was a big, raw-boned man. Danny noticed his hands were very large, and that his beret seemed shrunk on top of his head.

'Been fishing?' he enquired affably.

'Yes,' said Danny heavily. 'That's why we've all this tackle in here.'

'Catch anything?' The corporal sounded cheerful. He seemed quite interested in the gear.

'Yes. A few.'

'Been away for long, then?' The corporal had lost interest in the trunk, and he wandered round the side of the car. Careful, said Danny to himself, this big bastard isn't as thick as he looks.

'Three weeks,' he replied.

'Cor!' said the corporal, sucking his teeth. 'Three bloody weeks, eh! Can't be bad. Nice to be away from work that long.'

'Yes,' said Danny, catching the spirit of the moment, and falling neatly into the trap. 'Yes, very nice.'

'Good job?' It was half statement, half question. Danny was taken aback.

'What?'

'Good job? Yours. Get away easy, like?'

'Uh ... sometimes. Not bad ... building, mainly. Comes and goes, you know.'

'Of course,' said the corporal. 'Where did you say you were going, sir?'

'Andersonstown.'

'Ah! Back home, I see. That's where you said you lived, isn't it?'

'I didn't say that. You haven't asked me yet.'

'Oh,' said the corporal, and sniffed. 'Must be slipping.' He consulted his clip board. 'Well now, sir, where do you live?'

'Lower Falls, 26 Dornai Street. You've probably never heard of that.'

'Oh yes, sir! I have, I have.' He sucked his teeth again. 'Can I just see your driving licence again, please?'

Danny started losing his patience. 'What the hell are you on about?' he asked angrily. 'You've already seen it once, and I'm late and I want to get on.'

'Just your driving licence again, sir, if you don't mind.'

'For fuck's sake. . . .' he started shouting. Then he stopped. The corporal was looking at him without much interest.

'I have to stay here, sir,' he said, looking at his watch, 'for another three hours and twenty-one minutes. I don't mind what I do, but it would pass the time to strip a car down.' He held out his hand.

Danny glared, about to outface him. Then he realized this would only make him more conspicuous. Neither did he want the corporal to see any hardness in him, any strength at all. He took a step backwards, holding out his arms in a pacifying gesture.

'Sorry, mate,' he mumbled, fumbling in his pocket for his licence. He held it out without looking at the corporal, and waited while it was checked again.

'Thank you,' said the corporal, turning away. 'That's all.'

Danny drove off. The corporal looked after him. 'Nasty bit of work, that,' he reflected, sucking his teeth. 'Who was he again?'

The soldier checked his list.

'Daniel Loughran, corp, 26 Dornai Street.'

'Hmm,' the corporal sniffed loudly. 'I expect we shall see him again, somewhere. Somewhere, I suspect, where something bloody unpleasant is happening.'

This exchange was lost on Danny, who would have been even more worried about the incident if he had heard it. He was wondering why the hell that damned soldier had carried on like that, anyway. It was just a routine road block. Nothing suspect. Christ! It would be just something like that which would fuck everything up. Something small, and unimportant and unexpected.

However, he was through that, and he had better watch himself next time. He would bloody well cower on the road if necessary. No one must suspect he was anything other than one of the ordinary, wet people who moved around the province every day.

When he got home, the sun was high, and filled his tiny back yard with the gentle warmth of a summer which had stretched well into autumn. The usual muddy patches were baked dry and flaking into dust, and where they could, wild plants had taken root. There was some rank elder in one corner, and along the narrow path of broken paving stones, some dirty privet bushes struggled for survival. An old china sink lay broken, its bits and pieces merging into the dull colour of the untended yard.

There had been a sort of garden here once, long ago, and a straggling rose bush gave the place its only splash of colour. One solitary rose still bloomed.

Danny found a deck chair and pulled it into the yard. The back door lay open to the small, cramped rooms behind him. The front door was open, too, to catch the breeze. What little there was stirred around him as he dozed. His wife was out. He was waiting for Pat to show up. Pat, he had learned, had something interesting to tell him. The message had said very odd and very interesting, and when Pat sent a message like that, it usually meant what it said.

Letting his animal reflexes take over, Danny slumped further in his chair and slept soundly.

The same afternoon closeness had fallen round the presbytery garden, but here it was a little more bearable. The lawns were recently mown, and the smell of fresh grass was about.

There were flowers in the borders, and the bees bumbled purposefully about the long, blue stalks of the catmint, the petunias and the roses.

Here, too, the back door was open to allow the air to circulate.

In the drawing room, the sunlight fell through the tall windows on to the polished furniture, bringing out a warm glow from the red colours of the carpet.

There was a smell of well-polished wood, a faint touch of lavender. On the circular rosewood table in the centre of the room stood a large brass bowl full of flowers. Away from the brightness of the window the room had cool, shadowy corners. A grandfather clock ticked steadily, setting the pace of the afternoon.

In a high-backed chair, with his back to the sun-filled windows, Father Mulligan sat. He was leaning back, with one hand stretched out to stroke, slowly and thoughtfully, the carved griffin head on the arm rest. His thin face and slightly pursed lips were inclined towards his knees. His scant, white hair looked like a halo against the afternoon light.

It would be a very misleading thought, Father Farrell thought to himself. He found nothing saintly, in the accepted sense, in his superior. Rather he found him to be a shrewd and sometimes ruthless man, concerned more with the glory of God and His Church than with the niceties of saintliness.

Perhaps this was an uncharitable thought, Father Farrell reproved himself gently. There were times when a clear and unemotional mind was needed. This was such a time.

'I find it difficult to reconcile the natural feelings I have for law and order,' he said to the older man. They'd been talking together for some time and Father Farrell did not feel anything was becoming clearer at all. 'Especially when I see what is being done ... actually done to people by those very people who are supposed to be upholding the law.'

'You mean you've been watching your parishioners' heads being cracked open by baton-wielding squaddies?' Father Mulligan's nostrils flared on the last word.

'Not exactly. I haven't seen it happen. Certainly I've heard a lot about it....'

'Not quite the same thing.'

'No. No, of course not. But you can see the end effect of that sort of carry on. It's not just beating heads, it's the whole aggressive attitude. I mean, have you ever seen them come down a street, searching, kicking in doors....'

'You forget yourself, Father.' Father Mulligan's voice had hardened. 'I've lived and worked for many years in this city, and I'm well aware of what goes on. I've seen what goes on,' he emphasised.

'I'm sorry,' Father Farrell said quickly. 'I had no intention of....'

'Quite so, quite so. However, you mustn't let your feelings overrule your head. I know you are very close to a number of people in this parish who've been badly affected by all that's gone on – all that's going on even now!'

Father Mulligan looked down at the carving on the arm rest. The griffin's head stretched out from the end, aggressively. He put a long, bony finger on the top and then, slipping it forward, all his fingers came into play to feel the intricate outline of the wood.

'Your task, surely, is to bring the comfort and the teaching of the Church to those whom you can reach. You must concentrate on that, and cut yourself off from other matters.'

'What do you mean, cut myself off from other matters?'

'I detect a certain sympathy for the Republican cause.'

'Sympathy for their ideals, maybe. Not what they do.'

'Can you isolate the two?'

'Yes, I can,' Father Farrell said firmly. 'Ideals are something which need to be kept alive. That doesn't mean I agree with how people try to attain these ideals.'

'Doesn't it?' Father Mulligan clasped his hands together, putting his elbows on the arms of his big chair and his chin on the bridge they formed. He looked at the young priest. The blending of experience and enthusiasm was a difficult exercise, and he felt his experience weighing heavily on him.

'I think you need to examine your thoughts about this very closely. Anything that helps remove violence from our lives must be good. First, however, we must be sure about the source of that violence. That's the difficulty.' He shifted himself in his chair. 'Force must be met with force – perhaps I express myself inadequately there. Force should be met with firmness, but the norm is for it to be met with force. It rarely happens otherwise. You can't blame the troops for hitting back hard when they themselves are being attacked and killed. You can blame them for using excessive force, because then they are departing from the ideals of the society they are supposed to be defending.'

'Neither can you blame the youngsters for using force when it's been used so often against them,' Father Farrell interjected quickly.

'*Reductio ad absurdum.* I mean where do you stop if you

leapfrog your way backwards into history. We spend our lives blaming someone else for our troubles. It's the traditional Irish way of dealing with problems. There is the crusader in all of us, but I think we now take it too far. It's the fatal flaw in the Irish character, and it will be fatal for young Vincent Malone if he doesn't watch out. Fatal, too, for his family. As you yourself have pointed out, look what's happening to them.

'You know,' he went on, 'during the troubles here in the twenties – now you would be too young to remember that ... in fact you weren't even born then – in the twenties there were many more Catholics in the police force than there are now. That's the old Royal Irish Constabulary. It's incredible the number of sons, sons of Catholic policemen, who were at the top of the subversion movement. Many of them imprisoned and all that. Parents would have done anything to stop them. They were very much against it. But their lads were at school, mixing together, convinced that their parental advice was all wrong, and there was nothing much the other side did, mind you, to convince them they were wrong.'

The old man sighed and was quiet for a few minutes. He had worked in this city for many decades now, and he had seen men of violence come and go, and then come and go again. It seemed to matter little what was done, and he'd grown weary of it as he grew older. He had tried to fight this weary cynicism, looking to the Church to find a way of softening his outlook, but he found it increasingly difficult, and it saddened him to find his faith so battered.

'Is it that bad?' asked Father Farrell gently.

The old man stirred and sat upright, his eyes bright again. If he was tired and battered, there was no need to let this young priest see. He would have his own troubles to shoulder, there was no need to add to them.

'No, no. But I find I grow more pragmatic as I grow older. To be honest,' a slight smile came to his lips, 'that is really a euphemism for cynicism. The idealism of youth tends to fade. That's why you're here – to reburnish that idealism and take it on.'

'I take your point.'

'Take this point also,' he said, as Father Farrell got to his feet. 'With the Malone family, and Vincent in particular even if you don't see him, keep your pastoral responsibilities separate from political ideals. Blame is not always so easy to apportion as we're led to believe.'

12

They sat together in the small front room as they had done so often before. Mr Rafferty had his whiskey beside him, and his knees were covered by a black shawl. It belonged to his daughter, and it was strange to see it there, out of place, a woman's garment on a man's knees.

It had grown dark outside. Only the full moon lit the narrow street, and Vincent shivered at the sound of the cold, hard wind that funnelled down it, rattling the windows. He looked at the old man, remembering what he had been, and inside him grew a niggling fear, a doubt, and he wanted to cry out: 'Granda, what'll I do?' But he was afraid.

He thought of the times he had taken his granda for granted. The slow easy swing of his step along the sunny summer beach at Bangor: racing along the edge of the water until the years slowed him down, and he would have to stop, puffing and panting, and offer to buy you an ice. He remembered how he had protected him and Bryan from an over-fussy mother, gentling both of them along as they grew up to be men; how he filled the place left by his father, and filled his head with stories of Ireland. He had always made the boys think out things for themselves, and when they floundered at times, gasping with panic, he had always been there, waiting.

Now his granda was an old man, he could see that now. He, too, seemed to have been hit by the explosion that day, and Vincent knew he sat for long periods crouched in his chair beside the dead fire, staring at the wall.

The old man drew himself up as Vincent talked, for Vincent

was being bitter about that day. He felt stained with bitterness, and he told his granda that he was all talk, and that talk got no one anywhere except into a grave.

Mr Rafferty's large white head turned round, and his eyes snapped back into focus.

'Shut your mouth, boy,' he said, his years in the classroom coming through. 'You've no idea what you're saying.'

'I know that talking never got no one nowhere,' Vincent shot back angrily. 'What good's that ever done here?'

'There are times to talk, and times to act,' the old man retorted. 'No one's denying that. If we hadn't fought the British with guns and bullets, they'd still be here in the whole of Ireland, instead of just the six counties. And we'll fight on to get them out of here, too.'

'For God's sake....' Vincent shouted in desperation.

'Lower your voice,' ordered the old man, severely.

'You don't understand. Fuck the British. What do they matter? It's the people here who are doing the killing. It wasn't the British who killed Sheelagh ... nor Mairead. Don't you care?' he shouted, his voice cracking. 'Don't you care what happened to them?'

The old man flushed, angry, and he banged his fist feebly on the arm of his chair. 'I care. Of course I care.' A line of spittle came from the corner of his mouth. 'But what you should do is ... is join the IRA. I know they did you badly. But that was a mistake.'

'A mistake!' Vincent jeered. 'A fine mistake that was, that left me half crippled.'

'It was a mistake,' he roared. 'A mistake. Will you listen? Ill discipline, they're not what they were. That's why you should be back amongst them.'

'You're joking!'

'I am not.' He looked at Vincent, and a crafty look came into his eyes. 'I'll tell you what, boy, if you want to find who planted that bomb in the café, tha.'s where to look.'

'What do you mean?'

'Just that. I still have contacts, you know. The warning just didn't come in time, you see. It was shameful ... shameful.

'Tis the British they should be fighting, not themselves ... not their own. It's not what it used to be. That's where you should be, Vincent boy, in with the men I used to know. Sure now they'd as soon plant a bomb any old where as in an English barracks. It's them they should be fighting, and you –'

'Oh! Sod the British!' Vincent was distraught and not taking in all his grandfather meant. 'They've done nothing to us. It's not –'

'You're mad!' The old man was genuinely shocked, but Vincent wasn't listening.

'It's not them,' he went on, 'not them that blew up Sheelagh, and Mairead.'

'Until they're out of the country, and we run it,' he shouted at his grandson, his voice quavering, 'there'll be no justice.'

'Justice! Justice!' Vincent shouted back. 'Sure that's all you ever talk about. All talk, that's you. You don't do anything. You just sit on your ass and talk about Connolly and Pearse and Plunkett and what they did in 1916. You know full well what everyone thought of them after they'd finished fooling around in the post office for a week and half Dublin blown down around them. The people would have murdered them if they'd got at them.'

'Well, the British did it instead, even to shooting Connolly sitting in a chair because he couldn't stand.' The old man's hand shook a little, and he took some more whiskey. For a time he sat and said nothing, and all Vincent heard was the wind round the chimney pot, his own heart pounding and his granda's raspy breathing. All his grandfather would ever say was join the IRA. He'd be singing 'Dublin in the Green' any moment, he thought bitterly. But he didn't know what it was like now, and moreover, he hadn't ever been kneecapped.

Vincent put his fingers together and cracked his knuckles, taking in deep breaths to steady himself. Why couldn't his granda help him? he thought in despair. What was so different now?

After a while his granda started speaking again, slowly, as if he was on his own, talking to himself.

'It's primitive and barbaric,' he said softly from a long way

213

away. 'Vengeance for vengeance's sake is an appeal to base passions. Passions of cruelty and hatred. Is that the society in which we want to live? I wonder. For it will mean perpetual violence ... violence breeding violence and counter violence. The violence of the fathers being heaped on the children. Fight and kill, yes, but as a soldier, under discipline. There's some honour there.' He sank further into his chair, nodding his head. 'There's none in what you do, boy. Oh yes. I know ... I know about warnings, and I know about the ones that don't work. That's the way to murder women and children. Oh yes.' He raised his head with his eyes closed. ' "There are things a man must not do to save a nation." D'you know who said that now?' Vincent shook his head but the old man didn't notice. 'A great Fenian leader said that. John O'Leary. Now *he* knew where his honourable duty lay.'

'But they do murder our women and children,' Vincent said softly, controlling his voice now. 'Look what happened to Sheelagh ... your grand-daughter. And Mairead, remember her? You liked her.'

'Oh, I remember them, I remember them well. And I remember you, too, Vincent.' His eyes were held by the fire. 'This is a black time for me. To come to the end with so much left to do. There's a pain in me ... so much lost ... you slip away one by one, and I'm left and there's nothing I can do. You don't need my help. You don't need my advice. My Ireland's gone. You, and the likes of you, have the makings of it now.'

Vincent sat, hardly listening now, the rage in him burning. What did it matter anymore what anyone did? Everyone had had their say and they all did what they wanted. Nothing moved, nothing changed except his links with the old man, and that was gone now. Nothing held him – no doubts, no recriminations. He got to his feet.

'Are you away, then?'

'I am.'

'Are you not spending the night? It's wild outside.'

'No. I can't. You above all should know that.'

'Well, come and see your mother soon. Bryan's away and

I'm not much good. She needs you.'

'Good-bye,' said Vincent.

'Will you come?'

'I'll try.'

Far away to the south across the border, Mairead lay awake in her bed. The noise of the rain splattering down on the grey slate roof above and running fast down the gutters had almost died away. It was a noise that had kept her awake, on and off, for most of the night. But it was now gone. It was still too early for the birds, but the first signs of day were lightening the room. She could just see the soft outline of the rail at the foot of her bed, and the dresser by the wall.

The long night was nearly over, but she would have to be patient for some time yet, so she closed her eyes and practised her relaxing exercises. After a while, unknowingly, she dropped back into a fitful sleep.

The room grew lighter as she slept, pushing the night into the background. When she woke again the rain had stopped. She lay very still, thinking she must have spent the whole night awake, but knowing her drugs must have sent her off to sleep for some of the time.

Looking through the window, above the yellowing leaves of the chestnut tree she saw a mackerel sky, and it was a welcome sight: a sure sign that the stormy, unsettled weather of the past few days had gone. The dry, cold air had replaced the warm, damp air that had brought the rain in the first place. The small quantities of water vapour which were left produced the clusters of high, tiny cloudlets she could now see. She was pleased. Her ability to remember the details of the cloud formations was a link back to the time before the accident – to the time before the summer holidays.

One day flowed into another and she was getting better and stronger all the time. The days were quiet, and she would spend the mornings with Bryan and the afternoons resting while he and her father would go round the farm. It was always very quiet then, and she would lie, listening to the small movements round the house, a door shutting, the murmur of voices in the yard, the sound of the outside world filtering through the mild autumn days.

Her elder sisters were married and away, but her younger sisters who were still at school would come in before breakfast to sit on her bed and chat. Her young brother was at boarding school in Dublin and was furious at missing all the excitement of having Mairead home, and having Bryan there as well. He had been allowed a special weekend off when Mairead had first come back and his awe at seeing her, encased in plaster and with the rash across her face, had only been increased when he was introduced to Bryan – someone who actually lived in Belfast.

Her sisters, sitting round her room in their dressing gowns drinking morning cups of tea, had been full of questions. They had soon found out that Bryan wasn't the same man their sister had gone north with, and they thought it was fantastic that she'd come back with his twin brother. They'd been sworn to secrecy about it. They might think it great, Mairead told them, but the rest of the village wouldn't. They were scandalized she'd ever gone away in the first place, though they never said anything to her. She could see it in their eyes when they came into the drawing room to visit her, or to the bench where she sat outside. Always in twos or threes, never alone, and some still wearing their black shawls. They never stayed long, but they had known her since she was a child, and they wanted to come. If Bryan was with her she would notice their dark eyes widening and the hesitations in their voices. Sometimes she would try and joke with them, or joke with Bryan, making light of what had happened, but it wasn't in their character to see things that way. Once she had let some children play with her crutches, but the mothers had been so obviously disapproving she'd never tried it again.

She kept her days as full as her strength allowed, and she was glad Bryan was there to help when pain would wash over her like a tide, and she had to fight it and tell herself that one day it would all be gone. Other pains filled her mind at times – the doubts and questions raised by the whole visit to the north.

A soft-voiced, Irish-speaking priest had been to see her. For a time the measured cadences of his voice, the familiar prayers and phrases, had calmed her. When the fears and doubts came rushing back, though, he was not experienced enough to deal with them. Of course he had asked about Bryan, and she had resented saying anything about him at all. So she told him Bryan wasn't the man she had gone north with, and she enjoyed watching him struggle to hide his shock. He had really been out of his depth.

Mairead had been brought up in a convent – a world apart, of nuns and of veils and starched headgear; regulated by masses, and cups of hot senna ònce a week. The ordered calm at the time had frustrated her, and she had longed to be out. Now she drew strength from it. Her sisters, clattering their tea cups, wouldn't let her talk about such things. Instead, they drew hearts and arrows on her plaster, and took her pens away so she couldn't blot them out. They talked about the colours they wanted for their bridesmaid's dresses, and when she protested she wasn't even engaged yet, they'd throw their hands over their ears and chant 'we can't hear you, we can't hear you' and collapse into giggling heaps.

The evenings were always a rowdy, noisy time. She would sit with her leg stretched out, busying herself tying trout flies for her father, and everyone would bring whatever they were doing to sit round her and keep her company. She had let Bryan find his own way into her family circle. At first, whenever he had opened his mouth to say something, they had all stopped talking to look at him and listen. Once he had finished, the general conversation would start up again as if it had been switched on. This over-politeness soon wore off, she noticed, and once it had she knew he had been accepted. Her father would bring in news of what was going on in the district, and there would be shrieks of laughter over some stories. The North wasn't something discussed much when they were all together. Usually her father would leave that until they'd all gone to bed and he was left sitting with Bryan by the fire.

One morning Bryan drove her out in the car. It was a weekend but there were few people about and even less traffic on the roads. They drove for a couple of hours, stopping now and then to admire the view. As they came back to their own valley, Bryan pulled up by the lake. The mist was rising, leaving the autumn glow of the trees along the far bank reflected in the still waters. On the high land above there was less colour. The ash and larch had lost their leaves, leaving only the darkened yews and the wind flattened junipers to stand out boldly against the fading grass and the pale rock.

They sat quietly in the car holding hands.

'It's very beautiful here,' Bryan said. 'Very quiet and beautiful. I don't think I want to go back to Belfast.'

'I know. It seems so far away now.'

'I'll have to go back, but. Soon.'

'Soon!' she said, alarmed. 'Why soon?'

'I had a letter yesterday. From Father Farrell. He wrote me saying my mother's not well and Vincent's away and no one knows where he's gone to. England, maybe, to find a job.'

'I'm sorry your mother's worse ... and Sheelagh? What does he say about her? Is she all right?'

'About the same. It's the others who seem to be bad, you know. Depression. They can't take it all. It's all gone so bad this year, ever since Vincent got himself shot ... nothing's worked. I know it was bad before that, but then we could manage, we were all together. Ma was great, she kept the family together, especially after Dad died. Then granda came up and he was great gas. We had a lot of fun with him.'

'He's a lovely man. I like him a lot.'

'He thinks you're great, too.' He smiled at her. 'Someone to talk back at him about his Irish history was the best thing that happened to him. I'm glad you like him.'

'I do. I think your family's great, too. So do my parents. They told me last night.'

'Did they now?'

'Yes.'

'Mairead,' he said, after a time, 'Belfast's a terrible place now, least for us it is. There's nothing left there, and I don't want to take you there. You don't want to go there, do you?'

'No,' she said softly. 'Not really. But that's where your family is.'

'I know. There's no work for me there, but. And the family
. . well, you know what they're like now.'

'Do you have to live there?'

'No, I suppose not.'

'Have you ever thought of leaving?'

'Yes.'

'Where would you go?'

'Abroad maybe.'

'Bryan, you're trying to say something, I know. Why don't
you just say it instead of making me drag it out of you?'

He smiled at her. There wasn't much she missed. 'You're
right. I do have something, but it's two things really, and
they're both to do with you.'

'What's that?' she asked, opening her eyes wide.

'Well, first of all ... that is, I don't know quite how to put
this.'

'Try and make it simple.'

He looked away from her out the car window to the lake.
The low morning sun had burned away the mist and the sky
was blue above. It was a perfect day.

'Will you marry me?'

'Oh, Bryan!'

'Well?'

'Yes, of course.'

'Are you sure?'

She laughed. 'Oh, Bryan, you should see your face.'

'What's the matter?'

'Your face! You look as if you've seen a ghost.'

'Well ... I ... I....'

'What took you so long?'

'Took me so long ... ?'

'Oh, Bryan, catch yourself on! You've had the question
straining at your front teeth for days. Was it my leg put you
off?' she added, grinning hugely.

'Not at all,' he said, rallying quickly. 'That'll mend, and sure
it's more than your leg I'm after.'

'Bryan!' she said pretending to be shocked. 'What can I
say?'

'You've said yes. That's enough for me.'

He leant across and kissed her, and she held his head tight, running her fingers through his hair. 'Dear Bryan,' she whispered softly in his ear. 'I hope you'll not be as slow about everything else.'

'I will not.' His face was muffled in her shoulder. They held on to one another awkwardly in the car. Mairead's leg in plaster made it difficult for her to move. He brushed her cheeks gently with his fingers. Her eyes were very bright.

'You're grinning fit to bust,' he told her. 'What's so funny?'

'You,' she said. 'Just you. You're really very gorgeous.'

'Oh!' he said.

'You make me laugh. No. You make me happy, and then I laugh.'

'I'm glad. You need to laugh. You've had a bad time.'

'I know. And this all makes it worth while. That's probably the wrong thing to say ... with Sheelagh the way she is. She fights so hard ... she's very brave about it. I don't think I'd be so brave if it had been me that lost so much. Can you imagine ... never jumping out of bed again in the morning ... no running around in the country....'

'She'll walk again,' Bryan said firmly. 'You're right. She is brave ... and she'll fight. The doctor told me they start them off on low rockers. They get around on those and then learn on proper legs. He said it's bloody hard work. But you're to forget all that now. We can't change what's happened.'

'We can help.'

'Yes. Of course we can help. When we get back.' Mairead shuddered and he went on quickly. 'Now listen, there's something else I want to talk about.'

'What's that?'

'I've been thinking of moving from Belfast. I thought of it once before ... thought of going to Australia, on my own.'

'Oh!'

'Then I thought I'd try and get the family to follow, but Vincent wouldn't hear of it.'

'Why Australia?' Mairead asked in a small voice.

'I've some cousins there. I don't really remember them, but they are relations. That's something.'

'It's a long way away.'

'That's a good thing about it.'

'Oh, Bryan! Do you really want to go that far?'

He looked at her. 'You mean you don't?'

'How could you afford it?'

'We can't, to start with. The social security people, but. They say Sheelagh will get compensation. A lot of money, they say. We might use that. What do you think?'

'I think it's great ... to get away.'

'Not to Australia, but?'

'It's a long way.' Mairead paused, looking at the changing colours on the lake. There was a swishing noise over the car and she twisted her head to look upwards through the windscreen. Five large swans came into sight, dropping down towards the lake. They called to reach other, a loud bugle-like note, quickly repeated. It was really a double note.

'Bryan, look!' Mairead cried out. 'Aren't they beautiful?'

Bryan peered with her through the windscreen. The swans were heading away from them, circling once and then coming down fast with a splash and a wriggle and then there they were, pale white shapes against the coloured water.

'They are beautiful,' Bryan breathed. 'Swans, aren't they?'

She looked at him, and then gave his hand a squeeze. 'Yes,' she said. 'They're whooper swans. Did you hear the call they made? It's very clear.' They both sat looking at the swans floating on the lake. 'It's not just that Australia's far away,' Mairead said after a while, 'it's Sheelagh. Have you thought how she would take it?'

'Oh, Jesus!' said Bryan. 'I hadn't thought of that.'

'They've cut down on people going there, I've heard. They mi_ 't not be so keen to take someone like Sheelagh.'

Bryan sighed. 'No. I suppose they might not. That's something else I hadn't thought of.'

'There's no need to look so glum, now.' Mairead ruffled his hair. 'Australia's not the only place you can go.'

'What are you thinking of – America?'

'No, no, silly. Here. What's wrong with coming down here? We can get a place in the village. Dad will help. We can all live here, don't you see? You'll need help – not just Sheelagh, your mother too.'

'Oh, Mairead, do you think so?'

'Yes, of course. I've thought so all along.'

'Your parents would be pleased. I mean about having you around. They probably always hoped you'd marry someone from round here, and stay.'

'I expect they did, in a way. But they always thought I was a bit scatter-brained and would do something daft – like marry you.'

'Is it daft, then, that you think you are, marrying me?'

'No, of course not, silly.'

'You don't want to change your mind now? No one else has heard you say yes.'

'What would you do if I did?'

'Beat you ... till you changed your mind back again.'

'You would not!' she cried.

'I would that. Do you want to chance it?'

'No, no. I'll believe you.'

They looked at each other and Bryan, having finally brought himself to say what he'd felt all those weeks, found a relief he'd not known for a long, long time. The strain of the past few months had left his natural defences down, and he had had to fight very hard to keep himself, and his family, together. Then Mairead had arrived with Vincent, and the tight family world he lived in, and his special relationship with his twin brother, started to come apart.

Mairead was unlike any other girl he had ever met, and at first he had taken it for granted that only someone like Vincent would have a girl like that. He had watched from the background, fascinated by the difference between her and the girls he knew, and at how easily she fitted in with the family. Especially he had loved the way she had got on with his granda.

They drove back to the house and walked in and he felt faintly embarrassed at having to face her parents. The O'Donnells had treated him with great kindness since he had arrived, but this was something rather different.

'Oh, ho,' shouted Mr O'Donnell, when he saw them, 'what's all this, then? What have you two been up to?'

'Hold your tongue now, Rory,' his wife said, smiling at them and brushing her hair back. She left a smudge of flour on her nose, for she'd been cooking in the kitchen.

'Mother! Dad! We're going to get married,' said Mairead excitedly. 'He's just asked me. Isn't he lovely?'

Bryan blushed, and swallowed hard. 'Yes. Yes,' he said to them. 'I've just asked Mairead and she's said yes.'

'I'd have had something to say to her if she'd said no,' boomed her father, cracking Bryan heartily across the shoulder so that he staggered back a step.

'Rory, for goodness' sake take a hold of yourself,' said Mrs O'Donnell crisply, going to her daughter and putting her arms round her. 'Darling, I'm so happy for you.'

Mairead let her crutches fall, and balancing on one leg hugged her mother tightly. 'Oh, mum, I'm so excited. Isn't it lovely?'

'This calls for a celebration,' shouted Rory O'Donnell. 'We'll all have a drink right now,' and he moved purposefully towards his drinks cupboard. 'And listen,' he went on, throwing the words over his shoulder, 'now you're about to be my son-in-law, no more of the Mr O'Donnell nonsense. The name's Rory. Right? Right.'

'Oh good!' exclaimed Mairead. 'I'd love a drink.'

'Do you think you ought to, darling?' asked her mother. 'What's the time? Sure it's only half past ten!' She went to Bryan. 'Welcome to the family,' she said, kissing him on the cheek. 'Mairead's quite right. It is lovely to have you.'

'Oh, it's great!' said Bryan, the embarrassment only just starting to go from his face. 'Thank you, Mrs O'Donnell, I'm . . . I'm. . . .'

'Now, Bryan,' she said firmly, 'no more of the Mrs O'Donnell either. It must be Rory and Maude from now on. . . .'

'Since when were ye called Maude?' snorted her husband, handing her a glass of whiskey. ' 'Tis Maudie . . . Maudie she's called.'

'Rory! I can't take this now, we've scarcely had our break-fast. . . .'

'You might have just had your breakfast, but you'll drink that now because I tell you to and don't worry your wee head about me, for I had my breakfast hours ago. Now where's me daughter? Mairead! Come here, will you? Take this, and you too, Bryan ... my God, where are the girls? Call them, Maudie, call them in. Now, this is the drink to celebrate an engagement. The only stuff. None of that fizzy stuff, sure that's for namby-pamby townies, eh? eh?' He turned round with a sweeping gesture, 'Come on in, girls, come on now, here, you can all have a wee drop. Don't let your mother see now.'

Mairead's sisters came in, faces flushed from the cold out-side, squealing excitedly at the news, hugging and kissing Mairead, grinning at Bryan and then going up and kissing him too. 'Stand back now. Stand back,' shouted their father. He raised his glass. 'I give you Mairead and Bryan. *Slainte!*' and he hurled his whiskey straight down his throat.

'Rory!' Maudie squealed at him. 'What are you doing?'

'What do you think I'm doing, woman?' he roared. 'Having a drink with my future son-in-law. Come on, Bryan, get that down your throat. None of that sipping nonsense.'

Bryan grinned at them all and tossed his drink down too. '*Slainte, slainte, slainte,*' he said to them all, waving his glass before it was seized by Rory.

'Aha!' cried Rory, 'come on with ye. Drink up now. Sure we'll have to get some of the lads in this evening. What do you think, Bryan? Eh? Am I not to be a grandfather now before I'm sixty?'

'Dad!' shouted Mairead.

'Rory, will you hold your tongue?' said his wife. 'Sure you have five grandchildren already. What are you talking about?'

'Aha! Aha! But a grandfather again, I say, again. And this wee darling girl is going to do it.'

Bryan grinned sheepishly. My God! he thought, there's going to be some drink taken this evening.

13

As the days went past more and more quickly, Vincent welcomed the early darkness and the growing confusion of the violence all round him. Each night the city burned and bled, and each night he gained more confidence until he felt the blood run ice cold in his veins and he knew that he wouldn't be the one to make mistakes; he wouldn't be the one to blow himself up like so many others, nor would he be the one caught by the security forces. His bombs were simple and effective. When he ran out of commercial gelignite he'd stolen from the quarry where he had worked for a time, he turned to nitro-benzine and weedkiller. With a training manual he'd kept hidden since his early days with the Provies, he'd taught himself how to mix the explosives. Small mistakes would be fatal but he never realized just how critical the percentages were, and because he was lucky he grew more sure of himself.

After the last meeting with his grandfather, he had moved out of the house and taken lodgings some distance away. His mind closed in on itself, shutting out the warmth of family affection, locking everything together into his one overriding passion for revenge. He felt high and heady as if he were half starved, with his goals clear and beckoning before him.

Whoever laid the bombs, he argued to himself, it was the Orangemen to blame; they were at the bottom of everything that had been unfair or unpleasant in his life, and it was those people whom he would punish now. Not just for Sheelagh and Mairead, but. He would do it for all his people who had been beaten down by them over the years. His granda was quite right about that.

He had grown to hate them in the past few years, when they had come with their petrol bombs and set whole streets on fire and then paraded with their black bowler hats and Orange sashes, strutting and swaggering past Catholic homes with sword and stick and band. How he had longed to do something to stop them marching, but he always knew it was more than his life was worth even to dash across the road in between the passing Lodges with their huge embroidered banners and the ham-fisted men straining at the poles and ropes to hold them in the wind. The endless processions, clump, clump on the twelfth of July especially, with the twirling, whirling drum majors, some of them only youngsters, throwing their maces round their backs and under their legs and high in the air; the uniforms and kilts and the accordions and the flute and drum bands, ah yes! The flute players with their heads all leaning to one side, their cheeks puffed out with their blowing. Oh God! How he hated it all and the sheer bloody arrogance of it, and he remembered that as a child the Orange parades hadn't mattered at all, and they had all danced along the street beside them like the Protestant children did now. A Catholic wouldn't be seen dead near one these days, only to throw a stone or two, and the Orangemen had only themselves to blame for that.

Sometimes he clamped his head hard together between his hands to hold it all in, and sometimes he'd lie awake at night, his thoughts churning over and over. When his black depressions hit him now he knew what to do and he'd force his brain to cool down and he would make his way to where he kept his explosives hidden.

Heavy and bulky in their flak jackets, the soldiers stood close to the front of the house. They were carrying long, clear plastic riot shields. The one nearest the corner had his stuck out in front of him, and he was peering through it down the side street. When a milk bottle smashed into the road a few feet from him, he didn't move.

Across the main road from them, on the other pavement, stood a television crew looking straight down the same side-street as the soldier. Vincent stopped to watch them. They seemed to be just out of range of the odd stone or bottle that would come flying from the end of the street towards them. They would turn their backs, though, he noticed, if a bottle looked like landing too close, and he smiled to himself at that. He had thrown bottles himself, aiming them to break just in front of people so the fragments would bounce up into their faces, and this lot obviously knew all about that. The odd fragment that did reach them bounced harmlessly off their backs. One large bottle fell more heavily than the rest, full of some liquid. He thought it was probably battery acid.

It was quiet for a while and the man put down his camera and lit a cigarette. Over the road the soldiers did the same, still standing in a line close to the wall. They had stopped looking down the street and were chatting amongst themselves, their visors pushed up on top of their helmets. They didn't look as if they were going to move and neither could he while they were still there because he wanted to go down that street, and he knew he would be stopped by them. He put his collar up and lit a cigarette himself, leaning back into a doorway to avoid the wind and cupping his hand round the cigarette to keep its warmth.

Some sort of riot was still going on in the side streets off the main road, the sounds rising and falling and at times disappearing altogether. This happened so often now, he thought, but always in a Catholic area. The army hadn't taken on any Prods since the riot in the Shankill at the start of it all. Then, the Prods had shot dead one of their own policemen who with the army had tried to stop them pouring down the road towards a large block of Catholic flats at the bottom. He knew what had happened well enough, for he'd been walking out with a girl from those flats at the time and they had both been terrified. The large, uncontrolled procession had come down the Shankill behind a Union Jack, and the beat of the huge Lambeg drum had bounced off the shops and houses in an awful roar of endless sound. The army had sorted them out, but it had taken

227

all night in a hail of bullets, and yet another night of fighting to clear the whole road from end to end. What mad bastard, he wondered, had ever put a block of Catholic flats at the bottom of that road?

The cameraman had his camera back on his shoulder, and they were all looking down the street. He moved up behind them to see what was happening. They were watching a small boy staggering along towards the corner carrying a large bit of rock or broken paving stone. It was obviously too big for the boy to handle with any ease, and he put it down to have a rest. The camera switched off him and on to the soldiers talking by the house who couldn't see the boy.

He picked up his rock again and came on up the street. Behind him Vincent could see a makeshift barricade – old bits of furniture, paving stones heaped up, dustbins – anything went into those barricades, but this one didn't look as if it would stop much. There was no one around it, and he knew they would all be away manning another one where something was happening.

So just the small boy was left in the street on his own, and the cameraman was intent on him. They all stood there, saying nothing, watching. Vincent felt his fingers burning and he swore softly and flicked his cigarette away.

There was something strange about the boy with his straight black hair falling over his eyes. As he came closer, wobbling from side to side, Vincent peered hard at him. When he was nearly at the corner he had another rest, and now he was only some four feet away from the soldiers.

'Jesus!' Vincent whispered to himself as recognition came to him. It was Jamie. His first instinct was to rush across the road, but it was too late. Jamie picked up his rock for the last time, took a couple of quick steps forward and with a huge effort flung it round the corner. Then he turned and ran, his anorak flying out behind him.

The rock bounced off a soldier's leg and he leapt into the air, twisting himself round behind his riot shield. Instinctively the others caught the sudden movement and jumped themselves, their eyes automatically going to top windows and along the road. The soldier on the end of the line, whose leg had been hit, looked cautiously round the corner, his shield out in front of him. Vincent sensed his initial puzzlement as he looked at a street empty except for a small boy running away as hard as he could. The soldier turned and raised his hand to quieten the others, and shouted something over his shoulder. Vincent couldn't see their reactions under their visors, but the television crew laughed. 'That'll make a change,' said one.

He waited on but nothing else happened, and in the end the soldiers moved off down the street followed by the television crew and then himself. He walked slowly along, turning off as soon as he could to cut behind the disturbances and make his way to where he kept his supply of explosives hidden. He kept them in a derelict house at the end of a row of terraced houses which were still lived in, and so his comings and goings weren't much noticed. The front windows had been bricked up, but there was a way in through the back door which he was able to close so that it all looked undisturbed. He wouldn't keep his things there for long – just a week or two and then he would move them again.

He squeezed himself in and grubbed around, pulling up some loose floorboards to get at his board of explosives and the few tools he used to make his bombs. If the military did find it, he thought, they'd undoubtedly boast they'd got another bomb factory, but in fact it was a poor one ... at least, he corrected himself, it was poor in quantity, but what he had was quite good.

Working quickly and neatly he pulled out only what he needed for the first stage. If a military patrol came anywhere near he would have to pack it all up very quickly and get the hell out fast. From his pocket he took a small alarm clock and put it down on the floor and set to work.

'I don't know what to do about them,' Father Farrell complained. He was feeling tired and grumpy and Father Mulligan wasn't being too helpful. 'The old man ignores me,' he went on, 'Mrs Malone I can't get any sense out of half the time ... one of the boys has gone, disappeared, and his mother's

half demented because she thinks he's away to the Provos
... and the other boy's down South.'

'I know, I know,' said Father Mulligan testily. 'Sure you've told me all that before, more than once. What about the other children?'

'I'm beginning to think they're all children. . . .'

'Now, now then,' Father Mulligan reproved him.

'Well, for pity's sake, the other two *are* children, and they're in no great shape. The little girl is worse than her mother, and the wee fellow, Jamie, is out most days doing what he wants to do.'

'Do they go to mass?'

'The mother comes ... sometimes. She's not quite right ... in her mind, I mean. At least I don't think so. She's had to put up with a lot. Oh, my goodness, I had a fright last night. I thought the family had another tragedy on their hands.'

'What's that?' Father Mulligan asked sharply.

'I was riding down Ormeau Road, you know. Murder Mile they call it. Well, now, there on the pavement was this lad, slumped against the wall, and at first I thought it was one of the Malone boys. Looked just like them, black hair and all.'

'Dead?'

'Not at all, but in a bad way. He wouldn't give them his car, he said. . . .'

'Wouldn't give who his car?' Father Mulligan sounded very impatient.

'I'm just coming to that. He was too frightened, he told me, to know who they were. They must have been some paramilitary outfit, the Provos probably. When he told them to go away, but, they just dragged him out and broke both his arms. He said, what could I do ... nothing ... they had me.'

'That's terrible!'

'They said to him, put your arms up against the wall there, and they got out their hurling sticks and broke them – just like that.'

'My God!' said Father Mulligan, shocked. 'They must have been Provos if they'd hurling sticks. Mind you, he was lucky now he wasn't shot.'

'Lucky! And him with two broken arms – and no car.'

'He could have been dead,' responded Father Mulligan. 'Sure his arms will heal. Once you're dead, that's that.'

'It's enough to make anyone mad angry, but. Are you surprised that Vincent Malone is off to get vengeance for what's been done to his sister ... and indeed his whole family, as a result?'

'His brother ... what's his name now, Bryan, isn't it? He's not tearing round looking for revenge, is he?'

'No. He's very upset, but.'

'That is a rather different matter,' he answered gently. 'Being upset is quite normal. Bitterness is something else, and while I'm not always surprised at it, it does sadden me, specially in a family like the Malones.'

'What do you mean?'

'I mean that here we have – or had – a solid, God-fearing family – by and large, that is, I don't include the old man – anyway a family brought up as a good unit. They get badly hit ... it's very tragic, and the bitterness creeps in. It doesn't have to, you know. Tragedy has hit a lot of families here in the past year or two, and bitterness doesn't always follow.'

'I think you are asking rather a lot.'

'Listen to me,' he went on. 'I'll give you an example of this – it really is worth remarking. Now when that little girl died – was killed – Teresa Rooney ... we don't know if it was revenge or what, but all we know is that a little girl on the Shankill Road was killed shortly after. Within twenty-four hours. It could have been anyone, but it looked like Republican reprisals. Now the minute that happened Mrs Rooney, with her daughter's body still in the house ... she put on her hat and coat and went over to see the other mother on the Shankill. That is something.'

'I find it amazing,' said Father Farrell.

'Well, it won't be so amazing when you've been here as long as I have. I've encountered an enormous lot of incidents where someone has been shot, very often not in mistake but in folly. One of the times it was a mob down in one of the streets in the Lower Falls, and the military fired, and they killed this poor fellow who had a few drinks taken. Probably he was throwing bottles at them. The commander of the military afterwards nearly went into an air of ... a condition about it because he knew perfectly well he shouldn't have been shot. It was stupid. But he was killed.

'Now take if from his family's point of view.' They were both sitting on after their evening meal, and Father Mulligan poured himself another cup of tea. 'Do you want one?' he asked and Father Farrell shook his head. 'Well now, I went along to see his family the next day. There wasn't a trace of bitterness or anything else. They just said, "You know, Father, he was a good boy. He came in here every Friday and handed in his wages. He's done that since he started work. It's a pity he took a drink tonight."

'I said to them, "Well, don't you want any fuss about the funeral? You don't want one of these semi-military funerals?" and they said, "Oh no, no, no. We don't want anything like that.' Do you know what else they said? They didn't want any other family going through what they'd been through. We meet that attitude time and time again. On both sides. The ministers tell me the same.

'It's the Provos and the UVF and the likes of them who try to exploit the situation.'

'But if it's in people to be bitter, then they are going to be. I mean, what am I going to do about the Malones?'

'Pray with them. Talk with them. Teach them what other people have learned, and how other people have coped with their tragedies. That sometimes helps, you know. You must give them the inner strength to resist and overcome the tragedy. But you must keep at it. . . . You can't let it go.'

'I feel so inadequate for it. I feel just that it is sometimes all too much for me to cope with on my own.'

'You don't have to,' said Father Mulligan drily. 'You've forgotten someone up there,' he jabbed a finger at the ceiling, 'who helps you ... all the time. And will help the Malones too, so He will. Don't forget that.'

'I know, I know,' said Father Farrell sadly. 'If only I could get through to them. It's a lack of communication that makes things so difficult. Sometimes, of course, you don't even get the chance to try. I remember being stopped one night. There was this fight, you see, between a youngster I knew and three other lads who were beating him up. When I stopped – not to join in, mind you, but to try and stop the fight – they insulted me. They said I was wearing a Ben Sherman shirt back to front ... and implied I wasn't the spiritual Father of the youngster there, but the real father, you know. Ho, ho, ho, sort of thing. Then they got nasty and I think they'd have laced me if the army hadn't come along.'

'That sounds like very direct communication to me. Why are you complaining?'

'What? Oh! Seriously, but. The army came along and they all ran, but one was caught, the ringleader, and they got round him in a circle and they must have given him a thump for he went down. He's very bitter, that fellow, now. I would have loved to have ... to speak with him one day, with nobody else around – nobody for him to show off to ... just to see if I could get through to him.'

'Maybe you could. You're right about communication. I remember talking to Arthur Bishop once – you know he works in that community centre down in Donegall Pass – talking to him about the rivalry between our schools and theirs, and it wasn't just ordinary rivalry as you well know. Anyway, the whole question of what Tartan meant came up. We decided it would be a good idea if the boys confronted each other in debate in a situation where they couldn't actually clobber each other. So Arthur got a couple of lads to come across and talk about Tartan, and I laid on a class over here.

'I met these two lads at the door. They were dressed in their denims, with sleeveless waistcoats and big Tartan scarfs, and the first thing they said on coming in was "Holy Jesus, it's just like ours. It even smells like ours." They were astonished to find a Catholic school was just like their own. So they sat at the front of the class, with their scarfs draped over the desks, like banners. Then we brought our lads in. They were very wary about all this, but we told them it was the chance to discuss the kind of problems they faced, and it was up to them, but let the two Tartan lads have their say first.

'Now,' Father Mulligan went on, well in his stride, 'the two boys spoke very well. They were remarkably articulate. They talked about their backgrounds, which were exactly the same to the boys they were talking to. They talked about the current situation, which again was parallel, and they talked about the cult of violence and the Tartan. And they admitted they liked violence for violence's sake, and that sometimes in the heat of it all they reached heights of violence which frightened them.'

'And how did all this go down?'

'But wait, listen. They admitted that if they got the chance to beat up a Fenian, they enjoyed it. But if there wasn't a Fenian available, then anybody would do ... that was just as enjoyable.

'Now, to answer your question.... No, wait again. I'm talking myself dry.' Father Mulligan got up and went across to the dark, polished sideboard and took out two glasses and a bottle. As he poured, he went on talking. 'The questions weren't as aggressive as I thought they would be. Quite searching, in fact. Obviously trying to understand what made the other tick. They all admitted they liked having a go at a traditional enemy, but that it was a bloody stupid way to live. They would have a much better quality of life, and they recognized this, if they were free to walk through any territory without being attacked.'

Father Farrell sat forward in his chair, leaning on the table, listening intently. He would never have thought of doing something like that; he just couldn't imagine it happening. He looked at Father Mulligan, relaxed now, his arm lying on the table, his fingers turning his glass slowly round and round. With his other hand he rubbed the back of his head, fluffing up his white hair.

'You know,' sighed Father Mulligan, 'they all recognized there was a better way of life around. That once they had set themselves up in their ghettos, the very boundaries of these had the effect of shrinking their world. The Protestant boys with their Tartan scarves realized that their boundaries in particular were gettting smaller, that their own areas were being sub-divided, that it was dangerous for a Donegall Pass boy to go into Sandy Row ... that a Shore Road Tartan was likely to be beaten up if he went on to the Shankill. They realized all right they were reducing the availability of social intercourse.

'But they didn't know how to get off this merry-go-round on which they had been placed by others in their respective communities.'

They sat silently for a while, and Father Farrell thought how silly it all was, how much ignorance and fear there was around. He remembered a woman who had been vehemently outspoken about the Provos, and the way everyone around her let them come and go as they pleased. She wasn't going to stand for that, she told him, in confidence, of course. The next time he had seen her had been early one morning when a military patrol had been spotted in the area. She had passed him, hurrying along with her head down, to bang her dustbin lid on the ground with the rest of them. She never looked at him once.

'What you've got to do,' said Father Mulligan at last, 'is to keep on talking to those to whom you can talk ... and let them talk to you as well. That often helps. Does Mrs Malone talk to you?'

'Oh, yes,' he replied heavily, 'she does that.'

'The boy Bryan. You say he's away still?'

'He is. I've written to him, but. Told him he ought to be home, his family needs him.'

'Did you indeed! Was that wise?'

'Yes,' said Father Farrell, feeling more firmly about this that he'd felt about a lot of other things lately. 'Yes, I do think so. If anyone can hold that family together, it is Bryan Malone. So he'd better come back and do just that, for I'm sure I can't.'

'What's he doing down South?'

'He went back with that girl his brother came up with – Mairead her name was.'

'Oh!' Father Mulligan's eyebrows went up.

'I think he was just embarrassed with his brother, who took little or no notice at all of the girl after the bomb. I think he felt sorry for the girl, and wanted to help her back home.'

'Quite so, quite so.' Father Mulligan nodded his head.

'Thank you for your help, and the drink' said Father Farrell, getting to his feet.

'That's all right. I'm getting quite used to discussing the problems of the Malone family.'

The fire started early in the morning, and from the first dull explosion and tiny flicker of flame it had spread quickly through the huge, rambling mill. The glow lit up the sky over the eastern part of the city and showers of sparks soared upwards into the dense black smoke that poured out. Crowds gathered on the street corners to watch it, televison cameramen arrived to film it and the firemen could do little about putting it out. If they stopped it spreading they would be lucky – and content. They perched high on their slender ladders, the jets of water turning to steam as they arched out over the building; small figures silhouetted against the red and orange flames one moment and then were lost from view against the billowing smoke. It was one of the largest fires that had ever been seen in Belfast, and the crackle and roar could be heard halfway across the city.

Vincent hadn't stayed to watch this fire, as he had some that he had started. He knew what it would be like with the streets soon ankle deep in water and black slush and muck from the building. He had been well away when his carefully planted bomb had gone off, and he was pleased with the way the timing device had worked. It was very simply, really, with an alarm clock – an ordinary cheap one that could be bought anywhere. It was the placing of the explosives that had done the damage, however. He knew that well enough.

Only part of the mill was being used, but the people who owned it were fools, and had no idea about security. He had easily dealt with the old night watchman, hitting him over the head before he even knew he was there. He hoped the old man hadn't woken up before the bomb went off, as he had left his body lying beside it, uncertain whether or not he was dead. He hadn't the time to check, and he was safely in Ballymurphy, standing on the road eating a bag of chips, when it all went up.

Behind him an armoured car whined up the road and turned

into the heavily fortified school hall the army used as one of their bases. He heard the crack of a rifle, and a bullet singing and ricocheting off the armoured plate. There was no reaction, but he could imagine the sentries in their camouflaged pillboxes outside the entrance peering through the firing slits trying to spot the source – hoping for another shot so they could make sure. He moved further up the road. He knew they also had night-sights so they could see in the dark, and he didn't want to be seen.

The shot must have been a diversion, for he soon heard a lot more shooting further up the road. He sat down on some steps on a bank leading up to a row of empty houses and lit a cigarette. Protestants had once lived in them, but the endless trouble coming across the road had driven them off, and now the houses were empty, their broken windows boarded up. He was caught between the army post on his left and the shooting further up to his right. He didn't want to risk going either way, but he didn't really mind waiting as he had nothing else to do and he could always use the shooting as an excuse for having to stop where he was.

So he sat on, smoking, listening to the gun battle and looking at the glow of his fire over the city. He felt quite happy until he remembered Jamie that morning. Silly little bugger, he thought, and what the hell was his mother doing letting him loose like that? He should have been at school, working at his lessons. Strange, he thought, it wasn't like her to allow a thing like that. He would speak to her about it, and then, and then ... but he wouldn't be seeing her, for he'd left.

He sat for a long time in the darkness waiting for the shooting to die down, chain smoking until his mouth was dry. He wasn't keen to go back to his new digs because he wasn't used to living on his own yet and, pleasant though his landlady was, it wasn't the same as home. He had moved in some weeks previously, telling the woman he had just come back from England. She hadn't asked any questions, and he didn't know whether she believed him or not. Probably not, he thought, as she was used to people in trouble, having her husband and three sons all inside Long Kesh, interned for God knows how long. She had one daughter still at home who gave her a hard time, coming in at all hours of the night. What she needed was a strapping from her father, but of course he wasn't there. He thought of Mairead, far away in the South at the other end of Ireland, near the sea where they had walked that summer, bright blue and sun-filled. What a long time ago it seemed now. He had been mad to bring her to Belfast, though he doubted whether he could have stopped her once she'd set her mind to it ... and Bryan going down with her. Strange, he thought, how things worked out. Bryan was soft in the head going there. If she hadn't come up, then maybe Sheelagh wouldn't have been in that café when the bomb went off. If only ... if only ... His spirits started to go down and he pushed them all from his mind. He'd make everyone pay for it, but.

He got back to his lodging that night with some difficulty for there was yet another gun battle raging among the houses and across the fields that lay behind it. The street was deserted as he walked along, and he soon realized why when he heard the smack of a bullet hitting the wall above him.

His landlady was in a state when he got back, absolutely raging at what was going on. The military were nothing but a bunch of whore-mongering pigs, rampaging round the countryside upsetting and murdering innocent people. She had her grey hair still in curlers with not even a scarf over the top, and she grabbed him by the arm and yelled at him until he pushed her down in a chair.

'Catch yourself on,' he shouted back. 'Sure this goes on every night. What's the matter with you?'

'It's Brenda. She's out ... God knows where but maybe with those pigs.... Jesus, if she's caught they'll shave her head and pour tar all over her. Oh!' She screamed as the glass shattered in the window behind her, and Vincent saw, horrified, a hole appear in the front wall. The bullet had gone straight through. 'Now the bastards are shooting at me. Dear God! If any men were here they'd sort out them lily-livered scum. Oh, oh! What am I to do?'

'Come with me,' Vincent pulled her to her feet. 'Come on,

come on. You can go next door. You won't be on your own there.'

'Oh!' she cried, 'where are you going?'

'Where do you think I'm going? Out. To look for your damn daughter before she gets herself killed. Will you come on now?' he shouted again, opening the front door and looking out. 'Quick now, in next door, and Mrs what's her name will look after you.'

'Oh! Oh! Wait till I get my hands on them pigs ... them butchers.' She scuffled across the patchy grass to the next house and Vincent hammered on the door. When his hammering was answered, he pushed her in shouting to her to stay there, he would see what he could do. He had no idea at all, and he just wanted to get out of the place.

He walked down the road. He felt tired, but the adrenalin was still in him, and had been given a boost by the bullet that had come flying through the house. Straight through the front wall it had gone – he was amazed at it. Terrible damage that would do to a fellow, he thought. They said they tumbled, like, when they hit your body, and came out the other side leaving a hole as big as a dinner plate. He didn't like that idea at all.

He hadn't been walking for five minutes along the empty road, not really thinking where he was going, when an ambulance pulled up beside him. One of the men in it leant out.

'Is there some fields up ahead there?' he asked.

'There are,' said Vincent.

'Would you know your way round to the other side?'

'I would,' said Vincent. 'What's up?'

'We've a report there's a girl shot up there – something to do with the military. We're not quite sure.'

'Jesus!' said Vincent. 'I'm after looking for a young girl myself who's supposed to be out here somewhere. Is that where she is?'

'I don't know if she's yours, but jump in and we'll go and find out.'

They roared off in the ambulance, directed by Vincent, screeching round corners. The noise of the firing was getting heavier all the time. They could even see the flashes of guns. They stopped behind some buildings.

'Christ,' said the driver, 'that's bad, so it is. There's not a sinner around here. What do we do?'

'Control says whoever it is, they're badly wounded. So we keep going.'

'Right you are,' said the driver. 'Do or die, I say. Let's go.' He put his foot down, and they fairly whizzed up the road round a few more corners until Vincent shouted to him to stop. He pulled up behind a hedge. 'What's up?' he asked.

'We're here,' said Vincent. 'Can't go any further by road. Where's this girl now?'

The driver looked around him in the darkness. He could see they were on the edge of the estate, and the fields climbed up away from them towards the mountains. Vincent helped the other first aider to get some bags out of the ambulance. The firing was still going on, and someone shouted at them out of the darkness. The driver disappeared in that direction and they waited for him, their eyes getting used to the darkness. The houses below them were silhouetted against the lighter night sky and they could smell the dampness of the fields close by. To Vincent it all felt unreal – like a dream – except he knew it wasn't.

A few minutes later the driver came running back out of the blackness shouting, 'Follow me and keep your heads down,' and away they all went, scrambling over the walls and fences and across the back gardens till they came to an open space and a ditch. They flung themselves down into it, and Vincent suddenly became aware there were soldiers there. They stopped, puffing, and he caught the driver by the arm.

'What the hell's going on?' he said hoarsely.

'Sorry, mate. Didn't have time to tell you back there. The girl is out there. There's a squaddie with her, but. He's bad. Shot in the chest.'

'Shit!' said Vincent. 'What about the girl?'

'Shock ... shock. Don't think she's been hit. So they say.'

'Who says? Who told you this?'

'Officer back there. The man who shouted at us. He told me,

and anyway, how do you think we got here? It was his lads giving us covering fire.'

'Bloody hell,' whispered Vincent, dumbfounded at what he'd got himself into. If the military knew who he was, they'd make short work of him. He almost laughed at the situation, except the gunfire around him washed out any humour in it all. 'What do we do now?' he asked quietly.

'You do what you like. We're going to get them in.'

'Across there?' Vincent gasped, raising his head a little above the ground.

'Yes.'

'I'll stay here,' he said firmly.

'That's the girl you're looking for, I've no doubt,' said the ambulance driver. 'There's two of them there, and we need help.'

'You'll be on your own,' shouted a soldier at him. 'We're moving out. Run out of ammo.'

'Oh, God!' said Vincent. He'd better go anyway. He would only attract attention to himself if he pulled out now. 'All right. I'll come.'

Looking up, they could just make out some figures towards the centre of the field. What they were doing out there was anyone's guess, but if it was Brenda, and her mother was right, she had probably been there with the soldier when it all started. It might well have been they who attracted the firing in the first place.

'When the soldiers start firing again,' Vincent heard someone say, 'we go. Remember to keep your heads down. OK?'

'Right.' Vincent nodded.

They crouched in the ditch together. They were waiting to dash into the field, the other soldiers in the ditch were waiting to get out and back to where they could get some more ammunition. As the firing started, they broke in different directions. Vincent was almost knocked down by a bulky shape passing him in the darkness, and then they were out in the open, crouching and running hard for the figures lying out in front.

This is crazy, Vincent thought, as they threw themselves

down beside the wounded soldier. There was an officer with him, holding his head. The girl lay a few feet away, her dress pale against the grass.

'Thank God you're here,' the soldier croaked, and Vincent thought, he doesn't know whether to shout or whisper. He didn't know either. The bullets went zip, zip, zip in the grass around them as they lay spread out. The ambulance men worked on the soldier lying down as low as they could, but it was very awkward. Vincent crawled across to the girl.

'I think she's all right,' the officer said. 'She doesn't seem to be hit.'

It was Brenda. She was lying rigid in the wet grass, her eyes wide open, blood on her chin. She'd bitten through her lower lip. Vincent looked at her in sudden fury. She was barely fifteen, and by fooling around with some bloody Brit soldier, she had got him into this mess. He slapped her face calling, 'Brenda, Brenda. It's me, Vincent. Vincent Murphy, Vincent Murphy.' He was using the name he'd given her mother, but to no effect. She lay there, still rigid, unseeing in the night, and he crawled back to the others.

'It's her all right,' he told them. 'How do we get her out?'

'We'll have to come back for her. This squaddy's in a bad way. If we don't get him away soon he won't make it.'

Oh no, thought Vincent. Come back again through all this. Christ, what had he got himself into? The whole thing was becoming a nightmare.

They struggled together on the ground, the bullets still whistling overhead, and managed to get the soldier on to the stretcher. The officer was on his radio, calling for more support. It came in the form of two scout cars, and suddenly the noise of the firing changed as they swung their turrets and opened up with heavy calibre machine guns, spraying the far edges of the fields.

'I'll stay with the girl,' Vincent said suddenly. 'You need more than two on that stretcher. Only for Christ's sake don't forget to come back for us.'

'Right you are,' said the ambulance driver without hesitation, taking hold of one end of the stretcher. His mate and the officer took the other end.

'Let's go,' shouted the officer, his voice coming back to him, and away they went, bent double, back to the ditch, leaving Vincent and the girl alone, surrounded by the darkness. Above him in the cold night sky the stars shone brightly through the ragged edges of the clouds being blown across the province to the wild wastes of the Atlantic. The air was fresh with the smell of the country, of earth and rotting leaves and water. The wind ruffled through his hair and he shivered and crawled back to the girl who lay so still on the grass. He had never thought he would find her; he had only gone out because he couldn't stand her mother any longer, shrieking at him like a banshee. He didn't like being shot at either, but he didn't seem to have done very well over that problem. He pulled off his anorak and put it over her, and rubbed her hands and waited and hoped they wouldn't be long in coming back for him.

He heard them before he saw them, first crashing through the ditch, and then their heavy breathing as they got closer. The girl was light, and they lifted her easily on to the stretcher and she groaned. Then they were off again, back the way they had come. They weren't able to get the stretcher over all the back garden fences, so they went round the front of the houses where another ambulance was waiting for them.

The soldiers were cursing the Provos, quietly and bitterly as they smoked. He went to the ambulance with the girl, and the driver said he had better get in and come with them to the hospital. They slid the stretcher in and he went in after it and sat on the other stretcher. In his confusion he didn't notice there was someone lying on it.

'Jesus!' he shouted, jumping up.

The driver who was shutting the back door looked in.

'Don't worry about him,' he said. 'That's the squaddy you went out to fetch. . . . Her boyfriend,' he said, indicating the girl. 'He's dead. Died as we put him in.'

14

In her kitchen, Mary Malone sat quietly on her chair. Her hair, uncared for now, lay in wispy, greasy strands about her face. The small coke stove, which once shone so brightly with black lead polish, was dull and full of cold ash.

Dirty crockery sat on the draining board and in other odd spaces about the room. The frying pan, the most used cooking implement in the house, was covered in cold fat and the remains of unwanted cabbage. The bacon had long since gone.

The whole place was a mess, and Mary Malone, sitting in a heap and looking vacantly out of her dirty window at nothing, knew it was. She also knew there was little she was going to do about it. There was little she wanted to do about it. In fact, had she been able to string together even a short sequence of logical and constructive thoughts, she would have realized there was nothing she wanted to do about her dirty house, or anything else. Every time she moved to do something, the effort seemed too much, and she stopped.

She told herself that caring for her father and the rest of the family was more important. As it happened, she did little for them now either. She would, of course, fuss around Deirdre, and she had taken her to the doctor on a number of occasions. He had given her pills to quieten her down. They certainly made the child go to sleep more quickly, she thought. She had been so impressed she had tried some herself. It had meant going back to the doctor again rather soon for some more, and he had been cross when she told him they had got knocked over and washed down the kitchen sink.

What good was all that? she thought, as she slowly moved herself to put on the kettle. A cup of tea would help. Deirdre now? Deirdre didn't seem to get any better; not that she could see, anyway.

She pulled an old teapot towards her and was about to spoon some tea in when she found it was still half full. She emptied it into the sink, watching as the cold tea leaves swirled round and round and then disappeared. She splashed water at the leaves left behind. Most of them stayed where they were. She gave up and turned her attention back to the teapot.

She rested her back against the draining board while the kettle boiled. Her back was sore, and the change of position eased it a bit. What had she been thinking about? She scratched her head slowly. A bluebottle buzzed in through the open door, a momentary flash of bright green when the sun caught it. It settled on the edge of a plate.

Deirdre ... that was it, Deirdre. And the doctor. He didn't seem to do any good. The child, she thought, suddenly angry, still wet her bed for no good reason. It made her wild. How could anyone live with such a stink in the room? She had beaten the child hard, but it made no difference. A child of seven wetting her bed. She was too old for that; it would have to stop.

She made the tea, lettting it brew for a while, pouring it into a mug when it was ready and ladling in several spoons of sugar. It was hot and strong and very sweet, and she cupped her hands round it despite the warmth of the early autumn day.

She was on her own in the house. Everyone had gone out for some reason or another. Her father was away down the road doing a message for her. Jamie was away at school, and so was Deirdre. Bryan was in the South and ... her mind wandered fo a minute or two. Who else was in the house now? Someone had gone. Of course, Vincent.

Now where was he? she wondered. She hadn't seen him for some time now. Ah well, she said to herself, they have to make their own way these days. That's what he was doing. He was away to make some money.

Maybe, she thought with quickening interest, he had gone to

England. That was where her husband had gone once ... on the Liverpool boat. Gone to Liverpool on the boat to work. Yes, she decided, that was where Vincent had gone, and she felt a wee warm glow of pride that he was doing just what her husband had done all those years ago.

She heard the front door open and a voice, thin and wavering, call out.

'Mary! Are ye there, Mary?'

'Aye.' she said, flat and dull.

Philomena Conlon pushed her head round the kitchen door. It was a small head, covered by a scarf pushed up into odd shapes by the hair curlers underneath. She was dressed in black, mourning a husband who had been killed some ten years previously. She felt the black suited her, and, in these times, when so many husbands, sons and boys were being killed by the British, she felt it gave her an air of Republican respectability. That her husband had been run over by a bus, while coming home with too much drink taken one Friday night, worried her not at all. Those old enough to remember thought nothing of the matter, either. The younger ones would nod gravely to her, at least those who had been well brought up did, as befitted her station in life.

Philomena was a few years Mary's senior, having just been coming out of St Mary's Elementary School as Mary was going in. But when her old teacher, Mr James Rafferty, had come to the district, she had seized the opportunity to renew what she felt was an old friendship with Mary. James Rafferty's strong Republican sympathies and his knowledge of history had made him well known quickly. Dropping some of his more easily remembered phrases into her conversations, Philomena Conlon had basked in his reflection. She loved it.

For some time now she had been dropping by Mary's more than usual. She was worried at the way things were going in the Malone household; worried, too, that they might be about to disgrace themselves, and drag her down with them because of their long-standing friendship. That was not the way she wished to see matters progressing, not if she could help it.

'I see I've come at just the right time,' she said to Mary as

246

she came through the door, and arranged herself on a chair. 'Is
.it just made?'

'It is.' Mary rose stiffly, and looked around for another mug.
There was none hanging on the hooks where they normally
hung, and she finally had to take one out of the sink. Giving it
a quick rub, she poured her friend some tea.

'How is young Sheelagh?' enquired the thin voice of
Philomena.

Mary raised her eyes in some surprise. Sheelagh! Of course,
Sheelagh. She was the other person who had gone from the
house. Gone back to hospital. She looked at her friend. That
had been her doing, she remembered. It was Philomena who
had got the doctor down, and insisted that Sheelagh was too ill
to stay at home. She recalled, with some little satisfaction,
Philomena telling the doctor that she, Sheelagh's mother, had
too many other problems to be able to look after her daughter
properly at home; that Sheelagh required special treatment
that she could not get at home.

So Sheelagh had gone back to hospital. Of course she was all
right. Why did Philomena think there was anything wrong with
her? Granda had seen her ... when was it, she thought, yesterday, or maybe it had been the day before? Anyway, he had
seen her, and she was all right.

'She's all right,' she said at last.

'And the rest of the family?'

'Oh, they're all right, too.'

'Have you heard from Vincent?' The question was casual,
but Mary felt a pang. No, she had not heard from Vincent. She
wasn't sure where he was, even, though she pretended he was
away to England. Philomena had asked her that before. That
was what she had told her on the spur of the moment, and now
she more than half believed it herself.

Philomena prodded again 'And how is he getting on? Does
he have work over there?'

'He's well enough. He's about to start a job. It's a good job.
They've good wages over there, and plenty of work. Mind you,
they're very lucky to have him. He's very good.' She prattled
on, 'He'll do well, will Vincent. I know that, Philomena. Some

say he's a wicked fellow. But he's a good worker. He has a good job there now, which is more than he'd get in this place.' She moved herself round the kitchen to get at the teapot. It was a subconscious movement to change the conversation.

'Will you have another cup of tea?' she asked.

'I will that.' While she poured it she stopped talking. She held on to the mug firmly, her dark eyes fixed firmly on to the amber flow coming from the spout of the teapot.

Philomena switched targets. 'How is young Deirdre? Has that doctor fellow sorted her out yet?'

Mary clutched her mug and stared into it. The questions unnerved her, and she tried to put up a defence. The only defence of which she was capable was silence. She retreated into her mug of tea.

Philomena leaned across the table, pushing out a thin arm to tap Mary's elbow.

'Mary! Mary! Are you well?'

Mary didn't move. She could see part of her face, including an eye, reflected in the milky brown surface of the tea. She kept it very still so as not to disturb the pattern. She rather liked the look of just half her face, brown and gentle. She thought of herself looking back up from the warm safety of the tea. Now wouldn't that be grand, she told herself. Jamie and Deirdre and Sheelagh and Bryan could all be forgotten. And Vincent. Her thoughts hesitated. Maybe not forgotten, because she really loved them all, but perhaps they wouldn't be such a worry.

The reflection rippled and was lost, and she became aware of a tapping on her elbow. She looked up. Philomena was looking at her.

'Oh, Philomena!' she exclaimed, as if seeing her for the first time, 'you mustn't give me frights like that. Would you like some tea?'

'Are you all right?' Philomena said anxiously.

'Yes,' said Mary. 'Of course I'm all right. Are you?'

'You looked as if you went into a trance or something.' Philomena laughed nervously. 'You had me worried for the minute. I was after asking you about Deirdre.'

'Oh, yes! Deirdre.' She had been trying to escape from something, she knew that. But she felt she had failed, and the nasty cold feeling was back in her stomach.

She didn't want to talk about Deirdre. Deirdre worried her too much. She had been acting very strangely recently. Sometimes she would sit and clench her fists, going very stiff and staring in front of her. This seemed to happen often when she was watching television.

Once, when she had been fetching her home from school, they had been stopped by a road block and made to walk round another way. She had, she remembered, been with Philomena that time. They had to walk down the road and well away from them, but very clearly they had seen a mob of young boys and men throwing stones at the army.

The noise of all this had been funnelled down the street to them as they stood watching on the pavement. They had been standing in a group of women and children, some much younger than Deirdre. So she had been embarrassed when her daughter started acting in a strange way.

The acrid whiff of tear gas reached them. Just the briefest contact, but sharp and unmistakable. She felt she would have known what it was even if she had never smelt it before. There was only one thing it could be, she knew that. It had caught her up the back of her throat, and her eyes had started streaming. At once, Deirdre's hand had tightened on hers, and she had begun to moan softly.

She looked at Philomena.

'You remember, you remember, don't you? Deirdre's arm, all stiff, and her making that funny noise. You remember I shook her arm. I shook her arm but she wouldn't let go. You remember that ... don't you?' Her voice rose in an anguished whisper, hoarse and difficult for Philomena to understand. She grabbed her friend's arm.

'There, there. Quieten down. You're all right now. She's all right. It was a long time ago.' She stroked the arm, and Mary dropped her head on to it, and sobbed.

She couldn't forget it. She relived the moments too often. Sometimes she dreamed about it all, but it was worse when it came back during the day, and she couldn't force it out of her mind.

She remembered it only too well.

She had wrung her hand in instinctive fear when she found Deirdre would not let go. Then Deirdre's mouth had started to tremble, and, to her absolute horror, she had seen her daughter's eyes cross in a terrible squint. She had stood like that, stiff and trembling and moaning, for over half an hour. They couldn't get her to walk or sit down.

The other woman had fussed around her, making suggestions which she had never even heard.

The whole business had so upset her that she had not even told the doctor when she took Deirdre to see him. He wouldn't have believed her.

The teacher had told her to take Deirdre to a special doctor, but she couldn't remember exactly what she had said. Anyway, she hadn't wanted to talk about it to anyone.

Philomena poured her another cup of tea. She was very worried about Mary. She thought she was going a bit funny in the head, and what she had seen of Deirdre only strengthened her belief that something very odd was happening to the Malone family. Old Mr Rafferty, of course, was beyond reproach. She was filled with pride every time she spoke to him.

The others were different. Vincent was a wicked boy, and seemingly had disappeared altogether. She didn't believe Mary's story that he was in England, though she would never question it openly to her face. She had already raised the matter with a couple of friends in the street, and they too had their doubts.

Bryan, she supposed, was all right down South with the girl – what a carry on that was. Poor wee Sheelagh, but. She felt very sorry for the girl, and visited her in hospital quite regularly. She felt she had been quite right to insist that Sheelagh was moved back to the Royal. The state of Deirdre, and now her old friend Mary, had made that quite clear.

She sighed and looked at Mary, who was once more gazing vacantly out the window. Did Mary, she wondered, know about wee Jamie? She felt she maybe had enough worries at the moment without giving her any more. But she would have to find out somehow if Mary knew about her young son, before she could work out how to help her.

The street they all lived in was a small place. Everybody knew everybody else. There wasn't much that escaped anybody's notice. Why, she thought crossly to herself, some young hooligans had even come to her house to tell her, tell *her*, mind you, to stop paying her rent. It's to protest about internment and lack of political representation, they said. 'We know you're still paying,' they told her, 'because we have checked the rent collector's book.' She had rounded on them, her shrill voice quivering with fury, and asked one of them if he was a member of the IRA. He had been very firm and quiet, she remembered, and just gone on saying it would be better if she stopped paying. So she had. She had found out Mary had stopped paying as well.

'Is Jamie doing well at school?'

Mary stared out of the window. 'Doing well at school?' she asked in a faraway voice.

'Yes,' said Philomena firmly, 'at school. How is he doing at school?'

'Not so bad.'

'What do you mean, "not so bad"? Have you spoken to his teacher lately?'

'No ... no ...' she said slowly. 'His teacher? Well. ...'

'For pity's sake!' Exasperated, Philomena got up abruptly from the table. The sudden movement made Mary turn her head.

'You're not going?' she asked.

'Mary, you've to pull yourself together now. This won't do.' She put her hands on the table and looked at them. 'Listen, listen to me now. You've got to do something about Jamie. He's getting into bad company. Did you know that?'

'Bad company?'

'Yes. Bad company.'

'What do you mean, Philomena?'

'I mean he's been missing school,' she paused, and added,

'and running messages.'

'Running messages?' Mary's forehead wrinkled in puzzlement.

'Yes. Running messages.'

'For who?' Mary asked.

Philomena didn't answer her at first. She sat down again on her chair, and pulled it in until she was very close to Mary.

She leaned forward and lowered her voice. 'Mary,' she asked, 'have you no idea what I'm talking about?'

'I have not,' said Mary. Then her face brightened. 'Oh yes! Of course. Jamie. You were talking about Jamie. The poor wee lad. He's looking a bit pale. Working too hard at school, I suppose. He's a growing boy, you know. They grow so quickly at that age.' She nodded her head. 'They grow so fast their bodies can't keep up with them. It's a very trying time, you know,' she went on earnestly. 'I remember when Bryan was like that. It was the only time he wasn't the same as Vincent. Got very pale and peaky, he did. But we fed him up, and he was all right. Lots of good food, sleep and fresh air. That's all they need.'

Philomena was aghast. She couldn't understand what had come over Mary.

'He's half as likely to get his fresh air through his head as anywhere else now,' she said, under her breath, not quite sure how far to go with Mary.

'What was that?' The tone of her voice rather than what she had said had caught Mary's ear. 'What was that you said?'

'I was just after saying that wee Jamie was keeping bad company. You know, Mary,' she said urgently, 'he's getting tied up with the Provies.'

'The Provies!' Mary laughed. 'You must be mad! He's only a wee lad. You'll be telling me next he carries a gun.'

'I don't know about that,' said Philomena seriously, 'but he's running messages for them. Sometimes they get children to carry guns. Sure and wasn't there a case in the paper only the other day of some twelve-year-old spraying a soldier with a machine gun? Ha!' she snorted, 'he was so small, but, he couldn't hold it properly when it fired.'

Mary shook her head. 'You're daft, Philomena Conlon. Daft and an eejit as well. There's no son of mine going to carry on like that.'

'You're daft yourself, Mary Malone. You're the eejit, not meself, if you believe that. Sure and isn't your father one of the great Republicans? Don't you think your sons would follow him?'

'Listen to me, Philomena Conlon,' said Mary, as a small wave of normality washed across her brain. 'My da may be a great Republican, but it's all talk. I know that. He would run a mile if anyone asked him to shoot a gun. Talk! Do you understand? That's all these big Irishmen do. Talk about defeating the Brits and how glorious Ireland is going to be free. Holy Mother! If they were any good they'd stop the army and the Prods from rampaging up and down our street. That would do some good. It might even be a start. But they don't, do they?' The bitterness spilled out into her voice, and she started to cry again. 'When they do kill somebody, it's usually the wrong person. Or they hide behind women and children. Dear Jesus!' she sobbed, 'they have people who put bombs in shops and cafés. Blowing up ... killing anybody ... anybody ... my sons aren't like that. . . .'

She slumped back in her chair, her eyes glazing. 'Sheelagh,' she whispered, 'Sheelagh. Are you there, love? Where are you now? Have they taken you away again? I'll look after you. Mairead will look after you. You'll be all right. Don't worry, Sheelagh love. You'll be all right. . . .'

Philomena looked at her in despair. She just didn't know what to do. It was too much for her.

She put her arm forward slowly, and took her friend's arm. It felt very cold. She put out her other hand, and held Mary's between them.

'Mary! Oh, Mary! What have they done to you?' She rubbed the hand gently.

They sat on alone in the small, dirty kitchen, saying nothing. The sounds of the afternoon drifted in on them, unnoticed. The children playing in the street outside, the occasional squeal of brakes on tyres, the noise of the great city; all these sounds were muffled, held down by the late afternoon haze.

The sun sank slowly down, dragging the colour out of the sky and from the great copper dome of the city hall.

In long thin streams the people left the city centre, squeezing through the security cordons, clicking monotonously through the turnstiles. Like a giant slowly expiring, the city let out its life blood, surrendering to darkness, to wary army patrols and to killers who came from every side for the glorious revolution.

Bryan and Mairead arrived back two days later after a long and exhausting journey. They had come up on the Enterprise Express from Dublin, but shortly after they left Dundalk and had crossed the border into the North, the train stopped. The small fields stretched away on either side of the mountains of south Armagh. 'They call this bandit country,' Bryan whispered in Mairead's ear. 'In places like Crossmaglen they even fly the Tricolour.'

'Do they let them do that?' said Mairead, amazed.

'There's not much they can do about it,' he whispered back. 'Even with a whole bunch of the military there in a fort right in the town.'

'Is that so?' She couldn't believe it.

'It is that. The military are so tied down there they daren't move around the roads. They even have their dustbins taken out by helicopter.'

They sat whispering together for nearly an hour before they discovered what had happened, though everyone in the carriage had been very free with their opinions. Most of them were right. A large petrol tanker had been parked under a bridge just ahead, and there was a bomb on it.

'There's no moving past that tonight,' said Bryan when he heard the news.

'Can't the military fix it?' she asked him.

'They will. They usually sit and look at it, but. Maybe for a day or more, in case it's booby-trapped. Or maybe there's a fella on the end of a radio waiting to set it off when they get near it.'

So they finished their journey by bus, with Mairead's leg proving very awkward. She was worn out by the time Bryan got her home in a taxi, and she went straight to her bed in Sheelagh's room.

After a couple of days she felt much stronger, and she went with Bryan back to the hospital where her doctor had arranged for her leg to be examined. The sister greeted her warmly, and the doctor said her leg was coming along very well, and she could have the plaster off and leave it just bandaged. It was a great relief to have it off, and it meant she could have a proper bath again for the first time since the explosion. It seemed years since she'd last been able to lie fully immersed in hot water. Bryan offered to scrub her back, but she said no. The smallness of the house embarrassed her.

The news of their engagement they broke gently to Mary Malone, but they weren't sure she had taken it in. She looked far worse than when they had last seen her. Old Mr Rafferty, however was in fine form again. Sheelagh was overjoyed to see them, and the two girls clung together as Mairead told her about Bryan.

'Oh, Mairead, I'm so happy for you. Vincent was never for you really. He's lovely, but he's strange. Have you told him?'

'No,' she said. 'I haven't seen him.'

'Not seen him? Where is he then?'

'He doesn't spend much time at home now. He's always away. Your mum says he's away to England for a job.'

'Oh, dear. I didn't know that. Are things bad at home?'

'They're not so good, but we'll sort them out. Don't you worry your head about it. It's your mum and Deirdre that we're worried about, but Bryan's very sensible. We'll manage.'

It wasn't till a few days later that she found out just how wrong she was. There was Jamie to worry about as well.

She had been on her own most of the afternoon in the house, with just Mr Rafferty asleep in the front room. Bryan had taken his mother away to the hospital and Deirdre and Jamie were at school. Deidre came back about the usual time, and it wasn't for a while that she noticed Jamie hadn't come home. She couldn't get any sense out of Deirdre, and the old man wasn't much help either. She walked down the street as far as the corner shop, but there was no sigh of him. She asked some small boys if they knew where he was, and they looked at her in surprise.

'Sure he's away to the riot,' one of them said.

'Riot, what riot ... what do you mean?'

'The riot down at Divis Street.'

'You say Jamie's there?' She didn't want to believe what she had heard.

'Sure he's always away to the riots.' The boy looked at her, puzzled. 'Aren't you the one that's going with his big brother?'

Leaning on her stick, she stared over their heads. 'Oh my God,' she whispered to herself. 'Oh my God.' The boys said something to her but she didn't take it in and they ran away down the street shouting and pretending to shoot each other from behind imaginary barricades. She started to panic, hobbling down the street, wanting Bryan, knowing she could do nothing herself. She could hardly believe what she'd been told, but she knew from the radio that there was a riot going on. They said a soldier had been ambushed and killed ... and Jamie was there – there of all places.

'Can I help you?' a voice said from behind her. She stopped and Father Farrell drew up alongside her on his bicycle.

'Oh, Father, it's Jamie. He's not home yet, and the lads say he's away at the riot.

'He's not, is he?' said Father Farrell. 'Sure he's only a wee scrap of a fella.'

'Oh, but they say he is. What can I do? Bryan's at the hospital.'

He had got off his bicycle by now and was walking slowly along beside her. 'Slow down, or you'll trip,' he said to her. 'The pavements are none too smooth here.'

'Can you help me, Father?'

'Oh, yes, I expect I can, though I don't think there's much chance of finding him up there ... that's if he is there.'

'Thank you, thank you. Bryan would go if he was here, but

he's not. Do you mind very much? Oh!' she banged her stick angrily on the ground, 'I'll have his ears off when he gets back. He's a very bold boy.'

'He'll be around somewhere, quite safe I expect,' said Father Farrell soothingly. 'I'll see what I can do.'

An hour later he was back with young Jamie in tow, holding him with one hand and pushing his bicycle with the other. They crowded round him.

'There he is,' he said. 'Just where you said he'd be. I'm off now, but you'd better have a talk with him.' He let go the boy and got back on to his bicycle. 'Jamie,' he said, 'that's the first and last time I ever do that for you. I don't like riots and you shouldn't either. Don't ever let me catch you at one again.'

'You're a bold, bold boy,' Mairead raged at him in the kitchen, furiously cutting bread and buttering it for him. 'What do you have to go and do a thing like that for now? I nearly died when they told me. Do you want to get yourself killed?'

'No,' he said, putting some bread into his mouth. 'I won't get killed, but.'

'How do you know that .. and don't you be smart with me, or I'll have Bryan deal with you when he comes home.'

'They told me so,' he answered. 'It was all to get a Brit, and they did. That's another one dead.'

'Jamie Malone,' she said, the words hardly coming out, 'what are you talking about?'

'It's quite easy. We throw bottles and stones and the military can't touch us. We're just children, you see. And then we go away and the Provies can shoot them.'

'Dear Jesus!' she whispered, wondering what to do. Where was Bryan? She wished he would come home. 'Get you along to bed now. Bryan will see you when he's home.'

He turned in the door and looked at her. 'It's a great gas,' he grinned quickly at her and went upstairs.

The days passed, and Bryan and Mairead desperately tried to hold the family together. Bryan now fetched Deirdre and Jamie home from school every day, and kept them firmly indoors. It wasn't so difficult, as the nights were drawing in and getting much colder. Still the city burned every night, and the toll of dead and injured went up. Sheelagh, fighting hard from her hospital bed, was recovering well. She had been fitted for new legs, and was about to start the long and painful process of trying to walk again. Bryan was unable to find a job and, indeed, would have had little time for one with all he had to do at home.

Again and again they talked together about leaving, how they could take Sheelagh and how they could persuade Mary Malone to come with them. It wasn't easy.

'Bryan's talking of leaving again,' Mary said to Mairead one night as they sat, waiting for Bryan to come home.

'I know. He's been talking about it for some time. I think he wants us all to go ... to start again where there's no trouble. Wouldn't that be nice now?'

'I don't want to go.' Mary held Mairead's hand lightly in her own, but she hadn't any intention of letting it go. Small ripples of self-pity were reaching out to her, lapping on the edge of her consciousness; comforting ripples, like the warm, warm sea she had never known. Somewhere in her muddled mind the signals were going out, telling her to hang on to that hand because to let it go would be to slip back into a cold familiar world where she was lonely only in spirit.

'Sure and he was at it again last night. He's after losing his job on the site. He's not so good with his hands, you see, as Vincent. Least, that's what I think. He's a hard worker, you know.' She nodded her head slowly. 'A hard worker. No trouble, you know. Hadn't he been there near on six months ... or was it twelve? Never a day late or off work sick. It's not fair, with Vincent away.'

'What's that?'

'What's what?' She looked up in surprise, flustered a little by the abruptness of the question. She herself hadn't been following what she'd been saying.

'Are you saying he lost the job because Vincent was gone? Is that what you're saying?'

'Oh, yes,' she replied vaguely. 'Vincent was a great one with his hands now. See the table here. He made it.'

She stroked the ends of the table, tilting her head up and

down as she moved her hands. 'It's beautiful,' she said earnestly, 'and very strong, too. Look! It's a powerful piece of work for a wee lad now. It's a gift he has and 'twill do him well.' She said urgently, 'Isn't that a grand piece of work now?'

'It is that. Grand,' agreed Mairead.

'Bryan!' she cried, suddenly sitting up. 'He's just after losing his job.'

'Aye. You've just said that. But he lost it some time gone, not just now.'

'Did I say that?' She looked surprised again. 'He's talking of leaving, but.'

'I know,' said Mairead gently. 'We've all been talking about leaving.'

'Leaving home. Here.' Mary wiped her free hand across her face, pushing her fingers into her closed eyes, and smoothing back her hair. 'He will, he will,' she sobbed. 'Australia or some place else. I'll never see him again. Why does he want to leave me now? Sure Vincent's gone ... what will I do?'

'We want you to come with us,' she said patiently. It would have been difficult enough to persuade Mary to come with them in normal times, for she knew that parents traditionally stayed behind, waiting for the children to settle and send money back first. Now she couldn't even get through to her.

'No, no.' Mary waved her hand aimlessly in the air, and pushed some strands of hair from her face. 'Dad ... Deirdre....' Her left hand, slippery with sweat, slipped from Mairead's hand. Quickly she wiped it on her skirt, and grabbed Mairead again. 'Wee Jamie, too,' she wailed. 'What about him? I don't want to go, but. He shouldn't leave me.' She rocked back and forward on her chair, the tears running down her face. 'Oh, oh! He mustn't leave me now. He'll go, but. He'll go.'

'Hush, hush now.' Mairead patted her hand. 'Hush. You mustn't upset yourself.'

'Oh, Bryan, Bryan. You'll not leave me too? Vincent is gone and you're to go and what will become of us?'

'Mary Malone, will you listen to me? No one's to leave you

259

behind. If we go you're to come with us ... with us, do you hear?'

'He talks of nothing else. Australia this and Australia that. He's paid the fare already....'

'No, he has not. Will you listen to –'

'It's him losing that job that made him do it.'

''Tis nothing to do with his job. He'd want to leave even if he still had it.'

'No, no,' she wailed on. 'It was Vincent's fault altogether. If he hadn't gone, Bryan would still be here.'

'Holy Mother!' Mairead exclaimed, losing patience with Mary's ramblings. 'Will you come to your senses? 'Tis nothing to do with his job, and he's not away yet. None of us are away. Listen, listen to me,' she said urgently, forcing the woman's attention, dragging her back into the present. She had to get through to her. 'Mary,' she said slowly and clearly, 'we're thinking of leaving Belfast. Maybe not to Australia ... it's too far for Sheelagh ... she's hurt too bad. We're not to go there yet, if at all. We're all going to the South, Mary. Back to where you come from, and your dad ... and me. Mary, do you understand? We'll be all right there.'

The door opened behind her, and Bryan stood there.

'What's this?' he asked. 'Mother, what's the matter with you?' He looked at Mairead and she shook her head. He stepped to his mother's chair and put both hands on her shoulders. Slowly, he brought her rocking to a stop. 'Come now,' he said to her, 'you mustn't fret yourself so.'

'I'll make you some tea.' Mairead got up and moved around the kitchen. He nodded and sat down in front of his mother.

'Listen, mother. We've talked before about leaving. You know that ... I think you just don't want to understand. There's nothing for us here now. It's not just the job I lost ... there's what to do with Sheelagh, and Deirdre ... and Jamie.'

Yes, he thought bitterly, even Jamie now. Vincent had a lot to answer for. I did lose that job because Vincent left. He was the man they really wanted, not I. You're no more in England than I am, he said to himself, but he didn't say it out loud.

Instead he talked on with his mother, calming her little by little until at last the crying stopped and she sat there, exhausted.

'You get yourself to bed,' he said to Mairead. 'I'll sit here a bit. Just leave the tea there.'

'Thank you.' Mairead kissed him. 'Will she be all right now?'

'Yes, I think so. Good night.'

'Good night.'

Bryan and his mother sat on in the kitchen alone. The stillness seemed to draw them together, something born more of long association than spoken communication. Neither was given much to expressing thoughts which went much further than those needed for everyday contact, though Bryan was improving now, but there was special attachment between them. Mary felt very strongly about Bryan. He had been the second of the twins to be born and had come as an enormous surprise. Because she was so bad about seeing doctors, she had never had the proper pre-natal check-ups which would have let everybody know that twins were on the way.

She had badly wanted a boy as a first child; to get two at once was almost more than she could bear. Her joy had been intense, as the candles which burned in St Gomgall's had testified. Bryan, too, had been an easier child. Altogether an easier character, he was slow in thought and movement but kind and generous to a fault. He had been known to clean his own shoes, and even make his bed and get meals ready – of a sort – when his mother had been ill. This had always produced shrieks of merriment from Vincent and once, out of character, Bryan had hit his brother rather hard.

The details of all this now escaped Mary Malone. Her mind had been bombarded with so many awful, outrageous experiences over the past few months that she had retreated into herself, closing off the avenues of communication with the outside world in a desperate attempt to avoid any more unpleasantness.

In many ways she was only a few steps in front of the people around her. Alarmed by the relentless violence, terrified by their apparent helplessness to deal with the increased display of *force majeur* by the Protestant ascendancy, the ghettos of Belfast formed and re-formed. Each time they got smaller and more inward-looking as the need for closer identification grew stronger. At the first sign of stress, the veneer of normality had cracked, exposing the wounds of prejudice kept raw by long tradition. From behind their physical and mental barriers they peered out, always unwilling, and now unable, to communicate. The underlying bitterness which had given birth to the Protestant Orange Order over a hundred years before had once again come to the surface, but this time more intense than ever before.

Some links with her old world were still there, fragile though they might be. The residue of goodwill left after the years of happy family life had broken the complete slide into insanity. She knew she had to cling on to Bryan, desperately, because he was her lifeline.

'Mother,' said Bryan, 'you have to understand.' He took her tear-stained face between his hands. 'We've been through all this before. I have to go. We have to go. There's nothing left for me to do here. I have no job, and I won't go on the dole. It will be bad for you ... and the others.' He smoothed her face and her hair, wondering at the grey hairs coming through, the lines about her eyes.

'Australia is a long way away. Maybe we'll go there one day, I don't know. It would be difficult with Sheelagh now. So we're going south to Galway, as soon as she's fit to travel. Mairead and I will get married down there, and we're all going to go. All of us. You, mother, Mairead and me, Sheelagh, Deirdre and wee Jamie and granda as well. It's the only chance we have. Vincent has gone. He can't help you. I don't know where he has gone, but I doubt it's to England.'

'Not in England?' Her head shook. 'Not there....'

'No, mother.'

'Where, then ... where?'

'Never mind. He's not around, but. We'll find him later, and he'll join us. I know he will once he realizes we really have gone. We must go soon, but.' He thought of Jamie. 'Very soon.'

15

Joe Murphy had some interesting news for Danny. He had sent him a message to say so and suggested he should see him as soon as possible. He was in the city centre when word was passed to him that Danny was available. As intelligence officer for the unit, Joe should have known where to find Danny, but things had been a little difficult lately.

He walked through town to the car park about ten minutes away. With restrictions all over the place, the car parks near the centre filled up very quickly, and he wasn't going to leave his car where it could be picked up and used as a car bomb. He moved quickly through the crowd of shoppers, and past the army patrols and check points. They didn't worry him for he was clean, and unless they did a very thorough check on him, which was unlikely, he'd be through. They were a familiar sight now, and no one took any notice of them as they moved warily down the main shopping streets faces blackened, eyes constantly scanning the high buildings on either side. Even when they crouched in doorways or ran across corners, the shoppers just moved round them.

He drove out to the yard where Danny had his building business. It wasn't much of a business, and he did rather more repair work and decorating than anything else. He was able to run it and make a living from it because of the compensation the government paid out when buildings were damaged or destroyed. Joe knew Danny took a certain satisfaction from rebuilding what he himself had first destroyed. It was a good way, he'd said, of making the Brits pay for both his living costs, and the costs of the operations against them. Part of the costs, that was, for a lot of the money came from bank raids, drinking clubs and protection money. Joe knew how much it needed, for thousands also had to be paid out to the dependents of those interned in Long Kesh. It was a big drain on funds, but essential for morale. Luckily, regular funds from America helped as well.

Joe walked along a narrow back lane to the yard. A weed-covered embankment fell away on his right to an unused canal. He always used this back lane for it meant he could leave his car in a street totally unconnected with the yard.

Through the gate, he picked his way past untidy piles of brick, sand, old ladders and other debris of a builder's yard. Danny was in a small office where there was little else except a desk, a couple of chairs and an old filing cabinet. The cabinet was mainly for show; an inspection would reveal some old bills, invoices from the past, a plan or two of some minor buildings to boost the small amount of paperwork Danny had for his present jobs.

There was a phone on the table, but it was rarely used. Danny was worried about it being bugged, or getting the lines crossed. He preferred to give his instructions in person, face to face. He was talking now to a man about painting a room in Ballymurphy. Joe leant on the door frame until he was finished. The man nodded to him as he walked out, but Joe said nothing, and watched the man drive away. Then he came in and sat down.

'I've found the man we're looking for,' he said to Danny.

'You have? Good! Who is he?'

'He's just the man you want ... a carpenter, and he's got experience with explosives.'

'What's his name, Joe?'

'He's a fella called Malone. Vincent Malone.'

'Are you sure?'

'Oh, yes. I found him through a cousin of mine. He was telling me about a lad he had up after a job this summer, just now like, he's a foreman in a quarry, you see. . . .'

'Who's a foreman, Malone or your cousin?'

264

'My cousin, Tommy Ryan. This man now – Malone, that is – said he was a carpenter and wanted a job. Very good one, too, by all accounts. Tommy said there wasn't much work for carpenters at a quarry, but Malone said he'd be happy to do some blasting. Tommy thought it a bit odd.'

'Not odd at all, when you think of it.'

'No, maybe not. Well, anyway, as I was saying, this fella wanted to do some blasting, and Tommy thought he might be one of us. So he said nothing and let the fellow in. He did a lot of blasting. Asked a lot of questions, too.'

'You think this is our man, then? When did you find him?'

'I found out about him yesterday,' Joe said, not telling Danny that his cousin had given him the information weeks before, and he had not connected it with the man he was looking for. When it had suddenly dawned on him that the man might have some connection with the one he was supposed to be looking for, he had gone in search of his cousin. First to his home, but he wasn't there, and then out to the quarry where he worked. Tommy hadn't been there either, and so he headed back into town. He'd been given two possible contact points, and at the first he drew another blank. Tommy had already been and gone. He headed for the second in Smithfield Market, just behind the main post office.

This was a large, covered square where there were a host of small shops, many selling second-hand goods. You could buy almost anything in this place, and Tommy had apparently gone to a second-hand shop which specialized in electrical goods. Joe pushed his way through the throng of people who always seemed to be in the market; people browsing for books, examining pets or picking through the bits and pieces.

At the electrical shop he was relieved to find the familiar form of his cousin. A flat cap was on his head, and his boots were covered with the white dust of the quarry. He was talking low and earnestly with the shop keeper.

Joe waited outside the door. He would take Tommy to one side when he came out, and persuade him to have a quiet drink. That would not, he thought, be too difficult. He wanted not only the man's name from his cousin, but a bit of background on the man himself. Danny had raised a good point about the man's behaviour. He wanted a few good answers to give him.

Tommy was agreeably surprised to see him when he walked out.

'Hullo there, Joe lad,' he said cheerfully, 'what are you doing about here? Haven't been tracking me down now have you?' He looked around him in an exaggerated way.

Joe wasn't much amused. 'I've been looking for you for hours,' he said, rather untruthfully. 'I want to talk to you.'

'What's up? Trouble with the wife again?'

'No!' Joe snorted. 'Come and have a jar. This is serious.'

The two men walked off out of the market. There was a small pub close by which Joe sometimes used, Kelley's Cellars. It was a very old pub, furnished simply, its thick walls keeping out the noise.

Joe called for two beers, and then moved back on to a bench well into a corner. He waited till they were both well settled. Tommy took a long pull at his glass, wiped his mouth with the back of his hand, belched and looked at Joe.

'Well now,' he said, 'what's all this about?'

'Two things, Tommy. A name, and then some information.'

'Indeed now.' He leant forward towards Joe, nodding his head. 'It sounds serious.'

'It is. Remember that young fellow you took on at the beginning of the summer – or some time in the summer, I can't remember when ... anyway, a dark-haired fellow ... a carpenter?' Tommy nodded. 'Well, what was his name?'

'His name is it that you want? It's a reasonable return for a beer and no harm done. His name ...' he bent forward again and lowered his voice, 'is Malone. Vincent Malone.'

Joe sat back. Vincent Malone, he thought, turning the name over in his mind. Vincent Malone. What did that name mean? Was there something special about it? If so, what? It might come if Tommy talked about him.

'Tell me about him,' he said to Tommy.

'Tell you what about him?'

'Anything. What he was like. Good or bad tempered?

266

Efficient? Intelligent? Anything you remember.'

'Is it important?'

'Yes, yes,' Joe tried to restrain his impatience. 'I wouldn't be here asking you if it wasn't.' He drained his beer. 'Think about it while I get you another. Drink up.' He waited with his hand out while Tommy finished his beer.

When he came back, Tommy was ready to talk. 'Right,' he said, 'Malone was a young fellow, about nineteen. He came to me about the beginning of August. I had a temporary job for a carpenter. He seemed OK, so I took him on. He was OK, very good. Did some excellent work. He really knew his stuff. He was there every day, always on time, and always happy to do any overtime. In fact, he seemed to want to do it.' He shrugged and thought for a moment. 'Perhaps he was hard up. Anyway, it pleased me, and he was worth every penny.'

'Go on,' said Joe.

'He was strong. A well-built boy. Good looking, too, with dark hair and blue eyes. . . .' He looked over at Joe. 'Is this really what you want?'

'Yes, yes,' said Joe, impatiently. 'Just keep talking.'

'OK. Well, a good-looking lad as I was saying. But not very cheerful for all that. In fact he seemed bloody miserable a lot of the time. He was very quiet. Maybe that was it. Hardly spoke to anyone, and kept himself very much to himself. I thought at first it was because he was new. But not at all. He stayed the same.'

'Did he stick to carpentry?' asked Joe.

'It's funny you should ask that. Funny, because I very well remember telling you something about this lad some time ago. Am I right?'

'Get on with it, Tommy. I'm asking the questions. If you told me something before, it doesn't matter. I want to hear it all again. I haven't time to mess around. This is important, do you mind?'

'OK, OK! But like I told you once before, he was very interested in explosives. I mean, no one else would have noticed. But I . . .' he jabbed his thumb at his chest, 'I do notice these things. It's part of my job.'

'I thought you told me before you'd given him a job blasting. That you hadn't any other work for him.'

'No, I don't think I said that,' Tommy replied, scratching his head. 'No, he worked as a carpenter for me.'

'So, we have this man, this interesting carpenter who is shoving his nose into matters concerning explosives. Didn't that worry you?'

'No, why should it? At the time I thought he might be one of yours.'

'Well, he wasn't.'

'I know that now. I didn't know it then.'

'Did he learn much?'

'Oh, yes! I think he learned quite a bit. He was a bright boy, like I said. In the end he was doing quite a lot of blasting work for me ... helping out, you know. Maybe that's what gave you the idea I gave him a job doing that. It seemed as if he was desperate to get something done. Very single-minded, but for the life of me I can't think what about.'

Joe looked round the pub instinctively to make sure they were still out of earshot of anyone. 'Do you think, Tommy,' he asked very quietly, 'that this boy was the sort who would be useful to us?'

'I suppose he might.' Tommy pulled reflectively on his beer. 'I'm surprised you haven't got your tabs on him already. I did mention him to you before.'

Joe winced. 'That's another matter.' Joe remembered that moment well, and he hoped that Danny wouldn't spot his lapse.

Danny was looking at him. 'You say you found this all out yesterday?'

'That's right. You know, I think it was what happened to his sister that started him off.'

'What are you talking about?'

'Malone's sister. Tommy told me he found this fella one day moping over a bit of newspaper. A bit cut out of the newspaper, you know. He was looking miserable, but he flared up like when Tommy spoke to him. Anyway, they chatted a bit, and he showed Tommy the paper. It was about his sister. You remember the girl that got blown up in that café? The coffee shop place. You remember, it was just after you got back.'

Danny stiffened. He remembered very well. He had known nothing about the operation and he had been absolutely furious at the time. The Provies had lost a lot of sympathy and support because of that. 'Only legitimate military and security targets,' Danny used to pound the table and shout. 'Industrial and economic targets, yes. Catholic civilians, no.' But that bloody fool Hannahan had gone mad; he didn't care whom he killed as long as something was blown up.

'The girl,' Joe went on. 'The one that was badly hurt. Lost both legs and an arm and Christ knows what else. That's why he was so mad. I think his girl got hit as well.'

'If this is the man you think he is ... the one planting these bombs that we want to find ... then why? Why does he do it?'

'What do you mean "why does he do it"? Why does anyone do it?' Joe said. 'We do.'

'No, no.' Danny grabbed his arm. 'You haven't got it. Why is he blowing up Prod places?'

Joe looked at Danny in amazement. Was the man going out of his mind?

'What the hell are you talking about,' he exclaimed. 'The fella's had his sister hurt bad. His girl as well by all accounts. It's what you'd call revenge. That's it. Nothing very unusual about that. ...' His voice slowed down and he stopped talking. He looked at Danny.

'You've got it now, haven't you? Yes. Nothing unusual about revenge. Oh, no. But the coffee shop bomb wasn't planted by Prods, it was planted by our stupid fucking outfit. Hannahan did it. So what's your man up to, Joe? I think we'd better have him in and find out. Hannahan knows him well, send him. There's no love lost there.'

Mr Rafferty was about to go to bed. He was clutching a mug of cocoa and had one foot on the bottom step of the stairs when the front door burst open. He looked round about to say something when he saw it was someone standing there, a small man with a thin face.

'Who are you?' he said, crossly, stepping down in front of him.

'It's no matter to you,' said the man, trying to push past him. 'Where's young Malone?'

'Hey! Where d'you think you're going? You can't push in here. . . .'

The man pushed Mr Rafferty back with one hand and held up a revolver in the other. 'That says I can and you'll get it in your gut in a minute if you don't shut up. Stay where you are,' he said, sharply, 'and call your grandson.'

Mr Rafferty opened and shut his mouth. 'I'll do no such thing . . .' he began roaring, when the door behind him opened. It was Bryan.

'What's all this?' he asked, as his grandfather stretched out his arms in front of him. 'What . . .' and then he saw the gun, and the man behind it.

'What do you want, Hannahan?' he said, fear rising in him like a cold sweat. 'What are you doing to granda?'

'I'm doing nothing to this old fool, it's you I want. We thought you'd be here tonight, so just step past and be careful now for I'd love to use this on you.'

Bryan felt his mouth drying out. He thought of Mairead upstairs, and his mother and Deidre and Jamie. He must get this man out of the house. God knows what he wanted, but the little shit had been the one who'd shopped Vincent, he remembered that.

'Leave the old man alone, d'you hear?

'You leave my boy alone, that's what you'll do, you –'

Hannahan slapped the old man on the face.

'Don't you dare hit me,' he roared, and Bryan pushed past him, pulling down his arms.

'No, no, granda,' he said. 'It's not worth it. Leave it be, I'll go with him.'

'I don't like it, I don't like it,' muttered the old man, rubbing his face. 'Do you know this man?' he asked Bryan.

'Yes, I do,' Bryan replied over his shoulder, keeping his eye on Hannahan. 'Don't you worry about anything. I'll be back.'

There was a black taxi outside and Bryan was bundled into

it. He sat between another man he didn't know, and Hannahan, who kept his gun stuck in his side. They drove out towards the northern boundaries of the city, skirting round the Protestant areas and then climbing steeply up the Ligoneil Road to the hills beyond.

The lights of the city fell behind them and widened out as they went higher up the side of the valley. There was some mist around on the higher ground and then the city disappeared altogether, leaving only the red glow on the low cloud. It was colder, too, and Bryan shivered.

'Where are you taking me?' he asked, but no one answered, and he didn't try again. He recognized the road he was on, nothing was being done to hide that from him, and he knew exactly where he was. They drove up a narrow lane and stopped at a house, where the man sitting next to him got out. He came back a few minutes later, and muttered to Hannahan. Bryan missed most of what he said, but he did catch the phrase 'go back. . . .'

Hannahan cursed and got out of the taxi, and Bryan could hear that he was angry. They had what appeared to be a furious argument, and then Hannahan got back in alone and told the driver to move off. He told Bryan to sit on the far side of the seat, and make sure the back doors were locked. The gun lay in his lap, his hand resting on it, and he looked out of the window into the darkness, his face set in anger.

They drove back into town, and Bryan was surprised when they turned off the Falls Road and stopped outside the local stadium. The driver opened the gates and then drove them in. Hannahan walked cautiously round the taxi and said, 'Get out.'

Bryan clambered out of the back and looked around in the darkness. There were no lights on anywhere and obviously the last of the greyhound fanciers had all gone long ago. It was very quiet, and, as their feet crunched across the gravel, he could hear engine sound of the taxi driving away. He was alone with Hannahan, the empty stadium in front of him; the wall along the road behind. He was big and strong while Hannahan was small and slight – and armed.

271

'Walk straight in front,' said Hannahan, and he did, walking straight towards the back of the stadium which towered up above him into the darkness. He came to a door, and he stopped.

'Step to one side,' he was told, and he did, while Hannahan opened the door, and then they both went through and down a passage. Bryan wondered whether to jump Hannahan, but he was keeping well behind, and anyway, it would make enough noise to attract attention.

A voice came out of the darkness. 'In here, Jimmy,' it said.

'Turn the light on, Pat,' said Jimmy. 'I can't see where I'm going.'

Hannahan motioned Bryan with his gun, and they both went into the room. It had the damp, slightly musty smell of stale alcohol. It was the store room for the bar.

'What's up, Pat? Where's Danny?'

'I don't know,' said the large, powerful man sitting on a beer keg. 'All I know is he'll be late.' He looked curiously at Bryan. 'We'll have to keep your man in here till he comes,' he nodded at Jimmy, 'and I don't know how long that'll be.'

Bryan stood looking at the two men. By now he was really frightened. He couldn't work out why he'd been brought here and so he did nothing. Maybe the gun was for show – he couldn't think of any reasons the Provos would want to kill him.

He looked round the room. It was full of crates with empty beer bottles and metal beer kegs. There were a couple of unopened boxes of whiskey and in another corner crates of soft drinks. There were no windows, and the light came from a single, unshaded bulb hanging from the centre of the ceiling.

'Sit down.' Hannahan indicated a beer keg by the wall, his eyes locked on to Bryan's. He sat down. The whole thing was hopeless. Hannahan pulled out another keg and sat opposite him. There was silence. The big man, Pat, sat cracking his knuckles one by one and then he sniffed loudly and wiped a hand across his face.

'Is it a head job we have tonight?' he asked quietly.

'No.' Hannahan was abrupt. 'The boss wants to see him. Thinks he'll be some use.'

'Is that so?' said Pat.

'Why do you want me?' Bryan asked after some ten minutes. The silent waiting was unnerving, and he swung from total fear to amazed anger that this could be happening to him. He had never had anything to do with the Provos, indeed he'd always steered well clear of them. He thought of Mairead, and worried about her, because he knew she would be worrying about him.

'Why do you want me?' he asked again. 'What are you going to do to me?'

'Shut your mouth, or I'll put something in it.' Hannahan blinked hard and his tongue came out to moisten his lip. Bryan sat slumped on his beer keg, his shoulders hunched and his head down. Hannahan's foot tapped nervously on the floor, and this was the only sound.

Hannahan glared at Bryan, looked at his watch and jumped up. He paced up and down the room, stepping round the litter on the floor. Up and down, up and down he walked, and the minutes ticked by.

'Am I staying here all night?' Bryan tried again. 'If you want me for something, why don't you say what it is? What's the matter with you?'

'Shut your face,' Hannahan screamed at him, coming quickly round the room. 'Sit still ... look to your front.'

Bryan could hear him moving behind him, shuffling, breathing hard. He felt the hairs of the back of his neck ride. What the hell was Hannahan up to?

'Put your hands behind your back,' he was ordered, and suddenly he felt string go round his thumbs, bringing them tightly together and cutting into the skin.

'What are you doing?' He tried to struggle round, but he was hit hard on the side of the head and his ears sang, and then suddenly Hannahan was in front of him again, glaring.

'You're sitting here,' he said, his face close to Bryan's who recoiled from the smell of his breath, 'till you're seen. I've

273

been told to look after you, Christ knows why. I'd rather kill you.'

He moved away and started pacing up and down, looking at his watch, going to the door to look out and then back to his pacing again. 'If I had my way,' he said, not looking at Bryan, 'I'd have given you a head job, instead of knee-capping you. It would have saved a lot of bother.'

Bryan looked at him curiously, and then what he'd said suddenly dawned on him. Knee-capping! That wasn't him, that was Vincent. Sweet Jesus!

'What makes you think –' he started, when Hannahan leapt across the room and hit him hard on the side of the face.

'Shut up, shut up,' he screamed at him and hit him again and again, first with the back of his hand and then the front. Backwards and forwards and Bryan's head reeled but he couldn't get away from it. The man called Pat had got up and was standing watching.

'Will you ... stop ... that?' Bryan managed to get the words out between blows, tasting blood on his lips. Hannahan stopped.

'You'd do better to keep your mouth shut,' Pat said. 'The boss might want to see you, but he's not told us to take particular care of you.' He stepped forward and put a huge hand under Bryan's chin. 'Shut up, I said,' and he rammed Bryan's mouth closed with a snap. His head was pushed right back until he was looking at the ceiling and he felt he was about to fall backwards.

'I don't trust you not to open your mouth again,' Pat went on. 'So we'll do it for you ... our way.'

Bryan felt the fingers digging hard into the muscles in the side of his jaw, and his mouth opened again. The gag went into it and he retched, trying to protest. He hated it and started struggling to his feet but from behind he was pulled down again. He felt the gag being tied and then a searing pain across his head as Hannahan's revolver came down on his ear. He felt sick.

'Don't you move from there,' Hannahan panted from behind. 'If I hear you move I'll use this on you again. Pat,' he said. The big man was sitting down again. 'Keep an eye on him. I'm going to find out how much longer we have to stay here.'

The big man grunted and Hannahan went out, his footsteps fading down the passage. Bound and gagged Bryan fought down his rising panic. The gag was in his mouth like a horse's bit, forcing his teeth apart, pressing his tongue down and making it difficult for him to swallow. Why hadn't he told them he wasn't Vincent? It was too late now. God knows what they would do to him when they found out. What the hell was Vincent up to to get himself treated like this – and he swore silently at his brother.

Pat sat across the room, leaning back on a pile of crates, his eyes half closed. He was cracking his knuckles again, one after the other.

Vincent hadn't intended to visit home, but that was where he found himself, standing outside his front door. Something had drawn him down those narrow roads, and there he was. He would, he decided, only stay a few minutes – just to see how his mother was, and get news of Sheelagh. It would be dangerous to stay any longer.

The door, as always, was unlocked and he slipped inside. He heard voices in the kitchen. The whole family was there, and Mairead, too. He stood, shocked, looking at her. Her face was tear-stained and his granda looked white and angry.

'What ... what are you doing up here? What's the matter with youse all? What's happened? It's not Sheelagh, is it ... she's not...'

'No. Not Sheelagh,' Mairead whispered, her voice cracking. 'It's Bryan. He's been taken.'

'Bryan!' exclaimed Vincent. 'Bryan took? Who by, the military or the police?'

'Took, by God,' said Mr Rafferty, 'from right under my nose and I could do nothing to stop it.'

'Took, what d'youse all mean, took? Bryan's done nothing to get himself lifted.'

'No, no,' Mairead cried out. 'It's the Provies who took him.'

275

'Provies?'

'Yes. One wee bastard pushed his way right past me here, waving a gun in my face. A gun, I ask you! Bryan said not to worry, he'd be back. He's not yet.'

'Jesus!' said Vincent, exasperated about all this. 'How do you know? Are you sure it wasn't a UVF man now?'

'No, no,' said his grandfather firmly. 'The man who came to get him was a Provie. I know that rightly. Sure,' he looked at Vincent, 'you know him yourself.'

'I do? Who is he?'

'A fella by the name of Hannahan.'

'Hannahan! Are you sure?'

'Of course I am. Will you stop being stupid now? Didn't I see him with my own eyes, and didn't Bryan use his name when he was here?'

'Oh, my God!'

'And anyway, 'twas the same fella that did the café bombs ... the one that did Sheelagh, and Mairead here.'

'Hannahan!' whispered Vincent, the past flooding back. 'Hannahan did that? He planted the bomb?'

'Yes, sure I told you that some time ago.'

'You did not.'

'I did so. You weren't listening.'

'Oh, no!' Vincent grabbed his grandfather's arm. 'You say *he* came for Bryan. How long gone is he?'

'A couple of hours.'

Mairead was standing there looking at him, her eyes wide with fright. She looked very lost, Vincent thought. How long was it since they'd first met? It felt like years, and now she was here with Bryan. Vincent knew at once that it was himself they'd been after. To send Hannahan was madness, for if Hannahan had found him instead of Bryan, he wouldn't have gone with him. He was much too dangerous.

'Where did they go?' he asked, realizing that was a stupid question.

'I don't know. He just left.' Mairead was crying again. 'Oh, Vincent! Can you find him?'

'Yes,' said Vincent, more firmly than he felt, 'I'll find him.

I've been looking for that little shit for a time now. Only I didn't know it was him I was looking for. Oh, yes, I'll find him all right!'

''Tis Bryan I want you to find, Vincent. Won't you be able to find him?'

'I will if they're together now. Don't you worry your wee head. I'll get him back for you.'

'Do you know where they are?'

'I've a good idea. I think I've been there before. I'll be away now, I've a lot to do,' and he left.

Vincent got a lift up to Ballymurphy, and then back to the Falls Road, where he had himself dropped off on the corner. He didn't even bother to try the main gates to the car park, but just scrambled over the embankment at the end of the stadium. It was a well-worn path, he noticed, but it was dark, and he could scramble over unseen. He hoped he wouldn't bump into any youngsters out for a bit of sport in the stadium.

He moved round the edge of the arena keeping in the shadows, moving slowly until he had his full night vision. It was very dark, everyone had gone home hours before, but he knew this was a place Danny Loughran used, and he knew Loughran was Hannahan's boss. He also knew Hannahan wouldn't try something like this on his own, so he was pretty sure this was where they would be. He turned up his collar and stepped quietly round the back of the stadium. In his jacket pocket he felt the weight of the revolver he'd just borrowed.

He paused before he came out on to the back parking space, anxious to see if any guard had been posted. There was nothing: no movement, no sign of life. Had he made a mistake? This was where they had brought him after his so-called trial, waiting until dark before they dragged him out and kneecapped him. He remembered that all very clearly now.

He knew his way round the ground – he had often clambered in here with his friends to play on forbidden territory. Now, of course, anyone came in, smashing windows, tearing out fixtures, daubing paint and slogans all over the walls.

He was surprised it was so quiet, and he felt in his pocket again for his revolver. It was damp and cold, the air full of moisture making haloes round the street lamps beyond the concrete fence. A drop hung on the end of his nose, and he brushed it off. He waited, ears straining for any sound, but there was nothing. He moved on round the end of the building, and on to the terraces. Cautiously he made his way from those to the lower tier, climbing over the seats, up towards a window at the top which he knew he could open – at least he'd done it a long time before and he hoped no one had changed it since then.

There was a splattering of rain on the roof as he swung his leg through the window and dropped into the room. His eyes, accustomed now to the darkness, could just make out the dim shapes of a desk and other furniture. With his hands out he moved round them and across to the door where he paused, listening hard. He tried the handle gently, and the door opened.

Right, he thought, this is where I go in. He wasn't sure of the layout, but he knew there were stairs somewhere leading to the ground floor, and probably at the end of the passage outside. He went left and was lucky. With one hand on the rails he felt his way down, step by step into the deeper darkness below, and then he froze.

The footsteps he heard were coming along the passage below. Quickly he moved back up the stairs and into a doorway. The footsteps came up the stairs, and now he could see the light of a torch on the ground in front. Pressing himself back, he watched the dim shape of a man go past along the passage he'd just come down, and into the room he'd just left. He tip-toed after him, pulling his revolver out of his pocket. He waited by the door. There was the faint ping of a phone being lifted, and then he heard the sound of dialling.

'Is Danny there?' the voice asked quickly. There was a pause and then, 'I've been here an hour now. Will someone get him here quickly ... to deal with this man Malone, of course. ... What? Another hour? Jesus! Will you ... what's that? .... All right then, but don't be all bloody night.'

It was Hannahan all right, he told himself. That was one of them found. All he needed to do now was to find Bryan and without anyone else around. He stepped away from the door as Hannahan came out, his torch flashing down the passage in front of him. Vincent waited until he was going down the stairs, and then he followed.

As he turned he corner the light of the torch caught him full in the face.

'What the fuck!' cried Hannahan. 'Malone ...' and then he fired. The bullet hit Vincent below the shoulder, tearing through the muscle, glancing off a rib, twisting and tumbling down into his body. He was hurled across the passage and his gun dropped down the stairs. He sank down, clutching the wound, feeling the warm sticky blood on his fingers.

There was a clatter of footsteps as Hannahan ran down the steps. Vincent pulled himself up on to his feet again and went after him. He lurched down the stairs, using his back to support himself against the wall. At the bottom he could hear the footsteps going away, and then he heard a door opening. Light flooded across the passage. He looked on the ground for his gun but he couldn't see it. Maybe Hannahan had picked it up. He heard a shout, and then his name being called out. A door slammed and the light went out, and he went down the passage and stood with his back to the wall opposite the door.

'Bryan!' he yelled. 'Are you there?'

A muffled shout came from behind the door and he kicked it hard and went in. The light caught him in the face again, but this time the bullet missed and he put his head down and went for the man. Hannahan side-stepped him, and he crashed against a pile of crates and felt his strength seeping from him.

He turned, knowing he had made a mistake. Hannahan raised his gun, taking a step backwards to get a firmer stance, and then Bryan kicked out, catching Hannahan behind the knees so he fell. Someone was shouting – choking noises that didn't make sense – and he felt rather than saw a figure coming towards him. An enormous weight hit his shoulder and the pain stabbed down through his chest. Dear God, he thought, I must stay on my feet, and he swayed, but whoever it was had tripped on a crate of beer bottles and Vincent watched a huge man crash to the floor bringing with him a whole pile of crates.

As Vincent shouted in pain the big man roared. His flailing hands were hitting broken glass.

Then Vincent saw Bryan. He was standing still and he wondered what he was doing. On the floor the big man was starting to turn, and Vincent picked up a bottle. Dropping a knee hard into the small of his back he swung his arm and the bottle shattered against the man's head. He bent forward, panting and gasping with the pain that gripped his chest like cramp. Then he was flung sideways from behind. Hannahan! He'd forgotten Hannahan – that wee shit. He swung his arms round together in a wide arc missing him and then rolling over as Hannahan tried to fall on him. He felt the blood spurt from his arm, but he felt no pain. Hannahan yelled as he hit the floor and he rolled, too, into a sitting position, turning his gun on to Vincent. He was panting and scrabbling at his gun to get a grip with both hands. Bryan, his hands still tied behind his back, lashed out and caught Hannahan on the jaw and he screamed, dropping the gun and putting his hands to his face. Vincent dragged himself up and Bryan kicked at Hannahan again but missed and fell across a pile of crates, his feet failing to get a grip on the wet floor.

Pulling himself together with a huge effort, Vincent picked up one of the empty beer kegs. The pain shot through him as he tried to lift it above his head. Slowly from side to side trying to get himself off the crates. On the floor Hannahan, moaning, still clutching his face with one hand, reached for his gun.

Vincent could get the keg no higher. He was running out of strength and time as he watched Hannahan's fingers slowly close round the revolver. He felt himself draining away and he swayed on his feet.

As Vincent fell, he pushed himself forward two steps and holding the keg tight to his chest he aimed himself straight ahead at the gun pointing at him. It seemed to take a long time. Hannahan fired and the shot screamed off the metal keg. But in the end he got there, with an awful sound beneath him, to lie on top of Hannahan's crushed chest and stare into his popping eyes from a distance of five inches.

'That's for my sister,' he choked. 'You bastard!' But Hannahan was dead.

Where was his brother? Where *was* he? What was going on? 'Bryan! ... Bryan!' Bryan was always around when he needed him, so where was he now? He needed help to get away from this dreadful face beneath him. He turned his head and Bryan was on his knees beside him. Why didn't he say something?

'Aggh ... aggh. ...' Bryan gagged.

'Get me out,' Vincent said slowly. 'I can't see very well. ... What's that in your mouth?'

'Aggh,' Bryan shook his head, pointing with his chin. Vincent tried to push himself off the beer keg but nothing happened. He made another huge effort and slid off. He tried to concentrate on Bryan. What was he doing waving his head and making noises?

Then he saw. The big man on the ground was pushing himself up. Dear Jesus! The pain washed through him and he felt very tired. He watched Bryan go across and kick the man but the kick was shrugged off. The room swam before his eyes and he saw a blurred figure of the huge man getting up from his knees, his arms out and his hands reaching towards Bryan. On the floor in front of him was a revolver. Hannahan's revolver, he supposed. He wondered if he could reach it.

He reached out and sighed a little as his fingers closed round the butt. Bryan had backed against the wall. The huge man had pulled him back and banged Bryan's head against it. They were very close to him so he reached forward again towards the man's back and fired. The gun jerked back and he dropped it and sank to the floor beside it.

Bryan was kneeling by him again. 'I'm sorry, Bryan,' he whispered. 'Sorry for what happened ... isn't this. ...'

Noises came desperately from behind the gag.

'I'll miss you, Bryan. Miss you ... miss you all. How's mother? And Sheelagh's all right now,' he added in a stronger voice and his head fell forward.

Bryan knelt beside him and the tears rolled down his face. He was wild he couldn't say anything to his brother; couldn't help him or touch him. He wanted to put his arms round him, to stroke his hair, to tell him he loved him and he mustn't go – that this was all a terrible dream. His rage and grief came out in strange noises until in the end he was exhausted and he sank on to Vincent's body, his head lying on his shoulder, his face in his hair.

The army patrol that burst in a few minutes later, attracted by the shots, could get no sense from Bryan at all. He just stared at them, white faced, until an ambulance arrived.

16

Deirdre Malone sat cross-legged on the ground, her skirt pulled up above her skimpy knees. Her feet, sockless, were stuck into a pair of women's high-heeled shoes many sizes too big. Her hair hung, dank and greasy, down her back and over her face. Her old jersey had holes in the elbows.

She sat with her back to what was left of the old school wall. There was just enough of it left to hide her from most of the passers-by, and even from most of the other children who played on the site of what had once been a pub and four houses. Grass and weeds were already growing, covering the scars.

It was a low, grey afternoon, with the light already failing. A cold wind blew across the waste land, and Deirdre pulled the back of her hand across her nose and then wiped it on her skirt. Her face was pinched now, and her eyes large and black and just a little vacant. She scratched on her leg absentmindedly with one hand, while with the other she arranged her three dolls in front of her.

It was a daily ritual, and had been for over a month. She settled the doll on the right.

'No,' she said to it, 'you can't make supper for Daddy. Daddy is dead four years now. He died on Wednesday morning at half past six.'

She turned to the second doll.

'Now, Belinda, you've asked me before how he died. I told you, I did so. He was beaten up because he tried to stop them burning houses in our street. He was in hospital four weeks before he died. That's a whole month.'

She turned to the third doll.

'And I'm just after telling you,' she said crossly, 'that you can't say good night to Vincent. He's gone away ... gone away ... oh, somewhere far away ... to Heaven. You'll have to wait till he writes to you. Now don't be a bold girl or I'll smack you.'

She touched each one gently on the head, and sang them a little song she had made up herself, about a little cottage in the country.

'It's true, it's true,' she told them eagerly. 'You wait and see. Sure Bryan told me so, and Mairead.'

There was a slither of rubbish and gravel behind her. She didn't look round.

'Is that yourself, Tommy?'

A little boy appeared by her side, breathless from running.

'Am I too late? Say I'm not too late, please. I want to tell them about my da. It was me he spoke to.'

Deirdre looked at Tommy. She remembered he had to tell what his da had told him, but she had some news for him first.

'We're all away soon,' she said, and his eyes widened. 'Away South, and then maybe Austra ... Australia. That's a long way. You can't come.'

'Look. Got an apple. Want some?' he said.

She reached out an arm, took the apple and started to munch. The juice dribbled down her chin. She turned her head back towards her dolls and stared at them. After a few minutes' silence, Tommy cleared his throat. He stood with his hands behind his back, and started to speak.

'My da said to me when he was living, he said, when you grow up you can be a man like me. He said that because I bring frogs and budgies into the house, and so did he. He brought home fish and all.'

Deirdre swung her head again and looked at him. He glanced down and, catching her eye, blushed. He cleared his throat again, but before he could go on, Deirdre spoke.

'My mammy,' she said slowly and distinctly, 'my mammy

said my dad died happy because he died in his sleep,' and she turned to look at her dolls again. Tommy's voice started up over her shoulder.

'When the smoke started coming down the walls of our house, we ran out and down the street. Everyone ran and pushed. My budgie and frogs and my cat and my hamster were burned and all in the house. This was the third time we were burned out. When the slates were crackling in the heat, my mammy thought it was guns. So we went to granny's house.'

He stopped speaking and looked up at the sky. The clouds were swollen with rain, but here and there a pale blue patch could be seen. The air was fresh and cold. He seemed at a loss for words.

'Go on,' she said to him gently, 'you know the bit. The bit about the dog.'

He screwed up his eyes and thought for a moment. Then he screwed up his nose and opened his mouth with the effort of concentration. In a quick rush he spoke.

'My aunt gave me a dog. I call it Arkle. I have a piggy bank for to save my money in. When if I have enough shillings, maybe five or six, I will buy a goldfish.'

'Will you buy me one for to take away with me?'

'If you wait I will. Oh, yes, if you wait.'